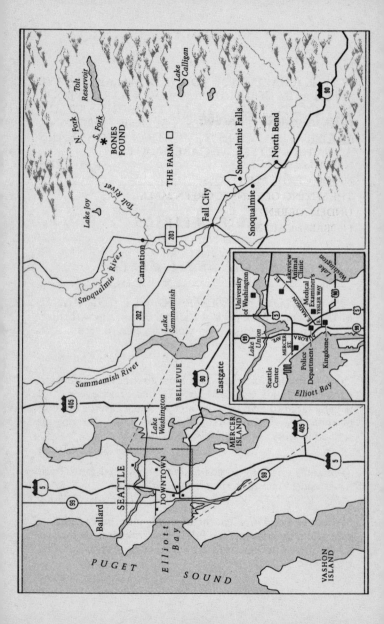

Also by Ridley Pearson

THE ANGEL MAKER

A NOVEL BY

RIDLEY PEARSON

Island
BOOKS

ISLAND BOOKS
Published by
Dell Publishing
a division of
Bantam Doubleday Dell Publishing Group, Inc.
1540 Broadway
New York, New York 10036

ISBN: 0-440-21632-X

Reprinted by arrangement with Delacorte Press

Printed in the United States of America

Published simultaneously in Canada

July 1994

10 9 8 7 6 5 4 3 2 1

Again, for Colleen.
You keep me in stitches.

I am a sort of phantom in life who has lost all beginning and end, and who has even forgotten his own name.

—Fyodor Dostoyevski,
The Brothers Karamazov

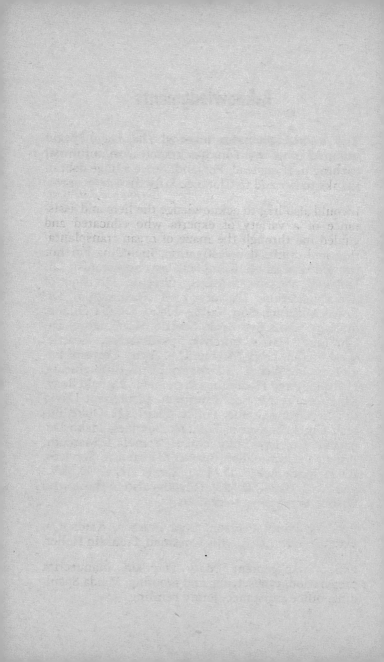

Acknowledgments

The original story that inspired *The Angel Maker* was told to me by Tona Backman on an autumnal evening in Hamstead, England. I owe a huge debt of thanks to her and to Clarence Stilwill.

I would also like to acknowledge the help and assistance of a variety of experts who educated and guided me through the maze of organ transplantation and criminal investigation, including but not limited to: Frances Campbell, psychotherapist; Dr. James B. Perkins, F.A.C.S., director, Division of Transplantation, University of Washington; Dr. Royal McClure, Sun Valley, Idaho; Donna Oiland, director, Lions Eye Bank, Seattle, Washington; Dr. Christian Harris, forensic psychiatrist, Seattle, Washington; Larry Merkle, U.S. Army Corps of Engineers; Joe Weber, U.S. Army Corps of Engineers, Hydrology and Hydraulics Branch; Dr. Donald Reay, King County Medical Examiner; Lieutenant David Reichert, King County Police; Charles H. Duke, Bureau Chief, Bureau of Forensic Services, Idaho Department of Law Enforcement; Pamela J. Marcum, Principal Criminalist, Bureau of Forensic Services, IDLE; Mark Acker, D.M.V.; Randy Acker, D.M.V.; and Steve Edsall, D.M.V. (Thanks also to those who wished to remain anonymous!)

Readers: Premi Pearson, Brad Pearson, Karen Oswalt, Colleen Daly, Ollie Cossman, Franklin Heller.

Office management, Mary Peterson; manuscript preparation, typesetting, and proofing, Maida Spaulding; office assistance, Jenny Femling.

Special thanks to: Mr. Albert Zuckerman, Ms. Carole Baron, Mr. Brian DeFiore, and Mr. Chuck Adams.

Also thanks to: The Fulbright Commission; Wadham College, Oxford, England; and to Sue-Todd and Chuck Yates, Mino Tomacelli and the gang at Kailuum, Michael Lewis, and all The Rockbottom Remainders.

WEDNESDAY

February 1

The young woman's pale, lifeless expression cried out to Daphne Matthews from across the room. Nearly all of the kids who sought out The Shelter were high on something. The hollow cheeks and dirty hair were common to all the runaways, as were the torn jeans, the soiled T-shirts, and the disturbing smell.

The windowless basement room in the King Center Baptist Church on South Jackson held thirteen beds and was void of any color except for the odd assortment of unframed art posters. The beds, arranged in perfect rows, were each covered with a gray wool blanket atop which had been placed a white towel and a dull green cardboard box containing a toothbrush, comb, bar of soap, a package of condoms, and a leaflet on AIDS.

The boys' dorm, across the hall and next to the room where the choir robes were kept, held only eight beds, because teenage boys were less likely to seek help from such places and because girls between the ages of thirteen and eighteen accounted for a larger percentage of the runaways who wandered Seattle's streets.

The other volunteers at The Shelter welcomed Daphne's expertise as a psychologist as much as her being a member of the Seattle Police Department, though this latter qualification was rarely called upon and never mentioned in front of the girls. For Daphne, each young woman who passed through The Shelter's door represented a challenge, each had her own unique, often terrifying story. By coming here they called out for help. Homeless. Penniless. Distrustful. Addicted. Pregnant. Filthy. Diseased. The job of each volunteer was to reverse all of that, to connect the runaway with counselors, doctors, halfway houses, government funds, jobs, housing, recovery programs and safety. To rescue and rebuild a life.

Daphne sat down quietly and slowly on the bed opposite the girl and forced a welcoming smile that made her feel cheap and dishonest: There was nothing to smile about here. She noticed a tiny scab on the inside of the girl's elbow joint and felt her heart sink. To her relief, she didn't see any other needle marks. Perhaps this was the girl's first time. With any luck, her last.

The girl never looked at her; she just stared off into the room in a catatonic daze.

Daphne suggested gently, "Would you like to lie down?"

The girl nodded slightly. Daphne moved aside the towel and box and supported her head as it traveled to the pillow. Some of the drunks felt this hot, some of the druggies, but this contact gave Daphne a sickening feeling in her stomach that told her this was something worse. Exactly what, she wasn't sure. She wasn't even sure she wanted to find out.

The girl cried out sharply as she leaned back, clutching her side.

Daphne cleared the tangled hair from her face, wincing as she noticed a pink circle on the girl's temple. Without looking, she knew there would be an identical mark opposite this: electroshock.

"Cold," the girl complained in a dry, raspy voice.

Daphne covered her with a blanket, told her she would "be right back," and hurried over to Sharon Shaffer, who had just arrived. Sharon, a remarkably petite woman with large gray eyes and an oversized mouth, a former graduate of The Shelter, was now its spokesperson, working the circuit of Rotary Clubs and ladies' luncheons in fund-raising efforts. To both the volunteers and the community, she was a symbol of everything right about The Shelter, its leader and patron saint. To Daphne, she was a dear friend.

Daphne asked one of the other volunteers to check the hospitals for a psych ward discharge or escapee. She briefed Sharon on the recent arrival as the two of them crossed the room: the needle mark, the evidence of electroshock therapy, the girl clutching her side.

"Are you thinking restraints?" Sharon asked. She had a way of reading Daphne's thoughts. Before Daphne could answer, Sharon said, "Let's hold off on that, okay? There's nothing more frustrating than a tie-down. It's horrible. I've *been* there." Daphne didn't argue. Reaching the girl, they perched themselves on opposite sides of her bed.

"Where am I?" the girl wondered aloud. "Why am I here?"

"The only requirement for being here," Sharon explained in a comforting voice, "is your desire to be off the streets." She hesitated. "Okay?"

The girl squinted painfully. It hurt Daphne to see that kind of pain—psychological or physical?—and it worried her too: The druggies usually felt *nothing*. Again, the combination of electroshock and that needle mark warned Daphne of an institution. Her policewoman instincts kicked in—this girl could turn violent without warning.

Sharon said calmly, "You're safe now. My name is Sharon. I'm a runaway. This is Daphne. We're all women here. Okay? We can keep you warm. We can feed you. We want nothing from you. Nothing at all." The girl began to cry. "We are not going to notify the police or your parents—you're home. You're safe here. Whatever you have done is behind you. Here, you are safe. If you need medical attention, you will have it. We want nothing more of you than your name. Something to call you. A first name is all. Can you tell us your name?"

"Cindy," the girl answered. "Can't you stop them?" she asked desperately.

Sharon repeated, "You're safe here, Cindy." She reached out and took the girl's limp hand.

The girl attempted to sit up. She cried out painfully, once again clutching her abdomen, and then shielded her ears. "Can't you stop them?" she pleaded.

The blanket fell away from her. A wet bloodstain colored her side. A stabbing? Daphne wondered. How had she missed the wound earlier? The girl pleaded, "Do you hear that barking? Can't you stop that barking?"

Daphne reached out and lifted the girl's shirt. Her skin was colored an iodine-brown from surgery. At the center of this stain was a three-inch incision laced with broken stitches. It was so fresh, it had yet to scab. She was losing an enormous amount of blood.

"Call 911!" Sharon shouted across the room. "We need an ambulance, *pronto*!" She caught eyes with Daphne then and whispered, "What the hell is this?"

2

Daphne's fingers gripped the handle, but she couldn't quite bring herself to open the door. From inside the nightclub came the muted melody of his jazz piano. She had carefully avoided coming to The Big Joke because new lives came at a price, and that price was distance. Two years had passed since that evening spent with him. A single evening, a single event long since over, but her nearly tactile memory of it remained. She had her feet firmly on the ground now; and he had a *family*. Why challenge any of that? She answered herself: She needed the best cop available; she needed Lou Boldt, retired or not.

A car pulled up. A young couple climbed out and approached. She had to make up her mind—turn back or go through with it. There were other people to whom she could turn. Not as good as Boldt, but certainly qualified.

To hell with it! She went inside. A short, stocky doorman with no head hair but a moustache waxed like an airplane propeller requested a two-dollar cover charge for the piano player. *The piano player*, she thought. *The sergeant*, she felt like correcting. The most celebrated cop in this city to ever walk away from the job—so important to Homicide that his departure was still technically termed an extended leave. She intended to play upon that fact. She handed the doorman the money. Cheap, at twice the price.

The club was dingier than she remembered. Its low ceiling hung over a roomful of small, cigarette-scarred tables and an army of armless chairs. Inset into the brick wall was a handsome fireplace. It was fake. So were the bricks.

The piano's sounds filled a pair of overhead speakers. To her left some guys were busy playing video games. To her right the piano, and the man behind it, remained hidden on the other side of an imitation Chinese screen, perched on the far left of a small stage where comedians performed stand-up on the weekends. She crossed the room toward the tables, nervous and even a little afraid. A single blue light shone down on him, his head trained on the keys in strict concentration. He shouldn't be in blue light, she thought, because it makes him look older than his forty-five. So did the thinning hair—a shade more gray if the light could be trusted. If there had been any question about the identity of the player, the half-empty glass of milk answered it. With his eyes in shadow, he looked kind of like an owl up there. This was how she thought of him, she realized, as an owl up on a branch, out of reach, wise, silent, even majestic. Terrifying to some, inspiring to others, he was both to her.

She negotiated her way through the tight furniture. Not a very good crowd tonight. Boldt was the kind to take that personally. She wondered if this was something to use in her attempt to win his help with her investigation.

The walnut bar had been imported from a British pub by the owner, Bear Berenson. Attached to the mirror using a decal from a local brewery, a happy-hour menu advertised peanuts, french fries and fresh oysters. A hard-faced woman wearing too much makeup stood watch behind beer taps, a hopeful gaze fixed on her customers, like that of a fisherman scanning the sea.

Daphne slipped into an empty chair and flagged down the room's only waitress, a tall black woman built like a dancer. In the process, Daphne caught Boldt's attention as well. He looked up, and their eyes met.

God, how she'd missed him.

===

Boldt felt her presence before he saw her, as close friends or former lovers often do. As they caught eyes he dropped a stitch, necessitating the recovery of the lost beat in the next measure. He felt himself blush—everyone had noticed the error, everyone but the bartender, Mallory, who never noticed anything but an empty glass or a waiting tip.

She looked real good. High, strong cheekbones, heavy eyebrows and shoulder-length brown hair that in certain light held a rusty red. Intense, concentrating eyes, and an outdoors complexion. He knew damn well she'd been home to fix herself up, and that made him wonder, all of a sudden, about her intentions. She didn't wear silk blouses and pearl necklaces around the fourth floor, unless a hell of a lot had changed in the past two years. Would she comment about the way *he* looked? A jazz rat wearing the same pair of khakis for a week. You could track his meals on these pants. His shirt was on its second day. He generally did laundry Mondays and Thursdays.

It was kind of strange to see her again, strange to have not seen her for so long. Not that he hadn't kept up with her through others, but seeing her in the flesh was altogether different. Nice flesh at that. But he felt none of the lusty urges he had been caught up in two years earlier. She felt to him more like a high school sweetheart, someone from long ago whom he had known before the rules had changed. Of course, the rules hadn't changed, he thought; he had.

He and his wife, Liz, had rebuilt their relationship from the ashes of overwork, failed promises, and a disintegration of purpose, interest, and spirit. It had required enormous sacrifices on both their parts: Boldt had left the department; Liz had borne the burden of pregnancy and a difficult delivery to bring them a son. New roles now: Liz, the provider, mother, and lover; Boldt, part-time jazz rat, full-time house husband and Mr. Mom. Together they had found a new rhythm, carved out a new existence.

Now, here was Daffy glowing in the limited light of the cheap seats, nervous eyes seeking him out.

He bought himself a few precious moments by delaying the ending of the song with a long improvisation. It would all be improvisation from here on out. He rose from the bench and interrupted Mallory before she could complain about the length of the set. "Push drinks on them," he suggested, feeding her one instinct. "I'll stretch the next set to compensate." Mallory grimaced but didn't argue. Daphne would call that a learned behavior.

He finger-combed what hair he could find up there. She kept her eyes on him as he approached. He wiped his palms on his pants and offered a smile. Two years had passed, and all he could think to say was, "Hey there."

She grinned and nudged a chair away from the table with her foot.

He felt big and clumsy as he sat down in the chair. He had added a dozen pounds and knew he looked it. Not her. They shook hands, and he was thankful for that. No need to be weird about this. He said, "Can't even see the scar," though he wasn't sure what possessed him to do so.

She tugged at the scarf and revealed it to him: three or four inches long, still slightly pink. It would always be there to remind her. He remembered the knife held there as if it were yesterday. Daffy attempting to *talk* a known killer out of using the knife on her; Boldt, the one with the gun. She in the way of the bullet, her throat in the way of that blade. Her weapons were her words and they had failed her. Boldt wondered if she had recovered from that one yet. Those things tended to haunt you.

"That was a stupid thing to say," he admitted.

"Is this the new you? Looking for my flaws?"

"Let me tell you something: There are women who would kill to have flaws like yours." He hoped a compliment might erase his mistake.

"Keep your shorts on, Casanova. That's all behind us."

"Hey, you think I don't know? I'm a father now. Though that's probably news to you."

"I keep up," she said. "I didn't think it would have been too appropriate for me to throw you and Liz a baby shower."

"It must have taken some courage to break a two-year habit of staying away. This is no visit, is it? Not dressed like that, it isn't. Have you been somewhere? Going somewhere? Are you selling something? Why *are* you here? Not that I'm complaining."

"I heard the piano player is terrific."

"Mediocre on his best nights," Boldt replied. "You must be hanging around with some critically tone-deaf people."

"They're *your* friends!"

"My point exactly. Homicide, right? You *are* selling something."

"How *is* the baby?" she asked.

"Miles? Terrific, thanks." Just the mention of the boy made Boldt homesick.

"And Liz?"

That took some real courage.

"Fine," he answered honestly. "Happy, I think."

"And how about you?" she asked.

He nodded. "The same." Why should it feel odd to admit such a thing? "You?"

"I'm good. I'm volunteering at The Shelter now."

"So I've heard," he said. "I've kept up, too," he added, wanting her to hear this.

"Through Dixie," she said, referring to King County medical examiner Dr. Ronald Dixon, a close friend of Boldt's. A short silence fell between them.

"Are you going to tell me about it?" he asked. "The case," he added, trying to sound smart. It worked; she gave him one of those impressed looks.

"She's sixteen-years old."

"Is or *was.*"

"Is," she confirmed. "She walked into The Shelter this afternoon in real bad shape. Drugs. Evidence suggesting the use of electroshock therapy. A fresh incision right here," she touched her side. "Too fresh. The bleeding kind of fresh. We thought she might be an escapee. We checked with hospitals and institutions. No one had record of her. Her stitches had popped, hence the blood. We admitted her to the Medical Center. I can't tell you what drew me to her, Lou. Not exactly. It was more than curiosity, more than sympathy. You run out of those after a few weeks at The Shelter. You're the one who taught me to listen to the victim—"

"Victim?" he interrupted. "They got her stitched back up, I take it." Exactly what was Daffy after? Why the compliments? She was a professional manipulator—he had to watch that. She knew her way around the human mind. Dealing with her was like playing blackjack with someone who could count cards.

She answered, "They stitched her back up. But they took X-rays. She's missing a kidney." She let it hang there a second. "No hospital record of any such operation. She has no memory of any surgery. None. No explanation at all. I'm looking for the explanation."

"Phil went along with this?" he asked curiously. As staff psychologist, Daphne reported to Lieutenant Phil Shoswitz, Homicide, the logic of which was known only to the upper brass. If there were to be an investigation and she part of it, it would more than likely be overseen by Shoswitz.

"He doesn't even know about it yet," she admitted, looking away—an uncommon gesture for her. "That's one of the reasons I've come to you," she added. "I need your help, your expertise."

Trouble! He knew her too well. "Help?"

"Her name is Cindy Chapman. She's been on the road for seven months. Left Arizona last winter after her stepfather sexually abused her. She went through Flagstaff, Salt Lake City, and ended up here about a month ago. Her long-term memory is fine. But she's lost a twenty-four-hour period during which she was exposed to electroshock and her kidney was removed. Let me tell you this: No two medical procedures could be less related to one another. I've studied this stuff, Lou. This is my turf. But investigating it? That's why I'm here."

He felt the stability of his marriage was at stake. Police work swallowed him whole. He and Liz had come to certain agreements. "What are you saying? Someone *stole* her kidney?"

"If a hospital or an institution is involved, it has to be local. These kids stick to a pretty small area. They develop small societies of self-help or self-abuse. When they move away, it's forever. On to Portland, San Francisco, L.A. *You* champion the cause of the victim. It's the victim that can tell you the most about a case, dead or alive. Right? You're the expert on the victim."

More compliments. He fought like hell to maintain his guard.

"She may have been raped. She won't admit to consensual sex. The evidence is there, but she doesn't *remember*. That's the electroshock. You see?"

She was beginning to frighten him. "No," he admitted, "I don't see."

A commotion at the front door attempted to steal his attention but failed. Daphne's eyes—convincing, terrified, searching, hopeful—held him firmly.

"Someone cut this girl open and stole her kidney. I'm convinced of it. The electroshock was used to ensure she didn't remember anything about it." Fire filled her eyes. "I can't prove it. Not yet." She placed her hand on her chest. "But I feel it *in here*. You know that feeling, don't you? I *know* you do."

He resented being cornered by her. Yes, he knew that feeling. Yes, he had been forced to defend it on a dozen occasions; and no, there was no real sense to it. But this was *her* feeling, not his, he reminded himself; her case, her instincts, not his. "What evidence is there?" he asked coldly.

She winced. "I'm not an investigator. I can't even take this to Shoswitz until I have something convincing. Hell, he's Homicide. He may not want it even then: She's *alive* after all. What do I do? Where do I turn?"

"The helpless female? I don't buy it."

She glared. "This young woman was violated in the worst, most heinous sense. Some monster"—*monster* was *not* a word that Daphne Matthews, the psychologist, often used—"cut her open, reached inside her, and removed an organ—a physical part of her! My God! Phil Shoswitz may be committed more to the dead than the living, but you? After they stole her kidney, they burned her short-term memory with electroshock. Am I getting through? Maybe one of them raped her just for fun. Evidence? Do I need probable cause, Sergeant, in order to investigate, or just the suspicion that a crime has been committed?" She stared him down. "Will you help me or not?" she asked, adding, "If for no other reason than as a parent."

He couldn't help but picture Miles—Einstein, the nickname belonging to his blond, curly haired son—involuntarily under the knife of such a butcher. She interrupted his thoughts. "The electroshock may have done permanent damage to her memory, not to mention her mind: She hears a constant barking."

"I'm out of the business. I'm off the force. My badge is collecting dust in Shoswitz's drawer."

"You're on extended leave."

"That's just Phil's way of holding a carrot out to me, of keeping my chance at twenty alive. That's the way it reads on paper, Daffy, but in here?" he said, repeating her gesture of placing his hand on his chest. "In here, I'm a father and a hack pianist."

He had never dared speak the words aloud, had seldom even thought them, for he wasn't one to lie, and he couldn't be sure this was the truth: "It's over." It felt sacrilegious to say such a thing. Just hearing it spoken confirmed its falsehood. He felt a terrifying loss of control, as if hitting a patch of ice on a dangerous curve. It wasn't over, was it? Someone out there had torn the guts out of a young girl. What surprised him most of all was the way he took to it so quickly. He wanted whatever evidence she had. He wanted the pieces of the puzzle. He wanted to put a stop to it before it happened again. Cop instincts—she was counting on them. Perhaps it was because the victim *was* alive.

A voice—a man's, big and thunderous—reverberated through the club. "Party's over, everyone. No more drinks. I'm going to have to ask you all to leave." Boldt looked over his shoulder expecting to see some drunk on the stage, but instead he saw a crew cut wearing a ten-year-old gray suit and scuffed wingtips with worn heels. A badge hung out of the breast pocket of the suit. Four or five clones of the man swept quickly into the club, fanning out to various responsibilities. It felt like a bank job to Boldt, an organized robbery. But when this guy announced, "Treasury Department," he realized what it was. The man continued, "These premises are being sealed." He repeated loudly over protests, "I'm going to have to ask you all to leave."

"Your idea?" Boldt asked her, nodding toward the T-man. "Trying to pressure me into this?"

She grimaced, looking past him toward the stage.

One of the suits was screwing a padlock clasp into the piano's keyboard cover. Boldt could feel the screws biting into the wood as if they were drilling into his own flesh. He rose angrily, Daphne following.

"What the hell?" Boldt hollered as he closed the distance. "That's a musical instrument, goddamn it!" The one with the big voice was smart enough to step aside. The assistant kept right on twisting the screwdriver. "Stop that! Now!"

"Don't make any trouble, pal," the assistant cautioned. The screw chewed more deeply into the wood.

"You don't do that to a musical instrument," Boldt repeated, wrapping one of his big hands around the boy's wrist. "You just *don't do that*."

The agent threatened, "You want me to call the cops?"

"I *am* a cop," Boldt declared. His eyes met

Daphne's; she wasn't going to let him live that one down. Boldt released the man.

"So am I," Daphne informed the agent, producing her identification. "I'd sure as hell like to see the warrant that authorizes the destruction of private property in the process of seizure. You want to show me that document, please, Agent—" she craned forward to read his I.D."—Campbell?"

The man's face went crimson. He looked first at her then at Boldt, then over at his superior. "You want to see warrants, you'll have to talk to Agent Majorksi. I got a job to do here."

"Leave it be," Boldt said definitively, grabbing his wrist again. Two screws had already violated the ebony.

Across the room, bartender Mallory struggled with one of the agents in an effort to lock the cash register, but lost. The agent took the key from her. They had practiced this drill well or had performed it enough times to execute it flawlessly. Piece by piece, stage by stage, the agents took control in a matter of minutes. Confused patrons were herded toward the door, several chugging beers on the way. Another commotion—Bear's arrest—grabbed Boldt's attention as the agent started twisting that screwdriver again.

The club owner was placed in handcuffs and read his rights. He glanced over at Boldt, shrugged, and smiled. "I should have hired H&R Block," Bear shouted over to Boldt. That was Bear: ever the comic. He threw a couple of one-liners at the agents who had him, but they didn't seem to appreciate the humor. "Drinks are on the house, fellas," he tried one last time as they escorted him toward the door.

"Hey, Monk," he called out, using his nickname for Boldt, "I thought all you badgers were on the same team. Hey, Elliot Ness," he called to the gray suit, Majorski, "this here is Lou Boldt. *The* Lou Boldt of the Seattle Police Department! Have a heart!" He was ushered out of the building.

"Louis Boldt?" Agent Majorski asked.

"That's right," Boldt answered, surprised to hear his proper name come from the mouth of a stranger. These guys were as stiff as cardboard. "You mind calling this guy off? He's screwing a friend of mine."

Daphne displayed her I.D. for the second time. "I'd like to see the warrant that permits him to do that."

Majorski looked over her badge and photo. "Tommy," he said, stopping the one at the piano. "Why don't you help with the files?"

Reluctantly, the rookie abandoned his task.

Boldt and Daphne briefly exchanged looks of triumph.

The euphoria was short-lived. Majorski consulted a typed list he withdrew from his coat pocket. "You'll be hearing from the IRS," he said to Boldt with a disturbing smugness. "I'd speak to my accountant if I were you." He moved off to reorganize his people.

"My *accountant*?" Boldt responded desperately, the man not listening. Liz handled their tax returns.

Daphne and Boldt were herded toward the door.

"Just let me use you as a sounding board," Daphne pleaded, ever persistent. "I can bounce my ideas off you. Show you what I've got." She feared she had lost him, that her effort had been overshadowed by the raid, that all was for naught. She couldn't leave it as it was, she couldn't bear the thought of facing Shoswitz alone; she *needed* Boldt.

"Daffy, I can sleep at night. My stomach is better than it's been in years. I take naps in the afternoon, with my little Einstein purring in his crib. I read books—imagine that! Liz and I actually find time to speak a few complete sentences to each other. You know what you're asking?''

"Please," she tried.

The way she said it. Boldt looked at her intently. "As a sounding board, but that's *all*."

"Sure," she said, unconvincingly. "That's all."

He hated losing.

THURSDAY

February 2

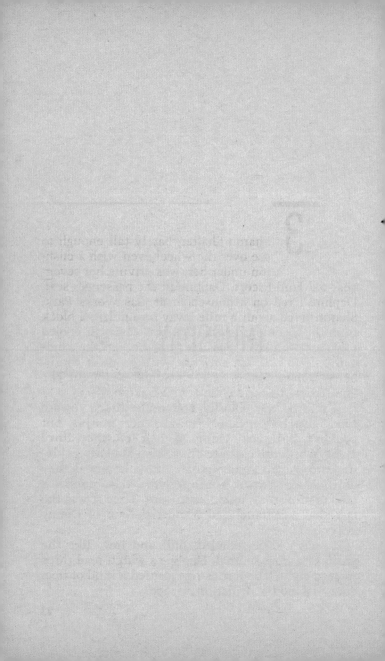

3

Sharon Shaffer, barely tall enough to see over the wheel even with a cushion under her, was driving her seven-year-old Ford Escort, Daphne in the passenger seat. Daphne lived on a houseboat at Gas Works Park; Sharon lived about a mile away on Linden, a block from the Freemont Baptist Church. They car-pooled together whenever possible, mostly for the company. Following her meeting with Boldt at the library, Daphne was going to spend the evening at The Shelter and then ride home with Sharon.

Crossing the colorful Freemont Bridge toward town, Daphne strained to see her marina but couldn't. With Lake Union to their left, they drove along Westlake, cluttered marinas gradually evolving into condos and corporate headquarters as they drew closer to town. Ninth Avenue was a no-man's land of struggling small businesses. Then it was the fast-food and franchised commercialism of Denny Way.

A ferry horn sounded, dull and low, like the groan of a huge animal. Daphne's watch read three twenty-eight. The ferries represented a kind of freedom—island life. Isolation, escape.

"Judging by yesterday's weather," Daphne said, "I'd say the groundhog *drowned*."

"We're halfway through the rinse cycle," Sharon agreed. "Four more weeks of this at least."

"Makes you really love the place, doesn't it?"

"You look a little tired," Sharon said.

"I spent the day poring over some autopsy files the medical examiner wanted me to see. It's exhausting."

"Sounds disgusting."

"I made some headway. I'm not sure Cindy Chapman is all alone in this."

"Meaning?"

"I need to run it all by a friend and see what he thinks," Daphne explained.

"I don't like the sound of your voice."

"I'm a little scared, that's all."

"I don't think I could ever be a cop," Sharon said. She ruminated on this for a moment. "Three years ago, if someone had tried to tell me that someday one of my best friends would be a cop, and a forensic psychologist at that, I would have tagged them for the bird house—the loony bin. It's weird how things work out."

"In your case, they've worked out rather nicely."

"It'll happen to you," Sharon encouraged. "It's all in your attitude, and your attitude is improving. Something's working."

"It's the therapy."

"Whatever it is, it's good to see."

"Have you ever worked with someone *after* you've had a thing with him?"

Astonished, Sharon cried, "Did you *sleep* with your therapist?"

"Not my therapist, dummy. Just answer the question."

Sharon stopped at a light and said, "On the street

I slept with *everyone*. You'd sleep with someone because they had the coke that week. Coke whores. We were all coke whores." She drifted off for a moment. When she spoke again, the pain was gone from her voice. "But I know what you're asking about, and it did happen to me once. I slept a couple of times with a guy I met in A.A. Then it fizzled out. I'm not sure why. But we kept running into each other at all the meetings. It worked out okay, except that no matter what we talked about on the surface, there was always this sexual tension—at least for me—going on underneath, you know? I wasn't after him—nothing like that—but you don't forget the really good ones, and this guy was *really* tuned in, really good for me."

"But you don't forget, do you?" Daphne asked, repeating her friend's comment.

"I sure don't."

"And it worked out?"

"Depending on who you ask. He's got a woman now. I have The Shelter. But," and she laughed, "it's hard to curl up with The Shelter. And there are times . . . Well, you know. But you can't project. 'One day at a time,' girl. 'An attitude of gratitude.' "

"Yeah, yeah. Don't preach," Daphne chided.

"Sometimes I think I'm lucky I got so messed up on the streets. Without A.A. Well, you've heard all of this."

"A number of times." Even three years into the program, Sharon was still on a sort of honeymoon. Sometimes it was all she could find to talk about.

"Who's the guy?" Sharon asked.

"Just that: a guy."

"Don't give me that." She laughed. "If *you* slept with him, he's not just a *guy*, he's an endangered species."

"Once. Only once. And I didn't even spend the night. It isn't the sex."

"Those are the dangerous ones," Sharon said, turning the corner and pulling over to the curb.

"Yeah, I know," agreed Daphne. She looked at her watch. Thirty minutes in which to do her research.

"You're meeting someone here, aren't you?" Sharon asked. "Him," she stated.

"I'll catch up with you later," Daphne reminded. She climbed out of the car, wondering why she felt so damned nervous.

4

The Lakeview Animal Clinic veterinarian offices occupied the ground floor of a relatively new business complex facing Madison. The reception area had vinyl flooring in a brick pattern and long benches against each wall. In huge letters a sign read: Keep Animals Caged or Leashed **At All Times.** Dogs, to the left benches. Cats to the right. There were a few of each in the small room, the air electric with possible conflict.

Pamela Chase, short and overweight, wore a yellow crew shirt with the words "Lakeview Animal Clinic" embroidered on her breast pocket. She inspected the form that belonged to the cat she was carrying. Camile hadn't eaten in three days. When she had managed to get food down, she vomited it back up. Camile, like so much of their work, was a referral—Dr. Elden Tegg was the one vet to whom the other vets turned.

The examination room had a chart on the wall

that diagramed the nerves, lenses, and muscles in a cat's eye. There was a large, framed color photograph of Puget Sound at dawn, a nuclear submarine just barely visible alongside a pod of surfacing Orca whales. The room had no window but did possess a large air grate in the ceiling. It smelled of rubbing alcohol and disinfectant.

Camile wrestled to be free but lacked the energy for a prolonged struggle. She resigned herself to Pamela's hold.

A moment later the door swung open and the veterinarian stepped inside. Dr. Elden Tegg, D.V.M., as his name plaque introduced him, stood close to six feet tall, in a wiry frame, with a dark complexion, brown eyes, and a black beard carefully trimmed. He wore a white lab coat, khaki pants, and brown leather walking shoes with rawhide trim. He had a protruding Adam's apple that bobbed as he spoke in a grating voice. His attention fixed immediately upon his patient.

Pamela Chase passed him the cat as he nodded. He had exceptionally long fingers, immaculately clean hands, perfectly manicured nails, and he wore a gold wedding ring.

He studied the cat thoughtfully, squeezing, probing. He looked into her eyes and glanced quickly into her ears. "Loss of appetite and vomiting," Pamela Chase informed him. He grunted an acknowledgment. "They sent pictures along." Tegg returned the cat to his assistant and approached the light board, turning it on and studying the X-rays.

"Well," he asked in a professorial tone, "did you have a look at these?"

She answered, "I was thinking we should try a milk shake," referring to a barium upper G.I.

"Have I told you how fortunate I am to have you?" he asked.

She glowed with the compliment.

"Let's sedate her," he said, "shall we?"

———

Fifteen minutes later, she reentered carrying both the cat and the new X-rays. Tegg slapped the large negatives into the clamps on the light box, studied them carefully, and signaled Pamela over to him. She responded without thought. "Here's what the others missed," he said confidently, running one of his clean fingernails over a section of the X-ray. "See here, and here?" he asked. "It's not what you see," he advised, "it's what you *don't* see, which might explain how it was missed so easily. Just a ghost, see?"

"Yes, now I do."

"There's some kind of obstruction in the stomach. Maybe a fur-ball, but I doubt it. Let's try an endoscopy and have a look." Pamela Chase prepared all the necessary equipment for the procedure and stood alongside him like a corporal at the side of a general. He inserted the black eel of plastic tubing down the cat's throat. The tiny fiber optic camera inside the animal's stomach sent back black-and-white pictures to the small SONY television that Tegg studied. "The problem with something plastic like this is that the veterinarian cannot feel it in the exam, cannot see it clearly in an X-ray, and yet to this poor creature it feels like her tummy is full all the time. She tries to eat, but the stomach rejects it. Probably picked it up off the floor."

On the screen, under his direction, a small set of pinchers moved like jaws. Tegg deftly maneuvered them to apprehend the foreign object. A moment later he extruded the endoscopy tube from the cat.

A small piece of soft plastic—a swimmer's ear

plug—fell into the stainless steel dish that Pamela held.

Tegg stated clinically, "That should do it. Send along the usual instructions regarding the anesthesia. Also some buffers to help out with the abrasion to the stomach lining. If the vomiting continues, they should reschedule immediately."

He moved toward the door. "What's next?" he asked her.

"You haven't taken a break all day," she said.

"What's next?" he repeated.

"A toy poodle," she advised, checking a list. "Blood in the urine."

"Are we set up for surgery?" he asked.

"All set," she replied.

"Give me five minutes," he told her. Then he added sincerely, "I hate toy poodles."

5

The downtown branch of Seattle's public library is two blocks from the Public Safety building, the police department's central offices. It is overshadowed by an intriguing skyline sprouting new glass and steel in amounts that ten years earlier would have seemed inconceivable. The Big Money had hit Seattle in the mid-80's, bringing with it a renewed downtown, renovations, public transit, and the ubiquitous shopping centers. The thirty- and forty-story towers competed for the best view of breathtaking Elliott Bay and Puget Sound to the west and the majesty of glacier-capped Mount Rainier to the southeast. By city standards, Seattle's downtown is remarkably small, contained to the south by the Kingdome and to the north by the Seattle Center, a holdover from the 1962 World's Fair. To the west is the green-marble estuary with its gray ferries and black freighters; to the east, downtown is stopped by Interstate 5, Pill Hill and Seattle College. Downtown is surrounded for miles by rolling hills blanketed in two-story clapboard homes and communities like Ballard, Ravenna, Northgate and Richmond Highlands. It is a city of water: the Sound, lakes, canals and rivers. For Boldt's taste, the city's growth and expansion was happening too quickly, seemed too uncontrolled. Seattle was learning life the hard way: theft, drugs, organized crime and shrinking budgets. Its art, culture and traditions kept it vital and unique: its music, dance, fine arts; its fishing, sailing, and Native American history; its festivals and celebrations; its libraries, museums, theaters and public market.

The library is a mixture of formed concrete and garden. Plate-glass windows and deciduous trees. As with any such library, entering it is like stepping into a silent movie. On the Thursday afternoon of their meeting, it was a little busier than usual, probably because of the drizzle, Boldt thought. In a city with a winter climate like Seattle's, the library took on a position of great importance, a kind of Mecca for the mind. The faces in these rooms were not pale, nor were they dispirited. The people of Seattle were a vibrant, red-cheeked, resilient bunch, whom Boldt counted as his own. The wet winter weather, extremely temperate considering the latitude, was essential—a few years of drought had taught the locals that much. This weather—or its reputation— was what kept the masses away. It was the city's best defense in its increasing battle against Californication.

Boldt entered wearing a baby carrier that supported his son Miles. He joined Daphne at one of the large reading tables on the second floor, as far away from others as possible. She steeled herself for what lay ahead. This was her chance to convince him they had a case—to win him over. That child hanging around his neck represented his other life. She couldn't allow herself to think of it in those terms. Boldt was a friend, certainly. But more importantly, he was a cop with the connections and talent to make this case happen. *This* was her focus. The image of Cindy Chapman's bleeding incision was lodged in her mind.

On the table in front of her lay three Pendaflex folders and a pile of photocopies from her research at the library. She felt both exhausted and afraid, and the two sensations fed on each other, injecting her with an anxiety she found difficult to overcome. Without him, without some *male* to support her— God, how she resented it—she had little or no chance of convincing Lieutenant Phil Shoswitz to open this investigation.

She wore gray stirrup pants, a white blouse buttoned high, and a crimson scarf to hide her scar. She had her brown-red hair pulled back off her face, a pair of simple silver studs in her ears. Boldt was, as always, disheveled, wrinkled, worn. Khakis, a Tattersall shirt, brown walking shoes with thick rubber hiking tread. He looked tired—probably was—and older than he had last night at The Big Joke.

"Meet my son, Miles," Boldt said proudly, speaking in a hushed voice, dropping into a chair and putting down the baby bag he carried with him. "Miles," he said to his sleeping six-month-old child in the carrier, "this is the 'other woman' I've told you so much about."

"He's adorable."

"I hope he gets his mother's hair."

"And her brains," Daphne said.

He glanced down at the folders and then up at her, disapprovingly. "You're not supposed to take these out of the office," he declared.

"They aren't ours. Dixie gave them to me," she said, referring to the chief pathologist of the medical examiner's office. "He thought they might help convince you that we have something."

"We?"

"I need a partner, someone with whom Shoswitz will *allow* me to partner. As of this morning, Dixie is a believer, but I can't very well partner with a pathologist."

"Wait a minute! I agreed to be a sounding board, that's all. There are a dozen guys who could run with this thing." His eyes strayed to the folders again, and she realized she was taking the wrong approach with him. For Lou Boldt, it was always the victims—the evidence—that did the talking.

She said, "You take each one of these autopsies separately, and they don't say much. You add them up, and we've got a problem."

Boldt leaned forward, his big hand shielding the boy's small head, and dragged the folders across the table. "Maybe I don't want to read these," he said, sensing the trap they represented. She willed him to open the top folder—just get him started, that was all it would take.

"Sure you do," she argued.

"Three of them? You're suggesting a pattern?" he said, thinking aloud. "Pathology reports—so they're dead. They're connected to what happened to Cindy Chapman, or I wouldn't be here, would I?"

She leaned forward and nudged the files even closer.

"If Dixie came up with these, then the pattern,

the similarity between them, has to do with the way in which they were killed."

"The way they *died*," she corrected. "And who they were or *weren't*. All three filed as unsolved cases. There may be more."

"Runaways?"

"They make such nice victims: No one knows they're here; no one knows they're gone."

"Don't do this to me."

"To you? This isn't about you." She ran her red nail down the spine of each folder. "This is about Glenda Sherman, Peter Blumenthal and Julia Walker."

He reached for the first folder, but stopped himself once again.

She said, "How do you prove something like this? He's counting on that—whoever is doing this. He's counting on our paying no attention. These kids are as good as John Does to us. They're nobodies."

"I want to help, to do what I can, but it's not easy. There are a lot of forces at play here. Even if I did reactivate, there's no saying I'd end up on this particular ticket."

"I'm not buying that. The lieutenant would do anything to have you back. He'd meet any conditions you laid out. Scheduling, day care, *anything*. What's the latest with the IRS?"

"You don't miss a beat, do you?"

The baby spit out the pacifier. Boldt caught it in a reflex only time or instinct had developed. She was in over her head. There *were* a lot of forces at play. He returned the pacifier to the waiting lips. He placed his huge hand on the boy's tiny head and encouraged him back to sleep.

"You're a natural."

"Cherish or perish."

"Maybe you're right. Maybe you shouldn't read these files. I don't want to take you away from him."

"Smooth. Very smooth."

"I *mean* it."

"I know you mean it. That's the problem."

"You didn't answer me—about the IRS?"

"We have to make an appointment. Liz and I. She's our accountant."

"Is it a big deal?"

"If it means more money, yes, it's a big deal. Liz had a horrible delivery . . ."

"Yes, I heard."

"It ran into some serious money. Insurance companies are wonderful until you show them the bill. Anyway . . . You want to remind me that I'm in a financial bind and that Liz and I could use a second income, that I could borrow from the credit union. I know what you're up to. Point taken. Okay?" He scrunched his nose. "Do you smell something?" He grabbed the bag and stood. "In a minute everyone in the library will smell it. My son and I are going to pay a little visit to the boy's room."

"You read these," she persisted, "and you realize he's a surgeon. Has to be. That gives us a place to start."

"A surgeon?" he asked, eyeing the folders.

She reached over and hoisted the top folder. "Can you read and change diapers at the same time?"

"Absolutely not."

"Then let me," she said, motioning for the baby.

"You won't like it. It's messy."

"You read the files, I'll handle Mr. Miles."

"You're a poet."

She motioned again for the child. Boldt unfastened the carrier and passed his son to her, along with the bag. "Cloth diapers," she noticed. "Classy."

"Environmentally sound. That's Liz—ever the proper mother *and* citizen."

"Read," she chided. She didn't want to hear about Liz.

═══

When she returned, wondering whether she could ever live with doing that several times a day, his face was buried in one of the files. The two others were spread open in front of him. Fast reader. Fast learner. Lou Boldt.

"How sure are you about this?" he asked. Accepting Miles, he thanked her and attempted to return him to the carrier. Fully awake, the boy struggled to be free, tying up Boldt's hands and attention.

"Cindy Chapman—the woman who sought out The Shelter—is missing a kidney." She touched the files. "All three of these kids died from hemorrhaging associated with a," and she quoted, " 'surgically absent' organ. Two kidneys: Walker and Sherman. Blumenthal was missing a lung. I think we may have a doctor selling stolen organs on the black market."

"A black market for *organs*?"

She fingered the photocopies in front of her. "Is it so impossible a thought? I have a half-dozen articles here: *Wall Street Journal, New York Times, The New Yorker, Vanity Fair, JAMA, New England Journal of Medicine.* In Third World countries, harvesting is an everyday occurrence. That's what it's called: organ harvesting. Nice ring to it, huh? Organized, well run. Quite the business. Fifteen thousand dollars a kidney—that's the going rate. Fifteen *thousand*. It's so obvious that something like this would grow out of the lack of donor organs. Transplant technology has outraced supply. It's all in here," she said, again tapping her copies of the articles. "There are not enough far-sighted people out there who think to become donors *prior* to their deaths. Livers, kidneys, lungs, hearts, ovaries, testicles, eyes, bone marrow, you name it. There's a shortage in nearly every category. And what happens when there's a shortage? It's simple economics. Third World countries are hit the worst because they lack the technology for life-support: the dialysis machines, the respirators. Egypt, India, Argentina, Brazil—kidneys practically trade on the open market. If you're an Egyptian farmer who's had a bad crop, you go into the city and sell one of your kidneys. You come home a few weeks later with ten *years'* worth of income. And when those organs are in short supply? Maybe the doctors there turn to their colleagues overseas."

"Fifteen grand a kidney?"

"Lungs about the same. Livers and hearts go for ten to twenty *times* that."

"But not here. Not in this country."

"Not in my backyard? Come on! What would you pay to stay alive? What happens when you find yourself number one hundred and fifty on an organ donor list where they're averaging three transplants a month and your doctor has given you six months to live? You start making inquiries. You beg, borrow, or steal the money necessary, and you *buy* what no one will *donate*. You establish a market. Where there's demand, someone will supply. It never fails. If you're a doctor, can you imagine how frustrating it must be to see your patients die because so few people will take the time to fill out a couple of forms?"

"You're right about it giving us a way to investigate it."

"Us? You said 'us.' "

"What *you* do is identify their method of selection."

"Meaning?"

"If it *is* organized—if it is a business just as you've suggested—then this surgeon must have some way of identifying, of selecting his donors."

"Meaning?" she asked, wanting to hear him think this through aloud. She could feel his enthusiasm. She almost had him.

"Listen, either they're stealing them, in which case Chapman and these others are innocent victims, or they're *buying* them, contracting them from people either desperate for money or sympathetic to their cause or both. Like your Egyptian farmer, right? Unfortunately, we don't know which. We need to establish that first. We need to know their game plan. How do they identify their donors? That comes first."

"These organs are perishable goods," she reminded. "There are time factors involved."

"Do they kidnap the donor, steal some kid off the streets? That's a hell of a risk to take."

"They're runaways. Who's going to notice?"

"But why take that kind of risk if you can cut a deal instead? What if the donor comes into the plan willingly? That makes a lot more sense."

"Cindy Chapman's a *victim*, Lou," Daphne said obstinately.

"We don't *know* that. What if she offered to *sell* her kidney? What if it was *voluntary*? Runaway teenagers are not exactly long on cash."

"I don't believe that. Why use electroshock if they're part of your conspiracy? She sure as hell didn't volunteer for *that*."

"Don't get all high and mighty, damn it. Your point is well-taken, okay? I *agree* with you. The electroshock doesn't fit. Okay?"

"You agree with me, but you won't help me."

"I *will* help you. All I can."

"But you won't take it to the lieutenant?"

"I can't get that involved. Not yet, anyway." He looked down, wiped some drool from the baby's mouth. "Extenuating circumstances." He added quickly, "But I *will* help."

"If Cindy Chapman dies, *then* will you take it to Shoswitz for me? Is that what you need, a fresh victim? She's in bad shape, you know."

"You can really piss me off when you try."

"Good. I'm trying real hard."

"I noticed. Have you run Chapman's clothes through the lab?" he asked.

She had been withholding this and another file from him, hoping to time their delivery correctly and sink the hook. Leave it to him to ask, she thought. "Courtesy of the Professor," she explained, referring to the head of the department's forensic sciences unit. She handed the first of the two files to Boldt. "He rushed this for me." It was the state lab's preliminary hairs and fibers report. "I used your name," she added reluctantly. She pulled both files to the table top, handing him only the one.

He opened it and read. The top of the page listed the identification numbers followed by how they had been received, in this case hand-delivered by Sgt. Daphne Matthews, SPD. The next section was divided into two columns: EVIDENCE DESCRIPTION and CONCLUSION. Boldt scanned the conclusions. He suggested, "LaMoia could handle this."

She answered quickly, "As good as his instincts are, John is about ten years short on experience and a lifetime short on manners. He just doesn't have the qualifications you do."

He waved a finger at her. "You're playing with me again."

"Don't you wish," she teased. "Not in your wildest dreams."

It provoked a grin. "What do you know about my dreams?" he teased right back. "Animal hairs found on her jeans," he said. "We dismiss them. Too common. Blood type O-positive." He rummaged through the other files before him.

She filled in, "These other three were *also* type O-positive." She indicated the stack next to her. "And when you read these medical stories, you'll understand why. Type O is the biggest blood group, the biggest market."

He glanced up, understanding. "They're all four the same blood type. They select their donors by blood type! *That's* our lead!"

"The Professor forwarded the animal hairs to the U-Dub," she said, meaning the University of Washington, "to attempt to identify the particular breeds."

"You're getting off track! It's the blood group match that's important. Let's stick with that for a minute!"

"The animal hairs are important too."

"I can't get too excited over some animal hairs. We all have pets, and if we don't, our friends do. Most of us come in contact with pet hairs on a daily basis."

"Most of us," she agreed, handing him the last file, "but *not* Cindy Chapman."

He started to say something but caught himself and opened the file containing a copy of Cindy Chapman's hospital admission forms. Scanning the contents quickly, he said, "You *have* been busy."

"Allergies," she hinted. She watched his eyes track down the form.

"Allergic to house pets," he read aloud.

"Severe reactions. Shallow breathing, elevated

pulse rate." It was how she felt at the moment. "There's no way she would have voluntarily been in a situation that would literally cover her clothing with animal hair."

"That's good police work, Daffy," he said, complimenting her, but she could sense a reluctance in him.

"But . . . ?" she said, waiting.

"But it's too broad a field. Too difficult to trace."

"It was the Professor's idea to run them over to the university, not mine. There were some white hairs that sparked his interest."

"The Professor will run down *any* hair or fiber. It's his job. It doesn't mean it's worth getting excited about."

She was excited. She hated to admit it. She also hated it when he was right—when he could read her so easily. She had long hours invested in this. She wanted something to show for it. How could guys like Lou Boldt stay with an investigation without victories along the way? Miles spit out his pacifier. Boldt plugged it back in.

Boldt said, "I'd say we focus on this blood group overlap. That's the closest thing to hard evidence we have, and it isn't much. Animal hairs won't convince Shoswitz you have a case."

"We have three victims—four, including Cindy," she complained, masking her relief at his use of *we*.

"Unfortunately, we can't choose the evidence these people leave behind."

"Dixie says each file indicates that there was some physical evidence stored from each autopsy. Tissue samples, that kind of thing. They do that for the unsolveds and John Does. He's having the evidence brought up. He seemed pretty optimistic."

"Dixie's *always* optimistic."

"He says that surgeons sometimes leave 'signatures' in their work. Style. Technique. He's going to review and compare autopsy photos when he has the time."

"That would help," Boldt said, "but knowing his workload I wouldn't count on it being very soon." He reviewed the files again. "So we're looking for a surgeon. That's another avenue worth pursuing. When in doubt, take the direct route."

"Not necessarily just surgeons," she corrected him.

He nodded. "A surgeon, another kind of specialist who wishes he were a surgeon, a medical student, an impersonator—a fake, a retiree. But of all of these, a surgeon is still the most likely. Can you draw up a profile for us?"

She nodded. She could feel him committing to the investigation. She wanted to hear it spoken. She wanted to snare him beyond any chance of retreat. She asked, "How many surgeons are there in Seattle? And of these, how many are *transplant* surgeons? A handful. And if we were both to question them—I mean you and I *together*—you could ask your questions and I could ask mine and we just might find this person. There are certain traps I could lay—psychological traps—that he might fall into."

"You don't want to tangle with somebody like this, Daffy. I don't have to remind you of that, do I?"

His cruelty hit her hard. Involuntarily, she tugged her collar up higher on her neck as she glared at him, hiding that scar. For an instant she hated him. "There was no need for that," she snapped. "Sometimes you're just another insensitive ape. You know that?"

He apologized several times, but she didn't buy it. He had wanted to remind her of her mistake. She had failed to react—she knew that; she didn't need him to remind her. She let it go; back to business. "When we talk to the girls at The Shelter about how they raise money out on the streets, one thing that comes up, besides selling sex, or running drugs, is selling their blood. They've all done it; all it takes is a fake I.D. Even Sharon's done it." She passed him several photocopies. They were from back issues of medical journals. "Both blood and tissue type are extremely important in transplants. That's where a doctor begins in what can sometimes be a long process of matching a donor with a recipient. These articles will fill you in."

He scanned the articles quickly. "Blood banks," he mumbled. Then he said outright, "They select their potential donors from blood banks?"

She said, "It's certainly a strong possibility. One worth following up."

"We'll divide and conquer," Boldt said. "Talk to Cindy Chapman. Press her for information. *Did* she sell her kidney? Did she sell her blood? I'll pay a visit to our local blood banks." He supported Miles as he stood.

She caught his eyes. She held him there, waiting. "Say it," she said. He stared at her. "You can't just walk out of here after all of this and not say it."

"Is it so important?" Boldt asked.

"It's a young woman's life," she reminded. "You tell me."

He nodded in resignation. "I'm in."

6

Dr. Elden Tegg retained the only key to the Lakeview Animal Clinic's refrigerated walk-in because of the drugs it contained. He never would have chosen to install the walk-in himself; but this office had previously been a small Italian restaurant, and the walk-in served a useful purpose, both as the repository for the medications and as a holding closet for the surgical waste and dead animals that were by-products of any busy surgical clinic.

The man he met at the clinic's back door was short and stocky, dressed in a black-leather jacket, with black hair that peaked sharply in the center of his forehead. Donnie Maybeck was hired freelance to drive the clinic's "chuck wagon"—transporting the various bags of organic waste to a private incinerator. Because they would temporarily store this waste in the walk-in, he made only two trips a week.

Tegg unlocked the heavy door to the walk-in and stepped back, allowing the man to do his job but keeping an eye on him because of the abundance of controlled substances.

"Wanna gimme a hand with this?" Maybeck asked Tegg. He had horrible teeth, chipped and gray with decay.

This question, posed as it was, signaled Tegg. He stepped inside the cooler and pulled the door behind him until it thumped shut, closing them in. "Make it quick," he said. You could see your breath in here. Tegg crossed his arms to fend off the cold.

The man in the black-leather jacket spoke softly. "Some guy called *me* about a meeting. Said it can't wait."

"What can't wait? What guy?"

"Sounded like a Chink. Said a doc up in Vancouver recommended you. Asked me to set up a meet with you. Wanted it ASAP. Like tonight."

"Vancouver?" Tegg knew this could only mean one thing. He felt hot all of a sudden.

"The guy says either you agree to meet him or no. There's no bullshit with this guy."

Tegg felt his knees go weak.

The man next to him continued, "Said he was prepared to pay some major bucks."

"And what did *you* say?" Tegg asked anxiously.

"I didn't tell him squat. Okay? I'd like to know how the fuck he got *my* name. I'm checking with you, Doc. That's all. No need to sprout a fuckin' hemmi! I got this covered."

Tegg attempted some measure of self-control. He slowed his thoughts down, separated them, and dealt with them one by one.

His thoughts tended to leap ahead of him, making the present something he saw only upon reflection, so that much of his life felt more like instant replay than the real thing. He lived life as much from recalling that which had just occurred as he did from experiencing it, making him feel like two different people—one moving through life and the other attempting to come to grips with his actions.

Could he allow an opportunity like this to pass him by? On the other hand, could he protect himself well enough from the possible dangers?

"Listen," the other man said, "you're my needle man for Felix tonight. Don't forget you agreed to do that for me. So, what if I got this guy to meet us out there?"

Tegg *had* forgotten about this commitment. It rattled him—it wasn't like him to forget *anything*, even something so distasteful.

Maybeck added, "Listen, I could run point for you. Get this Chink out there ahead of you. Check him out. Keep you close by. If it's cool, I give you a shout on the car phone. If you don't hear from me by, say, nine o'clock, I get rid of him and you hang until it's clear to come in and help me out with Felix. One thing about these fights, we got bitchin' security. If this guy's trouble, he's gonna wish he stayed home. Know what I mean?"

Tegg suddenly realized that in surgery his thoughts did not get ahead of him—his hands kept up effortlessly. He wondered if this explained his love of surgery.

He said to this other man, "What if he doesn't like the setup? *I* sure as hell wouldn't meet somebody at a dog fight! I've never even *been* to a dog fight."

"Hey, it's not our problem. Okay? This is pay or play," he said misquoting things he knew nothing about. This man's vocal drivel always set Tegg on edge. "If he doesn't want to show, tough titties for him."

Tegg contemplated all of this while the other man gathered the plastic bags of contaminated waste. "Set it up," Tegg ordered. He turned and punched the large throw-bar that released the walk-in's outside latch. He walked slowly down the hall, pensive and concentrating. He sensed that everything had changed. The closer he drew to the examination room, the more put off he was by the thought of cats and dogs. Boring, meaningless work.

Earlier in the day, he had simply wanted to do his job well—get through another day. Have some fun. Earn some good money, listen to some Wagner, all the while working a blade.

Now all he wanted was to meet this unidentified man. He glanced at his watch impatiently: hours to go.

He looked in on Pamela Chase, who was just bringing up another set of X-rays. Ever the diligent assistant. "We didn't get much on our first series," she explained.

"You do good work." She glowed at this comment. Tegg knew exactly how to play her, how to feed her needs. She fed his in her own way—her unending compliments, her adoring glances. Other ways, too.

He stepped up to the X-rays. Child's play, compared to the real work that lay ahead of him. He could feel her sweet breath warm against his cheek as she leaned in to share in this exploration. He moved over so that she could see better and allowed his hand to gently brush her bottom, as if accidentally. She didn't flinch, her eyes searching out the elusive fracture in the fuzzy black-and-gray images.

Besides, he thought, self-amused, she knew this contact was no accident. She loved it. She loved everything about him.

7

"Whose turn is it to heat up dinner?" Boldt asked his wife, feeling a little apprehensive about how to steer the conversation to the subject of his returning to work. How to negotiate his future with her. They had found a routine that worked. He was about to challenge all that, and he knew before he began that flexibility was not her long suit. She was changing clothes, out of her executive-banker look and into some blue jeans and a cotton sweater she had tossed onto the bed. It was past seven—he was starved.

Liz answered, "I suppose it's mine, but I refuse. Let's go out."

"What about Einstein?" Boldt asked, looking over at Miles, who was fighting to keep his eyes open, not wanting to miss anything. All so new to him. Each of his expressions meant the world to Boldt: an inquisitive glance, a furrowed brow. Simple pleasures.

"Okay," she said. "You win. Take-out, and I'm buying. If I make the call, will you pick it up?"

He asked, "Have you noticed how much we negotiate everything?"

"Chinese, Vietnamese, Thai? You name it."

"Fish and chips," he suggested.

"Too fattening."

"You said I could name it."

"I lied." She patted her belly. "How about sushi?"

"Where's your wallet?"

"The front hall I think."

"Make it a big order. I'm starved, and that stuff never stays with me."

"And get some beer, would you?"

While Boldt was gone, Liz had put Miles to sleep. When they finished eating, Boldt caught her hand and led her out to the living room where he sat her down. It was after nine.

"The IRS shut down The Joke last night. Confiscated all the books."

"The IRS? So *that's* what's bothering you."

"They want to talk to us."

Disbelief came over her eyes. "Us? Oh, God, I hope they don't know about the cash income."

"I don't see what else it could be."

"Oh, shit. I signed that return."

"We *both* signed the return."

"But *cash*? Cash under the table? How could they . . . ? Goddamn that Bear Berenson. He must have tried to deduct it. Damn it all. You realize the penalty we'll face? Oh, my God."

"And The Joke is closed down. I can look around for other work, but no one's going to pay me like Bear did."

"Oh, God. You realize the penalty? I wonder if they can send you to jail for something like this."

"Money's all they want. It's all anybody wants."

"But that's just the point! *What* money? Every available cent we have is going to pay off the hospital."

Boldt didn't want her thinking about this. He glanced back toward the room where Miles now slept and remembered the complications of his delivery as if it had been yesterday. Would he ever forget that night? Could any price tag be put on having them both alive? "We'll manage."

"Manage? You don't do the books. I do. We *won't* manage, that's just the point. We *need* that income. Are they going to audit us? Is that what you mean? Oh, God, I don't believe this."

He hated himself for manipulating her like this, for doing to her what in her own way Daphne had done to him, but on this subject Liz had Special Handling written all over her. "I heard an awful story today about a girl named Cindy Chapman."

"They *nail* you for unreported income, you know. You know that, don't you?"

"She's a sixteen-year-old runaway."

As he had hoped, Liz momentarily forgot about the IRS. "What are you talking about?"

"They *stole* her kidney," Boldt explained.

"Who did?" she gasped.

"Worse than that: She hemorrhaged. She almost died. Sixteen-years old," he repeated.

"Lou?" There it was, that flicker of recognition he had been expecting, but dreading.

"If I go active again, I'm eligible for a loan through the credit union."

Her eyes grew sad and then found his. She didn't speak, just stared. Boldt said, "We'd have to juggle Miles. I realize that. Maybe day care," he said tentatively, expecting an eruption.

Instead, she turned a ghastly pale. She rose, her back to him, and walked into their bedroom. She shut the door behind her, closing him out. He loved this woman. Her sense of humor. Her courage. The way she laughed when it was least expected. The way she reached into the shower to test the temperature. Little things, all of them important. The way she hummed to herself when she didn't know he could hear. Her sense of organization. The silly presents she would show up with on no particular occasion. Her pursuit of pleasure. The way she made love when she was really happy.

He could hear the radio through the closed door. The news. The weather. More rain. They couldn't take any more rain. The flooding was as bad as it had ever been. Suicide rate was up: bungie jumping off Aurora Bridge, without the bungie cords.

He looked around for something to do. Lately, Miles, this woman, and The Big Joke had been his whole life. Now he found himself thinking about Cindy Chapman and Daphne Matthews.

Maybe he'd try to talk her into this in the morning. Maybe he would admit to a promise already made. Maybe Cindy Chapman was an isolated case. Maybe there wasn't some guy out there carving up runaways after all. Maybe, maybe, maybe.

He went to the bedroom door and opened it cautiously. "Mind if I join you?"

She was on the bed, her jeans unbuttoned. She

shrugged. "More rain," she said, as if nothing had come before.

"Yeah, I heard."

She patted the comforter beside her. He knew that look. Forgiving. Cautiously optimistic. He loved her for it.

Boldt stepped inside, kicking off his shoes, and shut the door.

8

A hundred yards down the dark, narrow, overgrown lane, Elden Tegg encountered a truck blocking his way. A huge man with an untrimmed beard asked him his name, checked his driver's license, consulted a list, and finally backed out of the way, allowing him to pass.

He drove under a canopy formed by the limbs of trees. The road was all mud and leaves. He parked the Trooper amid a group of battered pickup trucks and hurried through the rain toward the large barn. A yellow light escaped the slats in the wood. He pulled open the door and stepped inside.

He smelled cigarettes, hay, manure and musty, rotting wood. He smelled a metallic, salty odor as well, one that as a veterinarian he knew only too well: animal blood. He stepped into shadow and studied the scene before him.

The fighting ring, a wooden box ten-feet square, had been hastily constructed out of gray barn wood. It occupied an area in the middle of the wide dirt aisle between the stalls. A hayloft, cloaked in dark-

ness, loomed above them. The building's only light
came from a single bare bulb suspended directly
above the center of the ring. It cast harsh shadows
on the rough faces of the nearly twenty men in at-
tendance.

This scene repulsed him. Pitting dogs to the
death. He repaired life; he did not waste it.

A head in the crowd turned and faced him. The
same man from earlier in the day, Donnie Maybeck.
His gold Rolex winked at Tegg as it caught the light.
He approached Tegg with an exaggerated stride. He
smiled, flashing his ragged gray-brown teeth at Tegg
like an old whore lifting her skirt at a would-be John.

"Are we set?" Tegg asked.

"Everything's cool." He indicated the loft with a
nod. "But before we get to that, we gotta do Felix."

Spurred by an act of local government that
amounted to canine genocide for all pit bulls, Tegg
had rescued Felix and others from certain death in
favor of lives devoted to science and research. These
dogs—his creations, in a way—were now hidden out
at Tegg's farm, where he maintained a surgical research laboratory. As much as Tegg hated the idea,
the only way to fully test the success of the latest
surgery was to fight this dog in the ring. Although
Maybeck had assured him that there was always
someone "competent" on hand to sew up any inflicted wounds—a so-called needle man—Tegg did
not want anybody else doctoring the dog. Besides, he
thought, this dog's insides would only confuse another vet, and raise suspicions about Tegg's prac-
tices.

"I'm not here to fight him, only to provide medical attention if he needs it," Tegg reminded.

"He's up next," Maybeck explained. "Up against
Stormin' Norman. You understand. Norman ain't
lost no fight in six go's. But I'm gonna need your
help, Doc. You're the only one can handle him."

"Where is he?" Tegg asked.

Donnie Maybeck led him to a cream-colored air-line travel cage perched high on a hay bale. The animal inside bared its razor-sharp teeth and growled ferociously at Donnie, who grinned back with his own ragged teeth, pressing his face close to the grid of bars on the door, teasing the dog with a growl. The pit bull charged the door so strongly that the cage nearly slid off the bale.

"Don't taunt him," Tegg protested. At the sound of Tegg's voice, the dog's behavior reversed. It quieted and pushed its wet nose tightly into the bars of the cage toward Tegg.

"See? This here is *your* dog, Doc. You're the one who saved him—and he knows it. You gotta help me do this."

"I showed you how to work the collar. What kind of fool can't work a shock collar? You can push a button, can't you?" It was a rare display of spleen for Tegg, a terrible sign of weakness. He regretted it immediately. Maybeck did not take well to denigrating comments about his intelligence or lack thereof.

Maybeck's eyes hardened. "I don't want to use no collar before the fight. It might weaken him, and I would hate to *lose* him."

The idea that Felix might lose cut Tegg to the quick. Maybeck was right—this was no time to shock the dog.

Tegg kept the shock collar's remote device in hand as he led Felix from the cage, leashed him, and led him toward the ring. To Tegg's delight, Felix behaved impeccably under escort. Maybeck followed, but at a distance.

Once alongside the ring, Tegg cradled Felix in his arms and removed the shock collar. Felix's opponent, Stormin' Norman, waited in the far corner. Around his throat he carried a dozen healed scars of a warrior.

A three-hundred-pound man with a beard of barbed wire peered out from beneath a John Deere farmer's cap and declared solemnly, "To the death."

The announcement sobered and silenced the spectators. The rain drummed on the roof. The air went electric with anticipation. Felix fixed his attention on his opponent. "I can't do this," Tegg told Maybeck. "Even in the name of research."

He was spared any such decision. As the other dog was released, Felix broke loose and dove into the ring. The dogs exploded at one another. A roar went up from the crowd. Tegg withdrew to the shadows.

He suddenly felt as if he was being watched. He looked around. No one. Again he scanned the barn's interior and again could identify no one interested in him. Then he looked up into the hayloft.

There in the soft shadows stood a man dressed in a business suit, his full attention focused on Tegg, who recognized him immediately as Wong Kei, an infamous Seattle mob boss. His face was constantly in the news. Though this was a different face tonight: pale skin stretched tightly across sharp bones. Hard, spiritless eyes. A man desperately sad.

An explosion of applause from the audience signaled the end of the fight.

Maybeck tugged on Tegg's arm and pulled him toward the ring. Felix was circling the bloodied corpse of his failed opponent. "Not a scratch on him, Doc. You understand? He dropped Norman like he was a toy poodle. Norman! Not a scratch! You're a fucking genius, Doc. A real fucking genius."

Expressionless, disgusted, Tegg collected the dog and returned him to the travel cage. Tegg glanced up into the loft. He told Maybeck, "I'll see him now."

═══

By the time they reached the hayloft via a set of rickety stairs, and Tegg had submitted himself to a frisk search by one of Wong Kei's two stocky bodyguards, another contest had begun below. There were no introductions; a man of Wong Kei's reputation needed none. In and out of the courts—always acquitted. They sat opposite each other on hay bales. Maybeck and the bodyguards remained standing.

Wong Kei got to the point. "My wife is fifty-seven years old. She is suffering from unstable angina that will shortly claim her life if nothing is done. She had her first myocardial infarction two years ago. As I am sure you are aware," he said venomously, "heart transplants are refused to anyone over the age of fifty-five. My wife's case is made worse by both a rare blood type—AB-negative—and the fact that she's an extremely small woman.

"I arranged a 'private' transplant surgeon some time ago. A man willing to help. He's out of Vancouver. He attempted to locate an unregistered donor heart but to date has been unsuccessful. He recommended I contact your associate. I understand you have found him a kidney from time to time. I must admit that I am not terribly comfortable turning to a veterinarian for a human heart. That is one of the reasons I wanted this meeting: to meet you." He paused as the crowd below erupted in cheers.

"I make no promises," Tegg stated.

"I have done my homework," the Asian said. "I would not be here had I not. As a veterinarian you have few equals."

"In a situation such as your wife's—one of life and death—time is the real enemy. Time forces certain decisions. I'm perfectly aware of that. How long does your wife have?" he asked, taking charge. But time wasn't Tegg's real enemy. Internally, a dialogue of a different sort began: Now that the opportunity had presented itself, how far would he go to erase a mistake he had made nearly twenty years earlier? Could he knowingly sacrifice a human being?

"She will be strong enough to move in a few days."

"To Vancouver?"

"Yes."

"Days?"

"If I put my wife's life into your hands, I will expect results," he announced sternly. "If you can't help me, you must say so now. If it's a question of money . . ."

Tegg waved his hand to stop the man. He did not want Maybeck to hear the amount being offered. A heart was worth no less than five-hundred thousand. If Wong Kei had indeed done his homework, as he claimed, then he knew that much. "I'm sure you'll be generous," Tegg said. The money accounted for only a part of his stake in this. There was more to be gained here.

"Are you interested?"

"Extremely."

"May I *count* on you?"

Tegg glanced briefly at Maybeck. The man looked frightened. You didn't fail a man of Wong Kei's reputation. The mobster was telling him that much by just the look in his eye. He wanted a commitment.

Tegg answered, "I will have to do *my* homework, hmm? We'll have to see what's available." He pointed to a file folder on a bale of hay. "Her records?" Seize control: That's how you dealt with people like Wong Kei. The Asian passed him the folder.

"We will begin looking for a donor immediately. How do I reach you?"

Wong Kei removed a business card, wrote a phone number on the back of it, and handed it to Tegg.

"You'll be hearing from me," Tegg said confidently.

They didn't shake hands. Wong Kei rose, crossed the darkened loft and disappeared down the stairs.

Maybeck sat in the shadow of a post. "We'll have to zoom the donor to get the heart. Am I right?" Maybeck asked.

Believing Maybeck was nervous about this, Tegg returned to a justification decided upon many months earlier: "If *one* human life is sacrificed to save *many*, then what harm is done? If not one, but four, five, six lives are saved, does this not balance the scales?"

Maybeck answered, "I just mean in terms of what we gotta do. We go zooming someone, this had better be *big* money."

Reading the file in the limited light, Tegg spoke without looking up, "Check the database for an AB-negative. She'll have to be small: a hundred pounds tops. All you do is bring me the donor. You'll be rich after this. Fifty thousand for your part. That's what you want, isn't it?"

Through the cavity in the hayloft came the chorus of barking dogs. Among them, Tegg could hear Felix as clearly as if he alone were barking. Felix's superiority in the ring confirmed Tegg's brilliance. There would be more tests, of course; there always were. Life, it seemed, was one long test. Victory came not from a single win but from a series of accomplishments.

He stopped to take one last look at Donnie Maybeck, who still hadn't moved. Mention of that number had numbed him. Just right.

As Tegg descended the stairs, he felt exhilarated. This was his chance to erase the slate, to prove something to himself, to give something back. He intended to make the most of it.

FRIDAY

February 3

9

Juggling his household chores and his role as Mr. Mom, Boldt visited two area blood banks Friday morning with his son Miles in tow. It was not until the second interview that he learned that the donation of whole blood was strictly voluntary. He had neglected to raise this question at the first location. Plasma centers paid, not blood banks.

BloodLines Incorporated, Seattle's only plasma center, occupied the back half of the ground floor of a former First Avenue warehouse which had, years before, been converted into retail space, then a dry cleaner/laundromat. Boldt remembered them both. A uniform rental shop now occupied the half that fronted First Avenue. Mannequins dressed as nurses and security guards stood at inanimate mock attention in the display windows. The entrance to the plasma center was from the side street, up four cement steps, through a set of glass doors stenciled in blue with the name BloodLines as well as a parent corporation, LifeWays Inc.—which in finer print turned out to be a subsidiary of The Atlanta Charter and Group Health Foundation. Boxes inside boxes, a reminder of Liz's banking world.

Reception held two orange-vinyl padded

benches, each fronted by an oak-veneer coffee table stained with white rings and littered with thumb-worn, outdated copies of *People* Magazine. A pair of dusty-leafed silk ficus trees stood forlorn in opposing corners. The dirt bucket that held the closest one had been used as an ashtray. A large sign thanked you for not smoking. A Coke machine, its light burned out, hummed from across the expanse of institutional gray carpet. There were several doors leading from this room. The one most often used, Boldt saw—noticing the accumulated dirt around the doorknob—was to the left of reception, a high counter attended by a matronly woman wearing a nurse's uniform that had probably been rented from next door. Behind her were shelves filled with files, marked with colorful alphabetized index tabs. Her name tag read, Mildred Hatch. She looked tired, suspicious and unhappy. A couple of Gary Larson cartoons were taped up for everyone to see.

"You been with us before?" she asked. She was apparently used to a regular clientele. Boldt's face didn't jog her memory.

"I'd like to speak to someone in administration, if I may." Miles nearly got his hand on one of the cartoons. Boldt arranged himself to prevent another attempt.

"Concerning?"

"One of your donors."

"Not possible. That's strictly confidential information. Can't help you." She pointed out a paragraph on a photocopied flyer, a stack of which waited to the right of a computer terminal.

Boldt explained, "I'm not trying to find out who the person is. I already know that. I just need a few questions answered. Someone in administration, if you please."

"I don't please. Not easily," she warned. She

found a pen. "Your name?" He told her. "Your company?"

Boldt said, "Seattle Police Department."

It shocked her. She flushed. "Why didn't you say so?" she asked angrily.

"I was hoping I wouldn't have to."

"The baby threw me off," she explained. "You always lug her around?"

"Him," Boldt corrected.

She looked closely at Miles for the first time. Briefly, she softened. He knew in an instant that she didn't have any kids; and by her ring finger, no husband either. "Name of the donor?" she asked.

"That's strictly confidential," Boldt said.

Her eyes flashed cold like green glass marbles. She had plucked her eyebrows thin and bleached the hair above her lip. A real beauty. She had missed with her eye shadow.

"Cynthia Chapman," Boldt told her. "The donor's name is Cynthia Chapman." She consulted her terminal, striking the keyboard with blunt, stubby fingers. When she paused, there was something in her eyes that confirmed she had found the name.

"She's in there?" Boldt asked, his heart racing.

The woman didn't answer. She picked up the phone and spoke too softly for Boldt to hear. By the time she started her third call he said, "Today, if possible."

A street person entered, a bum in his mid-fifties, although a quick glance and the clothes might have fooled you. Not quite pressed but not all that wrinkled. Not exactly clean-shaven but not disgusting by any means. It was his worn-heeled, unpolished shoes that gave him away. That and the pungent scent of a cheap after-shave which attempted to cover a week without a shower. Boldt watched as this man located the clipboard and ran the attached pen through the multiple-choice boxes with the practiced efficiency of a regular. The man knew the routine. He signed it, handed it to Miss Mildred Hatch, and headed for the Coke machine. Blood sugar, Boldt thought. They drink the pops to keep from getting light-headed. He seemed a man more accustomed to Muscatel. He headed over to the orange seats and a back issue of *People*.

Boldt wondered how they guaranteed a clean blood supply. Then he took one of the flyers and read, while Miss Hatch continued her two jobs simultaneously, the phone pasted in the crook of her neck, the bum's application form being studied box-by-box, answer-by-answer. The blood was thoroughly tested for drugs, alcohol and AIDS, the flyer explained, a process that took four to seven days. Donors were personally interviewed each time they gave blood. By signing the form you were verifying your personal activities, sexual preferences and your working knowledge of the condition of your blood. Anyone caught lying would be permanently refused acceptance by any branch of BloodLines. The plasma was paid for only after it had cleared the testing labs. They paid fifteen dollars a pint. You could donate every forty-eight hours but no more than three times a week. It seemed impossible. "How can a person give blood three times a *week*?" he blurted out.

Without looking up from her terminal, Mildred Hatch answered automatically, "We don't take your blood, only the plasma. The red blood cells are returned to you during the process. The plasma is removed by a centrifuge. Your body replaces the plasma within twenty-four hours." She glanced at him then, as if to say, "Don't you know *anything*?" Boldt folded up the flyer and slipped it in behind Miles, who chose that moment to become vocal. Boldt found himself bouncing around the room in an effort to settle the boy down, the waiting donor's attention fixed on him in a puzzled expression. Embarrassed, Boldt found the Men's Room and prepared Miles a bottle. Little murmurs of satisfaction, little slurps of joy.

Mildred Hatch signaled the man, who went through the more-often-used door A, the source of the medicinal odors that permeated this place. Five minutes later, following two more extended phone calls, Miss Hatch gave Boldt the nod, permitting him to enter the inner sanctum which, as it turned out, was through door B—just to the left of the Coke machine. He helped steady his son's bottle and found his way down a narrow corridor flanked by several workers tending computer work stations. Was the database of their donors available to any one of them? Was one of these persons directly or indirectly involved in the harvests? With this the only plasma bank in the city and a policeman's knowledge that *something* connected the four runaways, Boldt experienced the electricity of anticipation. He didn't believe much in "sixth-sense" phenomena, but there was no denying the quick beating of his heart and the internal sense that there was evidence to be uncovered here.

He put questions to a Ms. Dundee, a two-seater black woman with no neck and huge breasts. Her hands were swollen like some corpses Boldt had seen, and she wheezed when she spoke. She guarded all her explanations, and smiled in the same contrived manner as a used-car salesman. Her face was so bloated he could barely see any eyes and so round and wide that she seemed more a caricature of herself. Miles didn't like her either. On first sight of her he started crying and became a pest. He pushed his bottle aside demanding Boldt's repeated attention. An ever-cautious Ms. Dundee requested Boldt's police identification.

Boldt went through the ruse of pretending to search for it, realizing at that moment that events had led him to the inevitable. Would she call downtown and ask after him? Whether she did or not, Boldt now had no choice but to pay Lieutenant Phil Shoswitz a visit. Technically, he was impersonating a police officer. It seemed ludicrous to him, but he could be arrested for it.

"Just answer me this, please," he said to the huge woman. "Is Cynthia Chapman in your database or not?"

She nodded reluctantly.

Boldt felt a flood of relief. Curiosity surged through him. So many questions to ask. Could the harvester have selected Cindy from this database? Had he kidnapped her, or was a child desperate enough to sell her blood also willing to sell a kidney? Were the names of Dixie's other three "victims" in this database as well? "Does BloodLines keep an active database of all its previous donors?" he asked.

She viewed him suspiciously.

Their eyes met. "This can all be done formally," he informed her. "Warrants, subpoenas. Attorneys. Press. Have you ever been to our city police department, Ms. Dundee?"

"There *is* a database of all our donors, yes."

Boldt withdrew his notebook from his coat pocket.

"I have three other names I'd like to check," he said. He supplied her with the names of the three runaways—Julia Walker, Glenda Sherman and Peter Blumenthal—all of whom had been missing an organ at the time of death. Ms. Dundee entered these names into her computer terminal.

A moment later she said, "Nope. None of them."

"Damn it all!" he protested in disappointment. Then a thought occurred to him: "How far back do your records go?"

"A donor is kept active twelve months. The database is swept monthly."

"Swept?"

"Cleaned up."

"And what happens to those records?" he asked.

"Our data processing department in our home office maintains a complete donor list. That's required by the federal government in case health problems arise in the blood supply." She added, as a way of showing off the care they took, "You can't donate without a social security number, a current address and a phone number."

Boldt, having witnessed the street person in the reception area, wondered how careful they were in obtaining accurate identification, but he didn't press the issue. "Can you check these three names with the home office?"

Another expression of disapproval. Boldt's patience was running thin. How much could he tell her? "This isn't about traffic tickets, Ms. Dundee. A little cooperation now could go a long way toward protecting your company's image later. This branch's image."

"Just what kind of trouble are you talking about?"

"Why don't you make that call for me, and let's see where it leads? Then maybe we'll discuss it."

A few minutes and a brief phone conversation later, she informed him, "They'll call back. It won't take long."

Boldt used the down time to press for more information. Miles had dozed off. "How many of your employees would have access to your donor database?" he asked. She hesitated, unsure how much to share with him.

"A woman was *kidnapped*, Ms. Dundee. Kidnapping is a federal offense. The kidnapping may or may not be related to her association with BloodLines. Am I getting through?"

She answered, "At this branch, about two dozen of us would have access to our client base, maybe more. Hard copies of the files are kept behind registration."

"And is registration manned constantly?"

"Constantly? No, I would doubt it. No."

"You said 'this' branch? How many are there?"

"In Seattle? Just this one."

"And the others?"

"We're a regional corporation, Mr. . . . Boldt. Twenty-four branches in eleven states. I can give you the literature if you want. Or I could put you in touch with our home office in San Francisco."

"The database would contain a donor's blood type, would it not?"

"Blood groups. Of course."

"And personal information?"

"Meaning?"

"You tell me. You mentioned home address. How about age? Marital status?"

"All of those, yes."

"Accessible from any terminal?"

"No, the terminals deal with donors only by donor number. The personal information requires an access code. Only *I* have the access code, and only two terminals share the complete database: reception and mine. But there are the hard copies, as I mentioned, though they are locked up in a vault at night. We don't take our situation lightly, Lieutenant."

"Sergeant," he corrected. "No, I'm sure you don't."

"We take client confidentiality quite seriously."

Miles stirred.

Boldt asked, "What if I entered a particular blood

type into the computer. Would it be able to give me back the names of all those donors with that particular blood type? Can it sort that way?"

"You should talk to our data processing about that."

He hated these kinds of answers. "Back to your employees. How many of them do you know well?"

"Depends what you mean. I *know* them all. I hired them. I don't know about how well I know them."

"How long have you been with BloodLines?" he asked.

"Me? Goin' on nine years now."

"And your employees? Have any of them been with you, say, two or three years?"

She considered this. "Three or four, maybe. I could check for you if I had the home office's permission."

"And that would be up to me to obtain," he reasoned.

"Yes, it would."

Miles was awake and quickly losing control. Boldt resigned himself to leaving. He tried a long shot. "Of those three or four long-time employees, one of them has shown a particular interest in your computer system. Which one would that be? Maybe he or she helps you out with the system now and then."

She appeared both surprised and impressed by what he'd said. "You never did show me any identification," she reminded.

"No, I didn't." He paused. "Which employee?" he repeated, sensing she had the name on the tip of her tongue. "I need that name."

Her phone rang, sparing her from answering. When she hung up, she faced him with a dazed expression. "That was your call. The three names you gave me? They're *all* on our list. They were *all* clients of this office. Seattle. Were they kidnapped, too?"

Boldt repeated softly but severely, "I need the name of that employee. The one who helps you with the computer."

Ms. Dundee nodded ever so slightly, muttered, "I hate computers." She picked up her pen and wrote out the name: Connie Chi.

10

By five-thirty that afternoon, over one hundred cars had filled the lower parking area of the Broadmoor Golf Club. Mercedes, BMWs, Acuras, the occasional Cadillac and Olds. A spectacular turnout. In one corner of the enormous walled party tent, high-spirited kids dressed in Ralph Lauren's finest took turns, blindfolded, swinging a Louisville Slugger at a yellow-and-black *piñata* in the shape of a toucan. Heaters hummed softly, the champagne flowed, and the conversation reached a feverish pitch that all but drowned out the announcer's running commentary on the dog show taking place just off the practice putting green. A string quartet was all set up on a small platform stage at the far end of the tent, the musicians, in their formal wear, sampling the buffet as they awaited the "special guest" and a cue from their hostess.

Dr. Elden Tegg moved through his guests agreeably, if not comfortably, taking their hands, making small talk—charming, flattering. He wore a navy blue cashmere sport coat, a turquoise *Polo* shirt, khakis, and brand new leather deck shoes. He glanced over at his wife, Peggy, and offered a soft, appreciative smile—everything was going well. Two weeks earlier, Peggy had turned forty; to look at her, you might have guessed thirty. She was in her element here, mingling with the top of the heap, rubbing elbows with the real *power* of the city.

The banner behind the buffet read:

3rd Annual
Friends of Animals Benefit

Tegg mentally ran down the list of the day's events: the dog trials, a small wine auction, an awards presentation, and then the special entertainment Peggy had arranged. A few of the members of the opera's board of directors were already here. *All* of them had been invited. Tegg spotted James Hall and his wife, Julie, and crossed over to them.

"This is a better turnout than even last year," Jim Hall said, shaking Tegg's hand. "You'll raise a fortune."

"You must stay for the entertainment, James."

To his wife the man said, "The mystery musical guest. I've been hearing about this all week."

"Peggy's trying awfully hard to curry favor with the board, Elden. Don't you think?" Julie asked. She had a way of speaking her mind, of speaking the truth, that put you on the spot.

"How's the art world?" Tegg asked her, attempting to steer her clear of his wife's ambitions.

"Dodging the question, are we?" she replied.

One of the kids broke open the *piñata* right then, sparing Tegg an embarrassing moment. Peggy most certainly *was* trying to win favor with the board. Julie knew it. Everyone knew it. But it wasn't the type of thing you *talked about*! He had personally paid to fly in the winner of the Milano Festival to sing two arias here today. The string quartet, also brought in specially, had wowed Aspen last August. It had cost him a fortune! If this didn't impress the board, nothing would, except perhaps the donation he was planning to make.

With the prospect of the heart harvest now on the immediate horizon, Tegg faced the difficult decision of what to do with the enormous sum of money it would generate. He could "buy" his wife a seat on the opera board, or he could "buy" himself a transplant practice in Brazil. He knew whom to pay off; he knew which wheels to grease. Elden Tegg, M.D., F.A.C.S. Her dream or his? Could he leave all this behind?

He excused himself and hurried over to the children who were collecting the candy that had spilled. His son, Albert, and his daughter, Britany, ran up to show him their take, offering it like pirates' treasure. A bunch of the children gathered at his feet, excited eyes sparkling. They wanted another *piñata*, another game. It gave him great pleasure to bring the children this kind of joy, to include them in the event this way. How could you possibly benefit animals without involving children? The two seemed fundamentally linked.

Tegg signaled his veterinary assistant, the plump and officious Pamela Chase, and turned the children over to her. Pin the Tail on the Zebra was next. Last year some Democrats had complained about using a donkey.

Everywhere he went people called out softly, "Wonderful party!" "Terrific event!" "Having a great time, Elden!" He felt like Santa Claus, pleasing so many people at once.

He glanced out the door in time to see a collie—

Elsie was her name—paraded on leash around the circle. As Dr. Elden Tegg, he had healed a gunshot wound to Elsie's humerus. Scanning the field of contestants, he recognized several animals as patients of his. He knew each by name, knew each case history in detail; in a way, he regarded them as members of his own family. He hoped that Elsie won something—if for no other reason than to prove his own expertise with a scalpel. In another vet's hands, she would have been a three-legged dog today.

His wife's nervous voice came from behind him. "It's going beautifully, don't you think?"

He turned and kissed her. "Splendidly. The food is excellent. You've done a wonderful job."

"We might consider using these same caterers at our party next week. If we could get them. What do you think?"

"It's a great idea." This, he knew from the hopeful glint in her eye, was what she wanted to hear, so this was what he told her.

She kissed him lightly, as an excuse to whisper into his ear. "Be nice to the Feldsteins. He's had prostate cancer, you know?"

"Alan has?" He relied on Peggy to keep him up on such things. How she kept it all straight was anybody's guess.

She reminded, "Alan is very close with Byron. He has his ear."

The aging Byron Endicott, who ran a multinational shipping company, was City Opera's chairman and someone Peggy would have to win over in order to be invited onto the board.

"So, basically, what you're saying," he teased, "is I should avoid asking Alan what it feels like to be reamed with something slightly larger than a penlight."

She winced and chased a waving hand aimed at her from the crowd.

Tegg headed straight to Alan Feldstein. "Feeling better, Alan? Hmm?"

"They got it all, I'm told. Nothing like the big C to get you thinking, I'll tell you that." He studied Tegg and said confidentially, "You're a doctor. How much of what you tell your patients is B.S.? I don't believe half of what my doctor tells me."

"My patients have four legs. We don't enter into a lot of conversation."

"I suppose not."

"Have you seen Byron this afternoon?"

"I don't believe he's here," Alan Feldstein said, stretching his neck. He added, "If you had a wife that young, would *you* be here?"

"Well, at least we know your operation was successful," Tegg whispered quietly to the man. Feldstein grinned. Tegg bailed out while he was still ahead.

He was on his way to check how Pamela was handling Pin the Tail on the Zebra when he spotted a leather jacket out of the corner of his eye. Maybeck, pretending to be one of the public spectators of the dog show.

Tegg did his best to contain his anger. He brushed off several attempts to snag him, cut outside the tent, and walked over to stand beside the man, facing in the direction of the dog show.

"What are *you* doing here?" he asked.

"Connie found an AB-negative in the database," Maybeck said softly, screening those horrible teeth from sight with his hand. "Ninety-five pounds. Single. She ain't been an active donor in over two years, but she's in the phone book—lives in Wallingford."

Tegg experienced that weightless feeling in his stomach of being in an elevator that was falling too quickly. It was one thing to consider performing a heart harvest, another thing entirely to actually set it in motion. "Can you deliver?" Tegg inquired. They had never attempted a kidnapping.

"This ain't pizza we're talking about."

"Don't toy with me, Donald," Tegg said, knowing how the man disliked the use of his proper name. "Are there any other AB-negs?" Tegg asked rhetorically, knowing AB-negative accounted for less than four percent of the population. He was one himself. They were extremely lucky to have found even a single match.

"None."

"Age?"

"She'd be . . ." Maybeck attempted to add in his head. It bothered Tegg it should take him so long. "About twenty-six."

"That's very good."

"Why you think I'm here? I know it's good."

"Look into it. Find out if it can be done."

"We can do it. I already got it figured. I been watching her place. Back door is fucking perfect for this."

Tegg didn't trust his assessment. Maybeck was more than likely blinded by the possible money. What *wouldn't* he risk for that?

"But I'm gonna need your help."

"*My* help?" Tegg asked.

"You're the one who's going to get her to open the door for us."

Us? Tegg was thinking. Their relationship was symbiotic: Tegg needed a flunky, a go-between with the runaways and with Connie Chi at BloodLines; Maybeck liked the idea of large amounts of cash for relatively little work. But *us*? Tegg seldom thought of them as any kind of team. It was an *arrangement*, was all—often an unpleasant one at that.

"I'm telling you, Doc. I got it all worked out. We go for it tomorrow morning."

Tomorrow? Tegg wanted this chance at a heart. But how badly? How far was he willing to go? He glanced at his watch; he would have to make arrangements with Wong Kei. Could he arrange a meeting for later tonight?

It started to sprinkle. Rain would put a quick end to the dog show.

Maybeck said, "One phone call from you to this girl, Doc, and she's not only going to let us into her home, but she's going to make sure no one else is there. You want me to tell you about it?"

Tomorrow? Tegg was still thinking. "I'll call you," he said, turning and walking away. Then he changed his mind and headed toward his Trooper parked alongside the Pro Shop. He could use the cellular to call Wong Kei.

He could put this in motion immediately.

11

Dr. Ronald Dixon had something to tell him, and it pertained to Daphne's investigation—Boldt knew that much from the way Dixie had phrased the unexpected invitation to this dinner show.

The entrance to Dimiti's Jazz Alley is, appropriately enough, down an alley, opposite a parking garage. Boldt parked his seven-year-old Toyota and crossed the alley, feeling out of place. He was accustomed to The Big Joke's sticky floors and chairs with uneven legs. This place was aimed more at the BMW crowd.

Dixie's wife had allegedly been called to an emergency session of the local Girl Scout chapter, freeing the ticket he now handed to Boldt as the two met at the front door. Boldt didn't believe the story for a minute. Nancy Dixon didn't like clubs. That was just Dixie's way of sparing Boldt the fifteen-dollar ticket. Dixie confirmed his status as a regular when the two men were greeted warmly by the host and shown immediately to one of the best tables. Dixon placed a flight bag on the floor but kept it within reach. He could have checked it upstairs along with their coats. Why hadn't he?

Boldt ordered a glass of milk from the waiter who delivered a Scotch for Dixie—they knew his drink. The house began to fill. Good-looking women with good-looking guys. Computer whiz kids and aerospace experts. Older couples who remembered 78s and Big Noise From Winnetka—false teeth, false hair, but real lives. A couple of smokers relegated to the distant seats under the air vents. Bread roll baskets passing by in a blur. Nylons. Even a few spike heels. God, it was good to get out now and then, good to be out with Dixie again.

"I bet it's been a year since I've been here," Boldt said.

"Kids do that. It'll change."

"I hope not. I like things the way they are." Some part of Boldt, in spite of his rampant curiosity, wanted Dixon to leave that bag on the floor, wanted to keep the conversation personal, and off whatever that bag contained.

"I want to tell you a story," Dixie announced. Boldt's skin prickled with anticipation.

"What happens in my line of work as in yours is that cases come and go. Some are solved, some are filed. Some go dormant, though they never quite leave your mind." He sampled the Scotch and clearly approved. "Every now and then something triggers you, something goes off in your brain, and you think: 'I've seen this before,' or 'Didn't I hear somebody talking about something like this?,' or 'I *know* this is familiar to me.' You know what I'm talking about. It happens to all of us."

Boldt nodded. He felt impatient and restless.

"Cases overlap," he went on. Boldt fidgeted with his spoon, barely containing himself. "It happens all the time—more often than seems possible. There are reasons for such overlaps: There are only a limited number of murderers in King County at any one time—at least we hope so—more often than not, a relatively small number given the population base. We average less than ten in any given month. Sometimes zero. Right? From my viewpoint, it means there's a good possibility—even a probability—that any two bodies discovered around the same time, or in the same area, or relating to a similar cause of unnatural death may in fact be the work of the same person. It takes a certain jump in logic, however, to immediately reach that conclusion in *this* particular case, but that's my job, isn't it? Damn right it is. That's *exactly* what I'm here for. And my job is to pass along my concerns to the police if and when such suspicions bear investigation. In this instance, you, my friend, are the police, and I'll explain why.

"Nearly six months ago now," he continued, "a man carrying a brown paper bag arrived unannounced at our offices requesting to see 'whoever's in charge.' That's me, of course. He was of average height, in his early forties, with graying curly hair. He was of a slight build—a hundred and forty-five pounds maybe—the kind of guy who stays thin from an excess of nervous energy. You've met a dozen just like him. He was wearing a suit—a nice suit. This was his lunch hour. He was a corporate attorney by trade, name of Carsman.

"Mr. Carsman was a hunter. A bird hunter. Talked about not liking to kill. Talked about no one understanding hunting except other hunters. Said he liked to listen to the wind blow, the rain fall. 'The rain?' I asked. 'Is that why you're here?' He said no, it was on account of his dog. His dog? I verified that, then he lifted this paper bag, this grocery bag, the top of which was choked down tight so it looks like an old man's neck. He'd been sitting there holding it between his knees. I'm starting to think this guy is over the top and I'm part of his plan somehow. I'm starting to wish I carry some kind of revolver in my desk. I'm about to come out of my chair when he hoists this bag onto my desk. Thump, it goes. That thump worried me because I *knew* that sound: bone. I'm thinking it's a head maybe. He says he wasn't sure what to do with something like this. He said Stu Coleman's a neighbor of his. I know Stu from the state lab. Stu's all right. Stu told him to bring it to me. I asked him if I could see the bone. That threw him, but like I said: I knew that sound. There's no mistaking the sound of a bone on your desk."

"Whatever you say," Boldt said. His palms were moist. He wanted to order his dinner. He wanted Dixie to stop with his storytelling and get to the point, but Dixie spent a lot of hours with the dead, and he appreciated someone alive to talk to when he got the chance.

"He was hunting in a very remote location, timberland northeast of the city. He shoots a bird—a blue grouse, I think it was—and he sends his dog after it. Dog disappears a long time. When he comes back—the dog, that is—he has . . ." Dixie leaned over with some effort. Boldt heard the sound of a zipper. The bag. Dixie righted himself saying ". . . *this* in his mouth."

Dixon let the large bone down gently onto the table. To him, it was perfectly normal to show someone a bone—a human femur. Big and unmistakable. To the people passing by their table, it proved a source of great curiosity—and for some, disgust.

Boldt studied it, turning it over repeatedly, and said, "You could have waited until I ordered my dinner."

"After a little bit of searching the stream, he found this as well," Dixon informed him, placing another, much smaller bone on the table. "This is the one that interests you—it's a rib."

"What if I was planning on ordering barbecue?"

"I thought Liz had you eating vegetarian."

"Who told you that?"

"Word gets around."

"Yeah, well . . . What if I am?"

"Then you're not ordering barbecue," Dixon said.

The second Scotch arrived. This was followed by a dinner waiter whose attention kept drifting to the two bones. Boldt ordered the Greek salad. Dixon—just to be spiteful—ordered a rich pasta with smoked turkey and prosciutto.

When the waiter left, Boldt handled the rib. "I'm supposed to be interested in this?"

"Yes, you are. It's human. Just like the femur. Just like you." Dixie stared him down. "I took a personal interest in locating the rest of the corpse. Human bones discovered in such an isolated area suggest a buried body—and buried bodies seem to be epidemic these days. The discovery of any human remains has to be investigated if for no other reason than that it is illegal to bury a corpse in the watershed area where Carsman's dog discovered the bone. Maybe you remember Monty, my assistant, Lewis

Montgomery? He's our forensic anthropologist—and he's very good. Monty coordinated a search team using Boy Scout troops because at the time Search and Rescue wouldn't touch it."

Boldt interrupted, "Boy Scouts?"

Dixie ignored him. "Nothing turned up and the case was filed under *Unsolveds.* I haven't spoken to Monty about the bones since. He and I ran some tests on them back when Carsman turned them over to us. Measurement and calcification tests indicated this femur had once belonged to a woman between the ages of eighteen and twenty-eight. The pelvis, if it can be found, will not only confirm this but will also tell us whether or not this woman had children."

Dixon continued "To formally identify a person from his or her bones, one needs more bones than this, and a *lot* of luck. A young woman in her mid-twenties, buried fifty miles from nowhere suggests the obvious to me . . ."

"Homicide," Boldt finished for him.

He toyed with the partial bone on the table. "Look at the rib, would you?"

Boldt studied the rib more closely, taking it into his hands and spinning it around. The waiter arrived with their meals. Boldt moved his arms to accommodate the man, who remained fascinated by the bones. He bumped a water glass, nearly spilling it. The waiter offered ground pepper, which both men declined, and he left, backing away, still fascinated.

Boldt ran his index finger along the square end of the bone. "Some kind of surgical technique?"

"Interesting, isn't it?"

Boldt waited him out.

"We use gardening shears. They work the best."

"We?" Boldt asked.

"My office," Dixon replied. "For the autopsies,"

he clarified. "You've seen me use them; you just don't remember."

"But this was no autopsy," Boldt said.

"I have some serious hunches about that rib, about this skeleton, and the young woman it once danced inside. Once slept inside. The woman inside whom it grew and developed. My office closed the case. Another department could reopen it." He stabbed some of the salad. "*You're* the investigator."

"Boy Scouts. What did you expect?"

"We had some good people leading them. Nothing wrong with young eyes, young legs. That's rough country out there."

Boldt asked, "Did they look up river for the rest of her?"

"Of course. And found nothing. But there must be some way to find her."

"You want my advice?"

"I want more than your advice. I want your participation. How would *you* go about it?"

"I'd talk to the experts. Water Resources or Army Corps of Engineers. Someone responsible for flood predictions, for the way water would move a bone like that. We had some heavy rains last fall. Was that six months ago? I think it was. Those rains let up right after Miles was born. That's how I measure the world now, you know? In terms of when my boy was born."

Dixie said, "People bury bodies along rivers for two reasons. The wet soil speeds decay—"

Boldt interrupted, "And it's easier to dig in."

"Matthews showed you the autopsy files on those three runaways. I've put in a request for the tissue samples from those cases. But this . . . I had forgotten all about this case." He touched the long femur that remained between them on the table just as a young man in his twenties passed, noticed the bone and nudged his girlfriend.

"Oh, look. They have leg-o-man tonight." She giggled.

Boldt did not laugh. He was staring intently at Dixon.

"Patterns, my friend. We're in the patterns business—cops and interior decorators. This bone," he said, shifting his attention to the rib, "never healed. Never had time to heal. See the different color here? That means it was buried within a few days of the operation. Oh, yes: operation. This woman was cut open, either to heal her or to steal from her. But not at a hospital, not as part of the *system*. Quite possibly it killed her, if she wasn't dead already. Cut open by a surgeon—someone who has done enough rib work to use snippers instead of the medical school tools we're told to use. Snippers work better. Those runaways, the files I gave Matthews—Walker, Sherman, Blumenthal—they were also cut open by a surgeon. The same guy? The same reason? He wasn't after a kidney, I can tell you that. Lung or liver, those are your choices, the way he cut that rib. Are all these the work of the same doctor? Patterns. We both know that it's patterns that hang these guys. We're all—every one of us—victims of our own inescapable patterns."

Inescapable patterns? Boldt thought. He examined the bones once again. "An organ harvest?"

"It's a strong possibility. We have a lot of questions to answer: How long ago was she buried? Who was she? What procedure was done? We need the rest of her, Lou, or a good portion thereof. Why did he bury this one and not the others? She's been in the ground a long time. Those bones are picked clean. What sets her apart?"

Boldt sensed something in the man, as only friends can. "You're jumping ahead of yourself. You're linking her to the others with only supposition. Or are you? You wouldn't get this excited over hunches," Boldt realized, thinking aloud. "There's something else in that bag of yours, isn't there? Something even more convincing?"

"You were born a detective. Did you know that?" He seemed a little disappointed that Boldt had second-guessed him. Boldt's heart rate increased. Now, more than ever, he wanted the rest of the evidence. Dixie dug out a pair of black-and-white photographs which, because of their magnification, Boldt immediately recognized as lab work.

"Peter Blumenthal—one of the runaways who died as a result of surgery—also had several ribs snipped. He was a lung harvest. We saved one of his ribs, as is our custom with possible evidence. Yesterday, when those files reminded me of Mr. Carsman's visit, I ran both ribs—Blumenthal's and this mystery woman's—by the lab for comparison tool markings. Here's what they came up with." He handed Boldt the photos. He had studied hundreds of such photographs. When any tool—a knife, pliers, a wrench, wire cutters—interacts with a material—wood, wire, metal, in this case, bone—it leaves a distinct "fingerprint." A cutting tool leaves grooves that under magnification resemble scratch marks. These scratch marks form distinct patterns, like a comb with some of the teeth missing. In the photo, the two sets of scratch marks had been perfectly aligned, indicating the work of the same tool.

Boldt caught himself holding his breath. Whoever was responsible for the death of Peter Blumenthal and the two other runaways had also performed surgery on the woman who had once lived inside these bones. The cases were inexorably linked by this evidence.

Reading his thoughts, Dixie said, "The harvester buried this one, Lou. Why? Why when he turned the other three, and Chapman, back into the streets? Why treat this mystery woman any different?"

"Because she died on him."

"Maybe. But the way these bones were picked clean, this woman predates these other harvests by several *years*. These recent ones may have died by accident. He may not even know they're dead yet. But with her," he said, pointing to the bones, "he certainly knew."

"His *first*? Is that what you're saying?" Boldt knew the importance of such a find. The first incident in any criminal pattern typically told the investigator more than did any of the subsequent crimes or victims. It established method, motivation and a key look into the demographics of future victims. These bones suddenly took on an additional importance. This woman—whoever she was—just might tell them who the harvester was.

Dixon had reached the same conclusion. "If we locate the rest of her remains, she can tell us more."

Toying with the bones again, Boldt asked, "May I keep these?"

Dixon grinned. "I thought you'd never ask."

12

Tegg boarded the ten-fifteen ferry for Bainbridge Island at Pier 52 and waited until the ship was under steam. The wind blew out of the west, bitter cold upon his face. Gunmetal clouds moved overhead like a giant door shutting. When the ferry whistle reverberated out across the water, Tegg shuddered.

As ordered—he hated taking orders!—he worked his way down a series of steep metal ladders into the car hold.

It was dark down here, despite the occasional bare bulb and the wide openings at either end. Empty cars parked in long, tight rows. The smell of car exhaust and sea salt, kelp and fish. He wandered the aisles, as instructed, twisting and turning to worm his way through the cars. Sea spray kicked up by the wind blew through the open bow and misted across him, blurring the windshields. Many of the cars showed excessive body rot—even a few of the newer ones; these were the regular commuters. When Tegg turned around at the stern and started up the next aisle, he spotted a hulk of a figure some yards away. As he drew closer, he recognized the ape as one of Wong Kei's bodyguards. This was Wong Kei's world, not his. Wong Kei's rules. The ape stood alongside a black Chrysler New Yorker with mirrored windows. He opened the car door and signaled Tegg inside.

Tegg found himself alone with Wong Kei in the back seat. The emaciated man was drinking a diet Coke, holding the can with fingers as long and thin as chopsticks. "You are able to help me?" he said in an old man's voice. "You wouldn't have called otherwise, would you?"

"We have a possibility. What's your wife's present condition?"

"She's being flown north tomorrow, Saturday. I am told that surgery could follow immediately providing there are no setbacks. That will leave us in your hands, Dr. Tegg. We will be awaiting your call that the heart is on its way. She is running out of time. You understand this, I hope."

"I understand."

"You have found someone, I assume. Brain-dead? Dying? How long do we have?"

"You know as much as you need to." He didn't like the change in the man's eyes. Had he angered him? The Chinese are so inscrutable, he thought. "It's for your own good as well as mine," he added.

"I have a down payment for you. Call it good faith," he said. He pointed to the front seat where the ape belonged. The money was evidently up there.

"No money. Not yet. We can do that when it's over."

Wong Kei persisted, "I have a sum for you now which, as I have just said, is to show my good faith. Yours as well as mine. Please take it."

No mention of a final figure. Tegg liked it that way. "No hurry," he said.

The ferry rocked violently to the left. Dozens of cars complained.

"You are a trusting man," Won Kei put forward.

"Not really," Tegg said. "If you don't pay me, I'll take the heart back." He waited. "It was a joke," Tegg added.

"You joke about my wife's life?" His chin trembled. "Is that what I am hearing from you?" He drank more of the Coke, spilling some. "Allow me to explain something, Dr. Tegg. Allow me to explain the obvious." He finished the drink. He studied the empty can as if reading it. "I am relying on you. That is all I am going to say about it. That should be self-explanatory. Yes?"

Tegg didn't like the sound of that. "You will call me when your wife is admitted and ready to go," Tegg instructed. He wrote out his cellular number on a blank memo pad from his DayTimer. No name, just the number. "Only the cellular. If you call me on the land lines, I will hang up."

Wong Kei sat forward, reached over the seat and dragged a small Alaskan Airlines flight bag to him.

He looked incredibly tired. Anxiety and grief were swallowing him whole. Tegg knew the symptoms. "Take this. This is the *purpose* for this meeting— my purpose. Our time is wasted otherwise. I insist." He didn't shove it at him, but he made its handle available.

Tegg accepted the bag, his curiosity mounting. He understood the commitment his acceptance of it represented. He was crossing a dangerous threshold: He would now owe this man. He immediately regretted his acceptance of the bag, but knew it would be impossible to return it. Wong Kei's expression told him as much.

For emphasis, the Asian added, "We must not overlook the seriousness of the situation. Time is everything. There is *nothing* I will not do to restore my wife to health. Yes?"

Tegg thought he meant it as some sort of veiled threat, although it was difficult to interpret exactly. Perhaps he was offering his help. Tegg said, "If I don't hear from you first, I'll call when we're set to go."

The man nodded. The ferry slowed and bumped the loading dock.

From the ferry's deck, Tegg, all alone in the wind and the night, watched the black car as it and the others disembarked. In the glow of a few meager street lamps and a mercury light far in the distance, he watched sea gulls resting on pilings, standing on one leg. Balanced.

Tegg felt delicately balanced as well. Pamela would not assist in the heart harvest. They had discussed the possibility of it before—it was constantly on Tegg's mind—and she had rejected it outright. It would have to be a solo harvest, even more challenging. More risky. Perhaps it was time to sacrifice one of the dogs to practice. "Practice makes perfect," he said into the wind as the ferry lumbered through the chop and headed back toward Seattle. Toward his family. His children. And yet away from all of that at the same time.

Toward his future, he thought, however it was now defined.

SATURDAY

February 4

13

Dr. Elden Tegg attempted not to touch anything in Donnie Maybeck's van. Concern about leaving fingerprints behind had nothing to do with it—he was wearing gloves. The place was a cesspool. For a man repulsed by dirty environments, a man who had a fetish about cleanliness, this vehicle was a nightmare. A thick layer of dust and grime had baked onto the cracked vinyl of the dashboard. Some kind of solidified scum—soda? beer? coffee? worse?—had drooled over the engine cover that separated the two front seats and was now fuzzy with lint. The windows were tinted in a yellow filth, and the carpet—what was left of it—was matted like the hair on the backside of an incontinent dog. For a man accustomed to the sights and smells associated with invasive surgery, it was strange to feel nauseous.

"You don't look so hot," Donnie Maybeck said.

"Drive."

"Hey, I know you don't like this, but I ain't doing this alone. And Connie ain't no help in this kinda thing."

"We've been over this."

"Don't be so fucking pissed about it, because there's nothing can be done."

"Just drive.

"It's not the same as the others. You said so yourself. This here is kidnapping. This here is some serious shit. Connie could never do this."

"You shouldn't involve her in *any* of it." He saw no point in attempting to reason with a little person like Maybeck. There were fly specks along the bottom of the windshield. Donnie Maybeck was a fly speck. And what was that lodged into the defrost slot? A discarded plastic wrapper for a Sheik Elite with Spermicide! He recoiled, wanting to levitate and not have to touch *anything*.

"Hey, she's involved in it, all right. Okay? She's in this up to her short hairs. Ain't nothing can be done about it. Without her, without updating the database, how we gonna pick which donor to approach?"

"Humor me: Shut up and drive." Tegg felt uneasy. A mistake he had made years earlier had cost a human life. Now he possessed the skills and abilities to correct that wrong, even though it came at the cost of deepening his involvement with Maybeck.

"You're sure she's alone?" Tegg asked.

"You're the one who talked to her, not me."

Tegg had called Sharon Shaffer twenty minutes earlier and had introduced himself as a public health official. He apologized for calling on a Saturday but explained that this was something that couldn't wait. It was a question of some plasma donations she had made several years back. He suggested he and his assistant pay her a visit and that for confidentiality's sake, she would probably prefer to be alone. She had taken the bait, and she had sounded scared: just right.

"You understand she could recognize me," Maybeck said to him, interrupting his thoughts. "I mean chances are, since she's in the database, that I mighta sold her a fake I.D. at some point."

"If she says anything, tell her you work for BloodLines. We know she hasn't sold her plasma for over two *years*. She won't remember you. I do *all* the talking. Not a peep out of you. You're only there for control purposes—if things get out of hand, and only then *if I tell you to act*. Hmm?" The man didn't answer. Tegg felt nervous, a condition so foreign to him that at first it was unrecognizable. He thought maybe he was sick.

Maybeck sold fake I.D.s to underage runaways who needed them to sell their plasma. In this way, he won their confidence and obtained their vital statistics. He had been doing this ever since he had stumbled upon Tegg's Secret. The Secret had led to blackmail, the blackmail to a certain draining of Tegg's available cash, and subsequently to a new business for both of them: harvesting. With Maybeck assuming the streetside risks and logistics, connecting Tegg to the donors, this shaky alliance had begun. Now a kidnapping—their biggest risk to date. Tegg searched the dashboard's control panel, looking for a way to get more air.

Maybeck was in it for the money. Tegg, on the other hand, felt uncomfortable with the money. He gave every last cent of his share to charities in his wife's name, enhancing their social prominence. Feeling Maybeck's recklessness, he wondered how he would handle the man if he went too far—if he asked for too much. You had to watch the little people when they cottoned on to the smell of money.

Tegg knew they couldn't screw this up. Wong Kei was unlikely to be a man with a predisposition toward forgiveness. He had a mobster's reputation. If Tegg failed this harvest, it might be his last. His moral salvation commanded a high price.

Tegg finally threw a lever, and a gust of dusty air dislodged the condom wrapper from the defrost vent. He swatted at it frantically.

Maybeck slowed and turned into Freemont Lane, a dead end servicing a pair of apartment buildings to the right and, to the left, the back doors of houses on Lyden Avenue, including the green one, thirty-six thirty-nine and a half.

"Bring the laptop with you—it'll make you look more official. And remember to keep your mouth shut," Tegg reminded. He meant this literally: those teeth were enough to terrify anyone.

———

Sharon Shaffer had spent the last twenty minutes in terror. She had tried to drown out her recollection of that phone call by cleaning up, by running the vacuum. Public Health. The blood supply. It could only mean one thing . . . She answered the knock on her back door.

Two men. The bearded one was well dressed and looked distinguished, especially compared to his assistant, who reminded her of an aging James Dean. He carried the Toshiba laptop computer in his right hand.

"May we come in?" the distinguished one asked. She knew that voice from the phone call.

She felt afraid. If she refused them entry, would the reason for their being here leave with them? There were men she had been with during her years on the streets, complete strangers. There were things she had done that now, a few years later, she could hardly believe possible. She had not blocked them out, for she had no desire to forget her past; it was memories of her past that inspired her present work, that enabled her to so easily relate to the women who found their way to The Shelter. In an odd way, she was even proud of her past. But the characters she had encountered during that time were behind her now. She felt terrified. Was it true that your past always catches up with you?

She stepped back and admitted them. She knew what this was about. It was about dirty needles. About sex. About a different life, a different Sharon Shaffer. These two were about to ruin her new life. She felt faint. She waved them toward the dining table, for the place was small and there were only two stuffed chairs over by the television, and she wanted them all to sit. She had to sit no matter what.

The bearded man said, "BloodLines Incorporated maintains an active database of all of its donors, past and present." James Dean patted the laptop and set it down. The bearded man explained, "The donated blood is tested prior to distribution—for disease."

There was the word she had dreaded. Fear turned her palms icy. Her eyes threatened tears. As hard as the streets had made her, as welcome as death would have been back then, she felt weak and terrified now by this one word.

"What has happened," the man continued, "is that the state's department of health, in a routine audit, discovered a glitch in the software that drives the BloodLines' database. With that glitch removed, certain donors appear in an at-risk category, as concerns certain diseases."

"HIV," Sharon said. It was no guess. They didn't come to your door on a Saturday morning over measles.

"Yes, but we needn't jump to conclusions."

"AIDS," she whispered softly.

"What we need," the man continued professionally, "is a fresh blood sample. There's no need to jump to any conclusions until the results of those tests are in. *No need at all*," he emphasized. "The computer has been wrong once. It could certainly be wrong a second time."

"I'm shown as positive," she stated.

"It's only a computer. We need to run the tests again. I'm a doctor. We can take your blood now, or you can come downtown later in the week. It's entirely up to you." The doctor added, "It won't take us five minutes, if you'd care to get it over with now."

"Are you expecting anyone?" James Dean asked.

She shook her head. She found it difficult to speak.

The doctor said encouragingly, "One thing in favor of doing this *now* is that you will get the results much sooner."

"Let's do it now," she said. "How long until I know?"

"A few days. Four or five working days, usually."

"Oh, God. That'll seem like forever."

The doctor addressed his assistant, "I've left my case in the van. Go and get it for me." It was an order, not a request, and it struck her that there was no love lost between these two. James Dean stood and left through the back door, leaving the laptop computer standing on the carpet. "Our apologies for coming to your back door," the doctor said. "We've found most people would just as soon not explain anything to the neighbors. We try to park in the back and keep a low profile."

Again, she couldn't find any words. She nodded, just barely holding on. A lifetime lost?

"It's probably nothing more than a computer error. Really."

"That's what your voice says, but that's not what your eyes say," she wanted to tell him. He knew something, all right. He was as nervous as she was.

His lips tensed and his eyes hardened, and for the second time she felt a nauseating fear. She put her hands into her lap so he wouldn't see them shaking.

"I wouldn't worry," he said.

"Yes, you would. If you were me, you would." She stared at him. "You frighten me," she said without meaning to.

"It's the possibility of the matter that frightens you, not me," he explained in that harsh, grating voice he seemed stuck with.

James Dean returned with a small soft-plastic case and handed it to the doctor. It had tiered shelves, like a fishing tackle box. He tore a plastic bag off of a disposable syringe and took hold of her wrist to time her pulse. His fingers were ice cold.

He did some more preparations below the lip of the table, out of sight from her, and then slipped on a pair of surgical gloves.

He's afraid of contamination, she thought. She felt dizzy.

He swabbed her upper forearm with alcohol and then wrapped surgical tubing tightly around her upper arm. He asked her to make a fist. She looked away. These days, she hated the sight of needles.

"I'll need to take three samples," the doctor explained. "But just the one needle. It shouldn't hurt too much."

He pricked her arm then. She jumped with the sensation. All the ramifications, all the possibilities of what had been said here in the last few minutes swam through her head. Her life was finished. *Contaminated.* Contact with anyone at The Shelter would be minimized and eventually terminated. Worse than a leper. Society would shun her. She would eventually fall victim to the virus. They all did. There would be AZT—at a few thousand dollars a month! There would be counseling. There would be tears and lost friendships. There would be a long, grueling illness, weight loss, and death. She started to cry.

As she blinked away her tears, she focused on the contents of his medical case. She noticed an electric shaver, some leather strapping that looked more like a muzzle—*a dog's muzzle*? Next to it, a choke collar chain! This man wasn't a doctor, he was . . . "A veterinarian?" she asked.

At that same instant a stunning warmth surged through her system. It flooded into her like hot water. She *knew* that feeling only too well. Valium and some kind of narcotic. A slam like codeine. They weren't taking her blood, they were drugging her.

She snapped her head around in time to see the last of the injection administered. She looked up at the doctor—the veterinarian!—whose full concentration remained focused on the injection. She glanced up at James Dean, realizing now, for the first time, that they had not given her any identification. He was smiling at her. He had a mouth full of the worst teeth she had ever seen, like a rotten picket fence.

She tried to pull her arm away, but it barely moved—ninety-five pounds of dead flesh. She felt too slow, too heavy to offer much resistance. She felt terrified. She felt marvelously content. She felt tired, incredibly relaxed.

"You're going to be fine," he said in a fuzzy voice as if miles away.

Helpless. Powerless. Nothing she could do.

Across the room she saw a shadow move along the floor and believed at first it was another effect of the drug, but realized all at once that it was her housemate and hoped that she might yet be rescued. Agnes came around the corner, her seventy-year-old blind eyes open wide in curiosity.

"Help!" Sharon forced out numbly. Loudly enough to be heard? Had any sound come out at all?

The invasive warmth loosened every muscle. It felt like love. Pure and perfect love. Liquid love. Her eyes grew hot, and her lids fell like dark blue curtains. Agnes? Was Agnes out there? Anything but this, she thought. "Give me more," she felt like saying.

"Sharon?" It *was* Agnes.

Sharon Shaffer struggled to open her eyes, but only managed one last fleeting glimpse of the woman's silver-blue hair and pale white skin. Someone was dragging her.

The last thing she heard was the doctor's angry whisper—like cracking ice—as he demanded of his accomplice: "Who the hell is *that*?"

14

Homicide Lieutenant Phil Shoswitz loved baseball. He arranged his working hours around Mariners' home games and captained the police softball team. One of his favorite and most overused jokes was that he was the only guy on the force who was a captain and a lieutenant at the same time. His office, which remained constantly cluttered with stacks of pending case files, since Boldt's last visit had become something of a combination baseball locker room/museum. Its walls were crowded with autographed artifacts, photographs, and shelves of championship trophies.

As Boldt shut the door, one of the boys called out

a warm greeting. You don't know how many friends you have, he thought, until you return to a place after a long absence. He hadn't realized how good— how right—coming back here would feel.

"Thanks for coming," Shoswitz said in his typically tense voice. "I know it's a Saturday, but this is important." He had a dark complexion, a long, thin face, and ever-vigilant eyes, not unlike the hardened criminals he dealt with so regularly. A high-strung type, he chose his clothes poorly and shaved too fast. Married once, he was a weekend father now—at least if he wasn't stuck with a Saturday rotation. He had been a fair detective but was a brilliant lieutenant. Some people were made for a position of authority and a series of endless meetings.

"What are you and Matthews up to? First, she pays you a visit at The Joke. Now I get some inquiry from a place called . . ." he checked a memo on his desk, "BloodLines. A woman named Dundee is asking if we've got a cop named Boldt on our line-up. I'm wondering: Do we?"

"What'd you tell her?"

Shoswitz said, "That's not an answer to my question."

"Is that why the stern face?"

"That's why."

"Maybe we should get Daffy in here."

"Maybe we shouldn't. She's a cop, Lou, but she's not an investigator. You're an investigator, but you're not a cop—not active anyway."

"Ergo: We make the perfect team," Boldt said sarcastically.

"I decide the teams around here. I may manage from the dugout, Lou, but I manage. I don't need my players out on the field calling plays. Especially players who are sitting up in the stands, by choice."

"Foul ball," Boldt teased.

Shoswitz didn't appreciate it. "You learn to watch the foul balls. Sometimes they pull fair."

"BloodLines was just a quick little question-and-answer session, Phil. If I hadn't said I was a cop . . ."

"What's Matthews working on, Lou?"

Boldt felt that sinking sensation of losing your balance when it's too late to do anything about it. He had committed to Daphne, but he didn't want that to be the same thing as committing to Phil Shoswitz. If he handled this incorrectly, he would end up back on the force but off Daphne's investigation—if she was even allowed to continue with the case. Shoswitz was a tough negotiator. Boldt gave him the details, starting with Cindy Chapman's appearance at the homeless shelter, up to and including the "coincidence" that four out of four names were in the BloodLines' database. For now, he left out Dixie's matching tool markings, saving himself a trump card in case he needed it. He concluded, "You see why we were hesitant to bring this to you? We're a long way from any hard evidence. Bob Proctor wouldn't give me five minutes with what I've got." Proctor was the King County prosecuting attorney.

Shoswitz stared off blankly, deep in thought. He mumbled something about "Matthew's responsibility to involve the department."

Boldt fired back, "You just said she doesn't qualify as an investigator—which is unfair, mind you, since she took highest honors at the academy." He suggested, "She only came to me because she knew I would listen objectively."

"Objectively?" he asked. "She doesn't want objectivity. She's into the overwork phase. She's going through 'mental pause.' That incident with the knife set her way back. She's still not over it. You know how it goes: When you start to fight back you

go too far. She's haunted by that incident. She wants
to prove herself as a detective, wants to be more
than a psychologist. She's itching to get out of the
office and into the squad car. She tried to talk her
way out of something and it didn't work, so now she
wants it again, wants a chance to prove to herself
that she's over it. I see what you're thinking," he
added, heading Boldt off, "but it isn't that easy. I
can't very well recommend her for another rotation
when she's the only shrink on the force. That's her
specialty—that's what we took her on for, even if
she is qualified for investigations. Besides she hasn't
asked for any kind of active duty."

"What if she did? What if I signed back up on the
condition that we be allowed to partner together on
this harvester investigation? Fifty-fifty partners, no
seniority on my part, but I *would* be there to help
her out, maybe work her through this. At this same
time, she'd agree to continue to handle the more
pressing aspects of her job as departmental psychologist."

"You've thought this out, haven't you?" Shoswitz said.

"I know you, Phil. If I sign back up, you'll yank
me over to some murder-one ticket, and I'll never
see this thing again."

"What *thing*? You're the one pointing out the
lack of evidence in this *thing*."

"Give me the manpower and authority to run
with this. Give me a few weeks to come up with
something to convince Proctor we have a case. If I
can't, I'm yours—I'll see out my twenty."

"One week, no more."

"He's stealing organs, Phil. At least three kids
are dead. The deaths are a direct result of his work,
and that makes it multiple manslaughter, at least.
How many more are there? I thought that was the
point of Homicide. Three weeks."

"So it's hardball, is it?"

"Is it?"

"I want you back. That's no secret. I suppose that's half the problem," he said, allowing a rare smile. "But I'm not going to deal like this."

Boldt interrupted. "What a crock! You make deals like this every waking hour."

Shoswitz's face turned red and his nostrils flared. "Two weeks and that's final. Is this the new you?"

"Maybe it is," Boldt admitted. "I'm not feeling real 'new' at the moment, actually. Babies tend to make you feel ancient."

"You don't even have a formal complaint, do you? Is this on the books as a crime?"

"I'm complaining," Boldt said, carefully avoiding the second answer.

"The problem with you is you only see *your* side of things," Shoswitz said in a frustrated voice.

"Now you're sounding like Liz."

This elicited a smile from the lieutenant, and Boldt could feel he had won. Shoswitz glanced over Boldt's shoulder. Boldt saw a flicker of distraction in the lieutenant's eye and knew before turning that it would be Daffy. He turned to see her coming at them like a freight train—no stopping her. A beautiful freight train at that. A nice engine. She opened the door without knocking. In a desperate voice she said, "A friend of mine's been kidnapped. I need your help."

15

Pamela Chase climbed into her car, having decided on a drive because it was raining again and she couldn't stand it another minute inside her apartment alone. The occasional round-trip flight to Vancouver airport that she performed for Tegg did little to assuage her overall feeling of emptiness. Begrudgingly, she lived alone. Alone with her weight problem—with what she had come to think of as her ugliness.

A low ceiling of thick storm clouds blotted out the night sky and dumped more rain onto the drowning city. Four years of drought, now this! She didn't know exactly where she was going, but like a dog on a scent she followed her instincts away from the deafening drumming of the rain on her small balcony with its plastic fern and blown-out lawn chair. Another few minutes and that rain would have driven her right out of her mind. She pulled up to a red light and studied her reflection in the windshield. Mirrors were not popular in her apartment. She searched her face, trying to see it as beautiful, as Elden claimed to see it. She ignored the heavy cheeks and the squinty black eyes, the lifeless hair and spotty eyebrows. She saw someone else entirely. She briefly forgot all about her childhood—her parents' malicious remarks about her weight problem, her being left behind to "study" when her family went on social outings, the kitchen cabinets being locked, her being fed different size servings and different food than her siblings.

The neighborhood changed. Suddenly she left behind the stores and fast-food chains, the plastic marquees and 49¢ LETTUCE signs, and was surrounded instead by towering trees, manicured shrubs, and elegant homes.

This was familiar territory to her, not unlike her childhood neighborhood less than a mile away. This was where the money lived, the professionals, along the lake shore, away from the noise and exhaust.

The Teggs owned three cars. Since they had only a two-car garage, and his was the one always parked in the driveway it was easy for her to determine Tegg was not at home. She drove by here often, waiting for the hours to pass, waiting for work. She lived for business hours. For Monday through Friday. For late-night emergency calls. For something more than the boredom of that apartment.

She tried the clinic next, but he wasn't there either. The place was locked up tightly and the security was on. So where was he? Out at another of his social functions with *her*? The ballet? The opera? Out with the big names and big money? He loved that world.

The more she couldn't have something, the more she wanted it. Just like peanut butter. There was one way to make sure of his whereabouts. She pulled over at a Quik-Stop, bought herself a Reese's Peanut Butter Cup, and ran through the rain to a phone booth, getting soaked in the process. She thought about the voice she would use: Elden had taught her about image, about role-playing and acting. She summoned a convincing desperation, which wasn't too far from the way she felt anyway. The phone rang several times, which she knew from experience meant it wasn't the baby sitter answering, because the baby sitter always either occupied the phone line, keeping it tied up, or sat close enough to answer an incoming call on the first ring. The multiple rings confirmed her suspicions: The wife was home, Elden was not.

The wife answered: "Hello?" she said in that snobbish accent she had perfected.

"Mrs. Tegg, this is Pamela calling for Dr. Tegg."

"Oh, hello, dear," she said, now in a patronizing tone that implied a warmth between them that didn't exist. It came out of the fact that this woman was friends with Pamela's parents and felt obliged to a pretense of a certain degree of amiability. Resentment was more like it—the two of them had squared off on several occasions. "He's not here, I'm afraid."

"We've had an emergency call at the clinic—nothing too bad—and Dr. Tegg isn't answering his pager," she lied in her most appropriate voice: concern without alarm.

"He's out at the farm, dear. Working. *Incommunicado*, I'm afraid. That's what he loves about being out there, you know? You'll just have to refer this *emergency* elsewhere," she said in a not-so-subtle tone of disbelief.

Damn *her*, Pamela thought, it's getting so I can't fool her. The *farm*! Working? Without me? "Right," she managed to squeak out, strained though it was. She thanked the woman—she *hated* thanking her for anything—and hung up.

It was a long drive out to the farm, tonight even longer because her mind wouldn't rest, filled as it was with the force of her substantial insecurity—driven to discover what he was up to without her. Once off the Interstate, one road blurred into another. Trees. Darkness. The ceaseless rain hung in front of her like a curtain. Headlights flashed her windshield with silver. Taillights like animal eyes.

The farm was located far off the beaten track in a section of national forest that had been given over to timber lease some years before, the only access a series of unmarked, twisting, hard-pack roads.

She negotiated her way over these unmarked

roads, across the narrow bridges, and finally pulled into the rutted lane that led to the property.

To look at it, you might guess the place abandoned, except for the barking that emanated from the Quonset hut—the kennel—situated fifty yards down a sloping grade to the right of the old cabin and driveway. A light was on in the cabin. He was here!

She parked and hurried through the rain.

Her wet blouse glued to her chest. Her jeans—absurdly tight—were soaked from just below her crotch to her knees. Her hair was matted and a mess. She twisted the handle—it was locked. She crossed around to the cellar entrance and in doing so passed two glowing basement windows that had been painted over from the inside. She didn't need to see through these windows to know he was working inside. Now drenched, she approached the thick wooden door and pounded on it loudly. A moment later, he called out, "Who's there?" When she answered, he opened the door.

The hall was dark, though to his left the impromptu operating room glowed brightly beneath the surgical lamps. He stood in shadow, his face partially hidden. She slicked back her hair and shook the water off her. Behind her, the loud barking continued inside the kennel. She glanced into the operating room where a sedated woman lay stretched out on the operating table, green surgical cloth covering her. Pamela experienced the horror of exclusion. He was prepared to do a harvest *without* her! Unthinkable!

"So," he said in that grating voice of his, "you've come."

The fear of abandonment penetrated so deeply that she felt paralyzed, unable to move or speak.

But he touched her elbow and steered her into

the cabin's basement room—his operating theater—
and shut the door. The ceiling of exposed floor joists
hung low over their heads, woven with a network of
old pipes and electrical wiring. He had created a false
ceiling by stapling a thick clear plastic to the under-
side of the joists. He had done nearly the same thing
to the stone walls—had placed a series of two-by-
fours around the perimeter of the room and had fixed
the transparent sheeting to them, creating plastic
walls. This room was kept immaculately clean—
even the plastic was wiped down with disinfectant
following *every* surgery. He was a cleanliness fa-
natic—you only had to look at his hands and nails
to see that. And although in terms of equipment
they got by with only the bare necessities—anesthesia, lights, autoclave, and various monitoring devices—it was all state of the art. There was even a
backup generator in case the power failed. Tegg was
overly cautious with every aspect of his surgery. Obsessive. She considered him a great teacher. The
overhead lights burst with enough candlepower to
light a small stadium.

Only his eyes were visible above the surgical
mask as he studied her. He glanced quickly from her
to his patient on the table. He seemed briefly confused. She couldn't remember ever having seen him
with this particular expression—as if he had been
caught in some wrong. Perhaps he knew how much
such a discovery would hurt her. Perhaps he could
sense even *that*.

Her eyes welled with the tears of rejection. He
didn't need her. He had deliberately excluded her.
Just like her parents! Just like *everyone*! But then
he raised and dropped the green cloth as if it meant
nothing to him, as if discarding his patient, and
stepped toward her with a renewed confidence,
strong, even mesmerizing. "My pager must be bro-

ken," she said to him in a dispirited voice, looking for some excuse. She knew it wasn't broken, but she wanted to offer him a way out. Even now, she felt obliged to protect him.

He replied, "No, your pager is not broken. I didn't call you." Only now did she notice that he held a scalpel in his gloved hand. Devilishly sharp. Dangerous. "I didn't want to . . . bother you." These were the words he spoke, but it was not the message carried in his voice. This contradiction confused her.

"*Bother* me? You *never* bother me. I'm *always* available for you. For *any* reason. Anything at all."

She strained again to see the patient on the table, but he stepped into her line of sight and placed the scalpel flatly against her cheek. He clearly didn't want her looking.

She glanced into his familiar eyes and saw something new there. Her legs trembled. She felt herself flush a crimson red as sexual excitement rushed through her. Here? Now?

He stepped closer to her and ran the scalpel down her neck to between her breasts. "Elden?" she asked, her heart racing furiously.

One by one, he cut free the buttons. "Is this all right?" he asked.

She nodded. "I guess so."

Keeping his mask on, he kissed her then for the first time. He took her pouty lips between his masked teeth and bit down hard in a way that both thrilled and terrified her. She felt powerless next to him.

"Is it all right?" he asked again. "Hmm?"

She hesitated.

"You want this, don't you, Pamela? I know you do. Tell me you do."

Her shirt fell open. He pulled it back and studied the long scar below her rib cage. He touched it and hummed softly. "Tell me," he repeated. She thought she might faint. He used the scalpel to cut her bra. It too fell open, exposing her. He didn't look. He held her eyes. He said, "This *is* what you want, *isn't it?*"

"Yes."

"Good." He ran the flat of the blade over her breasts. A penetrating, exhilarating chill raced through her. The danger that blade represented . . . He then held out his empty hand and offered it to her. She kissed his gloved fingers then, one by one. She drew each of his fingers into her mouth, suckling them and curling her warm tongue around them, ignoring the odd odor of the latex. All the while, Tegg continued to stare into her eyes. What did he see? What was he after? He withdrew his fingers from her mouth, glanced once quickly—nervously?—over his shoulder at his patient, then quickly back at her and said, "You won't need these." He tugged her jeans away from her soft middle and drew the scalpel all the way down one pant leg, then the other. Her jeans came off like a pair of chaps. Her head swam, feeling his hand touch her there.

All at once she could smell her own excitement, and it embarrassed her. It mixed with the musty and medicinal odors of the cellar.

"You'll like it," he said, reading her thoughts. He pulled the severed blouse from her and left it on the floor. He led her—underwear, running shoes and peds—to the end of the operating table.

He positioned her facing him with her back to the patient, standing between the unconscious woman's bare feet. She resisted the urge to cover her belly, tried not to think of the way her flesh must look in the glaring light. His eyes glowed behind the operating mask. She could hear his coarse, exciting breathing.

She felt dizzy, almost drunk. This wasn't how she had imagined it. He was scarcely himself. Is this how men were? She ached with longing and fear. He reached past her and moved the patient's feet out of Pamela's way, clearing a small space between them on the operating table.

Suddenly, he scooped Pamela up and planted her sitting in this space on the end of the high operating table, centered between the patient's ankles. He took one of her hands and placed it on her raised knee, then the other, so she held herself open for him. He spun the scalpel before her eyes. Light glinted from its edges. He lowered it. He nicked the waistline of her underwear, and then threw the scalpel to the floor. He placed both hands on her underpants, and tore them open.

He asked, "Are you sure?"

She nodded, unable to speak.

"We can stop," he offered.

"No."

He touched her with his gloved hands. She rocked her head back and stared open-eyed into the harsh, sterile light. Her left leg cramped; she wanted to let go of her knee, but she didn't dare do anything. This was all so new to her, not at all what she had imagined. Better in some ways. Worse in others. He felt removed and distant, and yet his touch was intense and knowledgeable. She wanted him to want her.

He unfastened his belt. She grew light-headed. He took her legs and pulled them toward him, drew her to him, causing her to plant her arms and lean back, her head nearly touching the patient, her legs wrapped around him, her body half on, half off the metal table. The farther back she leaned, the easier it was to support herself, but the more contact she made with the woman behind and beneath her.

Humming one of the operas that he played during their surgery, he penetrated her. A sharp pain. She cried out. She could tell by his reaction that he liked it, so she didn't try to stifle the sounds that shuddered through her with each of his thrusts. He went after her with a frenzy. Her body went numb as all of her senses focused, instead of on herself, on him. His eyes closed. He smiled! He liked this!

Then nothing. He stopped. Was it over? He withdrew and shoved her away from him, back onto the table.

She was filled with a vague longing for something soft—muted light, a pillow, a kind word. "Was it any good?" she asked.

"You can't answer that yourself?"

"It was wonderful!"

"There, you see?" Then he said mechanically and without emotion, "Now put on a smock—there's work to be done. She won't stay under forever."

Pamela went into the adjacent storage room, cleaned herself off and changed into a smock, remaining naked underneath. The sensation thrilled her. Everything about this night thrilled her. With her clothes as they were, she would have nothing but the smock to wear for her drive home. Wild! She giggled with the thought.

When she returned, he seemed nervous, almost frantic, not at all himself. He kept checking his watch. She joined him at the table alongside the patient and the stainless steel tray of hemostats, scalpels, and needles.

Only then did she notice: "She's not prepped!" She blurted this out without thinking. "She isn't shaved." Their eyes met then, and she saw panic in his, so foreign a sight that it was made all the more obvious, like a virtuoso missing a note, or an actor forgetting a line. He had neglected to prep her. Inconceivable! Elden Tegg? He *never* forgot a single detail of any operation, large or small. Had the sex been *that* good? She didn't know this man. He had treated her so differently this evening, done things she had always wanted but had never dared ask for, that it was almost as if she was with someone else.

"You're right," he conceded, "she's not properly prepped."

Elden Tegg admit a mistake? He never *made* a mistake! What was happening?

He instructed her, "Get what you need and prep her." When she failed to respond, he commanded harshly, "Go on!"

She didn't like that voice. It wounded her.

A few minutes later, as she was soaping the patient's side and abdomen, she noticed that the surgical cloth covering the patient was damp in the center of her chest. It had been dry earlier, when Pamela had left the room. She shaved the woman, but her eyes wandered the room curiously and she spotted a surgical sponge stained with Betadyne resting on the edge of the sink. This too was new since she had been out of the room. She put the two together: The Betadyne had earlier been used to prep the epidermal for surgery, and then the patient's chest had been washed clean of it while she was out of the room.

A heart? Impossible! He wouldn't do that. They had talked about that recently. A lung perhaps. "All set," she said to him. All set? Her hands were shaking, her knees weak. Her eyes fell upon that sponge across the room. She thought about the sex, what he had done to her: Out of desire? Or had it been to distract her? To keep her attention off this patient. She glanced over at him. She felt a distance between them. If this was a scheduled harvest, why hadn't she been notified? Who was the courier if not her?

"All set," he said, his eyes dancing nervously, his hands trembling slightly—hands usually as steady as the steel he held. Yes, another man entirely.

He leaned over the patient, his dark eyes trained on her. Slowly, carefully, he lowered the blade. "Her name is Sharon," he said to Pamela. "Thank you, Sharon."

This was part of his ritual—every donor had a name, every donor was thanked for the contribution about to be made. He insisted on this.

"Thank you, Sharon," Pamela echoed in an unsteady voice that betrayed her inner thoughts and caused Tegg to glance up at her briefly. But not for long. Only an instant. The sharp blade came in contact with the woman's skin. The first drop of her blood seeped from the incision. Pamela lifted a sponge. There was work to do.

===

As Elden Tegg began the invasive surgery for the kidney harvest, thoughts swarmed inside his head like angry bees. The problem lay in the fact that Pamela would never approve of a heart procurement—the procedure for which this woman had been prepped prior to Pamela's intrusion. There was no predicting what she might do if she found out about it, hence the charade—the lovemaking, the distraction, the ruse that he had *forgotten* to prep— him!—and now an unplanned kidney harvest. Worse, Maybeck was due shortly, hopefully to inform Tegg that Wong Kei's wife had been successfully admitted to the Vancouver hospital, and then to act as courier for both the harvested heart and the other organs once the various procedures were completed. A single kidney harvest wouldn't interfere with any of that—this donor wouldn't need *any* kidneys where she was going, that was all part of

Tegg's plan—but Pamela's curiosity was sure to peak if she encountered Maybeck. Maybeck *delivered* donors, and he *returned* them to the streets, but this was too soon after surgery for a pickup; she would have to wonder what he was doing here this time of night. Pamela Chase was no idiot; she would figure this out in minutes. And then what?

There was one possible excuse, he realized, and he congratulated himself for thinking of it. On rare occasions they performed a "private" harvest, selling an organ directly to a friend of Tegg's, a transplant surgeon in Vancouver—as opposed to shipping it off to the Third World market. Patients on the low end of transplant waiting lists became desperate, and this surgeon in Vancouver—along with Tegg—was willing to do something about it. For a fee. This heart was a "private" arranged through the same man. Although Pamela had previously delivered the "privates," there had been talk recently that perhaps Maybeck should do it, and this provided Tegg his out.

He paid particular attention to his work, for he continued to see this woman's body as a treasure-trove, a chalice from which to draw life itself. *Several* lives. One begets many: It was almost poetic! He felt a small twitch in his neck but paid it no mind—just nerves.

He worked more quickly than usual, and Pamela did a good job of keeping up, of anticipating his every need. He wanted this finished. He wanted the kidney packed, readied for travel, and Pamela on her way *before* Maybeck's arrival. If Maybeck said the wrong thing, he could screw this all up. Tegg glanced up and looked around the room to rest his eyes. The plastic walls and ceiling gave the room a strange metallic sheen, reflecting the bright light like dulled mirrors. Again, the muscles in his neck and shoulder twitched; again, he fought it off.

"Doctor?" she asked.

He had actually blanked out for a minute, caught up more in his thoughts than his actions. His eye rest had gone on a little too long. He returned to his work, talking as he did. "Clamping the renal artery. Renal vein." He prepared to sever both. "Scalpel." She slapped it into his gloved hand before he completed the first syllable. She snatched it back just as quickly, and he knew she had spotted a possible problem. It was a tangled mess in here. He wormed his fingers around the various veins and arteries, double-checking to make sure his clamps were properly placed. What had she seen that he might have missed? Together they had successfully performed over thirty such human kidney harvests, and yet they treated each as if it were their first. He carefully followed the clamped artery to its source, confirming it was the renal artery and not the superior mesenteric, which for a moment she had obviously feared it might be. Satisfied, he reestablished his clamp and found the scalpel in his hand once again. He glanced into her eyes. Even with a mask covering most of her face, he could tell she was smiling. She enjoyed this precision teamwork as much as he. Too bad she would miss the heart.

"Tying off," he announced. He cut both vessels and tied them securely, testing first the vein—by carefully removing the hemostat—and then the artery. This artery carried over forty-five percent of the body's blood to the kidney. The pressure to the suture was significant. They both studied the two closures, alert for any leakage. Pamela reached in and sponged thoroughly, Tegg's dexterous fingers at the ready. "Looks fine," he declared, and went about severing the lesser vessels. Pamela washed the area in a steady stream of saline and antibiotic as Tegg continued his work. Several minutes passed. "Forehead," he warned. She mopped some perspiration from his brow. This tiny room lacked adequate ventilation, sealed in plastic as it was, and the intense heat from the light overheated it quickly.

"You know," she commented, "the heat is a lot more tolerable like this," referring to her nudity under the smock.

"I just bet it is," he said, close to having the kidney free and clear.

"It was nice."

"What we just did will carry more significance, mean more, if it is not discussed."

"Message received."

"I didn't mean—"

"Yes, you did." She added, "I'll live."

He glanced at her again. He didn't like to see her angry at him like this; he had come to expect that look of reverence in her eyes. He had come to like it.

"Here we are," he announced, as he slowly extracted the cherished organ from the retracted incision, cradling it in his cupped hands like a newborn infant. "Saline!" he commanded.

She presented the chilled stainless container to him. The clamped, pink organ sank down into the cool water. She added some saline to completely cover it and returned the dish to the bucket of ice where it had been waiting.

"Let's close," he said, pleased with their success. The organ in that dish represented a saved human life, and it was the product of the work of his hands. No such feeling of accomplishment could ever be properly explained, he thought, still looking at it. No one, not even Pamela, could fully understand the magnitude of his happiness at such moments.

They returned to their teamwork, four hands working as if controlled by a single brain. And maybe they were, he thought in a moment of conceit. Maybe this woman at his side was a far greater part of him than either of them understood. It had begun to feel that way of late. And why not? What was wrong with that?

As they closed the various levels of muscle and tissue he instructed, "There's a UNOS container in the back room." This transplant container, one of many stolen by Maybeck from the trash bins of the University Hospital, had been intended for the heart. It was a good size for the heart, slightly smaller than the ones they normally used for the kidneys. "Make sure you triple-bag the organ—use Viospan, as always—check for leaks, don't forget— and don't scrimp on the ice! We received a complaint the last time!"

"I *always* check the ice!" she protested. "It was the cabin temperature. It wasn't us. There's nothing we can do about some old pilot who insists on flying in a sauna."

"Just make sure."

"I will. You know I will." She then inquired, "What flight am I on?"

Tegg spoke quickly. "This is a private. Maybeck's delivering."

He awaited her reaction. He didn't dare look at her, she might see something in his eyes. To cover himself he added sternly, "We talked about this. Hmm? I think it's better this way. You said so yourself: You don't like delivering the privates."

She didn't say anything. Just right.

He didn't approve of the continuous stitch, subcutaneous closure he had performed. He removed it and began again, this time in silence. "Forehead," he warned. She caught the perspiration in time. This contact between them seemed to settle her down some. The remainder of their work went flawlessly.

He oversaw her efforts as she packaged the organ in the Viospan. She did a splendid job of it—he could have done no better. When the small Styrofoam container with its bright orange label was sealed and ready to go, Pamela retrieved her sliced-up jeans from the floor.

Tegg added quickly, attempting humor, "It's a good thing Maybeck's handling this one. After all, what would you wear?"

She forced a smile; she wasn't pleased with any of this. But hers was a role of obedience. Five minutes later, she was gone.

══

Like most of the rooms in the small cabin, the kitchen was in disrepair from years of neglect. Maybeck entered shaking off the cold, looking like a biker with lockjaw—he had the remarkable ability to talk most of the time without showing his grotesque teeth. "We got trouble."

Problems? Tegg wondered. He was proud of the way he had improvised with Pamela. The only problem he could conceive of had to do with transporting Wong Kei's wife to Vancouver. "She died?" he gasped.

"Connie says a cop was nosing around Blood-Lines yesterday. Had that girl Chapman's name. Knows she's in the database."

The police? The room suddenly seemed to be without air.

"Calm down," Tegg said, though rattled himself. The guy was pacing faster than a hungry pit bull, rubbing his thumb and fingers together like he was trying to remove something sticky from them.

The police? *Now?* He felt broadsided.

Maybeck said, "We're gonna shut it down, right?

You got plans for shuttin' it down, right? That's what you said before."

Tegg found it difficult to think with Maybeck circling the table like a predator. "Sit down!" he instructed. When issued this order for a second time, Maybeck sat.

"We *are* gonna shut it down, right?" Maybeck repeated.

"We *can't* shut it down," Tegg informed him. "We have Wong Kei to think about. I took an advance payment. He's *counting* on us. You know what that means as well as I do." Tegg had his own personal agenda, his own reasons for wanting to see this heart harvest to completion, but he wasn't going to share them with a little person like Maybeck who would never understand. Maybeck would respond better to his fear of the Chinese mafia than to Tegg's needing to right his own past mistakes.

"What advance?" Maybeck asked.

Tegg decided to play to the man's greed. "Don't forget: You have fifty *thousand* dollars coming to you from this heart harvest—*if* there is a heart harvest. No advance for you until the job is completed."

Maybeck brooded. Tegg needed to settle him down. He offered, "I have some vodka."

"Gimme some."

"Not too much," Tegg warned. "There's still work to be done."

He poured him a glass, no ice. Tegg seldom drank. He put the bottle away. A thought occurred to him: If worse came to worse, he could always *tell* Maybeck that he was closing up shop. He could courier the organs himself, if absolutely forced to. But with possession nine-tenths of the law, he would rather have Maybeck do it.

"No more work to do tonight," Maybeck corrected, spinning the warm vodka in the glass as if it were cognac. "Word from up north is that the old bitch barely lived through the flight. The Chink said that the doctor says we gotta wait at least a week. He mentioned *next* Friday."

"Next *Friday*? But that's *insane*!" Tegg protested loudly. "We've already abducted her. She's lying on my table downstairs right now!" He felt dizzy.

"Fuck her! It's the cops I'm worried about. We gotta shut this down, Doc. We gotta do something fast!"

"Whom do you fear more, Wong Kei or the police?" Tegg let the question hang there.

Maybeck drank half the vodka, swallowing it like water. He cringed and then coughed out an appreciative, "Ahhh." He answered, "The Chink, hands down. Goddamn gooks'll kill you for pocket change. I hear what you're saying, Doc—I hear ya, all right, but I don't know. I just don't *know*."

Tegg marveled at the incomplete mind of a little person. Most of all, little people wanted the answers decided *for* them. He debated several possibilities and said confidently, "I suggest the following: First, we explore the extent of their knowledge. Police muck about all the time. Doesn't mean they're necessarily onto something here. Hmm? Connie keeps us up to speed on *everything* that's going on at BloodLines. Her time has come to perform for us—this is where she earns her bread and butter."

"She gives us the database updates—*that*'s how she earns her bread and butter."

"Don't toy with me, Donald," Tegg warned, a mixture of anger and paranoia sweeping through him. The police?

Maybeck killed the vodka and looked around for the bottle. Tegg edged the glass away from the man using the back of his wrist—he wanted a glass with Maybeck's fingerprints on it in case he needed it later for damage control. *An ounce of prevention . . .*

"The point being: If the police remain interested in BloodLines, then we must know about it. You have to arrange this with Connie. No telephones, you understand, unless it's just a signal of some sort—no *discussions* on the telephones! That's imperative! Even a person like you can understand that. Hmm?" He didn't care if he insulted the man. He was beyond caring about such things: It was the police he was concerned about now. That and a successful harvest. Maybe he could up the schedule—a week seemed an interminable time—he'd have to look into changing that.

"If the cellular worked from out here, I'd call the man right now," Tegg said. "But as it is, we'll just have to wait on that."

He wrestled with the next thought that came into his mind because it was more something that Maybeck would think to do, not Dr. Elden Tegg; and yet it persisted, nagging at him, refusing to go away. They needed *time*. They needed to distance themselves from the police. There were ways to buy insurance that little people like Maybeck understood perfectly well.

He said, "You understand what kind of trouble you're in, don't you? You *personally*? After all, it was *you* who made the contacts with these donors—*minors*, don't forget. It was *you* who delivered them to me. *You* who arranged to steal the BloodLines database. *You* who paid them. *You* who put them back onto the streets."

"It was *both* of us," Maybeck complained.

"Oh, no, not at all. *Think* for just a moment—if you're capable of thinking—think about what I've just said, and I believe you will see that I'm correct. Hmm? Yes, I can see it in your eyes."

"It was you who sliced them open, Doc. What I done ain't nothing compared with that."

He wanted to encourage the man without directly giving him an order. "If Connie poses a problem for us, we should take care of her. She's the only direct connection between you and BloodLines. Perhaps I can advance the schedule. Another week and you could have your fifty thousand," he reminded, "and be out of town."

"Take care of her?"

"Is this stupidity an act of yours?"

That inflamed the man. Good. Tegg wanted him angry. Intense anger was a precursor to violence—Tegg felt this same anger himself at the moment—and violence was perhaps required of Donnie Maybeck.

"You're saying we zoom Connie?" Maybeck asked incredulously, trying to appear smart.

"I didn't say anything of the sort. I merely pointed out that you're in a hell of a lot of trouble if this investigation goes ahead. We can't stop the police from investigating, but we can stop them from having any luck. Things just might work out if Connie took a two-week vacation. Hmm?"

"But what if she freaks out?" Now he was catching on.

Tegg remained silent.

"Oh, I get it," said Maybeck. He smiled. Those teeth were anybody's nightmare.

"Yes, I think you do, Donald," Tegg encouraged. "I think you're finally catching on."

SUNDAY

February 5

16

Michael Washington was lost. He had followed the old railroad grade for most of Saturday, had slept near a marsh that wasn't on the topo-map, and now was stuck in a thickly wooded, second generation forest. A moment before, having climbed high into a tree-top, he had spotted a small cabin and Quonset hut poised in a remote and secluded clearing. He consulted the map once again, hoping this old homestead, a few of which appeared as small black squares on the map, might serve as a landmark and help him to determine his location. Nothing doing. He couldn't find anything like it on the map.

The problem was not the map, he thought, but him. For the better part of the morning he had been consumed with trying to debug a software subroutine, all in his head, while hiking the old railroad grade. He worked as a programmer for Microsoft in a division developing a database program that remained a closely guarded company secret. Weekends, he backpacked alone, exploring new territory—this part of the country was sure a hell of a lot different from Cleveland!—working out problems in his head, de-stressing. It left him mentally refreshed and physically satisfied by Monday morning when his twelve-hour, work-a-day world began again. Not infrequently, these sojourns left him briefly off-trail—lost.

This was not his first venture into this region. Through trial and error he had explored quite a piece of the South Fork of the Tolt and areas south toward Snoqualmie Falls. Even the old railroad grade was no stranger to him—it provided sure footing and a slightly elevated trail to follow. Each weekend, he expanded his knowledge of the area as he mentally ticked down imagined lines of source code in his head, searching for solutions to various problems inherent in the program. He was something of a superstar in a company of superstars. He didn't think of himself this way, but he knew that others did. Probably because he was Afro-American. If you had any brains at all, if you made it up even one rung of the ladder, coworkers and supervisors took notice. You were the *exception* not the rule. If you solved all the problems that stumped the Golden Wizards, they considered you a genius. Unwittingly, Michael found himself in this strange, even burdensome position. Now he was *expected* to solve the more difficult problems.

His immediate problem was to find his way to his car. By his calculations he was still a good two or three miles from where he had parked it, and none of this looked like familiar territory, especially the cabin and Quonset he had momentarily glimpsed. About all he could do now was to ask directions or try to connect with a dirt road that might eventually lead him to an identifiable landmark. It would be dark in another three or four hours; he couldn't afford too much more "exploring."

Despite the numerous NO TRESPASSING signs he encountered, Michael Washington walked in the direction of the buildings. He respected other people's right to privacy as much as the next guy, but lost was lost. Although it wasn't exactly an emergency, these people would have to be sympathetic to a person being lost.

Surrounded by thick forest, his only indication that he was nearing the small farm were these posted threats which occurred with an increasing frequency. When eventually he met with a sign that read PASS AT YOUR OWN RISK, he began to wonder what kind of people these were. He was no stranger to the occasional news story of the survivalists, racial extremists, and psychotic killers who hermited the woods of the Northwest. The warnings were quite explicit; perhaps it was a better idea to just move on and avoid the place. Obey the signs. But Michael Washington was too practical, too logical to pass up a chance to establish his location. He wasn't after a ride. He didn't need help. All he needed was the slightest indication on the map of where the hell he was. He stood in front of this final warning for only as long as it took the light rain to start up again. That did it! He was going to find his way out of here if it was the last thing he ever did.

It was.

—

The structure was thirty feet long and about as wide. At the far end, rain leaked in across the poured-cement floor. The canopy of corrugated metal that arched overhead reminded the woman of an airplane hangar. Rain beat down on it like hailstones. Her ears rang from it. She had awakened in a cage—a dog pen, she now realized by looking around. Constructed of chain-link wire mesh and galvanized pipe, the cage appeared to be about eight feet long by four feet wide, and too low to stand up in. There were dogs in nearly all the cages. She was naked, lying on a brown burlap sack. She had no idea what time it was, who she was, where she was, or what had happened to her. Some kind of nightmare. The reality of her situation slowly seeped in. She remembered the two men in her house. She remembered the needle in her arm. She tried to sit up. Pain screamed from her side; her arm tangled in an I.V. tube. She recalled a devastatingly bright light and another warm surge of drugs. Again, she tried to sit up, the pain even more intense. Her hand fell to her side, and she felt the bandage there. Panic overcame her. Dogs. A cage! Naked. There was a bucket behind her, a roll of toilet paper alongside of it. Against the wall, an automatic waterer. The I.V. bag was clamped to the overhead wire of the cage. Drip, drip, drip: She could see it feeding her. She rolled to get a better look at the bandage. It was several inches long, redness seeping into the skin around its edges. She felt overtaken by a sudden burst of nausea, rolled to her side, and vomited.

Had she awakened before this? She couldn't remember. She felt completely disoriented. There was nothing here that fit into her reality. It was almost as if this were happening to someone else. She really *had* believed it to be some kind of intense nightmare at first, one of those in which everything is *too* real, tactile, painful, and emotionally all-encompassing. But there was no question as to the reality of her situation. If she had awakened prior to this, her situation had not taken hold. Only now, as the dogs began stirring in their cages, as the pain in her side reached an excruciating level, did she begin to grasp her circumstances.

She began to collect herself. There were eight adjacent cages against each of the Quonset hut's two long walls, a cement aisle separating them. The building's only door was to her right. Her cage was sandwiched between two others that were empty. At the far end of the building, to her left, a cage was stacked high with sacks of dog food. Across the aisle to her left a gas heater suspended from the high ceiling emitted a warm wind which blew directly onto her. Perhaps, she thought, that heater explained her placement in this particular cage.

She counted twelve dogs. Some of them carried partially healed scars. She felt dizzy at the sight of those scars. A kennel? She sat up, slowly, overcoming the pain, driven by the need to get out of here. There was a weight on her neck. She grabbed for it, tugged, but it was thick and heavy. A collar of some sort. Only now did she realize all the dogs were also wearing such collars. Big collars, with a heavy black lump attached. She knew what that lump was—a battery; she understood the purpose of these collars. She pulled at it again; her fingers touched a small padlock—it was locked around her neck! She panicked. She crawled on hands and knees over to the chain-link door and grabbed hold. Her collar sounded a brief electronic alarm. It failed to register on her mind as a warning, instead, invoking further panic. She shook the cage door violently.

A jolt of electricity flashed from her neck to her toes like scalding water. Pain as sharp and severe as any she had known. She let go, fell back, and cried out at the top of her lungs.

The dogs leapt to their feet in unison and barked so loudly, so vehemently that it deafened her. Sharon Shaffer clasped her hands to her ears and screamed again, tears pouring from her eyes. The dogs roared on.

Perhaps this was hell, she thought. Perhaps she had died and gone to hell.

As Michael Washington tentatively entered the clearing that held a cabin and a Quonset hut, he heard a sickening cry that cut him to the core. A woman! It was immediately followed by the vicious barking of dogs, but he felt almost certain that he had heard a woman. Perhaps it was nothing more than his active imagination, he thought. He had, after all, only minutes before been thinking about the weirdos who lived in places like this. One of the newspaper stories that lodged in his mind was that of a father and son who had kidnapped a woman backpacker, keeping her in chains, raping and torturing her until authorities finally raided the camp. Had he merely projected the terror of that story onto what he had heard?

Or was there a woman trapped in there with a bunch of dogs?

He broke into a run. A minute later he reached the far end of the structure. The building's only door held an enormous padlock. Locked, with dogs inside? Why? He banged loudly on the door and pressed his ear to its cold metal.

There were so many dogs barking it was impossible to be sure exactly what he was hearing. And yet that sounded like a woman calling for help.

He abandoned his pack and ran toward the cabin, stopping abruptly before he reached it, because it occurred to him that if it *was* a woman's voice, then whoever was inside that cabin was responsible for her being there.

He returned quickly to his backpack, scooped it up, and made for the woods. He hunkered down and took a minute to collect himself. By all appearances the cabin was unoccupied, but the car tracks in the mud indicated this place was frequented often; and by the look of several of the tracks, recently.

How long would he have to check this out? He

left his backpack in the woods, returned to the structure, and circled it fully. Only the one door. Hinges on the inside. You'd need a stick of dynamite to break that padlock. He circled again, beating on the walls to check their construction—too stout to hope to bust up. At one point, he thought he heard that voice again—he was *sure* of it—but those dogs were so loud! The frustration drove him to a frantic circling of the building. Around and around. He finally caught himself and stopped.

He had to get help. That was all there was to it. He ran along the very edge of the primitive driveway that led to the farm, alert for any cars ahead of him, prepared to hide in the woods if he saw any. The driveway—the road—was the most obvious route to follow: Somewhere out there was civilization, and this had to be the fastest way to it.

The more he ran the quicker his pace, driven by adrenaline, driven as if pursued by someone.

The driveway, a half-mile long, joined a dirt road challenged on its edges by weeds. He followed this road to the right, convinced not only that town was this way—the sun lay to his right; he *had* to be running south—but also that his car was parked somewhere in this general direction.

He tried to think this through. Whoever lived in the cabin was gone. He decided that if a car approached from in front of him—a car returning—he would hide. But if a car or truck happened to approach him from behind—a car headed south, a car headed out of here—he would flag it down. He prided himself on his logic; the fact that he was able once again to think clearly restored some of his confidence and helped to calm him. He pumped hard and continued to run.

As time wore on, he considered flagging down *any* car he saw.

He encountered an intersection and then immediately another one. Here finally was an obvious landmark, but he had left his map in his pack! He sized up the dim glow of the retreating sun and continued south toward eventual civilization.

===

Elden Tegg was on his way to the farm to check his patient when he first spotted the boot prints coming down his road. These tracks stretched in a length and stride that indicated a hard run. His heart began to beat frantically. His cabin and kennel were at the end of this dirt track, nothing else. *Nothing else!* Fresh tracks at that, he realized.

Maybeck's warning of the night before echoed in his head. "The police!"

He drove quickly, skidding to a stop as he reached his property. The boot tracks led directly from the kennel!

For a moment he found it hard to catch his breath—him, Dr. Calm!

He leapt from the car, following the prints like a trapper, his fingers groping for his keys. Self-control was all-important. His strength. He settled himself and observed the scene before him.

Whoever it was had stopped in front of the kennel door, but there was only the one set of tracks: He or she hadn't made it inside. Tegg lost the prints in the grass around the side of the structure. His mind raced through a dozen possibilities, but he didn't like where any of them led: back to those tracks.

He unlocked the door, hurried inside and breathed a sigh of relief as he saw his captive in her cage, locked up tight. Bewildered, she didn't utter a word before he left and locked the structure again.

How old were these tracks? Minutes? Hours?

He had not seen anyone on the road, but there

were *dozens* of roads out here. Was he too late? Had the intruder taken a different road than he?

He jumped back into the Trooper and headed down the road as fast as the car would safely take him.

He followed the tracks on the edge of the road like a bloodhound. At the end of the lane they turned right. So did Tegg.

These boot prints dragged on for what seemed like miles, the distance between each print narrowing and after a while indicating the hiker was walking. Good, Tegg thought, walking is slower. He was still extremely nervous, once nearly foreign condition for him, but one that was beginning to seem familiar. He took long, deep breaths and calmed himself.

He reached the double-triangle intersection, where the aqueduct crossed the South Fork, and saw at once why he had not passed the hiker on the way in: He had followed the roads due south, but had taken the fork that eventually wound its way east to the reservoir. There was a lot of open road out here. Tegg drove faster, worried now. There might be people at the reservoir. He didn't want this hiker reaching anyone.

He rounded a long, sweeping corner.

A hundred yards ahead of him, he spotted the hiker.

As the hiker heard the vehicle, he—a black man—turned and waved his arms frantically. Tegg felt the blood pounding in his ears. He slowed the vehicle and rolled down his window. The hiker was young and handsome, with anxious eyes.

"Please," the young man pleaded. "I need a ride. I need some help."

"Help? Are you in trouble?"

"Please!"

Tegg said, "Hop in," releasing the car's power door lock, wondering how next to handle this. As the boy climbed in, Tegg felt charged with a keen sense of power. He couldn't weaken. He couldn't allow his fear to show. He asked his passenger to buckle up. He took control.

"Where are we?" the young man asked.

"Are you lost?"

"Among other things. My car's out here somewhere."

"Engine trouble?"

"No." The boy hesitated. He asked carefully, "Are you from around here?"

Tegg considered this briefly. A test. "No," he answered. "I have some work out at the reservoir." He pointed.

"The reservoir is *this* direction?"

"Yes, it is."

"Stop the car!"

Tegg slowed. "Problems?"

"I have to go the other way." He shook his head. "Oh, man, did I ever fuck up."

Tegg slowed the car to a crawl. "Can I help?"

"Could you?"

"Well, I wouldn't exactly feel right about *abandoning* you out here. What exactly *is* the problem?"

Hysterical, Michael Washington ranted and raved about being lost, about *dogs, a woman's voice*, and needing help. Something linking sexual perverts to backpackers.

"Calm down a minute," Tegg said, trying to convince himself as much as his passenger. He pulled to the side of the road. Stopping the car won the boy's full attention. Little people were so predictable.

"I'm telling you, there's a woman up there who needs help!"

"You *saw* her?" Tegg wondered if his heart could

endure this. The wheel was slippery from the sweat on his palms. He let go of the wheel.

An expression of doubt crossed the young man's face. It dissipated quickly as he reminded himself emphatically, "The barn was locked."

"A barn?"

"More like a small hangar. A Quonset hut. There were dogs."

"A kennel?"

"It was a *woman*, I'm telling you."

Tegg explained, "Well, we can be at the Sheriff's in about thirty minutes. Or we could call." He pointed to his cellular phone. "I can get a clear signal a few miles down the road. But you better have your story straight."

"Meaning?"

"Your name?"

"Michael."

"Michael, have you ever heard a cat at night? Hmm? Have you ever heard that peculiar screaming of a cat during fornication and thought you heard a woman?" Now Tegg's hitchhiker looked puzzled. "Don't get me wrong—I'm not telling you what you heard. I wasn't there. *You're* the one who'll explain it to the Sheriff, but you mentioned dogs and that made me think of cats and how much they can sound like a woman. A woman screaming. Cats fornicating. A mountain lion can sound that way. What was it you said you heard?"

His passenger didn't answer at first. Then he stated emphatically, "I heard a woman scream."

Tegg added, "I don't know how *you* feel about involving the cops, but they're not my favorite people. Were you on private property? Was that property posted? Did you have the owner's permission to be there? They ask you things like that. Don't forget that."

"I know that. I also know what I heard."

"And you're prepared to deal with them? Fine."
Tegg went through the motions of pretending to en-
gage the car. "You ask me, cops are stupid. They're
little people."

"What choice is there? I have to do *something*."
He added, "And what about those dogs?"

Tegg nodded. The important thing was to remain
in control, to give this person the sense that he,
Tegg, had all the answers, even though he was making this up on the fly. The key to such manipulation
was in allowing the other person to believe that all
the good ideas were his. To fill in gaps that were
never left in the first place. For so many animals in
the wild, the key to survival, the way they snared
their prey, was through convincing camouflage.
Tegg knew his most effective camouflage was to appear to be this man's friend. How quickly we place
our trust in those we like. And Tegg could be quite
likable when he tried.

"Listen, if you're saying I should go back there
with you," Tegg suggested, "I suppose that makes
some good sense. It's a good idea. The police are certainly more likely to believe the two of us, aren't
they? *Of course* they are!" He didn't wait for an acknowledgment; he had the boy right where he
wanted him: confused. No one likes to disclaim au-
thorship of a good idea. He turned the car around.
He would have to pretend he didn't know the way.

It was strange how long the ride seemed to take.
In reality it was only a few minutes, a couple of
miles. For Elden Tegg, attempting to work this out
in his head, those minutes passed slowly. Another
complication. This heart harvest had brought him
some bad luck, but he wasn't going to bail out. Not
with Wong Kei's money in hand. Not with a donor
all lined up. You seized a problem by the throat and

you squeezed until it died. It was as simple as that. Problems left breathing came back to life. You killed them the first time, or you suffered the consequence.

Michael directed Tegg through the turns that lead Tegg onto his own property. Tegg remarked convincingly, "I've been coming up these country roads for years. Never knew this place existed."

"Me either," Michael said.

"You're on foot, are you?" Tegg asked, needing as much information as possible. His hope was to discourage this person, to convince him he had heard wrong, send him on his way. But if this failed, what then? Where was a person like Maybeck when you needed him the most?

"Hiking."

"You're a long way from anywhere." He added, "I was under the impression this is mostly private land out here." It was *all* privately leased land now—timberland owned by paper companies. The hiker had been trespassing—probably knowingly— and this seemed useful ammunition. You preyed on a person's vulnerabilities. It was always the weakest link that broke first.

When his passenger failed to respond, Tegg said, "The thing of it is, the police may wonder what you were doing up here in the first place. Especially if it turns out to be a wild goose chase—a couple of cats fornicating. You say you were hiking? Are there trails up here?"

"There's an old railroad grade," the young black man snapped defensively. "I don't care *what* the police say!" Tegg knew all about the old railroad grade, about the Nature Conservancy's attempts to purchase much of this land. He remembered the tree spiking. The radicals who chained themselves to the trees.

He glanced over at his passenger, who seemed so righteous, so determined. Tegg rolled down his window and fished for air. What next? He thought of a possible way out. "We won't have any trouble with those dogs you mentioned," he said, once again getting the other's attention. "At least we shouldn't. Hmm? Did I tell you I'm a veterinarian?" There it was, the biggest risk to take, but if offered as an asset he hoped it might be accepted as such.

"No shit?" the young man asked.

"The rangers keep a couple horses out here," Tegg lied convincingly. "Out at the reservoir," he added, keeping his story straight. He glanced over at his passenger—was that *relief* he saw? He explained quickly.

"I have my kit in the back. If the dogs give us any trouble we'll be fine."

"It's just up here," his passenger informed him.

"Did you speak to anyone in the house?" Tegg asked as they rounded the bend in the road that revealed the cabin. He felt in more control now, though his adrenaline was still pumping. He felt slightly giddy with anticipation.

"Are you kidding? I mean, what if someone is in the house? What if there *is* a woman locked up in that hangar?"

"There isn't," Tegg said, asserting some authority.

"There are some strange people back in these woods."

"I know that."

"I mean *really* strange."

Tegg pulled the Isuzu to a stop. The dogs barked ferociously.

With one eye on the cabin Michael stated, "Leave it running. If they're armed . . . if there *is* someone here, and they turn out to be armed, we should be prepared to leave in a hurry."

"Agreed." They both climbed out. Tegg felt suddenly enlightened—what a *perfect* idea. "You've given me an idea. I just happen to have something that might help us." Feeling stronger now—himself again—he returned to the car, opened the back door, and rummaged in his veterinary supplies.

One thing was for certain: If he made it through this, a few things were going to change. He would leave Felix uncaged, free to patrol the aisle. Free to attack if a stranger opened the door. And he would muzzle the woman. The Bitch. No more screaming.

"This ought to help us," he said, showing it to Michael Washington.

"A gun?"

"A dart pistol. Armed with something called Ketamine. Quite effective, I assure you. Now, let's have a listen." He motioned the young man over to the structure.

"Over here. I heard her over here," Michael said, indicating the north side of the structure.

"We won't hear anything with this barking," Tegg said.

"Maybe if we just sit here," Michael Washington said, "they'll calm down." He seemed nervous about the possibility of somone coming from the cabin. He checked it continually.

"I haven't got all day, young man. Hmm?"

"If we could get a look inside."

"It's locked up tight. We've already trespassed. You don't want to add breaking and entering to that, do you? The police treat all crime the same, you know. I for one want nothing to do with breaking any more laws." Tegg felt a strange lightheadedness. The air seemed crystal clear. He knew what had to be done. He checked the dart gun.

Once again Tegg attempted to discourage him. "I for one have *other* things to do. What about you? I thought you said you were lost. Won't this delay of yours be noticed?" He tested, "Are you with anyone else?"

"Me? No. But I understand what you're saying. We can't wait around here forever. Maybe it *was* just a cat."

The dogs quieted. Tegg lifted his hand like a preacher and they waited in silence as the last of the barking stopped completely. It surprised him they should stop so soon; sometimes they went on for hours. "Nothing," he whispered.

Michael stepped toward the building. He raised his arm, preparing to bang on the wall!

"Without actually breaking inside," Tegg added, stopping the man, "there's not much more to be done. We're sure as hell not going to break that lock." Tegg's finger slipped onto the trigger. Despite the isolation, Tegg had no desire to do this out in the open. He had made a similar mistake once before in his life, and he was not prone to repeating mistakes.

"Helllppp!" came the distinctive cry of a woman's voice from inside. It was quickly buried in barking, but there was no mistaking it.

The hiker exploded into a frenzy. "What did I tell you?" He ran for the door.

The pistol was no good for moving targets; Tegg was no marksman. He hurried after him. Above all, he wanted them both *inside* before he used the dart gun. It would take anywhere from thirty seconds to several minutes for the Ketamine to take effect. He needed the man *contained* for this period, not running wild. Shoot him *inside* the kennel, then get out quickly and lock the door until the drug took effect.

In a calm, almost serene way, he examined his options. What was left? There could be no trusting this man. The threat was too great. Even if Tegg were to move the woman, his research laboratory was here in the basement of the cabin. Could he give it all up on account of one lost hiker? Problems tended to breed like rabbits. Solutions required quick decisions.

"Something has just occurred to me. What about a hidden key? A spare key for this shed? People *always* hide a spare. I certainly do. It shouldn't be too hard to find." Tegg said this as he fingered the appropriate key in his pocket.

"You're right!"

"All we have to do is think like him. Hmm? Where would you hide a spare key? I'll take this side, you take that."

It took Tegg only a few seconds to separate the key from his key chain, although he had to set the dart gun down to do so. He turned over a rock so that it would look as if he had found it there. Then he announced loudly, "I've found it!"

The man named Michael came running.

Tegg retrieved the dart gun and led the boy to the door. He inserted the key and turned. The padlock snapped open. "You first," Tegg said. "This was *your* idea." He added, "I'll back you up," and displayed the loaded dart gun.

The door swung open. They were greeted with a penetrating darkness, and foul, bitter odors. The dogs barked wildly. Michael Washington checked silently with Elden Tegg. Encouraged by him, he began a slow, tentative walk down the darkened aisle. The white teeth of the dogs, bared and snarling, challenged him at every step. The shock collars sang with warnings, and the dogs cried with pain as they threw themselves against the chain-link walls of their cages.

Elden Tegg, dart gun in hand, followed a few steps behind. With each cage Tegg passed, the dog inside went silent. Michael Washington took no notice, made no connection, his attention instead riveted on the inhabitant of the cage up ahead on the left. On the bare back and buttocks of the woman crouched into the far corner.

She glanced over her shoulder briefly, her arms tucked tightly, covering her breasts, looking first at Michael Washington, then at Elden Tegg. She hid her face.

"I was *right*!" Michael Washington proclaimed triumphantly, turning toward Tegg.

"But you'll soon wish you hadn't been," replied Elden Tegg, who was waiting several feet away, dart gun raised. He squeezed the trigger. The gun went off with a crack. Tegg had never fired a dart gun at a human. He had hesitated an instant too long. A shocked and stunned Michael Washington reached down and pulled the dart free.

Eyes filled with rage, he charged Tegg, who would be no match for the younger man.

The dogs' barking was deafening!

Tegg's mind worked furiously: the shovel! Leaning against the near wall, it offered possibility. He lunged toward the wall, jumping left toward the shovel as his charger misjudged his intentions and crashed into the door, slamming it shut. A drugged Michael Washington got out of his own way then and managed to crack the door open as Tegg seized the shovel and swung it in a long, unforgiving arc toward the other man's head. The shovel dropped quickly, only grazing the black man's arm. Washington caught hold of the shovel, and hand-over-hand drew Tegg closer—both of them struggling for possession. Tegg saw the man's pupils then, and he let go of the shovel, surprising Michael Washington, who staggered back, shovel in hand. Tegg witnessed the first major seizure in the man, a ripple of muscle contraction that ran from his feet to his shoulders.

Michael Washington fought it. With great difficulty, he managed to move one heavy step forward. Fear belied his intentions.

Tegg watched, catching his breath. He smiled. "There's no use fighting it now," he said.

Washington's entire body tensed as a second contraction hit him. He collapsed. Tegg stood over him, watching. Studying. He had never seen such a severe reaction to Ketamine. As a doctor, he found it fascinating. In higher doses, it was lethal.

"Oh, no . . ." the drugged man groaned.

"Oh, yes," answered Elden Tegg, another smile forming on his lips.

17

Boldt was driving his Toyota, Daphne riding with him. He had been warned that it might be days or even weeks until he could draw a vehicle from the pool. He didn't have an office cubicle yet, either. In many ways he remained the outsider, his return to the department more technical than actual.

A few miles passed. The Emerald City receded in the rearview mirror. He could see out across the Sound. Lush green islands like jewels. More pleasure craft than on the weekdays, their sails catching the brilliant sunshine like sun-starved flowers. Ferries like big bugs, back and forth, back and forth. The waterways came alive on weekends when the sun shone. His eyes refocused. OBJECTS CLOSER THAN THEY APPEAR read the message stenciled across the outside mirror. "No lie," thought Lou Boldt, studying Daphne's profile.

"You don't have to be so mad," he said to her.

"We should have done this yesterday."

"You *did* speak to her yesterday. It couldn't be official for twenty-four hours."

"That's a *stupid* law. Twenty-four hours? Sharon could be *anywhere* by now." She added, "And don't give me the statistics sermon! You'll see. Once you have spoken to Agnes you'll be convinced. I *know* you. I know you will be. Sharon *did not* take off somewhere. Those goddamn statistics weren't made for people like her. And don't hand me that *crap* about her having been a runaway. That's all behind her. I could have popped Shoswitz for that. He's a misogynist, you know that?"

"LaMoia's running the surveillance on the BloodLines employee, Connie Chi," he said, trying to distract her. She was worked up for nothing—they were almost there. In the police department *nothing* moved at the pace you wanted. Investigators learned to accept it; psychologists-turned-investigators suffered for it. There was a long silence.

"So how are things?" he asked.

"Things?" she questioned. "What things?"

"You know," he said.

"My sex life?" she asked bluntly. "Am I getting enough? Something like that?"

He felt himself blush. "Sorry." He wasn't asking about her sex life, but her happiness, though he felt helpless to explain.

"I'm on hold at the moment," she answered. "There *was* someone for a while, but I handled it all wrong. I wanted too much too soon. It wasn't even that I *wanted* it, I *expected* it. The truth is I don't know what I want, and that doesn't work in a relationship."

They stopped at a light, but Boldt didn't look at her. She sounded so *damaged*. "You seem happy," he said optimistically.

"I'm in therapy. It's fantastic! That's what I mean about being on hold. I'm working a little too much. Surprise! But it fills the hours. You know? And the therapy is helping a lot. It's nice to have some control again."

A single evening they had spent together. A dinner that had run out of control. Boundaries crossed. Honesties voiced. And now, strangely, as if it never had happened.

"Well, you look great," he told her, feeling stupid to have said it.

"Thanks." She hesitated. "No regrets. You?"

"None." He felt her look at him, and he warmed all over.

"I'm glad," she said.

———

Sharon Shaffer's housemate, Agnes Rutherford, was five feet tall with silver-blue hair that gleamed like silk and perfectly brilliant ice-blue eyes that belied their inability to function. Agnes Rutherford was blind. She wore a cardigan sweater littered with dandruff and a skirt that was losing its hem. Leather slippers worn shiny on the sides from sliding her feet along, like a person wearing boots on ice.

When Boldt and Daphne were only a few feet inside the door, Agnes Rutherford asked him, "How old is your child, Mr. Boldt? Or am I supposed to call you by your rank?"

Boldt looked over at Daphne in astonishment. She touched her nose in pantomime. "He's six months," Boldt replied. "Still a baby."

"And do you smoke, even with a child in the house?"

"Smoke? No. Not me. I'm a musician. On the side," he added, though he wasn't sure which side anymore. "A night club." He sniffed at his coat. "It's probably my coat that smells like cigarettes."

Agnes Rutherford grinned, proud of herself. Her teeth were too perfect to be hers.

Daphine repeated what she and the woman had discussed a day earlier.

"Hasn't been home, either," the blind woman said in a troubled voice.

Boldt asked, "Why is it you think something *happened* to Sharon?"

"Oh, something happened all right. Why else would that man have lied to me?"

"Which man?"

"You can hear it in a person's voice when they're lying. Did you know that? He was a very tense man. What a voice he had—like fingernails on a blackboard. Nervous. Not just because I surprised him—which I did, mind you—but out of fear. Strange as it may seem, he was afraid of me. *Me!*"

Daphne suggested calmly. "Why don't you start at the beginning, Agnes."

"I heard voices through the wall. Two men talking to Sharon. And Sharon was scared. Plenty scared. I couldn't hear the words, you understand, but I didn't have to. She was good and scared."

"Voices . . ." Daphne repeated.

"Yes, so I came in through the kitchen. We share the kitchen. My rooms are just off the back side there. Came in to make sure she was all right. That's why I say the man lied—he told me Sharon had gone out for a minute and that he and his associate were also leaving. But the other one—the one with the halitosis—I think he dragged Sharon out. I heard something dragging on the carpet. She had been sitting in that chair, right over there. That chair squeaks. I heard it. I heard her voice, too, though not her words, not what she said. Not exactly."

"Do you remember what was said?" Boldt asked.

Agnes Rutherford nodded. "Thereabouts. As I rounded the corner the one with the hard voice asked the other. 'Who the hell is that?' "

"Those exact words?"

"Yes. He didn't expect me. And then there was a long silence. Then the other dragged her out, I think. At the time, of course, I didn't know what was happening, but that's what I think was going on."

"And you didn't call the police?" Boldt asked, dumbfounded.

"I was—I *am*—afraid of you. I spent a good many years of my life avoiding you. Hiding. On the streets, you understand. Would anyone have believed an old, blind, bag lady, Mr. Boldt? Would they have? You don't believe me now. I can hear it in your voice. You can't believe an old blind lady can survive the streets, but I *did*! Daphne believes me, I bet, but only because she knows me." She added, "I didn't call the police, I called The Shelter. I called Daphne."

Daphne glared at Boldt then. He was trying to see this through the eyes of the law—Phil Shoswitz, or prosecuting attorney Bob Proctor—and he didn't like what he saw: There was no proof of a crime. No matter what Agnes Rutherford believed she witnessed, she had not *seen* it. Police work was as much practicality as it was instinct. Sharon Shaffer's history was that of a runaway. This would not be an easy sell, despite the cooperative relationship between the police and The Shelter. The prosecuting attorney's office was another realm entirely.

Boldt examined the room. He remembered the Stevie Wonder line: *Her clothes are old, but never are they dirty*. That was how this room looked:

pieced together from yard sales but clean to the corners. Vacuumed recently. He asked Agnes Rutherford, "Is this room still pretty much as it was?"

The woman answered, "Oh, yes. Exactly. I haven't touched a thing. My rooms are back there. I don't fool with Sharon's things."

Boldt walked slowly and carefully over to the table and chairs. The cop in him understood the significance of what, to untrained eyes, might have looked like nothing more than dust on the table. It wasn't dust. Tiny particles of shredded paper perhaps. He studied the table top and then, using his handkerchief so he wouldn't leave fingerprints, applied pressure to the back of the chair. It squeaked.

"That's the one," Agnes said.

Boldt told her, "The house had just been cleaned." He made it a statement. "She had vacuumed the carpet that morning."

"Now just exactly how did you know that?" Agnes Rutherford asked.

Daphne asked Boldt, "Lou?"

Boldt didn't need any more convincing, he was standing amid a pile of evidence. There were drops of blood on the arm of the chair. "Call the lab," he said. "And tell them to bring a lot of lights."

"Lights?" Daphne asked.

"For the carpet," Boldt explained. Variations in the nap of the carpet allowed him to see a pair of scuff lines and the perfectly formed impressions of shoe prints.

18 Boldt enjoyed watching the ID Unit —the Scientific Identification Department—at work. Educated as scientists, they didn't think like other cops. They worked as a team, speaking in half-sentences, using techie jargon unintelligible to the layman. With their nerd packs and a language all their own, these men and women remained on the social fringe of the police fraternity but played an increasingly important role in any investigation. The star witnesses in an investigation were no longer the boyfriend or the observant neighbor but these ID Unit technicians. Convictions relied on a foundation of incriminating scientific evidence. A jury, even a judge, preferred to believe a computer-generated enlargement of work from an electron microscope rather than a woman like Agnes who had heard voices through a wall. You didn't bother Bob Proctor and his band of PA's unless you had a file full of stats to support your case.

The only thing about ID that really irritated Boldt was how slowly they went about their jobs. If Sharon Shaffer had been abducted, which he now believed, he could only imagine how terrified she must be at this moment—providing she was still alive. No ransom call, no notification whatsoever. Impatience nagged at him.

The ID Unit continued its meticulous examination of the crime scene. The first round involved the detailed photographing, in varying degrees of enlargement and detail, of all angles and aspects relevant to the possible crime. Several general shots were taken, followed by increasingly specific studies of the carpet, the chair Sharon had apparently sat in, the table top, and the fixtures.

The area was vacuumed next—excluding the carpet—for fibers, using small, hand-held, filter-specific vacuum cleaners. Each filter was removed and labeled and then bagged in a white paper bag. Plastic bags were rarely used by Hairs And Fibers because of their static charge.

While several of the team continued to measure and photograph the "impressions" in the carpet, others began carefully dusting surfaces with dark and light powders using soft animal-hair brushes. Any developed prints were first photographed and then "lifted" using wide strips of transparent packing tape. The powder, print and all, came up with the lift, which was then mounted on card stock, labeled, and set aside.

All this while Boldt, consulting Daphne, wrote up a detailed first officer's report, describing the scene exactly as he had found it, his suspicions, and his findings. The report came to two single-spaced legal pages written longhand. They both signed and dated it for the specific hour.

———

Bernie Lofgrin ate too much and exercised too little. He had the coloring of an Irishman and the temper of a Scot. He wore glasses as thick as ashtrays and suspenders with full-frontal nudes hand painted onto them. When Bernie tugged them this way and that, the nudes did a belly dance. Everyone called him the Professor. He ran his squad like a Scout leader and put away more beer at The Big Joke than an alumnus on homecoming weekend. Over the past year he had become a regular during Boldt's piano sets. He had joined the Boldt-Dixon jazz record exchange—taping each other's albums. Bernie's collection leaned toward drummers and trombone players.

Boldt knew that with this being a Sunday it should have been only a skeleton-crew ID unit. But Lofgrin had come himself and had brought additional overtime help as a personal favor.

As he approached, his thick glasses were aimed at Boldt like unfocused binoculars. He seemed to have eyes the size of fried eggs. "One of the two suspects wears a shoe size eight-and-a-half wide. Maybe D, maybe E. The other suspect, some kind of running shoe. The way the nap in the carpet stood up for us, these guys might as well have left us plaster impressions. We might even have a make on the manufacturer of those running shoes by sometime tomorrow. We'e got a distinctive, triangular tread pattern in a couple of takes. Size thirteen, by the way. Big Foot. Fibers on the table vacuumed up just fine. Crisp paper by the look of it. We got another small piece under the table. Light blue ink on it reads 'USA,' as in 'printed in.'"

"Was that what the guy was waving a microphone over?" Boldt asked.

"You jazz guys think anything with a wire running into it is a microphone. That device measures low-level radioactivity."

"A Geiger counter?"

"Like that, yeah. The reason being that I suspected it was the paper covering to a Band-Aid or gauze, something like that. That paper has a distinctive look. That Geiger counter—as you call it—picked up a charge consistent with my suspicions."

"Radioactivity?"

"It's how they sterilize them. Band-Aids, gauze, nearly every self-contained disposable item in a hospital—they zap 'em with low-level radioactivity *after* they're packaged—that way they can guarantee sterility."

"Live and learn."

"Stick with me, kid. Evidence points to two possibilities: real careful junkies—doubtful; or a doctor—more likely."

"A *doctor*?"

"We've got some real obvious residual fluids—dried up you understand—discovered both on the arm of the chair and beneath the table. We got a good photo of the drip pattern. My guess is it was squirted. Size of the droplets suggest—"

"A syringe." Boldt interrupted.

"Either that or this guy is the original needledick and he came all over that chair." He smiled. "We'll get all this shit off to the state lab. Might have that blood you found typed sometime tomorrow," he said, answering Boldt's thoughts before he could voice them. "Mr. Eight-and-a-half-wide was carrying some kind of flat-bottomed case, fourteen by eighteen inches."

"Like a doctor's bag?"

"That's my guess, yes." Bernie went on. "Big Foot, the guy with the running shoes, was carrying a laptop computer. He set it down next to the chair and gave us enough of an impression for an educated guess that that's what it was, although you can't take that one to the bank. If you bring in these two in the next twenty-four to forty-eight hours, I *may* be able to lift some of these carpet fibers from the edges of their shoes. It's a cheap synthetic, loose weave, real prone to shedding. The static should hold the fibers on the shoes for a while. As to your idea that maybe the person in that chair was dragged out of the room, it's possible but we're not likely to prove it. *Something* was dragged—I can testify to that—and it had two legs or feet or posts, but that's as close as we'll get. Our other vacuum samples could give us a hell of a lot more to work with. Stay tuned." He slapped Boldt on the arm and returned to his crew.

Boldt looked around at an anxious Daphne, who had just returned from interviewing the neighbors in the apartment houses. He waved her over. "Nothing," she said. "Fourteen *families* of people and no one saw a thing!" He asked her to call the city's 911 dispatch, Sharon's doctor, ambulance services, and the two closest area hospitals, inquiring whether on the previous day Sharon had sought medical attention.

"What's up?"

"The Professor has uncovered some evidence that points to either a drug deal or a doctor."

"Not drugs, Lou. Not Sharon. I know her past says otherwise, but I know the woman."

"Would I have you calling hospitals if I suspected a drug deal?"

She eased noticeably.

"But if she didn't call an ambulance, then a drug deal is easier to believe."

"Not for me it isn't."

"Daffy, somehow two people convinced a streetwise woman to open her door for them. How? It also now appears that somehow she was further convinced to roll up her sleeve for them. You know Bob Proctor's reputation. It's going to be our job to *dis*prove any street-drug connection. The state lab will have a lot to say about that. But if we found her admitted to an area hospital, we'd all feel a hell of a lot better."

"That's not the way Agnes reports it. She says she was kidnapped."

"I *know* that, Daffy."

"Lou?" The Professor, Bernie Lofgrin, called out, kneeling by one of the chairs. Boldt joined him there. "You're the quintessential king of no coincidences," Lofgrin said. "Am I right?"

"So?"

"So we did the lab work-up on the Cynthia Chapman clothing—Matthews' runaway. 'Kay?"

"Okay." Boldt felt his pulse quicken. Why would the Professor bring up Cindy Chapman now?

Lofgrin, who was wearing a pair of jeweler's loupes clipped to his already thick glasses, found a magnifying glass in a bag and handed it to Boldt. "Get a load of this," he said.

He pointed. Boldt focused the glass onto the spot indicated. A clump of animal hairs clung to the fabric of the chair. Under the glass they looked like pick-up-sticks.

"What do you see?" Lofgrin asked confidently.

"Animal hairs," Boldt replied. "A pile of them."

"Notice the extremely long white ones? See how much longer they are than the others? They're unusually long. We lifted *similar* hairs off Chapman's clothes." He made a face at Boldt. A lab guy like Lofgrin would never use the word *identical*. In the scientific world, *identical* rarely existed. "What we've got here is a visual cross-match."

Lofgrin's magnified eyes looked like two veinmapped beach balls.

Boldt studied the hairs once again, blood thumping in his ears. Cindy Chapman and Sharon Shaffer connected? Abducted by the same man? Both runaways, one present, one past. Overlaps. Mounting coincidences he couldn't buy. He asked, "Any way to *prove* such a connection?" Evidence as ubiquitous as animal hairs was unlikely to hold up in court, but Boldt temporarily ignored this.

Lofgrin smiled; the Professor loved a challenge. "We'll sure as hell try."

Daphne kept a close eye on Boldt as he hurried her off the telephone, took it from her, and started dialing.

She protested, "Hey, it was *you* who wanted me to make these calls."

"Priorities," he replied.

He avoided looking at her because she was the kind of person to *sense* something was wrong. He didn't know the number, so he called information. "Seattle," he said. *Coincidences*, he was thinking. "BloodLines," hoping he had spoken quietly enough not to be overheard, but as he turned around, there she was, only inches from him, wearing a puzzled, frightened expression.

The woman who answered connected him to a man named Henderson, because Verna Dundee, the managing supervisor, didn't come in on Sundays. Boldt reintroduced himself and presented his case, Daphne listening in. He cupped the receiver and protested to Daphne, "Can't a guy get some privacy around here?"

"No," she replied, fear and irritation flashing from her eyes.

Boldt spelled Sharon Shaffer's name for the man. "I doubt it's a recent file. I'll wait," he said in anticipation. As he assumed, he was placed on hold. He would have to check central processing using another line.

"Lou?" Daphne asked, eyes squinting, lips pale.

Boldt felt impossibly hot. The seconds grew into minutes. He thought: I should hang up right now. I should leave this for others. I should stick to my family and my piano playing, because if it turns out . . .

It was Henderson telling him what he didn't want to hear. He wouldn't need the results of the Professor's tests. Not now that he had this. He felt sick to his stomach.

Daphne had desperate eyes. She had already guessed. "Lou?"

How did you put something like this to Daphne? Why, as a cop, were you always the bearer of bad news?

"Sharon Shaffer is in the BloodLines database. Three years ago she was a regular donor."

Daphne gasped.

"I think the harvester's struck again." He looked over at Agnes Rutherford, her blind eyes steady and untracking. "And she's our only witness."

MONDAY

February 6

19

Sharon Shaffer looked on as the black man in the kennel next to hers came awake for the first time. She remembered the terror of that moment and could do nothing to warn him of the horror he was about to experience, nothing to lessen its effect. The dogs started barking; she knew he would awaken—it had been the same for her. She couldn't remember exactly when. Had it been just yesterday? It seemed more like forever.

He looked around. Surprise. Astonishment. Terror. He clearly noticed then the chain-link cages; and a moment later, his own nakedness. She knew that his head ached miserably from the drugs just as hers had.

He spotted her then. She tried her best to communicate with her eyes, for her jaw was now held in a modified dog muzzle made of nylon webbing, one strap of which ran across her mouth, keeping a gauze rag stuffed into place to prevent her from crying out, as she had to this man. She felt responsible for his being here. She *was* responsible. His jaw was secured in a similar muzzle, although the gag had been omitted, probably because the doctor feared he might vomit on coming awake, which he did, repeatedly. She had to wonder: Was it the effects of the sedation or from looking at her? She could only guess at what she must look like. A bandage glowing a lurid pink at the edges. She had pale skin the color of cigarette ash. Her hair was matted flat. Or perhaps that expression of his arose from the dogs and their horrid smell. The deafening barking at the slightest instigation. It would take him a while to adjust to their situation, but she needed him to adjust—to settle down.

To help her escape. She was going to get out of here, with or without him.

She thought that if only she could stop him from what he would do next, she could spare him some pain. But the muzzle and gag prevented her from speaking; she could only grunt and gesticulate. And that, only quite weakly. She had little strength, drugged as she was by whatever was in the I.V. It felt like a combination Valium-Demerol to her. She was experienced enough to know. When she thought about it, it brought on resentment and anger, rage and indignation. She had spent the last three *years* of her life learning to live sober. Now, forced on her, she found herself drugged up again—enjoying the feeling, wanting more. She looked up at the precious drip, drip, drip of the I.V. Worst of all, she couldn't bring herself to disconnect the tube. If anything, she wished it would flow faster. She could take more. She had always been able to take more . . .

Despite her efforts to warn him, her neighbor reached out and touched the chain-link door of the cage. He actually laced his fingers into it and shook it with his considerable strength. He must have heard the collar sound its electronic warning—the buzz—but like her on her first time, he didn't associate this sound with the pain that would follow. And like her, he would learn soon enough.

She watched as his fingers met the cage, as a blinding pulse of electricity stung his neck, and literally knocked his knees out from under him. She heard his head thump against the cement as he wilted. His bowels loosened and he fouled himself. He lay there staring up at her, flat on his back, the pain, fear and terror so great in his eyes that she felt herself break into tears. A maddening frustration stole through her, and briefly she found enough strength to sit up, to sit forward and be as close to him as possible.

As his strength returned, he reached for the shock collar, and despite her shaking her head in discouragement, he tried, in vain, to rid himself of it.

How clearly she remembered those first few minutes; they seemed so distant now. He would deny his situation at first. She knew. He would think: This can't be. This is impossible. Then, as reality sank in, as his muscle strength returned, as he began to assess, to realize the hopelessness, he would recoil. A minute later he sat in the center of the cage, wrapped in the fetal position, sobbing and mumbling incoherently. "Impossible . . . What did I do? Can't be . . ." He mentioned God, he mentioned his parents. He glanced over at her several times, but seemed not to see her. He retreated.

She sat back onto the burlap and waited. In time he would come around. Given time, he would come to realize they were a team now and that their only chance of escape was to work together.

Her one single hope remained that he would come up with a plan. After all this time here, she saw no way out. Like the I.V. in her wrist, she was stuck here.

Not long after that—she could not determine the passage of time because of the drugs and the suspended states in which she found herself—the

ground rumbled. A car! The dogs paced restlessly inside their cages.

She turned quickly to her neighbor, charged with
adrenaline. She shouted at him through the gag, able
to win his attention but unable to communicate.
She resorted to an archaic pantomime, pushing her
hands along the cement as if to say, "Clean up!"
Demonstrating that he should scoop up the vomit
and excrement and get it into the bucket left as a
toilet. When he failed to respond, she twisted her
face angrily and screamed, shaking her fists, and
then pointed to the door. "It's *him*!" she mumbled.
She grabbed hold of her collar and shook it. That
reached him. He sat up with a jolt. Again she motioned that he must clean his cage. Her panic conta-
gious, she drove him to it. He worked quickly,
glancing over his shoulder all the while, both at her
and the door he expected to see opened any second.

Miraculously, he got most of the mess into the
bucket at the last possible moment.

The door rattled as The Keeper fumbled with the
lock.

The dogs erupted into barking once again.

Sharon covered her ears. The door opened.

The Keeper was dressed in a business suit. He
was smiling.

"Good morning," he called out, sounding more
like Captain Kangaroo than the madman she took
him for.

===

Elden Tegg walked down the narrow cement aisle
that separated the two sides of the kennel, carefully
inspecting the inhabitant of each cage. He knew the
medical history of each of these animals. He had
grown to love them. Each and every one despite—or
perhaps because of—their nasty dispositions.

"Time to eat," he said, pushing the wheelbarrow to each cage, the bag of dog food precariously balanced. At the end of the run, he reached the two newcomers, Sharon and Washington.

Sharon was huddled modestly in the corner, looking at him through the muzzle he had cleverly rigged out of nylon strapping. Her contempt for him never left her eyes, although he intended to correct that by harvesting her right cornea. "Come on," he said to her, encouraging her to show him her incision. When she failed to obey, he reached for the remote device that controlled her collar, threatening to use it. Use of this device had the same effect as coming in contact with the wire—it triggered the collar. She sprang into action, obediently duck-walking toward him, paying careful attention to her I.V. She clung to modesty by keeping folded up on herself. "Let the doctor see," he instructed, enjoying the title. He could care less about her nudity: It was the incisions that held his interest. His insistence on leaving the two of them naked had no basis in voyeurism. A determined person could hang himself with clothing. He couldn't afford to lose her, that was all. He waved the remote again, and she turned herself for him. The skin around her bandage was slightly pink but not bad.

He motioned her back into the far end of the cage and let himself inside, the shock collar's remote "wand" constantly in hand, constantly a threat. He changed her dressing, removed the muzzle, took her temperature—ninety-nine and change, nothing to worry about—and replaced her I.V. of Ringers solution with a fresh one, supercharged with Valium, a dash of Demerol and a higher dosage of antibiotics. He gave her new gauze for her gag, returned the muzzle, and handed her a bucket of a Quaternary-based disinfectant they used at the clinic. He stood by and watched her as she scrubbed the pen's floor. He directed her to a few missed spots and then took the bucket back, convinced of the pen's cleanliness. Locking her inside he told her, "Cleanliness is next to godliness."

He turned and faced Washington.

"Welcome," he said.

"You're insane," Washington whispered.

Tegg went rigid. His first temptation was to shock him, but he resisted. He had never felt clearer. "Sticks and stones," he answered.

"She needs medical attention."

Tegg shot back dismissively, "What do you think I just gave her?"

Sharon grunted at her companion, waving him off, asking him to stop.

Tegg added, "Perhaps you need some medical attention."

"Perhaps *you* do," Washington protested.

Tegg understood that such charges, if left unanswered, gained validity in some perverse way by simply having been spoken. He picked up the "wand" for this man's collar and reminded him with a short little *zap!* Washington responded with a spasm of pain. "You are out of your element. I would watch my accusations if I were you."

Washington backed into the corner. "Don't do this."

Tegg objected, "Do *what*? You don't even know what this is about. This is about basic needs. This is about life and death. That's fairly simple, isn't it?"

He clearly wasn't getting through.

Tegg paced the center aisle. He couldn't describe his present feeling. The air seemed to be vibrating, his thoughts precise—as in the middle of an operation. He felt righteous and angry—why was he forced to defend such obvious logic?

He checked his watch: eight-twenty. From the top of the hill closer to town, the cellular would operate. He could call Pamela. She could reschedule some of the morning appointments and be out here in a little over forty minutes. Why waste a specimen like this? he thought, pausing by Washington's cage. Make the most with what you've got.

"Some lessons," he told the young man, "are better learned first-hand." He returned the shock collar's remote device to its hook on the cage, clearly confusing his captives. "Remember our little skirmish yesterday? I certainly won't allow *that* to happen again." It wasn't a confusing situation to Elden Tegg: With a strong specimen such as Washington, the dart gun was clearly the only way to go.

20

"This is my son Miles."

"Hello, Miles." Dr. Crystal Light Horse, a transplant surgeon on the University of Washington's—the U-Dub's—medical staff whom Dixie knew through his lecture series, wore an oversized lab coat and a laminated name plate that included the hospital's insignia. She seemed young for a practicing surgeon, mid-thirties. She was a Native American with laughing eyes, barn-wood brown. She pursed her lips whenever Boldt spoke, her attention focused on him as if she were looking down a gun sight.

Boldt wondered at all the social obstacles she had overcome to get here.

He said, "We tried Miles in day care for about

three days, but we noticed this look in his eyes," he explained. "Do you have kids?"

"Two."

"Then you know what I mean."

"No."

"You see that look?" Boldt asked, pointing at his son. "That sparkle? Well, that's him, you know? And after day care," he waved a hand in front of his own face like a magician, and acted out the transformation, "gone. Just this glazed look like no one was home."

She bristled. "*Both* my children went through day care, and I never noticed any such thing."

"As a surgeon," Boldt asked, "have you ever had to remove a person's foot from his mouth?"

That won a smile. "Thankfully, no." She added, "It's a good thing you're a policeman. It looks as if you have a kleptomaniac on your hands." Miles had stolen a fountain pen off her desk—expensive by the look of it. Boldt wrestled it free and returned it. Miles promptly grabbed it again. His father stole it back and fed him a Bic.

Her office was buried in books and papers. He worried that she might be one of those more-diplomas-than-you-can-count type-A educators, quick to lecture, short on substance.

He explained, "I need to throw a hypothetical situation at you. I'm involved in an investigation that is really more your field than mine, and I'm at a loss for specific leads to follow."

"A scent."

"Exactly."

"I'll do what I can."

"Let's suppose you're a transplant surgeon— which you are—who, for one reason or another, finds herself in need of a great deal of money."

"You're broke."

He nodded. "You're broke and you hear that overseas or maybe right here in this country, this city, people are willing to pay big money for certain organs."

"There's no evidence that in this country—"

He raised a hand, interrupting; he didn't want her getting ahead of him. "Now as I understand it, in transplanting something like a kidney, you would want the donor to be blood type O."

"Not accurate: You would prefer the donor organ to match the recipient's blood group exactly."

"But to sell?" he inquired.

She bristled again. "Type O might indeed make it easier to sell," she agreed. "Type O is the largest, most common blood group, and Type O organs have the lowest rate of rejection in transplants into any other blood group."

He suggested, "So, if you put yourself in the roll of the harvester—"

"The procuring surgeon," she corrected. "We don't like the word 'harvester.'"

"Nor do I." He completed, "How would you, as the procuring surgeon, locate a potential donor with blood type O?"

"The procuring surgeon is looking for cadavers. I suppose the first resources I would draw upon would be the hospital morgue, the Medical Examiner's office, and any of a number of mortuaries."

Boldt took notes. Miles took his pacifier out and threw it across the desk at Dr. Light Horse, who scooped it up, brushed it off, and offered it back to him. Miles liked that. He accepted it gladly and sucked noisily. Boldt asked, "And if those resources weren't available to you or were exhausted for one reason or another, what then?"

She offered him a cold and puzzled look. "You're not suggesting?"

"*What* am I suggesting?"

"Someone *living*?"

"It's possible, isn't it? I've read about Egypt, India . . ."

"But those people are *desperate* for money . . ."

"There are people desperate for money in this country as well—in this *city* as well."

"But it's different there," she protested, clearly upset, "in terms of professional health services. It's true that some Third World countries have limited resources, limited access to technologies such as dialysis. The reason for the high prices, for the whole transplant mess in these parts of the world is that without those transplants people die. It's different here. Much different."

He admired her vehemence. She was morally and ethically undone by what he was suggesting. "Which means that your market is overseas, if I'm reading you right."

"Now you're scaring me."

"Good." He wanted her scared, because he felt scared for Sharon Shaffer, for whoever else was scheduled next for the knife.

"Here in Seattle?"

"You can't quote me on that," he said.

She thought long and hard. "Blood type? Depends what kind of resources you have, I suppose. You would need computer access, of course, but what comes immediately to mind are hospital records, the Red Cross, the insurance companies. Any of those databases would be likely to list blood type."

"A plasma bank?" he asked.

"Just exactly how far along in this investigation *are* you?"

He handed her several autopsy photos of two of the incisions. "Dixie suggested you have a look at these."

She studied them thoughtfully.

"Anything special?" he asked.

She continued to look them over. "Perfectly competent closures. Although the incisions are a little large."

As Boldt wrote this down, one of his notes caught his eye. "What kind of team does he need? How many assistants?"

"It depends on which organ we're talking about and which procedure."

"Kidneys," he said. "Harvesting kidneys."

"For a kidney procurement it's helpful to have an assistant. But again, I'm thinking in terms of cadavers," she corrected herself. "A live procurement? An anesthesiologist, a surgeon, a nurse or two."

"Could it be done with less?"

She nodded. "A surgeon and an assistant at the bare minimum." She added, "You'd be busy."

Miles was getting restless. Boldt contained him, but lost his train of thought.

"Have you thought about *where* this would be done?" she asked. "A location?" Then in a professorial tone of voice: "I see problems with this premise of yours. First, when a procurement is done in a hospital, the organ becomes part of the system. There's an airtight system in place. There has to be, because of the public's wariness about the whole transplant process. It's called UNOS—the United Network of Organ Sharing. The procuring institution assigns the organ a UNOS number. The recipient of that organ is assigned that same number. It all has to match. There is a paper trail a mile long the moment an organ leaves a body—hearts, kidneys, livers, marrow, it doesn't matter. The procuring surgeon lists an organ's destination as part of that paperwork—the name of the hospital or organ bank. The paperwork follows that organ everywhere. The organ is transported in specially sealed and labeled ice chests. It's all computerized. UNOS does an incredible job. I just don't see how someone could get away with what you're implying."

"And if the procedure was *not* done at a hospital? Could I get an organ into the system?"

"That's just my point. You can't without a UNOS number. No surgeon is going to touch an organ without the proper paperwork. At the end of every year UNOS follows up on every single organ procured or transplanted. Numbers have to match. If your numbers don't match, you come up for review—you're in deep trouble."

"And if it's *not* done in a hospital?"

She thought about this for a long minute. She nodded and nibbled at her fingernail, eyes on her desk. Boldt looked out the window at the weather. He felt tight-throated and hot. It was growing dark out there. More rain. She didn't say anything.

"You look puzzled." Frightened was more like it, he thought.

"The thing of it is," she said, "it's possible. You're right about the Third World market. If I'm the procuring surgeon, I don't want to mess with UNOS—they would catch something like this. I don't want to get anywhere *near* the system. I'm telling you, the safeguards in this country are just too established. But overseas? A kidney is good for sixty hours—these days, that's plenty of time to reach *any* foreign destination. And the money—the money would be phenomenal, I should think. You hear about prices like fifteen- and twenty-thousand dollars a kidney. Cash, no taxes. No questions. A couple of those a month, and you're doing just fine."

Excitement stole into Boldt so that his writing was illegible. He slowed and took down the same notes a second time. Miles snatched his pen and threw it to the floor. With the boy in the harness, Boldt couldn't lean down to reach it. Dr. Light Horse handed him a replacement. She seemed to be waiting for him to say something. He checked his notes once again. "So he does the harvesting outside a hospital?"

"Absolutely. This makes much more sense. But there would be a high risk of infection. Hospitals invest hundreds of thousands—millions—of dollars on their surgical suites. Filtered air, double doors, regular cleaning. You can't duplicate that on your own—unless you have more money than God."

Her fear fed his excitement. These were leads to follow, ideas to pursue. The more they talked, the more he saw an investigation developing. He now saw the investigation dividing into several areas: Connie Chi, the BloodLines employee, these technical leads, and the bones that Dixie suggested might have started it all.

She looked even more frightened when he asked, "Could I lease such equipment?"

"The scent you were talking about . . . something to follow?"

"Yes."

"Not my field. But I would *guess* that you could."

"What about transporting the organs? How difficult is it?"

"Technically, it's not difficult at all. You can use anything from Tupperware to stainless steel. Some Viospan. Ice. Depending on the organ, it'll keep anywhere from a couple of hours to several days." She added, "Ice chests—Igloo coolers or Styrofoam—are the most common ways to ship them. One of those small picnic coolers. UNOS uses disposable Styrofoam coolers with bright red labels sealing the joints. If you're going to walk a transplant organ through airport security, you're going to want a UNOS container. Now *there* is something you could check on." She brightened. "Stolen UNOS containers or labels. Air-freighted organs are usually hand-carried by the pilot or another member of the flight crew. The *legal* ones are. But a passenger could do the same thing if he or she could get through airport security."

Boldt wanted to grab for the phone. He wanted to rush out of here and put a team on it immediately. He wanted to reach across the desk and kiss this woman. This was the exact information he had hoped for: a different angle. A different point of view. If they couldn't trace the victims to the harvester, perhaps they could trace the movement of the organs: a courier. He said, "My feeling is that you overrate airport security. As long as an object doesn't appear to be a weapon or a bomb, they're not going to stop it."

"You're probably right." She picked up the autopsy photos and studied them intently. She was getting caught up in this as well. "That's a large incision for a kidney. Did I mention that?"

"Large?" Boldt asked. "Is that significant?" She *had* mentioned it, he realized; he'd even made a note of it on the top of the page. Was the surgical method unique? Would it provide them with a "signature" that they could later use to prosecute a suspect? He caught himself holding his breath, waiting for her.

She appeared so deeply in thought for such a long time that he wondered if she had forgotten his question. She tested her coffee and avoided his eyes in a way that prevented him from interrupting.

Miles was being a real pain in the ass. He wouldn't hold still. Boldt tried to occupy him with a plastic ring, but Miles wasn't having anything to do with it. He wanted some floor space. He wanted some moving room.

She finally said, "This incision is larger than necessary. These closure techniques are antiquated. It's doubtful that this is the work of a contemporary surgeon. A retiree is more likely. Unless the surgeon simply doesn't care how it comes out. But cosmetics are an important part of any surgery: Keeping the scar small. The subcutaneous closure is a continuous-interlocking stitch. It's an unusual stitch, but very strong."

Boldt wrote down in large letters: STITCHING. Retiree? This meant something, though he didn't know what. More to investigate; more to work with. Impatience stole into him—a cop's biggest enemy. Where was Sharon Shaffer at this moment? What had they done to her? What did they have planned for her?

Dr. Light Horse glanced at her watch, and Boldt took his cue. He packed up Miles, put his notebook away. As she walked them to the elevator, he stopped and said, "Let me ask you this . . . If type O is the best blood type for transplants, why would this harvester want someone with type AB-negative?" BloodLines had provided Boldt with Sharon's records that included her blood type. The Professor had confirmed that the blood found on the chair in her apartment was also AB-negative.

She appeared puzzled. "Is this person *soliciting* organs?"

He explained, "We believe he's kidnapped a woman. She's blood type AB-negative, not O." Her face tightened. "What is it?" he asked.

"AB-negative is an extremely rare blood group."

"So I'm told. But what's that mean for a transplant?"

She led him over to a string of seats by a Coke machine. He felt nervous, worried about Sharon. She obviously felt this would require some explanation.

Miles liked the lights of the Coke machine; he seemed mesmerized.

She explained, "The human body is blessed with an immune system to fight disease. The technical aspects of transplant surgery were pretty much worked out twenty years ago. Haven't been improved much since then. The main avenue of research has been into convincing the body's immune system not to destroy the transplanted organ. The body will reject *any* organ to some degree, unless it is from an identical twin. Blood is a tissue. A transfusion is the simplest example of a tissue transplant. Are you with me?" Boldt nodded.

"We all belong to certain blood groups, and many of those blood groups are incompatible with one another. An organ is made up of both a blood type and several different tissue types, making matching—for the transplant surgeon—even more complex. The focus for the last twenty years has been to suppress the body's immune system far enough to accept a transplanted organ, but no so far as to allow infection. That's a fine line. In the past five years, drugs have come a long way in helping to accomplish that. One day soon, immune suppression may be a thing of the past. But for the present, in the more critical organs—the heart, the liver, the pancreas—you need an organ not only the right size but also the best possible tissue match. The closer the match, the less rejection; the less you have to suppress the immune system, the less chance of a fatal infection. Okay? We talked about kidneys. It is true that type O organs transplant well because O is accepted more easily by the other blood groups. The body puts up less of a fight. If someone is selling organs, as you suggest, it makes sense to procure type O—it's your biggest market; not only the largest blood group but a good second choice if you don't have an exact blood-type match. Type AB-negative is less than four percent of the population. In the major organs, if you had an AB-negative recipient, you'd want an AB-negative donor to have any chance at all."

"A custom job, is that what you're saying?"

She cringed at the term. "It's a specific match. *That* is what I'm saying. A special order."

The elevator opened. Dr. Light Horse caught it and held it for Boldt and his restless passenger.

She walked him to the front of the building. She walked quickly, expecting him to keep up.

As they stopped to shake hands, she said, "The implications of what you're suggesting are horrible, of course. The medical community as a whole and surgeons in particular are just beginning to address ways of more closely monitoring the donor crisis. If more people donated their organs at death, we wouldn't be seeing any of this. If you're looking for a possible candidate," she continued, "I would start with surgeons reprimanded by the AMA—someone suspended and out of work. Frustrated. Angry. I assume we agree this person is deranged, and such thinking could easily distort the Hippocratic Oath. As doctors, we're sworn to save human life wherever possible. He or she reasons that the donor can get by on one kidney, that the recipient will die without that replacement organ. You have *three* dead, you said. Three out of a hundred or three out of five? That is how *he* is thinking. He may be playing percentages, I'm sorry to say." She touched his arm. "All this is just the long way of saying that it could be anyone disturbed enough to convince himself that what he's doing is not only acceptable, but ethically sound. He may see himself as an angel of mercy."

Mention of the word "angel" triggered vivid images from his youth. He remembered playing in the snow, lying down and fanning his arms and legs so that the impression he left behind resembled that of an angel. Only now he saw things differently: Inside that impression lay the bleached white bones of a skeleton. He said, "An angel? Hardly. An angel maker is more like it."

21

It gave Pamela Chase a sense of importance to be summoned at a moment's notice out to the farm. He needed her! Perhaps he would make love to her again; perhaps his calling her out here had nothing whatsoever to do with work, as his phone call had implied.

A low, mid-morning smoke-gray fog hung over the area where the farm sat, running from the ground to the tops of the tall trees that rimmed the ridges behind it. She spotted the fog only briefly before disappearing into it, and this made her wonder whether you ever saw things for what they were while you were inside them, a part of them.

The fog forced her to drive more slowly, and it gave her a few minutes to think. Seemed like all she did was think—that's how a person all alone spends her time, she thought, trapped inside your thoughts and dreams as this car was trapped inside the fog. Moving slowly. Crawling. Waiting for the phone to ring. Waiting for the workday to start. Waiting. Always thinking *ahead*, never really being where you are, but somewhere you hope to be. Strange way to live your life.

She parked alongside his Trooper and watched the mud as she climbed out, because she had been on her way to work when the phone had rung and wasn't very well prepared for the conditions out here. She loved the man—that was her problem. He knew it, too, which put her at a disadvantage because there was little she wouldn't do for him, and he made the most of it. With sex now part of their relationship, she wondered where it might lead next. Either it would turn magical or sour—no telling which. If those tics of his were any indication, then it was going sour. She wasn't sure where they had come from, but it gave her an incredibly creepy feeling each time one happened, and they were getting worse. No doubt about that.

She trudged around to the basement door and knocked. It was colder in the fog. She was shivering by the time he answered.

He locked the door securely behind her and started giving orders before he even said hello. "Run the blood tests, will you? Then scrub up and prep him please. Right kidney and spleen."

"Both?"

He stopped, turned, and looked her in the eye. "Are you questioning me?" It was just a flicker, just something passing across his eyes like a reflection on a pair of mirrored sunglasses, but it ran her blood cold. There was an implied threat behind this question of his. There was someone else—someone she didn't know—behind his eyes. Just a flicker, then gone, like the tics when they had first started.

"Right kidney and spleen," she repeated obediently.

"Good," he said, turning his back on her. He had one of those tics then. His head snapped violently toward his lifting shoulder, remained pinched there, intractable, and finally relaxed. She wanted to offer her hands to him—to rub the knots out of his back. She knew the pain of these tics because she had witnessed his face recently—all the muscles twitching and distorting like some kind of Halloween mask. It just had to hurt. A short backrub was just the thing for him. But she didn't offer it. They didn't talk about the tics; they both pretended they never happened at all.

She had to think: Was that the way their moment of intimacy was to be as well? As if it had never happened at all? It had happened right here in this room, and now she was to go parading about her work as Pam the Helper. Pam the Lover was apparently lost in the shadows. Burned to a crisp along with all the other contaminated waste.

He was starting to give her the creeps, the way he was so silent over there.

The donor was a black male between twenty-five and thirty. He was naked, face up, eyes open from the Ketamine, which paralyzed him but didn't actually render him unconscious. She was used to those eyes now, but at first they had really terrified her. Elden used Ketamine on all the donors, despite the dangers, because of its effect on memory. On some, he followed this up with electroshock. She didn't approve, but she understood. That was how she felt about much of this. Elden's strength, his power of conviction, left little room for argument. She noticed this man's upper arm then, and like so often in her life, words came babbling out before she could control them. "My God, Elden! What happened to his arm?"

"Hmm?"

"His arm! Did Donnie do this to his arm?"

"Donnie?"

"It's a mess. Lacerated, bruised. It might even be *broken* by the look of it."

"Yes, I noticed that. Perhaps we can help. But not now. Hmm? Right kidney and spleen, Pamela. Are you ready for me or not?"

The image of him, framed against the silvery plastic wall, was something surreal, something not of this world. It seemed fitting somehow, for a man of such talents.

She collected herself and asked, "Do you want me to dress it?"

"Prep him," he instructed. He never did pay much attention to what she said. He was in a mood today. More and more so in the last few days. You couldn't reach him when he was in a mood, so she gave up trying. She drew several samples of blood, labeled them, started the HIV test on one of them, the hepatitis A and B test on another, and placed the third in the waist-high fridge. There were a number of drugs missing from the door of the fridge. She was about to mention this when she caught herself. Antibiotics mostly. Some Demerol and Valium, too. The thought briefly crossed her mind that perhaps Elden was experimenting with the drugs himself; perhaps this helped to explain his recent erratic behavior. But not Demerol and Valium, she corrected herself. If anything, he seemed wound up and agitated of late, more like on an amphetamine high.

Donnie had probably stolen them; he was always sneaking drugs. Elden knew it, just as she did. They both did their best to police their supplies, but Elden never called Donnie on it unless he caught him in the act, and then he barely slapped his hand. A strange relationship existed between those two that she would never understand; why Elden would tolerate a man like that was beyond her.

She soaped and shaved the black man's side. Elden helped her to roll him over and she continued the procedure on his back.

"I made all the necessary arrangements," he said. "That is, Maybeck did," he corrected her. "You'll be back by this evening. I've written it all down." He hurried over to the work area and returned with a note written in his own handwriting, not Donnie's. Donnie could barely write at all. Elden never made the flight arrangements.

"You'll meet Juanita at the gate. The regular flight to Rio. Same as always."

"All right," she said, accepting the itinerary from him; but it felt wrong. Everything about this felt wrong. Was it just her? she wondered—expectations carried over from their encounter Saturday night?

"Now then," he said from over by the sink. He doused his hands in antiseptic and then snapped on a pair of surgical gloves. He turned his back to her to have her tie his mask in place, which she did. "All set?"

"I'm worried about you," she said softly to his back. She placed her hand gently on his shoulder. It was something she could never say while facing him.

There was a long, heavy silence in which she could hear the deep breathing of the man on the table behind her. She heard the plastic ceiling crinkle as it warmed. Neither she nor Elden was breathing. What she had said had stopped them both.

Finally his head bobbed slightly. He took a deep breath, filling his lungs completely, and said in a ghostly whisper, "It's him I'd worry about."

The way he said it frightened her. "Elden?"

His voice returned; he reminded her, "The patient always comes first."

22 They rose above the city, climbing an on-ramp at the end of Columbia that connected to the viaduct, then headed south toward the docks and Boeing Field. You could see the next wave of rain out over the water, hanging above the stunning green of Bainbridge Island—a mare's tail stretching down, a light gray mist feathered beneath charcoal clouds. If you didn't mind rain, it was a beautiful sight. If you minded rain, you didn't live here in February and March. Boldt turned on the wipers to fend off the spray from a van ahead of them.

Daphne crossed her legs and leaned over to check the speedometer.

"I don't like driving fast," Boldt explained.

"That's an understatement," she said. "At first I thought there was something wrong with this thing."

She had asked to come along with him at the last second. Boldt had warned her it might be a long meeting, but she had persisted. He'd been wondering when she would tell him whatever it was that couldn't wait.

Finally, his patience ran out. "So what's up?"

"I hate being wrong," she complained. "It doesn't come easy."

"You, wrong?"

"I had that talk with Cindy Chapman. I wanted to run Agnes Rutherford's descriptions of the two men by her—the grating voice, the bad breath. There are tricks you can play with the mind. Subtle ways to make it safe for a person to remember something they would rather not remember."

Boldt asked, "Where the hell is the toxicology report on Chapman? The blood workup?

"Are you interested in this or not?"

"Go ahead."

"She remembers Sharon and me tending to her at The Shelter. She's very clear on that. I worked with her on the events *before* the surgery. Could she remember being abducted? Could she remember faces, voices, surroundings? A week before, a day before, an hour before? As it turned out, you were right about the money." She added, "That's what I mean about my being wrong. I was convinced *you* were wrong about that."

His hands were sweating against the wheel. He rolled down the window for some air. "They paid her for the kidney?" he asked.

"It *was* a business arrangement. They offered her five hundred dollars."

"Five *hundred*?" he asked incredulously. "I thought the going rate is fifteen *thousand*. That's quite a mark-up."

"And there's no proof she ever received it."

"Well, it fills in a few blanks," he admitted. "It helps to explain why we never received any formal complaints against the harvester. If you're a teenager and you've cut a deal to sell your kidney, you don't turn the guy in. It also means there were—*are*—probably a lot more donors than we know about. The lucky ones lived to spend their five hundred. It may also explain the use of the electroshock."

"I don't think so," she interrupted. "Not the electroshock. Dixon's three victims—Blumenthal, Sherman, and the other one, Julia Walker, showed no sign of electroshock. If a few days had passed, that might be more easily explained, but in at least two of the cases—the deaths caused by hemorrhaging—those bodies would have been seen by the medical examiner rather quickly, wouldn't they? And that would indicate that those victims did *not* show signs of electroshock."

"You have something going," he said. "I can hear it in your voice."

"What if only the dissenters receive the electro-shock—the real serious memory blocking? What if you're right about there being a lot of others? A run-away, hard up for money, cuts a deal. Arrangements are made; the surgery takes place. They're paid up and returned to the streets. What if a person like Cindy Chapman gets cold feet once she looks around her and sees the reality of what she's gotten herself into? If you're the harvester, what then? You take the kidney anyway—you've probably already promised it somewhere—but you make damn sure your donor won't remember anything about it." She let the idea hang there. "You don't like it," she said.

"It makes sense," he admitted. "It doesn't mean I have to like it."

"So okay, let's say I'm right. Then why did they take Sharon?" she asked. "Except for her past, except for her BloodLines connection, she doesn't fit the donor profile at all: She's not broke, she's not out on the street, she's not desperate. At this point, she's even a few years older than the rest of them."

He didn't want to tell her about Dr. Light Horse's theory that Sharon might have been taken for a cus-tom procurement. If they were after a major organ, then Sharon was most likely already dead.

"And what have they done with her?" she added.

Boldt was spared giving an answer. He turned into the driveway of the Army Corps of Engineers and searched out a parking space.

——

The Seattle district office of the U.S. Army Corps of Engineers occupied an enormous brick structure a few miles south of the city on Marginal Way.

Boldt was hoping that as Dixie had suggested these bones might offer them a chance to identify the harvester. Locating the rest of the bones was the first, and most important, step in that process. The homicide victim was the last living witness to the crime and could tell an investigator much more than the murderer believed possible.

The receptionist greeted Boldt and Daphne warmly and made a quick phone call announcing their arrival. A few minutes later, a wiry man in his mid-forties bounded down the stairs and extended his hand, introducing himself as Harry Terkel. He had bright, enthusiastic eyes, and a lot less hair than Boldt. He wore khakis, black Reeboks, and a plaid shirt without a tie. He lacked the nerd pack of pens in his pocket that Boldt had expected of an engineer. He shook hands with Daphne and motioned upstairs. "I'll lead the way. It's kind of a maze."

At the top of the stairs they turned right down a corridor past scores of office cubicles.

They walked and walked and walked, finally reaching Terkel's enclosed office, where they took seats around a conference table. There was a Wipe-It bulletin board at the far end of the room, covered with math equations written in blue marker.

Terkel sat across from Boldt, rather than taking a place behind his desk. Boldt appreciated the gesture. He said, "Joe tried to explain this to me. Maybe I had better hear it from you."

Boldt explained, "Six months ago, a hunter recovered some human remains in the Tolt River. We have been unable to locate the source—the burial site—despite some exhaustive foot searches. The rest of those remains are important to our investigation, to our possibly identifying the victim and therefore the killer. The man I spoke with offered to set up your computers to help predict where the bones might have dislodged from the bank."

"Joe Webster. That's right." He added, "There's a book on this that might interest you," Terkel said. *"Fluvial Processes in Geomorphology.* River movement. River meandering and material deposits. Sediment actually 'cements' together—if you will—and moves downstream as a whole. Our job is the quantitative determination of water flow. Tracking flows. Predicting the sedimentation process. Erosion, deposition."

Boldt was wondering what language this was. *Fluvial Processes in Geomorphology?* Nice bedtime reading. Terkel recited like a student, "Material eroded from one bank will deposit on the same bank one to two bars downstream. That's two to four bends," he informed Boldt. "And that's a *fact.* That's something we can bank on. Pun intended. That's where the HEC computer can help us." Terkel saw Boldt's puzzled face. "HEC—the Hydraulic Engineering Center—runs the modeling computers."

"Maybe we should talk to them," Boldt suggested.

A few minutes later Boldt and Daphne were sitting alongside a Japanese woman, Becky Sumatara, staring at a color screen that offered a menu of choices. Joe Webster, a stocky man in his late forties, towered behind them.

Becky Sumatara said, "When we received your request, we updated our Tolt model for current flow notes, slope, sediment size, distribution, and areas of erosion based on our present data. That's what took us a couple of days. The updating is a lengthy process."

Boldt apologized, "When it comes to computers, I'm a techno-peasant."

The screen changed to a graphics aerial view of a map of King County. "Bodies of water, in all shapes and sizes, are represented by various shades of blue," Becky Sumatara explained, her red fingernail pointing out the Sound, reservoirs and rivers, "depending on volume. The darker the shade, the more volume. Elliott Bay and Puget Sound are a deep navy, while some of the smaller creeks are almost white. You're interested in the North Fork of the Tolt."

"Yes," Joe Webster answered for Boldt.

She dragged a blinking box to the area in question, bordering the box on Carnation, Monroe, Sultan, Skykomish and Big Snow Mountain. With two clicks of the mouse the screen filled with an enlargement of this area. "During enlargement, color reference is modified. You'll see the Tolt is now navy and its various tributaries are lighter according to volume. Also," she said with another click as the river, streams, and creeks turned various shades of red and pink, "we can view according to rate of flow—how fast the various volumes of water are traveling both in terms of quantity and"—the water all turned shades of green—"as regards land speed. All factors in erosion and flood control."

With the enlargement, a dozen smaller creeks had appeared. Daphne withdrew the topographic map from Boldt's briefcase. The exact locations where the bones had been discovered were marked. Becky Sumatara studied the map with Daphne and then narrowed the computer's target area yet again, creating a corresponding enlargement. "You're up into Snoqualmie National Forest there," she said, stepping the computer through maneuvers. "Rugged country."

"Yes."

"What does this tell us?" he asked.

"We have two views of each stream flow," she

explained. "Aerial and lateral. This gives us a visualization of lateral erosion as well as a cutaway of stream bed depth. Using the computer, I can increase or decrease volume and rate of flow as well as access any date in the past for visualization. Unfortunately, we've set this up only for the Tolt's stream bed profile, not the tributaries."

"The Tolt's our baby," Joe Webster said. "We have gravel moving one to two bars downstream. We'd like a look at those upper bars. That's all."

"The high-water mark for the Tolt reservoir should give us a fairly reliable benchmark for checking downstream erosion." She put the computer to work. Boldt felt some of the tension leave him. Finally, they were into it! On the left of the screen, she changed a date at the top of a table of numbers. The screen paused before redrawing.

"I'm going to ask the computer to compare this projection with one a month prior. It will color-code areas of the most severe erosion, red to black, red being areas of greatest damage." As she described all this, various images appeared and vanished. An arrow raced back and forth across the screen under her direction.

"You must keep in mind that this is all speculation. Without field reports we can't be sure of any of this. A fallen tree, a landslide, and we would have to start all over. This modeling is only as accurate as the data it's fed."

"The data is good," Joe Webster said defensively.

Boldt looked on as Becky Sumatara pinpointed some river bends that were bright red. "The computer takes soil composition into consideration," she explained, "which is one of the reasons it's of value to us in a situation like this. You or I could look at a map and circle the tightest switchbacks a river makes, but erosion is dependent on composition, and it's not uncommon for a stream to jump its banks on a straightaway where the soil is soft and relatively uniform. Stream beds generally make turns because the water encounters some form of natural obstacle, whether a rise in elevation, or a rock formation. A barrier. You could run your search party from turn to turn and never find this grave. My guess is that with flows like this, we're going to see a stream bubble-out well away from the turns. Although Joe may be right about the upstream bars."

"I'd like to see those upstream bars, if we could. I'd like to start there," Joe said.

"One thing to keep in mind," Boldt advised, "is road access. Our experience tells us that she would have been buried within a hundred yards of existing roads."

"That's a grisly thought."

Daphne fiddled with the ungainly topographic map. "There are logging roads in this area, even some old homesteads."

Joe Webster said, "There were hiking trails until they closed them down. I remember all that a few years back."

Daphne indicated the logging trails, one eye straying to the screen anxiously. "This will help," Sumatara said, referencing the map and comparing it to the screen. She made several small adjustments. The screen redrew itself each time. Boldt caught himself holding his breath again. As if from a descending bird's-eye-view, the screen showed an increasingly magnified area with each new redraw. She pointed convincingly to the screen. "Here are the two upstream bars you're after, Joe." The upper curve of the river was a deep blue; the cutaway of the stream bank showed as a bright—almost neon— red, clashing with her nail polish. "It's severely undercut." To Boldt she said, "That's why the

search teams missed it." She became distracted
then, as the screen seemed to call to her. Again she
worked the mouse. Again the screen redrew several
times. "You're lucky."

"How's that?"

"These most recent rains haven't yet caused the
Tolt to reach the high-water level marked last fall,
which means there hasn't been any additional
undercutting." Now her fingers flew through a volley of commands. Boldt looked over to see both
Daphne and Joe Webster glued to the screen. "Uh-
oh," she added, punching keys furiously.

"Becky?" Boldt asked, sensing from her sudden
silence that they had problems.

"You had better get someone out there quick,"
she said, pointing once again to the screen. "The
projected flow for the Tolt will pass that mark in
less than forty-eight hours."

Daphne asked, "Would you mark the area for us,
please?"

But Becky didn't seem to hear, still consumed
with working the computer. "And there's something else," she said, the screen changing colors
once again. "You're wrong about the depth. About
the grave being shallow." She switched to a lateral
view that depicted an overhang of brown earth and
the animated blue of the river water well below it.
"According to this, the undercut is at least six feet
below grade—below the surface. Those bones were
buried deep."

"He knows what he's doing," mumbled Boldt.

"It *is* a doctor," Daphne let slip, a look of horror
on her face.

"A doctor!" coughed Becky Sumatara.

"You never heard that," instructed Boldt. He
looked Sumatara in the eye, then Joe Webster. "In
fact, if it's all the same to you . . . for the time being

. . . you never heard word one of this. We can't afford any rumors, any leaks."

Joe Webster nodded, suddenly a shade paler.

Sumatara didn't seem to hear. "There's a doctor *killing* people?" gasped the woman, staring back into the glowing screen with its pulsing colors.

The red no longer appeared neon. To Boldt, it seemed the color of blood.

23

Sharon Shaffer had a hard time thinking through the drugs. It was like trying to write with her left hand—she knew the letters that were supposed to appear on the page, but they never came out looking right.

A car had arrived about an hour ago. It had left about forty minutes later. Forty minutes by her way of thinking.

The man was in the kennel pen next to her. He had two fresh bandages. Seeing this, she felt sick to her stomach. The Keeper was a butcher.

She didn't remember her neighbor having been returned, although there he was, and the collapsible wheelchair The Keeper used to move them was folded up and leaning against the wall. She must have fallen asleep again. She kept nodding out this way, which was one of the reasons it was so difficult to measure any passage of time.

She glanced to her right and literally jumped when she saw The Keeper in the pen next to hers. He had hold of her I.V. tube and was injecting a drug into the tube using a syringe. Separating the two of them was only the smallest amount of chain-link wire. Wire that would bite back if she so much as brushed against it. The intense look on The Keeper's face terrified her.

Felix, the biggest dog of the group, the alpha male, wandered freely in the center aisle. Pacing. Panting. Hungry and anxious. He was the sentry, the jail guard. He was there to prevent any chance of another intruder, any chance of escape.

The Keeper said softly to her, "I've canceled my morning appointments, but I'm in a bit of a hurry."

With the muzzle, she had no chance to respond. She was thinking, "Morning appointments!?"

"When you awaken your right eye will hurt. It will be carefully bandaged. Under no circumstances are you to toy with this bandage. Do you hear me? Do you understand? Nod, if you understand. Good. Now you're crying. Why are you crying? Do I scare you?"

She nodded, though somewhat reluctantly.

"Me? You needn't be scared. Stop that crying. I'm a *doctor*."

She couldn't. The more he said, the more terrified she was.

"Please," he said childishly.

She wrestled with her emotions and brought herself under control. She was shaking now, the crying turned inside. She wanted to see him as insane, but she couldn't. He seemed so *professional* in everything he did. So calculating. It made the chance of escape seem all the more distant.

"You will cause yourself an enormous amount of pain if you cry later. Hmm? The saline in the tears. You understand? You must not allow yourself to cry. You must apply no pressure to this bandage, none whatsoever, so be careful how you place your head when you sleep." He waited a moment and asked, "Are you listening?"

She managed to nod her head yes.

"Because of you—because of your cornea—some poor soul will be able to see again. Hmm? You will be giving someone the gift of sight. Can you imagine such a thing? A miracle is what it is, and without you, none of it would be possible. Hmm? How does *that* make you feel?"

Like escaping, she thought. Now, more than ever, escape was all she could think of. The drugs he injected brought a hazy fuzz to her eyes. Would she ever see again? Would she awaken? She glanced one last time into the eyes of The Keeper.

Perhaps, she thought, blindness wouldn't be so bad after all.

24

Boldt had a dozen thoughts crowding his head while staring at his phone. Following a morning with his father, Miles had been dropped off with their neighbor Emma, who was becoming something of a nanny to the boy. The phone wasn't exactly his, just as the coffee room wasn't exactly his office, but until they assigned him a cubicle he used both as if they were his own. People now knocked before entering the coffee room. In practice, Boldt had a bigger office than Shoswitz.

He was sitting in a fiberglass chair under a cloud of cigarette smoke left by a former visitor. Someone had stolen today's date off the Gary Larson day-at-a-glance calendar, so Boldt had to keep checking his watch to remember the date. The trash can was filled to overflowing because to save money the offices were being cleaned only every other day and Saturdays.

Unable to reach Dixie earlier by phone, Boldt had resorted to the newly installed electronic mail—asking a younger, more computer-literate uniform for help. He dictated a memo detailing his discoveries at both the Army Corps of Engineers and the details of his interview with Dr. Light Horse at the university, and suggested that Dixon follow up on some of Light Horse's recommendations, which included examination and study of the surgical techniques used to close Cindy Chapman's incision. With the push of a button, his memo—supposedly—flew across town, bleating like a lamb on some secretary's screen.

"Sarge?" John LaMoia called from across the room, a phone cradled between neck and chin. He waved some papers at Boldt. LaMoia, who was heading up the surveillance of Connie Chi, the Blood-Lines employee, was in an office rotation while other detectives watched their suspect. He was tall, with brown curly hair, and wore pressed jeans. He was a cocky, vibrant womanizer; everyone on the force liked him, male, female, uniform or suit. "The AMA printouts," LaMoia said.

Boldt crossed the room quickly, his own expectations increasing with every step. It was possible—in fact, more than likely—that the name of the harvester was somewhere on this printout. He took it from LaMoia. He scanned it quickly. And scanned. Page after page. His heart sank.

La Moia had anticipated his reaction. He hung up and explained, "Six hundred seventy-five surgeons. Discouraging, to say the least. Last page," he instructed. Boldt flipped forward. "By category it's a little better. *Any* of them could probably train to do those harvests—that's what I'm told—but if this guy is sticking with his specialty, then we've got thirty-one in thoracic, ten in urological. In general surgery we have," he honed in to read, "sixty-eight; thirty-four at the U-Dub. I wrote a total there: one forty-three."

The job before them was overwhelming, though not impossible—given a huge task force, which Shoswitz seemed unlikely to grant them. A careful interview would have to be conducted with each surgeon. Quiet inquiries about bank accounts and credit limits and life styles. Of schedules, phone calls and travel itineraries. Through this, they were to attempt to narrow this enormous list down to the one harvester—all without making him the wiser.

Reading his thoughts, LaMoia, who had reached the office and was still reading over his shoulder, suggested, "Are you thinking about bringing them in here one by one?"

"Thinking about it, but not very seriously. One: Doctors can make the kind of noise that finds the ears of the top brass. Two: Word would spread too quickly, the harvester would shut down shop, and that would be the end of any incriminating evidence. One of the difficulties here, don't forget, is that the law is hazy about all of this. If we're going to bust this guy, we're going to have to practically catch him in the act. We give him a week to clean up his act, and he'll skate—guaranteed. If we're right about this, this guy has been in business *at least* three years, which means he's extremely well organized and knows what he's doing. Who knows how many harvests he's done? He hears that we're coming after him, and he'll clean up so well that we'll never find so much as a needle out of place. We need the operating shears that connect Blumenthal to those bones. *That* would be some decent proof."

"So what *are* you suggesting?" LaMoia asked.

LaMoia could piss him off when he got like this.

The coffee room phone rang. It could have been any number of things. Besides interviewing Cindy Chapman and Sharon Shaffer's elderly roommate, Daphne was working with her contacts at the FBI's Behavioral Science Unit to come up with a possible psychological profile of the harvester. Bernie Lofgrin owed Boldt more complete lab reports on both Chapman and Shaffer. It might even have been Dr. Light Horse at the University, or Ms. Dundee at Blood-Lines, both of whom had agreed to call if anything else pertaining to Boldt's case occurred to them. But above and beyond all of these, Boldt hoped it might be someone—anyone—calling to tell him that Sharon Shaffer was safe and sound, or that some doctor had just turned himself in.

The call was from the surveillance team assigned to Connie Chi. Twice, the cellular phone from which the call was being placed went dead, and twice Boldt waited impatiently for the return call. The first news he heard, after the team identified itself, was, "We got a problem here . . ." The second time the voice asked, "How much of that did you get?" Boldt could tell by the ambient sound that the car was moving. "You rolling?" he asked. Again, the line went dead before he received an answer. The third time he answered, the phone remained in the clear, although he found himself rushing sentences in anticipation of another failure.

"Everything we're seeing here indicates she wants to lose us," the man said, referring to Connie Chi, the BloodLines employee.

"She made you?" Boldt asked.

"That's just the thing: I don't think so. But she's sure as hell acting like she did. We called in Danny and Butch. They're in the Jeep. We've been trading her off. I gotta think she thinks she's lost us. Way she's acting makes me think someone told her what to do. Know what I mean? All jittery-like. Constantly checking her mirror and shit like that. An amateur. It got a little hairy when she tried to ditch us in Nordstroms, but I gotta tell you: This gal is no criminal. Or if she is, she's the kind every cop loves 'cause she's so damn nervous that she sticks out like a sore thumb. I gotta hand it to ya, Sarge: You now how to pick 'em."

"Keep me posted. I'm on my way."

━━━

As he steered through traffic in an attempt to intercept the surveillance teams, Boldt heard over his radio, "I've got her, Butch." The voices surfaced only occasionally, rising from a sea of electronic hiss.

"Okay, good, we're falling off her. Keep us posted."

Mobile surveillance presented its own special logistical nightmares. To be effective it required an enormous number of vehicles, a central dispatcher coordinating them, and a lot of luck. Juggling the same two or three cars for an extended period usually failed. You either lost, or were spotted by, the mark. Boldt wondered what the hell was keeping LaMoia, when all of a sudden the man's voice crackled over the airwaves. LaMoia was like that: Just when you were about to lose faith in him, he came through. He seemed to constantly push everyone, everything, right to the limit. With him rolling, they were up to four cars. They had a fighting chance.

"She's turning right on 119th," announced detective John C. Adams, or J.C., as everyone called him.

"What the hell is she driving?" LaMoia asked.

"A red Saturn," came the reply. "But she ain't driving it. Some other woman is."

LaMoia asked for the license number and was given it. "I've got them," he announced. "Turning again—119th, now headed north on Greenwood. Go ahead and pass them."

Boldt ran two stop signs and a light and pulled to within a few lengths of LaMoia. "I'm with you, John, if you need me."

"Roger."

"Who's the Saturn registered to?" Boldt said.

"One Su-Lin Chi," LaMoia announced.

"Same last name," someone said.

"For the sake of the radio," Boldt announced, "We call the passenger 'Connie' and the driver, 'the Sister.'"

"Affirmative," came the various voices.

"What about Connie's car back at Nordstroms?" Boldt asked. "Did it occur to any of you goons to have it watched?" The resulting silence disturbed him. "This could have been some sort of drop, you know? Did it occur to *any* of you that maybe someone *wanted* us to follow her, to lead us away from the drop?"

J.C. offered, "We've always got a couple of patrol cars hanging around the mall. You want me to put dispatch on it?"

"We'll take care of it from here," came the voice of Phil Shoswitz over the radio. He had been monitoring the exchanges. It caught Boldt—and the others—completely by surprise. It was extremely rare for this particular lieutenant to listen-in with the dispatcher. He didn't like field work.

The red Saturn signaled and changed lanes. "I've got it, John," Boldt said.

LaMoia pulled past, leaving the Saturn and Boldt to turn off.

"They're slowing," Boldt announced. He added, "Maybe it's only a gas stop. I'm going to pull past."

His adrenaline rush was immediately replaced by disappointment as he saw the car turn right into a gas station.

"I'm pulling up short," said J.C. Boldt drove around the block and parked with a good view of the station. LaMoia coordinated his and the remaining car—a blue Jeep containing Butch Butler and Danny Wu—to cover either of two cross streets.

As Boldt looked on, he sensed that the driver of the Saturn was stalling. He announced this over the radio. The young Chinese woman filled up the small car's tank impossibly slowly, and only after it was full did she decide to check the oil, all the while looking around anxiously and consulting Connie Chi in the passenger seat. There was also a kid of about eighteen across the street who was looking on from over by a Dumpster. Boldt assigned Butch Butler to keep an eye on him, so his own attention wouldn't be distracted. A self-service gas station was an easy place to steal a car—too often, drivers neglected to take the keys with them. Or perhaps the kid was a runner—someone paid to make an exchange with Connie Chi. Whatever his purpose or intentions, the kid was a variable that Boldt didn't particularly like.

From down the street, a dark blue, slightly beat-up van approached at a pace uncharacteristically cautious for Seattle drivers. Boldt sat up in his seat, one hand grasping the radio's mike. The driver was nothing but a dark shape behind the silver impulse of the sky's reflection on the windshield. Boldt punched the button on the mike and said quickly, "Butch, Danny—incoming, right behind you!" He watched from a distance as the two detectives turned rubbery and slipped down in their seats so that as the van passed, the Jeep would appear empty. Slipping lower in his own seat, Boldt said, "I think we may have something here. Butch, you watch the kid. LaMoia, run the van's plates. J.C., if they break quickly, you take the Saturn with LaMoia. Danny, Butch, and I will take the van."

———

Donnie Maybeck drove past the gas station once to make sure the Sister's red car was parked there as it was supposed to be. When he confirmed this, he drove fully around the block looking for guys eating donuts in the front seat of their car: cops. Seeing none, he pulled in and parked next to an unleaded self-service pump. He climbed out and went through the process of filling up. In this way, he was able to carry on a conversation without ever looking at her. All of it had been the Doc's idea. Fucking genius. On cue, Connie's sister left for the bathroom.

"Tell me about the cops," he said to Connie. "What is it *now*?" When the shit hits the fan, he thought, it really spreads around fast.

"They asked about a woman named Sharon Shaffer. She's the AB-negative I gave you last week!" Involuntarily, he squeezed the pump so hard that gas bubbled out before the nozzle shut off.

"And Verna's been asking me about my computer time. What's going on, Donnie? I don't even know what it is you do with that database. Some extra money, that's all. That's what *you* said. I got a feeling I don't want to know." She paused, then contradicted herself: "What *do* you do with it?"

He tried to keep calm. When he got uptight, he tended to do stupid things. Same thing all his life. His big temptation right now was to lose her—to turn the hose on her, light a match, and watch her fry. He had stolen some plates and bolted them on before coming here—he wasn't *that* stupid. He could lose the van if he had to, torch it as well. Burn, baby, burn. If he had ever had a tattoo, that's what it would have said. Nothing he liked quite so much as seeing something burn. Except of course the sight of money. Cash. Or ass. He liked that a lot, too.

Squeeze goes the handle, poof goes the match. Zoom goes Connie. Her hair would go first, then her clothes. If she was wearing synthetics—anything stretchy or elastic—they would stick to her skin. She'd be staring at him screaming, bald from the flames, eyes beginning to swell in their sockets. "You don't have to worry about that," he said, answering her question.

"I'm scared," she replied.

Fifty grand. *Fifty*! A fucking fortune. A Harley. A trip somewhere. Who knows?

"What I want you to do . . ." he started, trying to think like the Doc, but losing his train of thought to anger. His temper was the problem. It had always been the problem. It ran away from him. As a kid on the streets—he'd been alone on the streets since he was thirteen—he had learned how to play tough. Tough, combined with a bad temper, meant violence. At fifteen he'd killed his first person—a junkie looking to roll him. He got pissed off and cut the guy with a bottle and then left him to bleed to death. At seventeen he killed a prostitute—*after* the act, which had been his first—because he didn't have the money to pay her. That had been Spokane. He left because her pimp was out to zoom him. In Seattle he'd been arrested for purse snatching. He served six months in a J.D. reform, and the offense was kept off his record. He was eighteen when he got out, and the state arranged vocational training that eventually led to a job with NorWest Power and Light. For nearly two months his life had been "real." And then that day doing shit work on the top of a newly installed high-voltage tower—he saw the

Doc digging a grave: The Secret. A chance at some real money. Things had been different since then.

"Can you take Sharon Shaffer's name out of that database?"

"What about the *police*?"

"I asked you a question." This was how the Doc dealt with him, and it felt good to pass it on. It felt real good. "Can you *erase* a file? Erase a file for good?" He pulled the hose from his tank and replaced it in the pump, still wondering if it wouldn't be smarter to hose her down.

"Erase a record from data processing, you mean? I don't know if I can. I suppose it must be possible. But I've never tried."

"I want you to try. The Shaffer file. It's *important*. You understand." He gave her a look then— Charles Bronson on a particularly bad day. Maybe Brando. How would the Big Man handle this one?

She hesitated. It pissed him off. Her sister was hovering around the candy counter looking impatient. He decided to pay up. He opened the van's door and took the keys. He left the door open because she answered just then.

"I'll try."

"Damn right you will." He gave her one last look and walked away looking tough. I *am* tough, he convinced himself.

When he reached the station, he looked away as her sister passed because he didn't want her getting a good look at him. You had to keep your options open.

He had to climb a small platform to pay at the cash register.

The gas cost him over twenty bucks. That pissed him off as well.

When he turned around, his added elevation gave him a view of two guys sitting real low in a Jeep parked down the street.

Cops! Connie had fucked up; she had led them here! Or was she *in* on it?

The panic hit him as hard as if he'd been slugged in the gut.

Out of the corner of his eye he caught some quick movement.

Some punk kid was headed for his van at a sprint. He reached it, leaned in, and came out with Donnie's laptop computer. The fucking *laptop*! The Doc had warned him to never let it out of his sight. The database! The kid took off at a run. Donnie shouted after him. He chased after him, one eye on those cops. If the cops got hold of that laptop it was all over.

The Doc would see to that.

===

"Trouble," J.C. Adams announced over the radio. Up until that moment, Boldt's full attention had been on the driver of the van, but now in his peripheral vision he caught sight of the juvenile crossing the street to the gas station and, a few seconds later, leaning into the open door of the van. When, on the end of that kid's arm, Boldt saw a laptop computer, he sat up so quickly he hit his head on the down-turned visor. The Professor had found carpet impressions that suggested that one of the two men who had abducted Sharon Shaffer had been carrying a laptop computer. With Connie Chi's connection to BloodLines, and BloodLines' connection to Sharon Shaffer, this *had* to be more than coincidence.

"Butch, Danny, you grab the kid. He's coming right at you," Boldt radioed immediately. "J.C., you've got the Saturn. John, you take the van driver on foot—I'll play backup. And listen up: I want *everybody* brought in, including that laptop. Okay. Go!"

As Boldt watched his team spring into action, Shoswitz came on the radio. "Lou?"

"How about a couple of radio cars, Lieutenant? We're losing this thing," he warned, as he saw their bust go south. Butch and Danny sprang out of the Jeep, weapons drawn, and took off after the kid. Displaying lightning-quick reactions, the kid veered down a driveway and vanished. Procedure would have had one of them pursue on foot, the other in the Jeep, but procedure didn't matter now. In the heat of the moment, they had both run after the kid, and the likelihood of catching him seemed slim. Boldt barked into the radio, "I need those backups now! Suspect proceeding on foot, northbound between 68th and 69th. If he gets into the park, we've lost him."

The dread of further failure choked his throat as he saw the red Saturn drive quickly out of the gas station, with none of his own cars following. Blocked by a recycling truck, J.C. Adams was forced to go around the block. Boldt punched the button on the radio mike to announce he would switch with Adams, but released it as he saw LaMoia going after the van driver on foot.

Misjudging the situation, LaMoia elected to take a shortcut—cutting behind the nearest house. But when the driver of the van saw Butch and Danny, guns drawn, he pulled an abrupt about-face, leaving LaMoia taking a shortcut to nowhere. This, in turn, made Boldt responsible for the van, which roared off, cutting in behind the slowly moving recycling truck and forcing Boldt to follow. Boldt was no fan of high-speed driving. He not only didn't care for it, he was no good at it, and he knew it. At the first intersection he braked for the stop sign, slowing considerably—out of habit. He should have been calling in his position and situation over the radio, but he needed both hands on the wheel. He was sweating; his scalp itched. He should have been all but ignoring stop signs, but his right foot kept betraying him and tapping the brakes.

The van remained in sight, but just barely. It was suddenly making big speed. It ran two lights and negotiated a series of quick turns. Boldt managed to keep it in sight, but at this rate he knew he wouldn't keep up for long. On a brief moment of straightaway, Boldt reached for the radio to call in his position. Just as he grabbed hold of it, a skateboard shot out from between parked cars. Fast on its heels was a boy of about twelve. Boldt jerked the wheel sharply to the left and slammed on the brakes. The car swerved in a squealing of rubber. A pencil skidded across the dash and disappeared down the defrost. The driver-side sun visor slapped Boldt in the forehead and forced him to duck beneath it in order to see. The front right tire crushed the skateboard.

The bumper missed the boy by inches.

Boldt kept his foot on the brakes. The van continued on up ahead, growing smaller. It turned right. Boldt checked the rearview mirror. The boy was okay. In his right hand he discovered the radio microphone, its coiled wire disconnected and dangling like a stretched spring—he had ripped it out of the radio housing. He had lost all communication with dispatch.

He took the same right, following the van's route. Three blocks ahead of him, he saw it turn north onto Aurora, State Highway 99. A four-lane road with occasional lights, the traffic was typically congested and unpredictable. Boldt slowed at the next red light, but ran it. Getting the hang of this. Maybe he would attract the attention of a traffic cruiser. He craned across the front seat and located the dash-mount flasher. He tossed it up onto the dash and threw the switch, facing the blue, pulsating light forward. He forced his place into the left lane and put his foot down. By switching lanes repeatedly, the van continued to pull away from him. Boldt was no match for such maneuvers. He lost sight of it as it followed a long, arching turn to the right. He stepped on it.

A police cruiser approached in the opposing lanes. Boldt rolled down his window and beat on the side of his car, signaling—he hoped—for backup. His eyes left his lane for only a second, but when he looked back, the traffic ahead of him had come to a complete stop.

He slammed on the brakes, the car in an immediate skid, the remaining distance shrinking impossibly fast. He then pumped the brakes as he'd been trained to do—a half dozen times in quick little jabs. He cut his speed in half. The unforgiving back bumper of a pickup truck loomed directly ahead. Thirty yards to go. Twenty. An adrenaline rush choked him. His hands tightened on the wheel. Miles . . . Liz . . . Bear Berenson saying, "This here is *the* Lou Boldt . . ." More brakes. Still too fast. Too close . . .

Mentally, these last few seconds slowed perceptibly. He could *feel* the shrinking space between his vehicle and the pickup, he could somehow measure it precisely.

In desperation, he hit and held the brakes. The back tires cried out. The car fishtailed.

The pickup truck—this entire lane of traffic—rolled forward as drivers anticipated a green light. This added one vehicle length of roadway between Boldt and the pickup. He skidded to a stop inches behind the pickup.

The van was sitting four cars up.

He grabbed for his weapon. Weapons were not

his way, this kind of street cop work was not his work, but he saw little choice.

The driver of that van was connected to Sharon Shaffer's abduction.

The stopped traffic was nothing more than a red traffic light, not a traffic jam as he had first believed. In a moment the traffic would begin to roll again. In a moment Boldt would be doing sixty again chasing him. He checked his rearview mirror: That patrol car was nowhere to be seen. All alone.

He threw the car into PARK and approached the van in a squat from the passenger side in order to avoid the chance of being seen in the driver door mirror. He hurried between waiting cars, his back cramping. Too old for this shit. Someone behind him honked, pissed off, no doubt, that he had left his car. Oh great! he thought. Let's attract as much attention as possible.

The light changed to green. Engines revved, and traffic began moving again. He caught up to the van and, arm outstretched, took hold of the handle to the side door. He yanked, now pulled along by the van's progress. Locked! He lunged for the front door next, the van moving even faster. From behind him the volley of protesting horns continued.

He took hold of the passenger door handle and jerked upward to open it. At that very instant, a finger appeared and locked it as well. The tie didn't go to the runner: Boldt stumbled and fell. The van pulled away.

By the time he reached his car and was driving again, he couldn't see the van for the trucks, the Hondas for the hatchbacks. He stayed with it a while longer, but the van was nowhere to be seen. Without a radio and without backup, Boldt resigned himself to failure.

Depression overwhelmed him—not for what was

coming from Shoswitz, he could handle Shoswitz—but because a woman was missing, and Boldt was convinced the driver of this van was an accomplice in her abduction.

It was time to start all over, he decided. Time to do things right.

Time to have a little talk with Connie Chi.

25

Tegg had never seen Maybeck look this desperate, otherwise he might have objected to Maybeck's barging into his office unannounced. Maybeck was relegated to the back hallway, the walk-in, the *disposal of waste*; he was overstepping his bounds.

"What is it?" Tegg complained.

"The laptop's been stolen," Maybeck announced.

Tegg felt a sharp pain in the very top of his skull, and one of his tics hit him hard. He felt his shoulder lift and his head strain to meet it. He recovered and said, "Tell me about it, Donald."

"Don't call me that!"

"Start talking, Donald. This instant!"

Maybeck suffered through an explanation, trying to make himself into some kind of hero in the way he had avoided the police. Tegg was beginning to see him in terms of a corpse—just exactly how would he dispose of a person that size?

The laptop? He blamed himself for having ever entrusted such an important matter to Maybeck. It had all been by design: trying to distance himself from incriminating evidence wherever possible. But now? He had to assess his situation, to take control. The planned date of the heart harvest was inside that laptop—the entire *history* of their operation, if you knew what to look for.

"First you handle Connie. She *must* be dealt with. Hmm? Nothing violent, I'm not suggesting that, just see that she's out of the way, out of town. Now! Then we get the computer back," he said. "One thing at a time. Hmm?"

"Connie's first," Maybeck replied like a magpie echoing his master's voice.

"Immediately."

"No problem. I know where to find her. I set that up like you told me to."

"You'll watch for cops."

"I know."

"This 'punk,' as you called him," Tegg said distastefully—he had no use for such slang—"is there some way to identify him?"

Maybeck said brutishly, "I could always report it to the police."

Tegg waved a finger at him. "Don't challenge me, Donald. Insolence will get you nowhere with me." A bonfire, Tegg was thinking. That size body was just made for a bonfire. One fire to burn the flesh, a second for the bones. Maybe even a third for those teeth. "This is *your* error we are attempting to correct here—let's pay particular attention to responsibility, shall we? We've discussed this all before. All before." How strangely seductive the lure of violence could be. He *wanted* to hurt this man.

"I can handle it."

"Spare me such indulgence, would you? Dream on your own time." Tegg felt another tic coming. He squashed it with anger. Interesting how that worked, he thought—perhaps anger, always heralded as the enemy, was indeed a friend. "We will go to whatever means necessary to obtain that computer. A reward, a ransom, I don't care what you have to do."

"I can put the word out. We offer a reward, and we'll be onto this thing like flies on shit. It's password protected," Maybeck reminded. "That's one thing good about it."

"There's *nothing* good about this!" Tegg announced. He cleaned out his wallet—one hundred and fifty dollars—and practically threw it at Maybeck. "That kind of thinking is poison! Do you hear me? Poison! We need that computer back immediately. That computer is *evidence*, Donald! Get that into your head. That laptop is *exactly* what the police want. That's our battle, don't you see? And it's not one we want to fight, believe you me. No, sir. But we'll fight those we must. Hmm? You bet we will."

"I can get it back." He waved the money at Tegg. "I have friends."

This seemed unlikely, if not impossible—especially the latter statement. "What an idiot you are!"

"Shut up!"

"An idiot, do you hear me?" He leaned toward Maybeck. "You get that laptop back, and you destroy that database *before* the police are any the wiser! Get rid of the van, too. If you fail in any of this, you will regret it!"

"Doctor?" His receptionist's voice. "Is everything okay?"

He'd been shouting. "Out in a minute," Tegg replied in a friendly voice to the closed door. How much had his employee heard? How could everything come down around you so quickly?

Maybeck whispered, "I say we zoom the girl we kidnapped and take our chances with Wong Kei."

"Is that what *you* say?" Tegg asked, standing and approaching him, daring to put his face up against Maybeck's. Breath like an open sewer. "I'm not terribly interested in what you have to say, Donald. But you had better be interested in what *I* have to say. Extremely interested." He whispered, "Connie, then the laptop, the van: That's your order of business, your priorities. If Connie won't play along . . . well . . . Use your imagination."

"No problem," Donnie said.

Was he actually condoning such a thing? He felt a disturbing pressure in his head, like a tire taking too much air. He wondered why he couldn't just step away from it all? Let it go. How far would he go in order to make up for that mistake of his? He didn't like himself; he didn't even know himself. He had studied the psychology of cornered animals in college; only now that he was experiencing it did he begin to understand.

Only now did he see clearly what exactly was to become of the black man out in the kennel. He too was a liability, one that at this point they could certainly not afford.

But not for long.

26

With the surveillance a complete disaster, with no one to be mad at but himself, with no appetite, Boldt left work and headed directly to the back door of The Big Joke. He didn't want Liz to see him like this—he wasn't sure *what* he wanted. Had he been a drinker, he would have gotten drunk, but booze only gave him a sour stomach and a bad case of the blues. The blues themselves seemed the best way out—eighty-eight keys of refuge, where voices sang in his head and drove out all thought. The club was closed to the public by order of the Treasury Department, but since Bear Berenson lived upstairs, access was still available through the back. The piano had never been confiscated—just the financial records—and only two of the six screws intended to lock it shut had violated it.

Boldt let himself in, found the piano in the dark, and started playing. A while later Bear settled himself into a chair at the table farthest from the stage, because Boldt hated the cigarette smoke and because this table sat immediately under a light which Bear needed to read his trade paperback, *How to Beat the IRS*, a gift from Boldt. He studied it like a preacher with a Bible, his reading punctuated by grunts of disapproval and sighs of supplication. A captain going down with the ship, he paused and looked up only to relish a particular phrase from Boldt's piano or to roll himself another joint.

It had been several days since Boldt had played, and he took to it hungrily, tuning all else out. His pager—switched off—his holstered weapon, his shield and his wallet all occupied a leathery heap by the glass of milk that Bear occasionally refreshed on his way back from the bar.

The investigation would occasionally surface, like a prairie dog lifting its head from its lair, but Boldt would send it into retreat with the stomp of a foot or the stabbing of a dissonant note.

Bear disappeared sometime during the marathon. Boldt didn't look to see what time it was. He heard the phone ring several times, glad it wasn't his. A while later, needing the bathroom and unable to use the club's because of the dark, he found his way upstairs. Bear was asleep in front of the television. With that much pot in him he wouldn't be worth trying to awaken and put to bed, so Boldt left him.

He was back at the piano and into one of his better renditions of "All The Things You Are" when he detected movement out of the corner of his eye.

He turned to see Liz standing in the darkness. Like him, she had entered through the back door. Arms crossed, she observed him solemnly, in quiet contemplation. No telling how long she might have been there: Liz was not one to interrupt his playing.

"Bad day," he offered.

"They happen," she reminded.

A wind moved through the room carrying the scent of her with it. Perhaps this was what had stopped him in the first place. She smelled gorgeous. She explained, "We need you, Miles and I. We need you even when you feel like this—especially when you feel like this. I worried. I was picturing a hotel room. Something like that."

"Not likely."

"But possible. Anything is possible. Have I let you down? Have you let me down? Can I blame it on your work? Can I blame it on you? I want to. I try to."

"I miss the music, that's all. I miss you more, you and Einstein. Where is he?"

"Emma is pulling emergency duty."

Their neighbor. She pinch-hit when they needed her.

"You don't get it, do you?" she asked.

"Maybe not."

"I *love* you." When he failed to reply she added, "*I* want to be your piano. *I* want to be the one you turn to when you feel like this. *I* want to be the one to help."

"You do. It's not you, it's me," he said.

"It's both of us. It always is."

"I screwed up a surveillance this afternoon."

"Do you see what this stuff does to you?"

"Please."

"But do you? He's killing you, too. He *is*! And me and Miles. What about your son? I hate this. It's as if we never worked any of this out. But we *did*, once."

"I love this work. I live to stop guys like this."

"But when you don't? Look at you."

He glanced at the piano. "This is the other me."

"No, Lou: This is the same you. I won't give you permission to love your work more than your family."

"Who said anything about *that*?"

"I did."

"I'm talking about me."

"You never talk about you. That's one of our problems."

"*One* of our problems?"

"Things are far from perfect," she advised him.

There was a spider in one of the spotlights, searching its web for food, seemingly supported by nothing. Boldt felt like that at times: alone, hanging by a thread, caught at the focal point of all that heat.

"People die. You see enough of it, it makes you think."

"Shit happens," she said. She was angry.

"Do you wish I hadn't signed back up?"

"I wish you were happy. You're not. Not with me. Not with yourself. I want to understand that. I want to help."

"Do you want me to quit?"

"Do you?"

"I will."

"You need an excuse? I'll give you one if you want."

Sometimes she knew him better than he knew himself. Boldt shifted on the bench. "Maybe there's a way to balance the two."

"Which two?" Was she asking about Daphne? Was she haunted by *that*?

"Music and work. Friends and family. Work and family."

She forced a smile. "Honesty is a good place to start."

"I love you," he said.

"I need some evidence, Sergeant."

He stood, crossed the room, and offered his arms. She folded into him naturally and wrapped around him like a vine. "More evidence," she said, and he hugged her tighter. He slipped his hand inside her skirt and cupped a buttock. She purred. Her hair caught in his unshaved face. It tickled. "I'll try to be there for you."

"Me too."

"It's hard," she said.

"That's because it hasn't felt you this close in a while." That made her laugh, which was good. "We need more laughter."

"We need a lot of things," she said softly into his shoulder, and giggled self-consciously.

It felt fresh, wonderfully fresh, as if he had never touched her before. Each movement of hers, each probe, carried a tingling electricity. She pulled out his shirttail; her hands felt hot on his skin. She was fully off the floor, hanging off him. Her lips smeared him with lipstick, her smell invaded him. He groped for the door, stumbling with her along as baggage. She unfastened his belt—how he wasn't sure—and went for the button to his pants. He kicked out the door's stopper. She threw the bolt, as if they had practiced this.

She refused to be let down, clinging to him like Miles. Giggling playfully. His pants fell down around his knees and he staggered. "No," she protested, as he tried to lower her onto a bar stool. "No," again when he aimed for a table. As he limped around waiting for approval, she lifted her skirt into a ruffle and tugged on her underwear, but with her legs clasped around him in a straddle, they weren't going anywhere. "Damn," she gasped urgently, charging him with excitement. The room was dark and strangely hot. He felt like a klutz, scanning the room for somewhere to satisfy her. She felt anxious, alive, nervous, hungry.

She hung off him, head lowered back, her lacy chest exposed from an unbuttoned blouse. She pointed like a lookout on the bow. He leaned his head down, took her bra in his teeth and tugged until he freed her breast which he sought with his lips. He found her, and she gasped as much from surprise as pleasure. He felt her heat pressed against him, and it drove him to an impatient frenzy. He was about to drop her, she was so far cantilevered off him. Her legs gripped him like a vise. He found the other breast and went after it with his tongue. She cried out. Her legs gripped even tighter and she worked herself against him in an unmistakable motion. "Oh, God!" she said in a way that called for him. "Down," she commanded.

He lowered her onto the piano bench, her head dangling off the far end, her skirt gathered at her waist. He jumped—fell—out of his khakis. She struggled free of her last barrier with an ambitious bend of the knee. Her scent overwhelmed him, and he lost any sense of their surroundings. It was just them. Joined. Athletic and driven toward fulfillment. Wild. She coached with sharp cries of approval and overactive hips. An elbow smacked the keys and sounded a dissonant chord.

Red light from an EXIT sign. Her hair stretched like spilled water toward the floor. He could see darkness down her throat as she laughed a pleasure-ridden, gutteral laugh. He had been a long time waiting to hear that laugh again.

He warned her, and she liked that.

"Wait . . . wait . . ." she pleaded.

"I can't," he cautioned.

What started as another of those laughs gave way to him and ended with the sharp sounding of satisfaction, loud and honest. Honest as anything she ever said to him. Honest in a way he lived to hear.

For a long time her head hung limp, her chest rose and fell toward recovery. With some effort she managed to look up, holding onto him so he wouldn't move. Wouldn't leave her. Her face was a glorious red, her eyes filled with wonder, hope and promise.

She took him by the hair and pulled him to her. She whispered in a husky voice, "We've gotta get a piano."

TUESDAY

February 7

27

A homicide. Boldt had been to too many to count, but each was different, each sickened his stomach. It was something you never got used to, and if you did, then it was time to change departments. A human life. So precious when you saw it taken away. So ugly a sight, a murdered human; so different from a mere dead body. The first dead body he had ever seen had been his grandfather's. He wasn't supposed to see it. He had been told not to go upstairs, but he had sneaked up while his father poured his mother a drink from his grandfather's bar. Dead on the bathroom floor, his pajamas down around his knees. Eyes open and squinting. Little Lou Boldt had dared to touch him, and when he did, the man's entire body jumped as if he were hooked up to electricity. Boldt had run from that room blindly, screaming, "He's alive! He's alive!" Dead bodies still terrified him.

He had to park out on the asphalt. They had taped off the sandy road hoping the Professor's boys might lift some tire or shoe impressions. But with this rain, it was unlikely. Things washed away pretty quickly. Boldt crossed a spongy fairway. A weird place for a homicide, a golf course. The guys hadn't touched the body. They were still doing pho-

221

tographs when Boldt reached them. The back of the
station wagon was open. Connie Chi was wearing
relatively new shoes by the look of the soles. Her
underwear had snagged on the right shoe. Both
ankles were tied to opposite ends of an umbrella,
spreading her legs.

Sadness washed through him, replaced a few seconds later by an intense and unforgiving anger.

"Sexual assault for sure," the Professor's side-
kick told him—Boldt had forgotten the man's name,
"though Dixie will have to confirm it."

"Where is Dixie?" Boldt asked.

"On his way. Be here any minute."

Boldt looked in at her. Naked from the waist
down. Hands tied with plastic grocery bags, spreading her arms open like Jesus on the cross. Tied to the
back seat door handles. He glanced just once at the
head. A car flare was thrust deeply into her mouth,
sticking out like a cigar. The phosphorous had
burned a white hole through her throat. No blood at
all. Just an ugly two-inch hole.

The other guy said, "Doing her Groucho imitation." Trying to be funny. There was always a ten-
dency toward humor around crime scenes.

Boldt got away from there quickly, over to the
bushes in case he puked. He'd been away for two
years—his stomach had forgotten about this. Fifteen
years earlier he would have been embarrassed to
puke; now, he wished he would, just to make himself feel better.

He wanted to think that some monster had done
this to her all by himself. But the inescapable feeling
was that *he*, too, was responsible. He and his crew
had blown the surveillance. He and his crew had
made their interest in Connie Chi apparent. They
had marked her.

"Over here," one of the Professor's boys hollered.

Boldt and some others joined him. At the end of the man's Bic pen was a spent condom and a blue wrapper. Looked pretty fresh. One of the others said, "A place like this, the bushes are probably full of one-finger gloves. You want it, Sarge?" he asked Boldt, inquiring if it should be collected and marked as evidence.

"I want everything," Boldt replied in a voice that cracked. *I want her back alive*, he felt like saying. *I want a second chance at that gas station surveillance*. He could picture himself running alongside the van, his hand on the door handle—he could *feel* it. He could see that finger lock the door before he got it open. He could see the van pull away into traffic. "We're looking for animal hairs—white animal hairs. Carpet fibers. Fingerprints."

"Prints are out. The vehicle is wiped clean," one of the technicians called out.

In an authoritative voice that rang with anger Boldt ordered, "Don't forget to check under the back seat. He may have folded the back seat down at some point. He may not have remembered to wipe it down." Had this guy thought of everything? "And get someone from Sexual Assaults down here. I want the rape angle treated just as carefully as if she had survived. This is a hell of a lot more than . . ." He caught himself. The entire group of maybe ten guys, including the uniforms, were looking at him. Staring at him. Only then did he realize he was crying. Crying buckets.

Only then did he wish he had never come back at all.

28

Donnie Maybeck entered the First Avenue storefront that advertised "Peep Show $1." Inside, behind a black velvet curtain, a row of well-used nickelodeons showed endless-loop adult videos. Loners, who smelled bad and couldn't keep their hands from shaking, pressed their faces to the viewing lens, squinting. Donnie thought that if someone had been running a camera in the back of his van when he had knocked those runaways or when he'd jumped Connie that he'd be a porno star by now. Donnie Does Debbie. Live Healthy: Eat A Vegetable. He could see the titles now. Worthless dirt bags, these guys. They should all be zoomed.

The one behind the counter was called Bogs. He had a tattoo of a skull on his left cheek, and he chewed gum so fast he sounded like a dog eating. Bogs knew everything and everyone. When the word had reached Donnie that Bogs wanted to buzz, Donnie had made tracks to the shop.

Donnie said, "Hey," because that was how Bogs said hello. You had to know these things.

Bogs said, "Hey," though his mouth never stopped chewing. "I hear you got a C-note for me."

"The laptop?" Donnie shouted it. He couldn't control himself.

"What the fuck do you think?" The man winked slowly at him. His right eyelid was tattooed with the word "Fuck." When he winked his left eye, Donnie read "You." He repeated the sequence proudly— FUCK YOU—just in case Donnie had missed it. Donnie could see this guy doing this into a mirror, reading the words backwards, smiling, chewing his gum. Probably chewed gum in his sleep.

"You got the scratch?" he asked Donnie.

Donnie dug into his pocket and withdrew Tegg's money. He hated to see it go.

Bogs said, "I ain't promising you it's *yours*, you know. I got no way to know if it's *yours*."

Donnie realized he should have split the reward into two payments. He *hated* it when he did stupid things like that. He said, "If it's not mine, I'm coming back for the scratch."

"A Toshiba, right?"

Donnie answered this with a nod.

"Young kid, dark hair?"

Another nod.

"It's yours." Bogs pocketed the money. "North side of Pine between First and Second, just up from the market. You know the place?"

"I'll find it."

"You're never going to get it without the stub. You know the way it works. But that's *your* problem."

"You got a name for me? Someone I could grease?"

"Grease someone at a hock shop? What kind of dumb shit are you?"

Donnie was sick of taking insults from everyone. "Up yours!" he said, losing his temper. "I'll get it back."

Bogs shook his head at him. That really pissed Donnie off. "You'll see," Donnie said childishly.

Bogs offered only the same winking of the eyes, that same message flashing back from his darkened eye sockets: Fuck . . . you.

29

Boldt was folding laundry when the car pulled up out front. The image of Connie Chi's murdered body still lingered in his mind's eye. Liz was on the couch reading a novel. Miles had fallen asleep in the Jonny Jump-Up, effectively guarding the way into the kitchen and preventing anyone from attempting to clean up. Scott Hamilton played sensuous sax from the stereo. Boldt knew every note, every nuance. But tonight it all seemed so trivial. In his mind lingered another image as well: Sharon Shaffer, her chest cut open, her heart removed. Were they too late to stop it?

The plates on the van had turned out to be stolen. No real surprise to Boldt but still a disappointment. They had alerted area pawn shops to notify them of any hocked laptop computers. It was pretty much wait-and-see at the moment. It was frustrating as hell.

"That's a brown and a black—just in case you care," Liz said, pointing out the socks Boldt was in the process of rolling together. She was like that: She could split her attention among several things at once. Not Boldt—he tended toward obsessive. His mind, his emotions locked on and wouldn't let go. Despite the present activity of his hands, his attention was not on the socks. He was on autopilot, stuck with the rookie cop dilemma of reliving his mistakes. He broke the pair apart, said "Thanks," and started again. *She* cared—that was the point—about the socks, about him. She looked after him, and he was thankful for it. She didn't nag, she observed. She didn't force herself on him. She reminded him to shave when he forgot. She threw his shirts into the wash—even though he *did* the wash. Right now she was probably worried sick about his skipping dinner.

They had a visitor.

Boldt heard the feet trodding up the wooden steps of the front porch and announced, "It's Dixie," before the man even knocked. "I'll get it."

"You amaze me," she said. Boldt stopped at the door. He felt tempted to turn the lock rather than the door knob, tempted to crawl up her skirt and make some trouble, or another baby.

"He's going to want me to go with him somewhere," Boldt informed her when he saw the glare of the headlights and realized Dixie had left the car running. He opened the door. "Be with you in a second," he told Dixon before the man could utter a word.

Dixon managed to ask, "But how—?"

"He's psychic," Liz interrupted, helping Boldt to locate his gun and jacket. She asked Dixon, "How long will you be?"

"A couple hours maybe," the befuddled man replied.

She asked Boldt if he had his keys because she would be asleep by eleven. She hated the way policework robbed them of their private time. Tuesday was his night to put Miles down. Now she would have that chore as well. She whispered into his ear, "Wake me," following it with a quick dart of the tongue. Boldt returned a kiss and heard the door close and lock behind them as he and Dixie descended the steps.

"What's up?" Boldt asked across the roof of the car, after reaching the passenger door.

"They've found the remains," Dixon told him. "Water level in the river is high, and rising. We excavate tonight, or we lose it. Monty's on his way—our forensic archaeologist—and I've asked an entomologist from the U-Dub to join us as well. We would rather do this by daylight, of course, but not if we risk losing the remains by waiting."

Boldt's depression vanished instantly, replaced by an elevated pulse and a tingling sense of curiosity. A dozen questions crowded his brain once again: When had the body been buried? Exactly what was the cause of death? What could it tell them about the harvester? Was this his *first* kill? They needed the rest of the remains and the identity of the victim before they could answer any of these questions.

"You're certainly talkative," Dixon said, a few minutes into the ride. Another fifteen minutes later they were away from the lights and the traffic, the density of the darkness increasing around them. It rained lightly for a few minutes. Boldt felt hypnotized by the motion of the wipers. Dixon asked Boldt to pour him a cup of coffee from his thermos, knowing better than to offer any to Boldt.

"The blood toxicology workup on Chapman came in today," Dixon baited his friend.

"Am I interested?"

"Ever heard of a drug called Ketamine?"

"No. Should I have?"

"You're about to."

"Good."

"It's a drug used by veterinarians."

For a moment, Boldt actually thought his heart had stopped. "Animal hairs," he said, recalling that a variety of such hairs had been found on both Chapman's clothing and Sharon Shaffer's furniture.

"What?" asked Dixon.

Boldt recalled Dr. Light Horse's comments about the closure appearing unusual. A veterinarian—when you looked at the evidence, it suddenly seemed so *obvious*. The road ahead of the car was clear, but there was plenty of traffic in his head to make up for it. "Talk to me."

"You ever watch *60 Minutes*?" Dixon asked.

"You know better than that." Boldt hadn't owned a television since Walter Cronkite went off the air.

"It's a drug used in surgery by vets. It paralyzes the patient from the neck down. The dog, cat, whatever, remains semi-awake—that is, doesn't require ventilation or other life support during surgery—but can't feel or move. It's often used in conjunction with gas. It's a very serious drug to use on adult humans because of its psychological effects. Oddly enough, some pediatricians are now using it on children. *60 Minutes* did a thing on a guy who evaporated Ketamine down to a powder, slipped it into the drinks of women he met in bars, and then took them to motels and raped them."

"I read about it," Boldt said. "I remember the case."

"Well, apparently you're not the only one. The interesting thing about Ketamine, especially in large doses, is its devastating effect on short-term memory. None of the rapist's victims ever remembered what happened to them. And I mean, they remembered *nothing*. It was only because one of them escaped before the drug fully took effect that he was ever caught. He was lucky he didn't kill someone. In large doses it's lethal: convulsion, asphyxiation, death."

"A vet?"

"He's using a knockout intravenous dosage of Ketamine combined with Valium. Throw in a dash of electroshock for good measure and there's no one—*no one*—who's ever going to identify him." Dixon turned off the darkened road onto a muddy dirt road and slowed down to where the rear end of the vehicle wouldn't fishtail.

"A vet?" Boldt was stunned. Suddenly he was having to rethink his line of investigation—it was like starting all over. He couldn't manage any other words.

"There's more. Once I discovered the Ketamine in the workup, I knew what to look for. I told you we saved some tissue samples from the ones we lost to hemorrhaging."

"Daffy told me."

"We save those things for a reason. Reasons like this." The car was acting squirrely, having a hard time with traction. More than once Boldt was tempted to reach over and grab the wheel, but Dixon did a good, albeit disturbing, job of talking while driving. "Vicryl had been used in two of the three cases. It's a woven suture made by a company called Ethicon—it's used internally for closures. But the Vicryl used in both Peter Blumenthal and Glenda Sherman was a number two. That's *huge*, way too big for human use. Horses, cows—gorillas, maybe; not humans. The point being that oversized woven suture will loosen up on you. Your knots fail. In the case of a kidney, let's say you've tied off an artery with it. It comes loose and you have forty-five percent of the body's blood flow pouring into the back side of your intestines. You're dead real fast. *Real* fast. Like walking down the street and keeling over, which is how Sherman was found by 911. Do I have your interest yet?"

There was a red flare burning like a Roman candle on the left side of the road up ahead. Dixon slowed and turned at the flare, following a good number of rutted tire tracks. They wouldn't be the first on the scene.

"A vet?" Boldt repeated. "May I use your

phone?" he asked, taking the car phone from the cradle before Dixie consented. It took him three calls to find Daphne. She was staying at Sharon's, looking after Agnes Rutherford in Sharon's absence.

"How do you feel about unpaid overtime?" he asked rhetorically, not waiting for her answer. "It's not a surgeon, it's a veterinarian. Dixie has the proof. Roust LaMoia. Make a list, just like the AMA list. All the local vets capable of this. Think of ways to narrow it down. Find out about the distribution of a drug called . . ." He looked at Dixie.

"Ketamine."

Boldt repeated it. He added, "We're closing in, Daffy. Search and Rescue found the bones."

"I'll find LaMoia. We'll be at the office."

"And I want a psych profile, ASAP," Boldt reminded, though the phone had gone dead. "Out of range," Boldt said. He hung up.

"There's more," Dixie announced proudly. "The Ethilon—a suture used for the subcutaneous closure—followed what we call a continuous interlocking stitch. I'm talking about Chapman now, about those photos you took to Dr. Light Horse. I got your memo. She's right about the technique used on the closures. And it all fits with a vet, incidentally: They use the interlocking because of its strength. The giveaway is the subcutaneous stitch, the continuous interlocking stitch. It is *always* done right to left by right-handers and left-to-right by left-handers. This one was left-to-right."

"A leftie?" Boldt asked excitedly. "That certainly narrows the field, although whether a person is right- or left-handed is not the kind of thing we have access to." He realized that it would require a hell of a lot of manpower to chase down a lead like that.

"I thought that would interest you."

Boldt nodded but was thinking how difficult it would be to verify or investigate. And if they sent out detectives asking questions, they would only serve to tip off the harvester, to give him time to clean house and shut down shop. They needed the cart before the ox: They needed the pair of snipping shears that Dixie believed connected at least two of the victims. They needed a witness. Even a dead one.

"We're here," said Dixie, pulling over.

====

The air smelled impossibly good, and the sound of the raging river, growling from below them in the darkness, brought back memories of twenty years earlier when Boldt and Liz had found time to explore the peninsula. The four-wheel drive vehicles were parked below, their headlights and search lights revealing a dug-up area that looked like the surface of the moon. The entire landscape was riddled with deep test holes, the work of a yellow backhoe that now sat off to one side. As Boldt's eyes adjusted, he saw that they had worked their way up this bank of the river—some sixty yards worth of excavations. Those lights were now aimed onto the grave, an angry black hole that looked like a huge mouth locked open in mid-scream. There were maybe ten people—all men—crowded around the hole, some leaning on shovels, some in sheriff uniforms, most drinking coffee from plastic thermos cups. Their attention fixed on this hole in the ground and its contents, which remained out of sight for Dixon and Boldt as they slid down a small incline, the sound of the river growing even louder. It no longer sounded peaceful. The closer they drew to this hole, this grave, the more menacing that sound. Two of the four-wheel drives were running. The light was a blue sterile wash, out of keeping with the natural surroundings, like the illumination at a photo shoot or movie set.

They avoided the other holes as they approached. One of the uniforms from the sheriff's office introduced himself. This site was well outside of the city limits, outside of Boldt's jurisdiction, but still in King County and therefore within the professional domain of Dr. Ronald Dixon. Jurisdictional differences could create tremendous headaches for all concerned if ego and territory became issues. Boldt kept this in mind and let Dixie do all the talking. The deputy sheriff was nice enough. He asked to be brought up-to-date. Dixie managed to tell him as little as required, without reference to Sharon Shaffer's abduction or the harvesting linkage, for which Boldt was grateful. To date, they had managed to keep this out of the press. The press could be a nightmare.

A light mist began to fall. Boldt turned up his collar. One of the Search and Rescue guys offered him rain gear but he declined. They had hand dug a series of terraced shelves descending from surface grade to the partially exposed bones below. Boldt felt impatient: This site could be the harvester's first kill, perhaps his first harvest, and as such might hold clues to both his character and methods. Criminals made mistakes the first time around that they often eliminated as time wore on and the number of their crimes rose. As the depth of the hole increased, different strata of soils could be seen. "Remember," one of the men warned from overhead, "this sucker is undercut something fierce! There's not enough floor in the very bottom to support you. Stick to the shelves. That last step is as low as you dare go." It looked as if a shovel had pierced the tender layer of soil that still supported the skeletal remains, causing a hole through which the fevered gray foam of a dark angry river could be seen threatening. Some water splashed up and into it. Over the roar of the white water another of the crew shouted, "It's dangerous down there. That hole you're looking at was caused by my foot!"

Dixie stepped onto the first terraced landing, standing about knee deep in the wide mouth of the excavated hole. Boldt followed, the two of them standing side by side. Dixie reached up and was handed a powerful flashlight, the size of a small briefcase. He turned it on, illuminating the haunting mask of a hollow-eyed skeleton that stared back at them. Boldt could clearly make out an arm and part of a leg. Dixie said, "She's beautiful."

"If you say so," answered Boldt.

Dixie ran the light down her extremities, and as he did he recited the names of the various bones he saw: "humerus, radius, ulna, tarsus, metatarsus." When he reached the "proximal phalanx," he accidentally directed the bright light into Boldt's eyes. "Skull and pelvis; most of the remaining ribs. We're lucky."

Boldt reached out and steered the light back to their subject. "Not her," he was thinking. He said, "One thing about a murder: There are always *two* witnesses."

Dixon said, "Now, if she'll only tell us who the other one was."

"The harvester," Boldt said softly. There was no doubt now. Two of the ribs were cut sharply, their ends clearly missing. A whole section of her rib cage cut away like an empty box.

To the Search and Rescue team whose glowing, dirty faces rimmed the enclosure, all of them looking down into the grave, Dixon said, "Let's get to work."

30 Inside the farmhouse, a single light burning in the other room, Elden Tegg sat in the relative darkness. He missed Pamela. She was essential to the team. Without her, this procedure was going to be much more difficult, though not impossible by any means. Even so, he remained quite angry with her for wanting no part in this, for forcing him to hide it from her.

Tegg accepted his solution to the Michael Washington problem, because he felt justified in blaming it on others. The police were a force to be reckoned with; he had no desire to be an object of an investigation. He also blamed Washington himself—a victim of his own foolishness. He prepared mentally for the task at hand, experiencing a stimulating warmth in his neocortex. He felt high. He felt ready.

He headed toward the kennel through the chill night air, drawn to the barking like a mother to a baby's crying. As he unlocked and opened the door, Felix—left free to defend—and the others went silent. Tegg stood before Washington's cage, his doctor's case in one hand, the collar's remote device in the other. Washington's hot, terrified eyes revealed a man overcome with fear. Even though excited, Tegg didn't feel good about this; but he accepted it just the same. Did the man know what fate awaited him? Sharon looked terrified as well. We're all in this together, Tegg thought, each inexorably linked to the other.

He waved the "wand."

"You don't want me to use this, do you?"

Washington replied through the muzzle in words

surprisingly clear, "What *right* do you have to do this? Who made *you* God?"

Tegg's knee-jerk reaction was to light him up with the "wand" and watch him squirm. But he didn't do that. He felt compelled to answer this, if for no other reason than to hear the explanation himself. "I am doing what must be done. We *all* are. It is not without sacrifice on all our parts. No. Not without sacrifice."

"But you're a fake! You aren't even a doctor. You told me yourself: You're a veterinarian! An animal doctor! How can you pretend like this?"

"Pretend?" Tegg's nostrils flared. His eyes flashed hot. Auspiciously, the dogs, who had been pacing anxiously inside their cages, all stopped at once, as if on cue. The building went deathly silent.

Tegg depressed the button on Washington's "wand." The black man repeatedly danced around the cage like a marionette. Sharon screamed soundlessly. The dogs barked.

Tegg stopped. Enough. Washington collapsed to the cement, a magnificent erection rising from him.

Tegg said to Sharon, "What do you make of that?" He indicated Washington's erection, but she wouldn't look. She curled into the fetal position, trembling.

Washington was weakened to the point that he couldn't move quickly—the perfect target.

Tegg used the dart gun next, administering a strong dose of Valium. He would hold off on the Ketamine until he had him up in the cabin. "He's going to sleep, that's all," he told the woman in a blatant lie. How many times had he spoken this line to pet owners? What a strange euphemism. Washington did not attempt to remove the dart. His will was broken. Strangely, that hurt Tegg most of all.

The first few incisions went beautifully. I should be videotaping this, he thought. His patient lay before him, an eight-inch incision in his chest. Again, he longed for Pamela's assistance and support. He had grown to depend on her, an uncomfortable feeling, a sort of attachment that he couldn't fully accept.

He thought through the procedure carefully now, for this was *exactly* where he had made his mistake twenty years before. He pushed the thought of the police from his mind. He pushed away his temporary anger at Pamela. He tried to transcend it all—to establish a quiet place in his mind from which to commence.

He reviewed each detail: He would split the sternum with the sternal saw; place and lock the sternal retractor, opening the chest cavity; open the pericardial sac; identify and immobilize all the vessels leading in and out of the heart; flush the heart with cold solution; place ice around the heart; collect and centralize all the vessels; cut the heart out and place it immediately in ice. He congratulated himself on how effortlessly he recited the various steps. Not so terribly difficult. One step at a time. He checked, insuring that any and all instruments he might possibly need were within easy reach. They were. Ready now . . .

He switched on the sternal saw. The Ketamine, Valium, and Versed paralyzed and relaxed the man, but left his eyes open in a vacant stare. Tegg was distracted by those eyes. Without Pamela by his side, whom he normally used as a sounding board, describing each detail of the procedure like a pilot running down a checklist, Tegg found himself looking at those eyes, engaging his patient in a monologue. The electric saw hummed noisily. A sternal saw requires an upward pressure in order to cut the bone and still remain at a safe distance from the tissue beneath it—the heart. With the sternum exposed, Tegg fed the saw under the lower edge of the sternum into the chest cavity, slipping the edge into the slot made to accept it.

This was *the very same* procedure Tegg had failed to execute properly twenty years before. Seemed like yesterday, now that he had this saw in hand. Seemed so much like yesterday, that yesterday came right out of his subconscious. His mind played tricks on him: It wasn't Washington on the operating table, it was Thomas Kent. His eyes were open. He looked dead already. One second Washington; the next Thomas Kent. Back and forth: black skin, white skin, positive, negative. *"You're a fake!"* He recalled this man's words clearly. But I'm not, he thought. *I'll show you. Sternum goes in the mouth of the saw*—he could remember performing this procedure on cadavers, never a hitch. He could remember assisting Millingsford a dozen times. Never a hitch.

"Stop staring," he told his patient. He hadn't bothered with conventional anesthesia because Washington wouldn't be around after this, and it was usually Pamela's job anyway. The harvest would be over in thirty minutes or so—what was the worry?

It was those eyes. Was he *awake*?

"Stop staring," Tegg beseeched the man for a second time.

He flipped on the switch. *Sternum goes in the mouth of the saw* . . . Only for a fraction of a second did he glance at those eyes.

"A fake!"

Too long. He neglected to maintain the constant upward pressure required of the saw. Suddenly, the donor's warm blood, like water from a burst pipe, sprayed into Tegg's eyes and blinded him. At the same time, he was flooded by his memories again. Was this nothing but the same nightmare he had lived with for twenty years? For a moment he stepped back, believing it was, but his surroundings—the plastic walls and ceiling—alerted him that this was for real. He jumped back to work, literally throwing the saw to the cement floor with a crash.

He attempted to contain his mistake, which was like expecting the Dutch boy to hold back the flood, like trying to piece a blowout back together from the scraps of a tire found in the breakdown lane. He enlarged the chest incision, gaining access to the heart by reaching beneath the sternum. He quickly packed the wound with cloth, applying pressure with his hand. He plugged the hole in the man's heart with the cloth and pinched the tough muscle shut. But he was all out of hands. The hemostats—the clamps—were just off to his left, lying there waiting for him, *staring* at him, glinting in the light, but his hands were fully occupied. *Pamela*! If only . . . Frantically, he released the heart and made for the clamps. Blood erupted like a geyser. He began furiously clamping anything he touched. The bleeding slowed and stopped. For a moment he thought he had contained it, but then he looked up at the monitor and realized the patient was dead. In abject horror, in fear of total failure, Tegg worked at a frantic pace. There was far too much blood on the chest for him to see what he was doing. His movements, usually smooth and controlled, came out of him as small explosions. He retrieved the saw, opened the chest and let his fingers be his eyes. The organ was ruined. The saw had inflicted a two-inch incision in the left ventricle. Had it only been the pulmonary artery . . .

Tegg ignored the error—not his, but the saw's, he tried to convince himself—and removed the heart properly. He cradled it in his hands and sank slowly to the floor, exhausted. Could he never get it right? he wondered. Only one more try, and if he failed at that what would Wong Kei do to him? He'd have *his* heart, that's what! The police, Wong Kei, the heart he held in his hands, Pamela's refusal to help him. It felt like some kind of conspiracy! He had to rise above this, to overcome. "Practice makes perfect," he mumbled, looking down at the heart still cradled in his hands. "Practice makes perfect."

===

Sharon Shaffer trembled in the center of her cage, wrought with fear. There was nothing to measure this fear against, nothing to compare it to. At first, the pain had distracted her. Pain was a matter of tolerance, tolerance a matter of attitude, attitude a matter of choice. She chose to be strong, calling on her higher power to see her through. Thus far it had. Her wounds were both terrifying and painful. She could only see out of her left eye now, but maybe that was a blessing, for all she saw were the vicious, angry eyes of the restless pit bulls boring down onto her. She concentrated not on her losses but her strengths. In order to regain the confidence required to escape, she would need every available faculty.

Her central focus had been, and continued to be, gaining her freedom. People made mistakes, even people like *him*, and she was ready to seize the moment.

Fifteen minutes after The Keeper had left the building, she went to work with a determination she had not allowed him to see. She hoped that his impression of her was that she was weakened to the point of total exhaustion—a necessary ruse if she was to have any hope of taking him by surprise. In fact, quite the opposite was true: She was much stronger than she looked.

That morning she had spotted a hypodermic needle covered in dust, pushed into the corner of the adjacent cage where the building's corrugated metal met the chain link of the kennel wall. She saw it not as a needle but as a potential weapon.

Given the right moment, she could take an eye out with it. Blind him. Jump him. When he returned with Michael, he would be distracted. If she could only get that needle, it might be the perfect time for an attack. Lure him into the cage by moaning and gripping her side . . .

The problem was how to reach clear across the adjacent cage, snag the needle, and drag it all the way back. She had decided to craft a fishing line out of the only two materials available: the plastic I.V. tube hooked up to her arm and string from the burlap sack. Having spent the last twenty minutes unweaving a portion of the burlap sack and knotting pieces of it together, she now had an eight-foot length to use as a fishing line.

As she disconnected the I.V. tube from both the needle in her forearm and the overhead I.V. bag, she considered using the needle in her own arm as a weapon—a needle was a needle, after all—but she feared he was too observant for that. He always stood there examining her prior to opening her cage. If he noticed the needle missing, if he sensed her intentions, all hope was lost. He would shock her into semiconsciousness, and her "weapon" would be lost. She would have only one chance to use the needle. She couldn't risk his catching on.

She prevented the I.V. from leaking by inverting it and re-clamping it to the top of the chain-link cage. She fashioned a "fishing pole" from the tubing by doubling it on itself. She knotted her burlap line to the end of it.

Her blind eye gave her unexpected problems. She felt time slipping away. How much longer until he returned Michael to his cage? The more she tried to hurry, the more awkward her motions. She quickly realized that above all she had to remain calm. Steady.

The door banged. She glanced toward it in terror. *Him*—or just wind rattling its hinges as it often did? If he came in on her now . . . She studied the dogs, for their pacing and silence had become warning signs of The Keeper's approach. They showed no such signs at the moment. Sweat trickling down from her temples, she went back to work. She tied a few pieces of dry dog food onto her line to act as weights. They kept breaking apart and falling off. Her frustration grew to the point where she could hardly use her fingers. She had to stop, take a deep breath, and try again. Finally, she formed a small loop—a lasso—on the end of her line, with enough weights to do the trick.

The door banged again, but the dogs remained complacent, dozing for the most part. The sweat now trickled down her jaw. She fed the tubing and line through the chain link, careful not to touch it. Any contact with the cage would trigger the shock collar. She jerked the tubing back and forth, driving her weighted line toward the far corner and the needle. She couldn't judge distance well. She kept casting toward the needle but the end of her line didn't even come close. It took some practice. The tubing sagged if she extended it too far. The line hit the cement floor if she didn't keep it high enough. With each new attempt, her lasso inched toward the target.

The door, the wind, her imagination, all worked against her concentration. The harder her heart pounded, the more pain she felt in her wounds.

The loop hooked the needle! Slowly, she pulled it toward her.

Suddenly, the dogs sat up in unison, their ears perked, eyes alert. *Him*!

Him!! Her bad eye screamed with pain as she squinted. Her good eye blurred with tears from overuse. The needle was only halfway toward her. Come on! She pulled the line more quickly. The dogs paced anxiously—he was *close*.

Her hands shook. Panic overtook her. She tugged on the tubing and lost the needle, stranding it in the middle of the adjacent cage. To her, it looked as big as a Coke bottle, lying there. It called out: "Here I am! Look, she's trying to escape!"

Her hand brushed against the chain link. Her collar sounded a quick warning and then delivered a devastating jolt of electricity. She fell back, letting go of the tubing. It slid through the chain link, threatening to fall into the next pen. She snatched it back quickly, but in doing so made contact with the fence once again.

The dogs circled their cages frantically. He was coming! He was certain to see the needle!

She stuffed everything under the burlap and sat down on top of it and looked up, only to see the I.V. bag still clipped to the top of her cage. This, of all things, would give her away.

Then she saw that the I.V. needle in her had leaked blood onto her forearm. What to do? Think!! With the door coming open, with far too many loose ends to tie up, with no clear idea what she was doing, she pulled the I.V. bag down, its contents leaking out onto the floor. She grabbed the plastic tubing from beneath her and slipped the string off its end, leaving a knotted tangle—a mess—on the floor. Now it might look like an accident—it had tangled in her sleep.

With all these thoughts swirling inside her, she dared not look at the needle. *Don't draw his attention to it.* She looked away.

As the door opened fully and he stepped inside, she vomited.

Drenched in blood, he held a human heart in his outstretched hands. The heart looked so small. So pitiful.

"Nothing to worry about," he said strongly. The door banged shut behind him. The barking stopped. With the scent of blood in the air, all the dogs hurried to the front of their cages. Tegg moved down the center aisle. "Practice makes perfect," he stated. Sharon caught herself pulling at the shock collar—a forbidden action—not because she wanted out of it, which she did, but because she found it hard to breathe. Her teeth chattered uncontrollably; her hands went numb.

"Who's been good?" he asked the dogs.

She screamed into the gag, but little sound came out.

"What I bring you today, my friends," he addressed the dogs, "is an example of the human condition: the pursuit of perfection." He hoisted the dripping heart aloft as a kind of sacrificial offering. "Who's been good?" He sounded so *normal*: a father to his children.

She glanced at the needle; it seemed so insignificant now.

With the heart clutched in his hands, he said to her, "Be thankful this wasn't you." He tossed the heart up lightly and caught it playfully. It slapped into his gloved hands with a sucking sound. He did this several times, like a child with a ball.

He marched down the center aisle. "Felix, for you," he said as he made the dog sit. "Hold," he said. He dropped the heart in front of the dog. "Not yet," he said. "Not yet."

He walked back to the main door. It sang as it opened.

Felix's full attention was on the chunk of meat in front of him.

"Okay," Tegg commanded.

The dog lunged forward and ate the heart.

WEDNESDAY

February 8

31

"Okay. I've been on the phone all morning consulting some of the best in the business: Dr. Christiansen here in Seattle; Shires in Denver; Rantner and McCullough at Quantico—and the picture is not a pretty one. If this guy has done three, he's done thirty. He likely views the runaways as street scum—but it's unlikely he knows he's killed them. He is trying to prove himself, as much as help those who need the organs. The fact that he's done at least two kidneys *and* a lung indicates this is not strictly business—it's a competency test as well. He's in his early to middle-forties, married, with children."

Shoswitz huffed.

She explained, "That's the demographic on veterinarians, Lieutenant. It's my job to play the averages. He's probably attempting to overcome some prior grievance. With a vet, the most obvious is being turned down by medical school."

"He's playing doctor," Shoswitz said.

"Exactly. Maybe he lost someone close to him either because of a failed organ transplant or, more likely, because of a lack of organ availability. He's now both proving his own abilities and making certain there are plenty of organs to go around so that it doesn't happen to anyone else.

"He's had extensive medical training. He may have flunked out of medical school—that may be his grievance. He or an associate has or has had exposure to the runaway and homeless community. He can deal with these kids without raising suspicions."

"So what you're saying," Shoswitz tested, "is that these three deaths you turned up are the exception, not the rule."

"That's the opinion, yes. Cindy Chapman is more likely the rule: Harvest the organ, drug and electroshock the donor, and return him or her to the streets. A few of the unlucky ones didn't make it."

"Thirty?" Shoswitz asked.

"That was Dr. Rantner's minimum estimate based on pattern cycles, his expertise. Two of the victims, Sherman and Blumenthal, occurred within three weeks of each other, suggesting a three-week cycle. But the indication is that this has been going on for at least three years—if, as these bones indicate, the harvests are the work of the same person. Somewhere between twelve and fifteen a year. It could be two or three times that."

"And the body count?" Boldt asked. "Is that consistent?"

"It fits well. Yes. Three deaths that we've uncovered. At a ten-percent failure rate that still adds up to thirty or more."

"Jesus!" Shoswitz said. "This guy's fucking out of his mind!"

"Not necessarily, Lieutenant," she corrected, taking him literally. "Christiansen profiled him as bright, charming, even active in the community. He sees himself as going a step beyond—going the extra mile—to save lives. He feels perfectly justified in what he's doing. He feels good about it. Empowered by it. We're dealing with a substantial ego here."

"Robin Hood?" Shoswitz asked incredulously. "Are you telling me this guy believes he is performing some kind of civic duty?"

"Absolutely. That's very well put, Lieutenant. That's it exactly."

A uniformed patrolman knocked and opened the office door. "Lieutenant? We're ready for you."

===

Fifteen people were gathered in the situation room. J. C. Adams, Butch and Danny—all working surveillance; several nerds from Tech Services, including Watson, who ran it like it was its own department, which it wasn't; two women, Maria Romanello and Trish Leidecher, veteran Sexual Assault detectives currently assigned to Special Operations. Boldt, LaMoia and Shoswitz followed in behind Daphne.

Shoswitz paced the room rubbing his elbow, and spoke in a commanding voice. "Here's where we stand, everybody: Robbery has quite possibly located the laptop computer that was lifted from a van we had under surveillance. A pawn shop on Pine called in serial numbers to a Toshiba laptop yesterday. The timing and the description of both the laptop and the kid who hocked it were a good match. We sent Watson and crew to have a look at it. Subsequently, we've been informed by them that the laptop is password protected. Watson," he said, turning it over to a man with thick glasses and wet, red lips.

He spoke with a slight lisp. "Given the existence of an unknown password, we are unable to retrieve any file on the hard disk in full. We can only grab data a few sectors at a time, and copying in any kind of order is out altogether. We have programs capable of testing sequences of passwords—trying to 'break the code,' if you will—but with this particular hardware/software combination it's a terribly time consuming process."

Shoswitz cut him off. A couple of the wise guys applauded. Watson sat down. Shoswitz said, "Obviously we need that password. Interestingly enough, a *different* individual approached this same pawn shop late yesterday afternoon, claiming *he* had hocked the laptop, which we know is incorrect. He wanted the laptop back. He was told to return this morning. This individual fit the description and through in-store video has subsequently been identified as the driver of the van in question. We would not only like the driver of that van under surveillance, we would also appreciate it if he would give us the password so we could have a look-see at the data. I hope you're following this because I'm not going to repeat it. Sergeant Boldt has decided we will not—I repeat, will *not*—detain this individual when he returns this morning to claim the laptop. We will place him under surveillance and hope he leads us to bigger fish. Okay? Got it? But we need this friggin' password in order to get at the laptop, and Sergeant Matthews has some ideas on how we might get it. Sergeant . . ." he said, turning it over to her.

Daphne scanned the crowd, making eye contact with each person. "What we're going to do—*all* of us—is 'trick' the suspect into volunteering the password. Each of you has some role to act out. You've already been briefed on that. What I'm going to be talking about applies to how you approach that role, how you approach the suspect.

"We know what this guy looks like—you've all been shown a photocopy of a shot lifted from the store's video. We'll be fully wired. Watson will be set up in the back of the shop." She studied a report. "I've had the chance to study the in-store video of the suspect. This guy is the nervous and anxious type," she said. "He's cocky. He's used to being in control and is not at all comfortable about his present situation. He *wants* this laptop. And that's why he plays into our hands so well. He's suspicious, which means he'll respond best to *negative* reinforcement—reverse psychology. We want to play him like a fish—let him run. We act like we don't give a damn. That's what it amounts to. We're in no hurry to help him out. None whatsoever. If he senses our *trying* to help him, it'll tip him off. He's looking for us—remember that, too. Those of you who are going to be on the shop floor as patrons, I want you to put him down at every opportunity. That shouldn't be too tough for most of you." More laughter. "Get in his face. Call him an 'asshole.' Call him 'stupid'—"

"Just don't call him late to dinner," someone shouted out.

"Cute, Meyers. Bet you thought that up all by yourself," she said quickly, stealing the laughter that Meyers had hoped for, boosting her confidence. She looked Boldt in the eye and was gratified to see respect there. "We want to use his insecurity against him. He *wants* this laptop. You must remember that *at all times*. He'll do what's necessary to get it back, *including* giving us the password as long as we make *him* think of it. It may take us several times. We must be prepared for him to walk. We can't be afraid of that. Let him go; he'll be back." Lots of doubting faces on that one. "This is *my* territory," she reminded. "Trust me: He'll be back. That is, if that laptop contains the kind of information we think it does and if our surveillance boys don't tip him off to us." She allowed them time to talk among themselves and then interrupted. "We're going to push and pull him. Toy with him. It's essential we make this tough for him."

Boldt interrupted, his confidence apparent. "Once we have the password, we're going to copy files from the laptop's hard disk. That may take a minute . . ."

She reinterrupted, "Which is when he will grow the most suspicious. Those of you acting as patrons—that's your moment to cause the most confusion. We want to make it safe for him to be delayed. If he wants to leave—fine. Once we have the password, we don't really care."

Boldt corrected, "But we *do* care about his catching on to us. The whole reason we're letting him skate is the hope he'll lead us up the ladder. It's like a Narco bust that way—which is exactly why those of you from Narco were assigned here. We need your expertise."

Meyers asked, "How do we know this guy ain't the cutter?" Some heads nodded.

"We have a profile of the harvester. This guy doesn't fit," Boldt answered. Daphne witnessed the glum faces and felt tempted to defend herself. He glanced at her from the side of the room where he was standing. "We have reason to suspect that the harvester is a veterinarian." They both allowed a few seconds for the resulting chatter that always followed such an announcement. This was the first time anyone had been told this, other than Shoswitz, LaMoia and herself.

Daphne offered, "There's also some physical evidence. We believe the harvester has a harsh voice. Our pawn shop suspect does not. We believe the accomplice wears size thirteen running shoes; the suspect in the pawn shop was wearing large running shoes.

"The important thing," Daphne continued, "is to use his impatience against him. To criticize him: his looks, his intelligence, anything to heighten his anger. If we keep him angry, he won't be thinking clearly, he'll stop being observant—his focus will be on directing his anger." She asked the two women, "Which one of you is the prostitute?"

That caused all the male heads to spin.

Maria Romanello raised her hand. She was a good choice: dark skin, sultry attitude, with an eye-popping figure. But she was a gum-chewer and not at all glamorous. The guys applauded her. Maria flipped them the bird.

Daphne explained, "You'll want to turn it up pretty hot. Not for him—just in general. Lots of eye shadow. Some skin—as much as you feel comfortable with. Anything to keep him distracted without going over the top." Maria nodded. One of the men let out a wolf whistle. "What we're looking to do," she told them all, "is pull this guy in as many directions as we can. We make the environment busy. We make him feel unwanted. We piss him off, if possible. Maria keeps his hormones active. The more compartments in his brain we can activate, the less mental power he has to concentrate on what's being asked of him. We make him believe he's *offering*. We make him think this is all *his* idea. We play this right, and he'll volunteer that password without thinking about it."

"If we blow it," Boldt said, "chances are we've sacrificed a nice piece of evidence. Maybe even the smoking gun."

Daphne looked up at the clock. "The pawn shop opens at ten. That gives us one hour to get into place. Any questions?"

A single hand raised. Meyers again. Daphne nodded. "Anybody thought about what we do if he pulls a piece and *demands* the laptop?"

Boldt said, "We'll have an identical laptop on hand. If he tries to rob the place, we'll substitute it and give him the wrong one."

"Anything else?"

No other hands surfaced. Daphne felt herself perspiring as she watched for the lieutenant's reaction. Shoswitz looked his crew over. He hesitated but finally nodded, giving his approval. Boldt glanced over at her. She felt a real connection to him.

As she passed closely to him on her way out, she whispered, "What'd you think?"

He said softly to her, "I'm glad you're on our side."

She was thinking about Sharon again—it was all she could think about anymore. What had become of her? Where did this man at the pawn shop fit in? And what fate awaited Sharon if they failed in the task before them?

32

The receptionist left for lunch.

Pamela locked the front door and placed the CLOSED clock in the window—back in an hour—because they had a surgery to do and they couldn't be disturbed. In truth, this wasn't the only reason she locked the front door. It was for privacy as well, for while it trapped the public out, it also trapped the two of them inside, together. They had *work* to do.

She had lost two pounds in just three days. Some kind of miracle! She attributed this newfound strength to *him*. She placed the phones on the service, unbuttoned the top button of her shirt, and headed for his office. If she was honest with herself, she was worried about him. He wasn't himself today. He had spent the morning brooding in his office, his nose buried in medical journals and textbooks. He had outright refused to see several of their patients, passing the work along to her. Not like him at all.

She knocked.

"Enter," he called out in a threatening voice that reminded her of her father. No, he was not himself at all. She opened the door.

He looked worried behind his desk. Others might not see it in him, but she knew him better than anyone. He picked at his beard nervously. "What about that stray?" he asked. "What's become of him?"

"We've called around. No one is claiming him. He's headed for the pound later this afternoon."

"The pound? But they'll kill him in three days! I saved that dog's leg!" he protested.

"The farm? Is that what you mean? You want him out at the farm?"

"Are we prepped for surgery?" he asked.

"A knotted intestine. Routine. It's all set up for you, prepped and ready to go." She added as a hint, "I've locked up. The phones are off." She wondered if he noticed her exposed cleavage. He didn't seem to. She reached up and undid the next button as well.

"Very well," he said, rising from his black leather chair. "But not the lower G.I. Set up the stray for thoracic."

"Excuse me?" she questioned.

"Prep the stray. Now!"

A few minutes later, they were standing alongside one another ready for the first incision. He studied the animal for what seemed like an interminable amount of time.

"Doctor?" she said, breaking the silence.

He glared at her. He looked down at her breasts

and told her to button herself up. "This isn't a porno movie, you know. We have work to do. Correction! *I* have work to do. I'll handle this alone."

"What?" she gasped, fishing for the buttons.

He glanced around the room. "Get me some ice," he said.

"Ice?"

"Now!"

She left the room and headed into the small kitchenette. She collected ice from a freezer there. She heard a buzzing from the surgical suite. The *saw*?

"Saline!" he called out loudly. She had to go to the back room to find it. It took her longer than she wanted. She hurried back into the operating room, because he blamed her for any problems, even if she was off doing something he told her to. "Where's that saline? Penicillin! Where's the ice?" he repeated sternly.

When she rounded the corner and saw him standing there, she stopped abruptly. "My God!" she exclaimed, seeing the chest cavity splayed open.

"A perfect job," he proclaimed proudly. "And fast, at that!" He turned to face her, his outstretched hands cupped firmly together.

There, still beating, was the dog's harvested heart.

33 When Donnie Maybeck entered the pawn shop, he had no way of knowing that his every word, his every movement was being monitored and recorded by the police. No idea that everyone in the place—the cheap-smelling skirt with the cleavage, the lame Jimi Hendrix impersonator, and the half-dozen others who crowded the counters—were all undercover cops. No clue that the big hairy bastard in the undershirt who was giving him such a hard time was a Homicide cop named Lou Boldt.

The man behind the counter was supposed to have been Hymie Monros, but Hymie had missed the briefing because of an asthma attack that had later sent him to the emergency room. Daphne, through Shoswitz, had tapped Boldt for the job. Boldt, notorious for avoiding an active role in setups or stings, had argued he might be recognized from his pursuit of the van.

Shoswitz had been carefully coached to convince Boldt to play the part. He said, "It was late afternoon. Dusk, if not dark. It was raining. You were running, which means you had your head down. It was a panel van, which means it had no windows on the back or on the side, except the passenger door, and you never made it that far, by your own admission." Boldt had smelled a conspiracy.

"The side mirror," Boldt had argued. That was when he *knew* it was a conspiracy and that Daphne *had* coached the lieutenant, who immediately produced a still photograph of the gas station surveillance taken by J.C. Adams. It clearly showed that the van was missing its passenger-side mirror. In fact, there was no way the driver might have seen him, and it even helped to explain why the man had reached to lock the passenger door so late—blind on that side, he had not reacted until he had *heard* Boldt try the cargo door.

Boldt, his skin going itchy from nerves, told the suspect once again, "What I'm telling you, *asshole*, is that any sleazeball could come in here off the street, ask if we had a Toshiba laptop, and then claim it was his." Boldt carried a huge wad of pink gum in his cheeks. It looked like a pitcher's abscess. It had been Shoswitz's idea. "Read the fucking sign."

"Just let me see the thing."

"Show me the receipt," Boldt repeated, finding it difficult to stay with Daphne's script, but doing so. What if she were wrong? What if they pushed too hard, and this guy went south on them? "Show me the ticket, *then* you'll get the laptop, providing you've got the money."

"I got the money," the man complained anxiously, producing a hefty roll of bills.

That's blood money, Boldt thought. Sight of it made him sick. He wanted to arrest this guy. Now. Why wait? "Money won't help you without the ticket," he warned. "The sign, pal. Read the fucking sign."

"But I *lost* the ticket," the guy protested, color rising into his pale face. He had horrible breath; the blind woman, Agnes, had mentioned that. He kept his hand loosely over his mouth, half covering a set of the worst teeth Boldt had ever seen. "I suppose I'm the first fucking guy to lose a receipt, right?"

"Maybe you can't *read*." Boldt pointed to the painted sign. "You blind or just plain *stupid*?" Boldt was beginning to enjoy this. It gave him a vent for his anger.

The woman edged over to them and said to Boldt

in a sexy voice, "Hey, sweetheart. You gonna jerk off all day or what? I got some rocks I wanna hock."

"Get lost," Maybeck barked at her.

"Get fucked," she said to him. "Wasn't tawkin' to you."

"In a minute," Boldt told her.

"Those really your teeth?" she asked Maybeck. He popped her shoulder with the butt of his hand. She stumbled back and flipped him the bird.

"I don't need your business, pal," Boldt said. "Take it somewhere else. *Now!*" He felt terrified to say such a thing and yet he went with Daffy's assessment.

"Hey! Hey!" the guy said, raising his hands as if the woman had stumbled all by herself. "I'm cool, man."

"You hit her again, I'm gonna see you through the front door—without opening it."

"You and who else?" the guy asked.

"Who's next?" Boldt called over the guy's head, ignoring him completely now. He looked over at Maria Romanello. Her skirt was about as big as a fly swatter, her legs, in black tights, a mile long. "What kind of stones?" he asked her.

The guy was looking at her, too. Damn near drooling. Meyers let loose on electric guitar so loudly that Boldt couldn't hear himself think. Boldt hollered for him to knock it off.

"Come on, man," the suspect tried once more.

Boldt felt relieved that Daphne's ideas seemed to be working. He *never* would have played it this way. Not in a million years. He said strongly—a teacher losing patience—"My floor manager told you yesterday: You lose the ticket; you come back *after* the grace period; you buy it back at floor value. *If* no one has bought it by then, it's yours. Those are the rules, pal. And I gotta tell you: A laptop computer is *not* going to be around that long. No way. So give it up. Get a fucking job for all I care."

"You got to make an exception." He offered Boldt two twenties he had cupped in his hand. "What do you think?"

"Put the fucking cab fare in your pocket, pal. You're going to need it. Wrong guy. Listen," he said, conceding a point, "the only exception I ever make on something like this is if the customer can describe the item in such a way as to convince me they're the rightful owner. But with something like this—with a laptop computer—they're all the fucking same to me. I don't know shit about computers—so you're plum out of luck."

"But they're not the same!"

"To *me* they are."

"Diamonds," Maria interrupted, leaning in so the man could see down her blouse. "Diamond earrings."

The guy was staring right along with Boldt. "Get outta here," the suspect said to her, but he didn't seem to mean it.

She adjusted her blouse. "Keep your fucking eyes to yourself," she said.

"In a minute, darling," Boldt told her. She pumped her way over to a stool and sat down on it with her legs set wide apart. Meyers broke a string on the guitar. Who could blame him?

The suspect was still staring at Maria when he said softly, "Jesus, what a package."

"I hear ya," Boldt agreed. It brought them together. It allowed Boldt to soften.

"But what if I could *prove* it's mine?" he asked Boldt.

"You mean a serial number, something like that? Maybe. We've done weirder things before." It was an awful chance to take. If the guy produced the serial number then Boldt would have to change his mind. Or he could pretend to check in the back and "discover" that the serial number indicated the computer was hot. Something. But this was clearly the turning point. He felt warm again. He wondered if the guy could see him sweating. "You got the serial number?"

"Better than the serial number. A password. Who else besides the owner is going to know the fucking password?"

"A password? What the fuck are you talking about?"

"The thing won't *work* without the password."

"You kidding me?" Boldt shouted over to La-Moia, who was also in a grungy undershirt, "Hey, Benny! Know anything about computer passwords?"

"Password? I thought that was a TV game show!" He laughed. "Check Deloris in the back. She's the only one around here with any brains."

Maria shouted over to LaMoia, "Hey, buddy? Yeah. You interested in my diamonds?"

"Can't keep my eyes off'em, honey," he shouted back. She strained up off the stool and sauntered over to him, brushing past the suspect on her way, keeping his attention off the fact that Boldt had gone into the back room. Meyers managed to get the rock guitar sounding like a jet airplane. LaMoia swore a blue streak at him until he turned it back down.

Boldt mopped his forehead when he reached the back room. There were a couple techies waiting with the laptop. Some expensive-looking cameras were locked away in wood-framed chicken wire cabinets. A belt of cigarette smoke hung in the air like a layer of cloud. It came from the real owner, who was chain-smoking from a corner seat. He looked nervous.

The techies had the laptop up and running, the

cursor blinking on a line that awaited the necessary password. Daphne rushed up to Boldt. "You're doing great," she said. "Tell him to write down exactly what steps to take and that Deloris will try to get it running. You're going to have to convince him that under no conditions will you allow him or any client to work the machine. No exceptions."

"No exceptions," Bolt repeated, his system feeling overloaded. "Now I know why people smoke," Boldt said, looking over at the nervous owner. He walked back into the main room.

One of the guys working undercover shouted, "You guys all on fucking *vacation* or what? I want some fucking service."

Maria turned to him, "I got some friends who are in the fucking service, honey, if you're serious. But they ain't cheap."

"Up yours," he said.

"That's the general idea, in case you're new to it." She returned her attention to LaMoia and went through the act of selling him her "stones."

Boldt was so entertained by this—so surprised at how convincing his people were—that the suspect had to shout over at him to get his attention. "So?" It worked in Boldt's favor.

Meyers launched into a dreadful rendition of "Purple Haze," badly out of tune. A woman with kitchen brooms for eyelashes entered through the front door inspecting her nails. Her facial skin looked like old boot leather.

Boldt worried about her. He didn't want any civilians in here just now. She might realize that he and LaMoia were new faces. Boldt went into the back room again and told the owner to put one of his people out front. The owner agreed. The new person handled the woman.

Boldt hurried back to the suspect who was

clearly losing patience. To Meyers, the would-be Jimi Hendrix, he shouted, "You gonna *buy* that thing? This ain't rehearsal space!" To the suspect he said impatiently, "I gotta have two forms of picture I.D. from you, and you gotta write down how I do this password thing."

"I can do it for you."

"No fuckin' way. Do you *read*? Do you *listen*? We got state rules, and we got our own rules here, you understand? And I don't got all day, neither, so move it or lose it." He pushed a piece of paper in front of him. To one of the undercovers he shouted, "How can I help you?" in no mood to wait around for the suspect. As he stepped over to help this "customer," the suspect said, "I'm with you!" He fished for his wallet. "But I only have one picture I.D."

Boldt wanted that wallet so badly, wanted this man's name so badly that he felt like diving across the counter to get at it. Instead he had to sound uninterested. "I'm not gonna do this computer shit twice, pal, so make the directions simple. Understand? Far as I'm concerned, you can come back after the grace period. Guys like you are a real pain in the ass."

The suspect slid him his open wallet. Boldt hadn't realized how hard it would be to suppress his exhilaration. He felt *high. Donald Maybeck*, he scribbled out, taking down the name, address and pertinent data. This had to be the rush that poker players felt. "I gotta have a second I.D. of some sort, Mr. Maybeck," he said. "You got a credit card . . . something like that?" Boldt had to bite his lip so he wouldn't smile. By the end of the day, he felt like telling the man, I'll know more about you than your mother does.

He owned a Shell Oil credit card. Name: Donald Monroe Maybeck. I'll have your full credit history—

taxes, debts, income. You just became public property.

It took everything in his cop's brain to slide the wallet back across the counter without searching the rest of its contents. He couldn't allow even the slightest indication of pleasure to cross his face. He drummed up annoyance—this *asshole* was keeping him from his wife and kid—and moved down the counter to the waiting "customer" while Maybeck wrote out the computer instructions. The temptation to burst into a victory smile proved incredibly difficult to resist. Finally, he faked a sneeze in order to look away. He took a deep breath, regained some composure, and returned his attention to the undercover cop.

Meyers shouted from the floor: "Hey, fatman, I'll give you two bills for the guitar and the amp."

Boldt shouted back, "Wait your turn."

LaMoia called out, "Hey, dick-for-brains, watch who you're calling fat. Put the guitar down and get the fuck out of this store. Now!"

"Eat shit!" Meyers called back. He turned the thing up loud and hit an ear-blistering chord.

Maria marched over to him. He stood up bravely. She planted her hand into his crotch and squeezed strongly. "You're hurting my ears, Beethoven. You want to trade hurts?" She squeezed again.

Boldt was distracted as well. The entire store was distracted.

"Out!" LaMoia shouted. Meyers left, red in the face—which wasn't all an act.

"Okay," Maybeck called out to Boldt, waving the instructions at him. Boldt was thinking that had they brought this guy into interrogation and *requested* the password, he never would have volunteered it. Now, here he was waving it at Boldt like granny with her flag at a Fourth of July parade. *Take it!* he seemed to be saying. Each step closer Boldt drew to that piece of paper, his heart beat a little quicker. Finally, his fingers took hold. To his surprise, Maybeck refused to let go. They stood face to face, eye to eye. There was nothing in this guy's eyes—like looking down into a dark cellar. Maybeck's breath was foul; again Boldt recalled the comments of Sharon's housemate. It was the same guy—the one who had dragged Sharon from the room; Boldt felt certain of it. He wanted to take the guy by the neck and choke him down. He wanted to hurt him.

Still holding the instructions—the password—Maybeck said, "You get the thing running, then I can buy it back for what you paid me, right?"

"Right."

"You'll look that up. You're being square with me. Right?" Could he sense Boldt's anger? No, it was the silence. The room had gone still. Boldt looked up a fraction of a second before the suspect. He saw LaMoia first, whose panicked eyes gave Boldt a sinking feeling in his gut.

And then he saw the uniform. A patrolman—a beat cop doing his job—had wandered into the pawn shop. Chances are he knew at least some of these undercover people by name. It had shut everybody up instantly. Maybeck went white as a sheet. Seeing this, Boldt improvised. He said strongly, but not loudly, "You've got no problem with the police, do you? We don't do business with people involved with the cops." He wanted to sound as if he were protecting *himself*. Being selfish. All-American.

"Not me," Maybeck replied. "I'm cool." He looked terrified.

LaMoia crossed through the counter. "Officer Barnes! We're all out of Uzis this week."

Maria Romanello laughed and started mouthing

off at the cop who, looking around, stood dumb-struck. He must have realized that he had walked into a sting, and now he wasn't sure how to act.

Boldt kept one eye on the cop.

Maybeck kept one eye on the cop.

LaMoia said to Barnes, "I got a hell of a nice car stereo you might like." He led him over to the counter. Smooth as silk, he leaned in and whispered something when Maybeck's head was turned.

In a frightened but contained voice, Maybeck said to Boldt, "I'll be back later to pick it up." He turned.

Boldt caught him by the arm. He held on tightly. "Suit yourself, asshole. But I'm not wasting any-body's time on this unless you're here."

Maybeck glanced down at the way Boldt was holding onto him. Only then did Boldt realize that he was wearing his police academy ring. He *never* did this kind of undercover work, had never even considered taking his ring off. But now it glared back at him like a neon sign. He released the man imme-diately. Had he seen the ring? Had Boldt blown the entire setup? Had he sacrificed Sharon Shaffer?

The patrolman said goodbye to LaMoia and left the building. Maybeck, still watching the front door, said over his shoulder, "I'm hanging. Just hurry it up."

Boldt could hear Daphne's coaching. Against his better judgment he said to the man, "You *sure* you're clean with the cops?"

"I'm clean, okay? You gonna do this or not?"

"Wait here."

As Boldt entered the back room for a second time all eyes were trained on him—terror in most of them. One of the techies snatched Maybeck's in-structions from him and hurried to the computer. Boldt felt stunned. He was tugging at his ring when

Daphne caught up to him. She looked a few years older than just a couple of minutes before. She stared at him. "You all right?" she asked.

"I'm taking Grecian Formula into the shower with me tonight."

"You did good," she said, intentional in her cop talk.

Boldt glanced over at the techies. "Any luck?" he asked.

One of them signaled a thumbs-up. "We're copying now," he said. Adding, "Database software, a couple of big files, Sergeant. That's good news I think."

Boldt studied Maybeck on Watson's television screen. The entire ordeal had been captured on time-coded videotape. They would relive his every move, study every word for significance. The prosecuting attorney's office would examine the tape for signs of entrapment and rule as to its admissibility in court. A process would begin. Maybeck was in their file as of now. Boldt handed Watson the slip of paper that contained Maybeck's name, address, and credit card number. "Fax this back to the office and have them run him through the computer. Do the same with the Bureau. I want to know this guy's birthmarks, if he has any."

"I'd like a copy of that," Daphne said, explaining to Boldt, "for the handwriting sample. The instructions as well."

Boldt looked at her skeptically. He didn't put much faith in handwriting analysis. She said defensively, "I'll make a believer out of you yet."

"Don't count on it."

"He's looking for you," Watson warned.

Boldt faced the television screen. Maybeck looked restless. Boldt looked to Daphne for advice.

"Make him wait," she said. "We've got the password."

Watson added his two cents: "You're going to lose him. He knows it shouldn't have taken this long."

"We *need* him," Boldt reminded. To the techies manning the laptop he said, "How long?"

"There are a couple big files. We're doing everything we—"

"How long?" he reemphasized.

"Not long."

"Stall him," Daphne said. She *ran* over to the computer table, snatched up the instructions. "Tell him to step you through it."

"He's leaving," Watson said to Boldt. To Daphne, he added, "I told you."

As Boldt reentered the pawn shop's show floor, Maybeck was on his way out the front door.

"Hey, asshole! Mr. Toshiba! Where the hell are you going?" he asked. "Fuck you!"

Maybeck stopped. He didn't answer. He looked scared. Maybe he'd figured it for the setup it was.

LaMoia shouted to Maybeck, "Hey! What do you want a computer for anyway, Mr. Toshiba? I got a hell of a car stereo system over here." It broke the ice. Maybeck allowed the door to shut, remaining inside.

Boldt argued, "You crush my stones about how important this is, and now you're gonna blow on me? Get gone—and don't show your face in here again."

Another agonizing silence as everyone looked at Maybeck. The amplifier spit static. It was the only sound except for traffic noise.

"Why so long?" Maybeck asked.

"What? You think I'm Einstein?" Boldt asked, wondering how Miles was doing. "You got the handwriting of a moron, you know that?" He waved the sheet of instructions at him. "My first-grader's got better lettering than this! Get out of here. Get gone. But don't come back here. Not ever."

"What? You can't read my handwriting?"

"What did I just tell you? You gonna leave? Go ahead, leave! You got a lotta nerve wasting my time. Yanking my chain."

"What can't you read?" Maybeck asked, taking his first step back toward the counter.

Boldt felt a huge sigh of relief pass through him. "How about you *explain* it to me?"

They worked it out between them. Maybeck talked Boldt through the whole thing. It took several minutes, Boldt watching the wall clock.

When he finally returned to the back room, the techies were standing there anxiously awaiting him. The laptop was all ready to go. "We got it!" one of them said excitedly. "We got every file in the thing."

Boldt took the laptop. One of them said, "Better give it another minute." That minute stretched on indefinitely. "Okay," he finally said.

Boldt asked, "What the hell *was* the password, anyway. I forgot to even look." Donnie Maybeck stood less than fifteen feet away, on the other side of the closed door to this back room.

"*Zoom*," the man answered. "Whatever the hell that means."

34

Inside the chilled, damp confines of Elden Tegg's wilderness kennel, Sharon Shaffer sat bare bottomed, her arms hugging her knees, her weak grip clutching the discarded needle she had recovered, her mind off in an imagined fantasyland where the cement she now sat on was a hot, fine, Mexican sand, and that god-awful smell in the air was the sweet perfume of a trade wind. Each day she challenged herself to come up with another image, for without them her mind would decay into the depths of self-pity and her body surrender to disease. No one needed to tell her—she knew. She had seen it on the streets, usually at the receiving end of a bottle or a needle similar to the one she now cherished as if it were a key to the lock on the door that impounded her. She assumed from her diarrhea that he had her on a powerful course of antibiotics. Weakness was her biggest enemy. He was both feeding and drugging her through the I.V. She didn't know how much longer she had in her.

Strength was everything. She knew that.

Her will carried her hour to hour, but for how much longer? She continued to remind herself that as terrible as this was, she had seen worse, had lived worse, for she had lived without faith. Faith alone now carried her forward. Perhaps this suffering was her punishment for years of recklessness.

His words haunted her: "Practice makes perfect." This said while he held Michael's heart. Did that mean what she thought it meant? Was her heart next? Her life?

Her years on the street had taught her some things. She had learned how to fight, how to survive, how to lie, how to deceive. Cunning, she had found, could get you out of more problems than any amount of reason or talk.

The needle remained coiled in her fingers. An eye for an eye, she thought.

The obstacles she faced seemed overwhelming. The doctor, the *vet*—she still thought of him as The Keeper—was using Felix to patrol the building. The dog would tear apart any intruder or her, should she manage to escape. She needed more of a plan on how to deal with that. As part of an incentive program, The Keeper had also left the dog without food. Felix used the automatic waterer from the cage to her right, its door wired open for him, but as each day wore on into the afternoon, in anticipation of The Keeper's arrival, of food, the dog's restless pacing increased. He would enter the cage adjacent to her, sit there and drool while staring at her. It often went on for hours; it frightened her. She would motion at him, scold him through her gag, but the guard dog just sat there impassively, smelling her. Wanting her.

What worried her most about her planned escape was the way The Keeper used the shock collar to subdue her. The collar could be triggered either of two ways: if she touched the chain link or if The Keeper used the button on the remote "wand" that corresponded to her collar. His routine was to deliver a few devastating blasts to her collar, weakening her before his entry into the cage to change her dressings. By the end of those blasts, she was feeble and in immense pain—she was putty in his hands. He knew exactly what he was doing. He was taking no chances.

It would require all her strength if she were to use the needle on him. She had it all worked out: needle to the eye, out the cage, out the door, lock it,

into the car, gone. But his liberal use of the shock
collar warned her that she would not have all her
strength when the moment arrived.

After hours—days?—of contemplation, the only
solution to this problem that she could arrive at was
to condition herself against the effects of the collar.
She had to beat him at his own game—to take more
than he could deliver.

Getting started was not easy. Knowledge was one
thing, execution another. For hours now, while Felix
stared at her, she had been staring at the chain link,
daring herself to willingly reach out and touch it.
It required a morbid perversity—a masochism—that
she found impossible to summon.

Nothing, she reminded herself, *is impossible.*

She closed her eyes, bracing herself for the power
of that shock, reached out and took hold of the
fence. The collar sounded its warning—an electronic
buzz—and then delivered its full voltage. The kick
snapped her spine straight, lifted her chin, and filled
her with a savage heat. It felt as if her neck were
burning. She released the fence and tumbled heavily
to the cement, at first unable to catch her breath—
numb, her joints welded, her muscles locked tight
in an impossible, unforgiving cramp. She only realized it had temporarily blinded her when her vision
returned and she saw Felix up on all fours, his stub
wagging, his eyes locked onto her.

She sat up, prepared herself, and took hold again.
She held on a few milliseconds longer this time, en-
dured the seizure, the spasms, the white-hot fire at
her neck, finally surrendering and letting go. Again,
she collapsed to the cement. Again, her vision failed
her briefly. Again, she was met by the hungry eyes
of her sentry watching from the other side of the
wire wall.

Escape was all that mattered. Since this pain was

a means to freedom, she would gladly repeat this routine a dozen times, a hundred. He would shock her, she would act the part, and she would be free. Perhaps, given enough times, she might drain the collar's battery and render it useless. She repeatedly reminded herself that there was no easy way out of here, that sacrifice was the only means to this end.

Her mouth was dry. She felt as if her insides were shaking involuntarily. She denied her fears. She combated the pain with desire.

She reached out and took hold of the fence again. It sang through her like music. It made her dizzy and light-headed. It challenged her to let go. But she fought it, refusing.

"Noooo!" she screamed into the gag that rubbed her mouth raw. "Nooo!" as she gripped her fingers more tightly.

Felix looked on with the white-rimmed eyes of disbelief. Awe. He was her audience. Respectful. He sat back on his haunches and cocked his head in question.

And then she realized she could see! Her vision had overcome the shock from the collar. No more blind moments. A small victory, but for Sharon a milestone.

Encouraged, she grabbed the fence again and again, her collar sounding its warning buzz each time before the voltage surged through her.

One step at a time, she told herself. One step at a time.

35

With Daphne looking on, Boldt struggled at the coffee machine, trying to turn it on so he could make hot water for some tea. LaMoia entered the office, bumped Boldt out of the way, flipped the on-off switch twice rapidly, tapped the machine on the side and proclaimed, "No *problemo*." Sure enough, the light came on, and a moment later the water started dripping.

LaMoia bought himself a Coke. The three of them took seats around Boldt's table.

Boldt asked LaMoia, "Well? Anything from Watson? Anything in that database?"

"He's on his way. What I have is Maybeck."

"I'm more interested in the database."

"I know that," LaMoia said.

"We *all* are," Daphne added.

"Go ahead," Boldt instructed, attempting to contain his impatience.

"Donald Monroe Maybeck has no priors, no outstanding warrants, and only a couple of delinquent parking citations. As far as we're concerned, he's clean."

"Shit," Boldt hissed. He opened a file folder just to occupy his hands, to keep busy. He had been hoping—praying—that Maybeck's record might tell them something about the man. DMV records—all LaMoia had to go on—offered you precious little information.

LaMoia continued, "He owns a blue 1981 Ford panel van. Other than that, officially we don't have squat on this guy. I did, however, put in a call to a buddy of mine who is able to pull credit records—no questions please," he said to Daphne. "I supplied him with the gasoline credit card number. He's going to poke around for us. No promises." He sipped from the soda can. "You hear about the laptop?"

Boldt shook his head. LaMoia was one of those cops who knew anything of importance before anyone else. He prided himself on it.

LaMoia said, "J.C., who's working the first shift of surveillance along with Butch, just called in that Maybeck already deep-sixed the laptop. He got a photo of him tossing it into Lake Union. I suppose we could pick him up for littering."

"Well," Boldt said, trying to see the positive, no matter how small the victory, "if we ever get as far as trial, his tossing a perfectly good computer in the drink may help reinforce the possible criminal nature of the data he had in there. We can assume he erased the data, so chances are that he also knew that the laptop was hot—maybe he even stole it himself. He's protecting himself. It's not much, but it's something."

"There's a downside to that," LaMoia reminded. "If he's trashing evidence, there has to be a reason."

Daphne said, "He's already onto us?"

Boldt felt an added pang of urgency. Bile stung the back of his throat. His stomach had turned on him. *Welcome back*, he could hear it saying. If Maybeck and the harvester knew about the investigation, then the laptop wouldn't be the only evidence being destroyed. They would have to move quickly now. Every day, every *hour* gave the harvester more opportunity to distance himself from his work.

He scanned his current checklist. Addressing Daphne, who was still glowing with their success at the pawn shop an hour earlier, he asked, "Do we have the count on the number of vets in King

County?" He had asked her for this the night before on the way to the gravesite. It felt like a week ago.

"Not officially, but we have a bare minimum." She hesitated.

Boldt knew that disappointed look of hers, knew that he didn't want to hear her answer.

She told him, "Three hundred and seventy."

The number hit Boldt like a truck. "That's a joke, right?"

"That's only the veterinarians who advertise in the US WEST Yellow Pages. There's probably a third again as many who don't elect to advertise."

"Seriously?" A number that size seemed impossible. It *was* impossible in terms of the investigation. Boldt instructed, "We've got to narrow that down. Fast. That's way too big a list to even *begin* thinking about." There were background checks to make, bank records to scrutinize, interviews to be conducted. A number like that would take a team of twenty investigators over six months to whittle down.

She added, "Some of those are clinics. A clinic can have one or as many as ten or more vets. We're going to need an army if we're going to go after these guys one by one," she suggested, having come to the same conclusion as Boldt.

Boldt fought to maintain some optimism. Given his fatigue, it wasn't easy. "I'll hit Shoswitz up for the army—for task force status. You try to narrow that list down to surgeons. Or maybe tighter—internal surgeons? Transplant surgeons? I don't know. See what's possible. We've got to cut that list in half at the very least. Half of that, if we're lucky."

"I'll do this during all my free time, right?" she asked sarcastically. He wasn't the only one showing fatigue.

"Listen, I know it's hard—"

"It's impossible," LaMoia interrupted, supporting Daphne. "I'm not laying this on you, Sarge, but we gotta have a bigger team. I've been pulling office hours *and* surveillance duty. Not only is the lieutenant gonna shit when he sees my overtime, but I'm a walking zombie. A guy makes mistakes when he gets this tired. Even me. We could be overlooking something here—something major—and we wouldn't even fuckin' know it."

"Any suggestions?" Boldt asked. He'd been up all night with Dixie at the bone dig. He could hardly keep a thought straight in his head.

LaMoia said, "Like you said, a task force would sure help. We could pull guys from County Police; the FBI boys would be able to help out maybe. We've got to have more manpower."

"And womanpower," Daphne corrected.

"I said I'll try," Boldt snapped irritably. "Sorry," he apologized.

LaMoia drained half the Coke. Daphne wrote herself a note.

She said, "I'll do what I can to narrow down the vet list. Maybe Maria can help me out."

LaMoia offered tentatively, "I'm overseeing the Maybeck surveillance, but J.C.'s got it pretty well handled. I'll still be putting in a lot of office time. I'm available."

It was times like this, when everyone reached deep and suddenly rallied around each other in the crunch, that Boldt remembered what it was like to be a team, what he had missed about this job. Just yesterday he had wondered why he had come back; now he wondered why he had ever left. God, was he tired.

He consulted his list again and said to LaMoia, "There's more."

"Always is."

"Now that we've located these bones, I want a follow-up. Granted, anybody and their brother with a four-wheel-drive has access to that area of the Tolt River, but I want to search county records for any landowners out there. Forestry leases—anything we can think of. We cross-check anything we get both with the AMA's list of surgeons and with the list of vets that you put together," he said to Daphne. "Sometimes people bury bodies a million miles from home—just as often, in their own backyard. Let's check that out."

"I'm on it," LaMoia said, writing it down, trying his best to mask his discouragement.

"I know that it's a long shot and a hell of a lot of work," Boldt admitted. He also knew that LaMoia didn't like this kind of paper research; he preferred street work. "But these bones are part of this thing. Dixie proved that with the tool markings. We can't let this slide." He encouraged, "If we go to task force status, we may be able to wrestle loose a chopper to do an aerial search of the Tolt region. Maybe that would speed it up."

Daphne suggested, "U.S. Geological might have satellite maps of the area. We could look for structures, identify locations, and check county records. Kind of work it backwards. Our friends at the Army Corps might be able to help us with the maps."

"I'll call them," Boldt said, making a note. "What else?"

Watson entered and took a seat in a chair over by Daphne. His glasses were filthy. He needed new blades in his electric razor—his face looked like an old weed patch. He adjusted his glasses and said, "I won't bore you with the details."

"Good," LaMoia said, intimidating the man.

Watson looked a nervous wreck. His domain was wires and cathode-ray tubes. He didn't take to a meeting like this.

Daphne advised him, "Don't worry about John. He has a testosterone problem."

"To every problem, a solution," LaMoia chimed in, trying to stare her down.

"Not in your wildest fantasies." She stared back.

"Watson?" Boldt asked. When people came under too much stress, it found strange ways of manifesting itself.

"That's not my name, you know," he complained.

"With a name like Clarence, you should be grateful," LaMoia advised him.

"The database?" Boldt reminded. "The laptop. Did you print up the database for us?"

He handed Boldt a sheet of paper. The database looked like a spreadsheet, a grid of rows and columns. There were seven columns and had they been titled across the top, which they were not, Boldt guessed they might have been labeled, DATE, NAME, (?)FILE NUMBER, ADDRESS, PHONE NUMBER, BLOODTYPE, (?). The rows were created by the names of the donors, listed alphabetically. "The minute we had this list, we faxed it down to BloodLines for comparison. According to them, what distinguishes ours from theirs—in terms of layout—is the addition of a new column—the last column over—which contains as yet unexplained four-digit numbers. This column is unique to this laptop database; that is, there is no such column in the BloodLines database. The other distinguishing feature is that the date column—far left—has also been modified so that only a small percentage of the records now contain a date. They should *all* be dated.

"It is sorted alphabetically by the donor's name," he continued. "What's interesting is that if a name has a date, it also has an entry in this new column. There are twenty-eight such dated fields."

"Twenty-eight?" Boldt asked, flipping forward.

"It's the donor list," Daphne speculated. A silence hung over the room. Daphne broke it. "Is Sharon on there?"

"Twenty-eight donors," Boldt repeated, looking ahead on the list. How many dead? How many victims of electroshock? He spotted the name. "She's on here," he confirmed.

Daphne went a sickly pale and excused herself from the room.

Boldt fought his stomach.

LaMoia killed the Coke.

Watson toyed with his glasses nervously.

Boldt waited for Daphne's return. She didn't look much better.

He ran down the column of names, calling out: "Blumenthal, Chapman, Shaffer, Sherman, Walker: They're all here." He felt it as both a nauseating moment of reality and a major moment of triumph—the extra care they had taken with Maybeck had proved worth it.

He noticed for the first time that the date alongside Sharon Shaffer's name was not a date in the past, but was for two days from now: Friday, February 10.

"Lou?" Did it show that easily? Or was it her? She always seemed to know his thoughts.

In less than forty-eight hours, Sharon Shaffer would be cut open. According to Dr. Light Horse, it was likely to be a major organ. There would be no time to organize a task force, no time to sort through a list of three-hundred-seventy veterinarians. They would have to force every lead they had. Every suspect. Sharon Shaffer's life had a burning fuse attached to it now. Look for the good, he reminded himself—they were too tired to take a setback like this. "Accentuate the Positive"—it was one of those songs occasionally requested in a piano bar. He missed The Big Joke; he wondered how Bear was doing with the IRS.

"She's alive," he said. "Sharon Shaffer's alive."

"Lou?" she asked again, sensing something wrong. He slid the printout over to her, pointing to the date. He watched as her eyes glassed up.

A confused LaMoia asked, "But that's good, right?" Daphne slid the sheet to him, and he too fell silent.

"What did I miss?" Watson asked.

Boldt inquired, "What do these four-digit numbers mean?"

"I can tell you what we ruled out," Watson explained. "We know it's not phone numbers. Not social security numbers. Not zip codes."

"But what *is* it?" Boldt asked angrily. "What *are* they?" Watson leaned away from him sheepishly.

The coffee room's phone rang. Boldt answered it. He listened. He said to the receiver, "Can't you just *tell* me?" He paused. "I'm on my way." He hung up.

"What's up?" Daphne asked.

"Dixie's got something."

===

Boldt turned the car into the back of the Harbor View Medical Center and started hunting for a parking place. Five minutes later, two blocks away, he found one across from the Lucky Day Grocery.

He climbed out of the car. A student cycled past him on a mountain bike. The tires splashed street water onto Boldt's shoes and onto a section of newspaper that was stuck to the pavement. A display ad for an American Airlines special to Hawaii looked up at him. This meant something. He studied it more closely. It was the airplane in particular. And then it occurred to him. He unlocked the car, so nervous with the keys that he dropped them. When he finally got inside, he shoved the key into the ignition, turned it to battery power, and punched in the cellular's security code.

He dialed the downtown office and asked to speak to Daphne. She had to be paged. Boldt was losing patience when he finally heard her voice. He said immediately: "They're flight numbers. The extra numbers in the database are *flight numbers*."

There was a long pause as she processed this. A woman bought a newspaper outside the Lucky Day Grocery. He added, "They had to connect these organs to specific flights in order to get them to their destination in the allowable time. It all had to be arranged in advance—the timing just right."

"A courier!" she said.

"Track down those flight numbers. See if we're right. Move it to the top of your list."

"Don't spend all day over there," she cautioned.

"You know Dixie," he said. "When he makes a discovery, he tends to drag it out a litte."

"A little?" She *did* know Dixie.

"I'll try to hurry it along."

The medical examiner's offices are in the basement of the Harbor View Medical Center. The ceilings are low, the windows rare—and then just half-windows looking out at the sidewalk. The hum of computers, the active ventilation and fluorescent lights, the percussion of typewriters, and the electronic purring of telephones were the only sounds as Dixon led Boldt into a back room, where the excavated skeleton was now laid out on a stainless steel slab.

"It's a damn good set of remains," Dixon announced. "All but the teeth. We're missing the lower mandible. Several teeth in the upper jaw were chiseled out. He used a screwdriver, maybe. He didn't want us identifying her. I *like* that," Dixon said. "That means he had something to hide. That kind of effort always makes me all the more determined." He pointed to what remained of the rib cage. "He cut ribs six and seven," he leaned closer, "here and here, immediately above the abdominal cavity. We got a nice set of tool markings off the butt end of number six." He handed Boldt a set of black-and-white lab photos just like those he had showed him at Jazz Alley, only with today's date, February 8, photographed into the upper right corner. The upper set of magnified tool markings was labeled *Peter Blumenthal*. The bottom set, *Jane Doe*. The tool markings matched.

Dixie continued, "A liver procurement, a liver *harvest*, is one of the most difficult surgeries there is. Extremely technical. It's not uncommon for the procuring surgeon to do what's called a radical harvest." He demonstrated using the skeleton. "You take far more tissue than you need, leaving all the connecting vessels intact. The transplant surgeon then does the actual harvest."

"Dead or alive?" Boldt asked in a whisper. "Would the victim have been dead or alive?"

"Prior to surgery, I can't say." Dixon looked at the gaping hole in the rib cage. "But *after* this technique," he said, "definitely dead."

Dixon crossed the room, returning with several jars that he placed under the harsh light. He talked quickly. "The next piece of the puzzle we went after was timing. In order to identify her we need to know as precisely as possible when she died—when she was buried," he corrected himself, "in order to match her with missing persons for the same period." He asked Boldt, "How are you with bugs? Larvae? Maggots? That sort of thing?" Before Boldt answered, Dixon said, "I hate it when people toss their cookies in these little rooms."

"I've never been a real fan of maggots. And I *hate* things with lots of legs. Can we speed this up?"

"You'll live." Dixon frowned and pointed to the jars. "These are courtesy of our entomologist who helped out." Each was labeled, but Boldt wasn't wearing his reading glasses. "Forensic entomology is an exploratory field," he warned. "The courts have not made it clear exactly where they stand, but thankfully that's Bob Proctor's problem. Tissue decomposition is the first thing you look for when trying to date remains. Lacking any tissue, as in this case, we turn to bugs—insects living and dead. Graves within graves."

Dixie drummed on the lid of the first jar. "We found a breeding colony of woodlice on the bones. They feed off a fungus that grows *only* on bone. It takes woodlice two years to establish a breeding colony."

"Two years?" Boldt asked, thinking he had a date. Pushing.

Dixon raised a finger. He tapped the second jar. "We also discovered a past infestation of phorid fly maggots, a close relative of the coffin fly. The phorid fly consumes decaying flesh. We're estimating the weight of the deceased, judging by skeletal size, at between one-hundred-ten and one-hundred-forty pounds. At that weight, it would take the phorid flies no less than two years, no more than three, to consume her." Boldt felt himself blanch. "Woodlice will not coexist with phorid flies, so we add the times together: two plus two—four to five years, minimum. To further substantiate this estimate, we have evidence of a beetle that would not attack the body for at least three to four years after burial."

"So we can safely say that she was *in the ground* at least four years, maybe as long as five?"

"Correct."

Dixie hoisted the third jar to eye level and said, "Meet the blue bottle fly. The blue bottle lives above ground and lays eggs in decaying flesh. These eggs form larval cases that house pupae that grow to adult blue bottles. I discovered ten such cases—blowfly puparia—in the soil samples. No colony of blue bottle, just ten such larval cases. Lack of a colony is important. The body was exposed to air long enough for the blue bottle to deposit its eggs, but *not* long enough to form a colony. That means her body remained above ground for three to four days prior to burial. Whoever buried her has a strong stomach—that's consistent with a veterinarian—and he had to have someplace to keep a decaying body for at least four days that didn't raise suspicion." He added, "And that's not easy; she wasn't pretty by the time she went in the ground." Dixon asked, "You okay?"

Boldt said, "A four-year-old homicide with an unidentified victim? It's interesting stuff, Dixie, don't get me wrong, but it's an investigator's nightmare, and like I said, I'm pressed for time."

Dixon encouraged, "Would I drag you over here for bad news? I can give you bad news over the phone. Would I *waste* your time?"

He waved Boldt out of the room and led him through the offices to a distant storeroom that had recently been converted into an office.

A video camera atop a tripod was aimed at a skeletal skull that sat on a pedestal in front of a backdrop of white oaktag. To the left, within range of the camera, photographs of women had been tacked to the wall. Boldt said, "Missing persons."

"Yes," Dixie acknowledged.

Dixie switched on the computer screen. "Caucasian women aged eighteen to twenty-six. All nearly the same height. All went missing not less than four, not more than five years ago. All *remain* miss-

ing to this day." He added as a caveat, "All but *one*."
That awakened Boldt. Gooseflesh raced up an arm
and tingled his scalp. The screen was divided in half.
To the left was a freeze-frame of this same skull.
"It's a new technology developed by the Brits we're
calling Cranial Imaging. It isn't infallible; it may not
even hold up in our courts, but it knocks months
off of clay reconstruction. We superimpose properly
sized images of the missing person's photographs on
top of the skull and look for a perfect fit. Remember,
all eleven went missing during a six-month period
four years ago. That's where the entomology helped
us."

Dixon took control of the computer's mouse.
"On the left is a frontal of the skull recovered from
the river site. On the right, a frontal of one Peggy
Shulte." She was an average-looking woman. Not
glamorous, not taken to fussing over her looks.
"Miss Shulte went missing in the Tolt River area
two years ago, not four. The county police suspected
these were Shulte's remains, but: Voilà!" The photograph of Peggy Shulte overlapped with the skull, but
the fit was bad, the shape of the head all wrong.
Dixon made several adjustments attempting to improve the fit. "No matter how we work this," he explained in an excited voice, "we just can't make
them fit. See? There's no way that this skull we dug
up belonged to Peggy Shulte."

Boldt inched his way up to the edge of his chair.
We tear people's lives apart right down to the bone,
he thought, all in an effort to explain their deaths.
"Who *is* she?" he asked impatiently.

Dixon snapped his head away from the screen.
Light flashed from his excited eyes. Once again, he
worked with the keyboard and mouse. The photograph of Shulte disappeared, replaced by a different,
even more innocent face. She had a number below

her face. How many missing each year? Boldt wondered, knowing that it was so many that the police and FBI flushed their active files after twelve months to make room for the new. Too many for milk cartons. You counted these people—mostly young women—in graves.

Sliding the color photo over the skull, Dixon said, "She was number eight of eleven." Remarkably, the two images—the face and the skull—joined like a hand inside a glove. Dixon described the fit in technical detail, his finger spitting static sparks as he touched the screen. Boldt wasn't listening. This picture was indeed worth a thousand words: one and the same woman. Dixon concluded proudly, "This woman went missing while working in the Seattle area fifty-one months ago—which fits our window of time. Furthermore, her dental records, faxed to us this morning, show fillings in the exact same uppers that had been chiseled out from our victim's remains. This guy would have been smarter to knock out a few other teeth as well. As it is, in a roundabout way he's actually helped us to identify her."

"By knocking out a few teeth? How so?"

"By knocking out *the same* nine teeth." Dixon pointed at him. "I *knew* you would ask me about this. Picky, picky. But I'm prepared for you." He fished a piece of note-paper out of his chest pocket. "I called a mathematician friend at the U-Dub—asked him the probability of the same nine teeth, and only nine teeth, having had dental work. You ready for this?" He slipped on some glasses and read: "One in twenty-eight million, forty-eight thousand, eight hundred. Ergo: Odds are there's only one of her in this city." He added, "Lou Boldt, meet Anna Ferragot."

"Anna," Boldt said, leaning forward. He placed a hand on Dixon's back. "Always a thorough bastard, aren't you?"

"Goes with the turf." Dixon pressed his face close to the screen. In a tired but proud voice he said, "The harvester kept you around for four days and *then* buried you—why? He harvested your liver—for whom? Can you help us? Did you know your killer? Was he a stranger?"

Anna Ferragot's photo showed her to be an attractive young woman with sandy hair and gentle eyes. Boldt said, "I bet you thought we had forgotten all about you."

"Guess again," said Dr. Ronald Dixon.

36

Elden Tegg hugged his wife and kissed her hello. Despite his ongoing concerns, he felt calm. He would not allow himself to lose control. That was for the little people. When he began to feel unstable, he fought against it and overcame it. Strength was everything.

"I like your haircut," Peggy told him. "It's better for the party." Her eyes sparkled. He knew what this party meant to her. Even a few days earlier, it had still seemed important to him on some level. But now?

For the past few years, every cent of his share of the harvest money had been donated to the city arts—dance and music mostly. *Large* sums of money. It made him feel even better about the work. Save lives and give something back to society. What could be better?

This money from the heart harvest was something altogether different. He was at a crossroads now, an intersection of past and future where the present took on a dreamlike, transitional quality. There was *so much* money at stake: hundreds of thousands of dollars. Enough to *buy* him a practice if placed in the proper hands. His past and present— the interdiction of the police—pushed him toward this future now as surely as the wind pushed a sailboat toward untraveled waters. There were calls to be made, plans to be finalized. A future set in motion. With each step forward, his present identity slipped further behind, as if he had divided into two people and could actually see his former self receding in the distance. Growth is change, he reminded, steeling himself for the immediate challenges that lay ahead. This woman, this house, this existence, belonged to that other man now, a person he hardly knew at all.

She said something to him, but he missed it. He was thinking. Maybeck had called the office with the message that the "truck was fixed." It meant that the laptop was taken care of. Good news in itself. But not enough to convince him that things would work out. Change was in the wind. A quick exit was called for. All predicated on the harvest taking place.

He snagged a few pieces of leftover New York steak and tore off bites with his teeth, carefully brushing at his beard for errant food particles. Beards could be dirty and foul if you did not groom properly.

"Have you decided a menu?" he asked, attempting to be that other man, the other Elden Tegg he planned to leave behind. He didn't care about the menu; he cared about the disposal of Michael Washington's body, but he had a role to play—certain attitudes were expected of him.

"It's being catered. Remember? Same people as the animal benefit. Nothing to worry about," she informed him. "I'm handling the flowers, that's all. They're taking care of everything else."

"And the kids?"

"What about them?" she asked. She was a nervous creature. He found it irritating.

"They'll be introduced, of course. After drinks, but before dinner. Allow a few minutes in the schedule for that."

"Do they have to?" she asked.

"They're your children. They're a reflection on us both. You want this seat on the board, don't you?" He stood there impassively.

"Of *course* they have to!" she said. "What am I saying?"

"Of course they do," he agreed.

"You look so tired," she said, studying him. "The color of that tie is all wrong. You've been working too hard. You might want a new pair of shoes. At the very least you'd better have those shined. Are you getting enough sleep? All those trips out to the farm. I feel as if I haven't seen you in weeks. What *are* you working on, anyway?"

"Nothing much," he mumbled. That body had to be dealt with. No question about it. But how to do it?

"What's that?"

She never seemed to hear anything he said, always making him repeat himself. He felt it coming then—one of his tics. He didn't want it to happen in front of her, because it was worse lately and even the small ones terrified her. But there it was: His head snapped toward his shoulder. He recovered quickly, but not without an ungainly effort. She had the frightened eyes of a stranger. Would she dare mention it? He gained an unusual sense of power from this tic because *no one* mentioned it.

"Have you seen a doctor?" she asked.

"I *am* a doctor!" He was thinking: *I could burn it. I could bury it.*

"If you do that at the party—"

"Of course I won't." *Dismember it—bring it to the incinerator as contaminated waste.*

"As if you can control it. You really should see—"

"I *am* a doctor. It's nothing. A little nervosa is all—fatigue. Besides, it's not so bad." *It should be done soon. Tonight, if possible.*

"You should stay home tonight. You should rest," she recommended warmly, touching him. "We could . . . you know. It's been a long time."

"Tonight?" he gasped. *Other plans!*

Oh, God, here came another one. Worse than the last. Triggered by her suggestion, no doubt. Her fault. He charged himself with a manufactured anger: "Don't look at me like that!" he shouted. The tic never came. He had overpowered it.

He straightened himself out. She was crying. She looked pitiful with bloodshot eyes and tear-streaked cheeks. "I'll see someone," he lied. *Bury it!* he thought. He believed it best to comfort her before going. He might not be back until morning. "The party will be just fine. We're both just under some undue pressures, that's all. Nothing we can't handle."

"If you do that at the party . . . Can't you take something for it?" she asked.

She fueled his anger with such talk.

"Drugs?" he asked. "Medication?" Oddly enough, he hadn't considered such a thing. "It's a fine suggestion, dear. Very well, I agree. You talk to the caterers; I'll investigate the drugs. Don't wait up," he said.

He left his house feeling very good indeed. In control. He had work to do.

He had a grave to dig.

37

Sharon Shaffer sat in the middle of her kennel pen, clutching the recovered needle like a worry bead. She kept staring at the stain on the cement where the heart had been for the few seconds before Felix consumed it. She had been forced to stop conditioning herself to the effects of the shock collar when her neck had swelled up to the point where it nearly cut off her air. For a moment, about an hour earlier, when she had first realized what was happening, she had actually debated going on with it—suffocating herself by swelling her neck beyond the tolerance of the collar. Committing suicide. But she had put that consideration behind her by reminding herself of her life on the streets, by studying the old scars on both her wrists: She had been through the worst and had lived to see another day. She looked around her. *This too shall pass*, she thought, warming the needle, awaiting her chance to use it on The Keeper. She said a series of prayers, some for herself, some for those she loved. She looked at that stain again and said a prayer for the man who had belonged to that heart.

Felix wandered the aisle and occasionally used the waterer in the kennel cage next to her. The dog was hungry and tense. How would she deal with him even if she managed to blind The Keeper and make her break? He wore a collar. One of the remote devices would control that collar, though she wasn't sure where The Keeper kept it. She was considering all of this when the heater kicked on and warmed her. It roared loudly, blowing a strong wind into the building. As always, a few of the dogs, one in particular, barked at it. This only served to make Felix more restless. His pacing increased.

She thought it strange that she hardly heard the barking any longer. It had become a part of her, like the drip of the nourishing I.V. and the pain in her side that worsened by the hour. She was sicker than even he knew.

"Practice makes perfect," echoed through her mind like a disturbed mantra. More than once she found herself with her hands pressing firmly on her chest—hiding her heart. She knew what he had planned for her. The only question remaining was whether or not she could stop him.

The ground shook. The dogs who weren't barking came to their feet and began to pace. They knew the sound of his car engine, even at an incredible distance.

Shuddering from fear, she turned to face the door, and like the others in this building, waited for it to open.

═══

Tegg was running late, delayed by his wife and her plans for tomorrow night's party. He wanted to get started with this well before dark, and that meant he would have to hurry. Deep in the trees there was a ninety-minute dusk leading up to sunset when the grayness of the air blended images, making it difficult to see. He intended to capitalize on that time period.

He intended to dig a grave.

There were other ways to dispose of a body. He might have dismembered Washington, sealed the various pieces in the red contaminated waste bags and left them for Maybeck or one of the other chuck wagons to incinerate. But that would have required transporting the five or six bags back to the clinic, off-loading them, storing them in the walk-in—all elements that afforded too much risk. He might have built a large bonfire and incinerated it himself. In fact, he had given a great deal of thought to this possibility, but had decided against it on the off chance that such a large fire might attract the attention of someone beyond Tegg's control—overflying aircraft, another hiker—again, too much risk.

In the end, he had decided to repeat himself. The banks of the Tolt had kept Anna Ferragot cozy these last four years, the soil there dug easily—though not without effort—and what was good for one was certainly good for another.

He backed the Isuzu up to the cabin's cellar door and spent fifteen minutes struggling with Michael Washington's rigid cadaver, finally depositing him in the back, where he covered him with a blanket. He was losing light; given the time restraints, it wouldn't be nearly as deep a grave as it had been four years ago—two feet; three at the most. Wearing a handkerchief across his mouth and nose, he set off, all windows down, as fast as he dared to drive.

Three roads, six turns and two logging roads later, he was driving alongside the south bank of the North Fork of the Tolt River, trying to remember where it was that the road fell away toward the river steeply enough that he could launch the cadaver in order to get it near the bank. Right along here somewhere . . .

Suddenly he noticed the enormous number of tracks in this road—a deep-woods logging road that only saw a minor amount of traffic, even in the peak of October's hunting season. It struck him as strangely curious. Then just as quickly he realized he had reached the perfect spot. The tire tracks widened here, spreading all over the road, and it took another second or two for him to realize that there had been *dozens* of vehicles parked here, and by the look of those tracks, quite recently.

Then he saw the bright orange tape stretched between several consecutive trees, with the boldly printed warning:

KING COUNTY POLICE DEPT.——DO NOT CROSS

Instinctively, he slammed on the brakes. The Trooper's wheels locked and the back end skidded out of control. His heart pounded ferociously in his chest. The vehicle drifted toward the edge of the road, toward the trees and the steep incline. He could just imagine himself getting the car stuck right here, a dead man in the back. Once again, his reactions were well behind his thoughts. He released the brakes, over-corrected the wheel, applied some gas, and lost the tail end once again. It slid so far to the left that it smacked into, and bounced off of, one of the trees, actually breaking the police tape from this tree. He saw the tape flapping like a flag in the rearview mirror. His only saving grace was that there was no one here. They had packed up and left. He did manage one quick glimpse of the area below, just enough to confirm his fears—the entire area was excavated, including one massive hole, the location of which he recognized.

All this brought back memories, rushing as quickly as the dangerous waters of the river below. This grave was The Secret that Maybeck had held over him these last four years. Tegg could recall the day with an alarming vividness.

Anna, unaware of her mistake, had neglected to latch one of the dog pens. Unlike Pamela, who had all the right instincts, Anna could never get close to the dogs, could never "speak their language," could not control them by tone of voice and attitude. She had been attacked from the back, while Tegg was out of earshot. And by the time he did hear, it was too late. Or was it? he remembered thinking at the time. The most important part of her had survived. Could he waste that?

After the harvest, he had to dispose of what was left of her or face unanswerable questions. He had driven out here with her body, selecting a burial site that assured him what he thought was complete privacy and, being near the water, promised a quick and thorough decay. What he had mistakenly overlooked on that day was the construction of a high-voltage power line nearly a mile away. A young man named Donald Maybeck had been atop one of those tall towers, performing labor for NorWest Light and Power, looking out over this most secluded of spots.

A streetwise Maybeck, sensing easy money, quickly drove to this site rather than to the police, and confronted Tegg, offering to remain silent for a price. That uneasy partnership had continued to this very day.

And now, The Secret had been dug up by the police! Maybeck's doing? Had he cut a deal with the police?

For the next few minutes Tegg drove fast, putting as much distance between himself and that site as he could manage, as if hoping to drive away from his past. Later, he didn't remember the driving or the turns he had made, just that gaping hole in the riverbank. He refused to backtrack; he didn't know the area well enough and he got himself lost several times trying to find an alternative route. There were so many thoughts banging around his brain, so many internal voices arguing that he couldn't hear himself think, couldn't sort them out. Every thought an explosion. Every conceivable explanation terrifying.

Somewhere along the way he had rolled all the

windows up, leaving himself enveloped in the nauseating smell of the decaying body. He pulled off the road, hurried into the bushes, and vomited. From the odor or from nerves? He couldn't remember vomiting in the last twenty years. What was happening to him? He didn't know himself anymore.

And what about that thing in the back? he asked himself.

Maybe a bonfire was the answer after all.

38

Boldt, carrying Miles in the sling, found Shoswitz on the third floor of an old brick ice-house that had been converted into The Body Shop, a fitness center that provided everything from a lap pool to high-tech game rooms. It was located only a few blocks away from BloodLines, and Boldt couldn't help but think about the donor agency and the parade of twenty-eight young victims who had passed through its doors. SPD had a contractual agreement with The Body Shop that allowed cops and civilian employees a discounted rate to use the facilities. Boldt passed a weight room crowded with the after-work set, grunting and sweating. Young, finely tuned women wearing Day-Glo Lycra like a second skin. He passed a step-aerobics class, voyeuristically pausing to watch. These people looked too good to be working out. *He* was the one who needed the aerobics, but he wouldn't be caught dead in a T-shirt and gym shorts in the company of people in this kind of shape.

He came here, armed with the most recent information and evidence, to seek Shoswitz's help. The lieutenant, ever skeptical of the harvester investigation, and always politically sensitive to his own position in the department, would not be an easy sell. All that Boldt needed was for the man to place a single phone call. It had to be made by Shoswitz because only he had the necessary contact inside U.S. Immigration. But to *ask* him outright to make that call was certain to fail. Boldt had to trick him; he had to lead him into it. He had to make Shoswitz *offer* to make the call.

On the third floor, alongside an office door marked PRIVATE, were three doors, each individually marked in computer graphics: GOLF, TENNIS, and BASEBALL. He didn't have to guess behind which one he would find Phil Shoswitz. He knocked and entered, stopping abruptly. The room was small and dark. He was standing on the playing field at Yankee Stadium. *The* Yankee Stadium. A series of surround screens filled his vision, the rich green playing field seemingly stretching for acres, the spectator stands rising into the imaginary sky. The player, Shoswitz, stood inside a chain-link wire box that had been painted black so you couldn't see it well in the relative darkness. A pitcher—surprisingly real—stood out on the mound.

"Oh, it's you," the helmeted Shoswitz said, looking impossibly foolish. "What's-a-matter, never seen this before? The Japs are geniuses. They call it virtual reality. That's Tommy John out there. Or at least his stats. And that's the *real* Yankee Stadium." He tripped a button on the floor. The pitcher on the mound wound up and delivered the pitch. A hardball came flying through an unseen hole in the projection screen. Boldt jumped aside, not realizing the chain-link fence would have stopped the ball if Shoswitz hadn't connected well. The sound of bat against ball made Miles jump, but, surprisingly, he didn't cry. A born fan. The ball flew toward the screen's projections, hit a net, and fell to the floor with a thud. Simultaneously, the image of a baseball in the same trajectory was picked up in the screen. It flew in an arc into shallow left field where it dropped and rolled. "Base hit," Shoswitz announced proudly. The roar of approval from fifty thousand electronic fans filled unseen speakers. A scoreboard far in the distance registered the hit, as a baserunner reached first base and removed his batting gloves. "Japs are incredible, aren't they? You ever seen the golf?"

"Saw it in a movie once."

"Fuckin' incredible. You can field, too. You know, play a position like shortstop. Genius. You don't catch any hits, but when you throw the ball, the screen registers how accurate you were. This time of year, the weather like it is, this thing keeps you polished—know what I mean?"

"Can we put it on pause or something?" Miles caught Boldt by the lip and tugged.

"You kidding? You know what they hit me up for this—above and beyond my regular fees? A good chunk of change, kiddo. No way. I'll keep hitting. You talk if that's what you came for."

"Please?"

"No fucking way. Talk." He tripped the button on the floor and hit a foul ball. "You can change pitchers if you like. Stadiums too. But I love the old Yankee Stadium, don't you?"

"No thanks," Boldt said, misunderstanding this as an invitation and not knowing the names of more than two or three pitchers, most of them hopelessly out of date. "The bones we dug up alongside the Tolt River have been positively identified as those of a woman named Anna Ferragot—"

"Old news, Lou. What's your point? I'm busy

here." He turned and eyed Miles like an unwelcome guest.

"LaMoia just got a peek at Anna Ferragot's state tax records." That caused Shoswitz to turn his head—such records were not easy to come by. Boldt continued, "For the two years prior to her disappearance, Anna Ferragot was employed by the Tender Care Animal Clinic."

Shoswitz swung and missed. The ball crashed loudly into the protective cage. Shoswitz gave Boldt an angry look. Boldt didn't like competing with a batting machine, but this couldn't wait until morning. Sharon Shaffer had less than forty-eight hours. Her chances of survival diminished with every passing hour.

Boldt reminded, "The suture? Dixie's pathology report? Did you happen to read *that*?" Miles leaned forward, groping for the cage.

"Where are you going with this?"

"Going? Veterinarians! Tender Care *Animal* Clinic. The suture used in the harvests points to a veterinarian; so does the use of Ketamine."

"This same suture is used in every hospital in this county. Animal *and* human. Do you read your *own* reports?"

"But the *size* of the suture indicates a vet. And Ketamine is *never* used on adults."

"The effects of Ketamine were broadcast into the homes of thirty-five million Americans. Listen, it's good police work, Lou. I'm not knocking that. I think we put a vet at the top of our list. But none of this *proves* anything. You want to talk to the people at this Tender Care Animal Clinic about Anna Ferragot, I got no problem with that. But talk is all, until and unless you have something more. We're not going to get a search-and-seizure based on this." He swung and missed again. "You're fucking with my average here, damn it all. Are we through here? If not, get to the point!''

He couldn't get to the point. *That* was the point! He had to take it step-by-step, leading the lieutenant into his trap.

Shoswitz tripped the pitching switch. A ball flew at him. He fouled into the stands.

Boldt and his son waited him out. Some guy in the stands to the far left was wandering the aisles selling either hot dogs or popcorn. It made Boldt hungry. He couldn't remember the last time he had eaten a real meal. He hadn't seen Liz—awake—since their encounter at The Big Joke, although a mostly form letter about her meeting with the IRS, a meeting he had missed, had been left for him on the kitchen table. Between back taxes and penalties, they owed the IRS seventy-three hundred dollars. For them, in their present financial condition, it might as well have been a million. He intended to talk to the credit union as soon as possible.

Shoswitz struck out. He flashed Boldt an angry look and asked, ''How many vets in this Tender Care clinic?''

''Four years ago—note that the date coincides exactly with the disappearance of Anna Ferragot— there were three partners in the practice. They broke it up. Two of them went their separate ways. Three clinics now: Tender Care, Lakeview Animal Clinic and North Main Animal Center.''

''So *if* you're right about this—and there's no saying you are—the cutter could be one of those three vets. So you and LaMoia nose around a little. You shake them up. I just told you: I have no problem with that.''

''Asking questions isn't going to do any good. I need to kick the place. I need to locate a pair of snippers that did both Anna Ferragot and Peter Blumen-

thal. That's our hard evidence, Phil. That's our way
to lock this guy up, to stop him while Sharon Shaffer
is still alive.''

Shoswitz stopped batting. He asked, ''Were Ferragot's tax records obtained legally?''

''You know they weren't. A formal request to the
IRS can take weeks. We don't have weeks.''

''They're your only link to this animal clinic, I
take it. So in point of fact, you've got zilch.'' Shoswitz tripped the pitching switch again. High and inside. He swung and missed.

For no reason at all, Miles shrieked at the top of
his lungs. Shoswitz scowled.

''Look at it this way,'' Boldt said amiably. ''You
can blame all your strikes on Miles and me.''

''Don't think I won't.'' Shoswitz hit a grounder
past third and seemed pleased with it. Boldt played
with his son's fingers attempting to distract him.
Shoswitz wanted them out of there. Good. He took
his foot off the pitcher's switch, turned to Boldt, and
said, ''You've been away from this too long, Lou.
You've gone soft. What's the next step? Think about
it.'' The lecture mode. Perfect. ''You need warrants,
right? Either that or you're talking about bringing
these vets in and chatting them up, and we both
agree that's no good. Am I right? So if you're going to
get paper on this, you've got to have probable cause,
you've got to have a nice clean chain of evidence.
And what have you got? You've got squat! Some suture? Some drug that's been on *60 Minutes*! Come
on! Four-year-old skeletal remains? What? Exactly
which judge were you going to take this to? Or
maybe you intended to run it by Bob Proctor, our
broom-up-the-ass prosecuting attorney. You know
what Bob would do? He'd laugh you right out of that
office! Swear to God.''

As Shoswitz turned to face the plate, Boldt

smiled behind his back. Daphne had coached him on
how to handle the lieutenant: "Let him be right. Let
him tell *you* what you need." Boldt said, "We *have*
those tool markings linking the victims. If we could
only raid all three vet clinics at the same time . . . If
we come up with the surgical shears responsible for
those tool markings, we've got a conviction."

"You're ahead of yourself," Shoswitz advised.
"It's a Catch-22, Lou. You need those shears *in order*
to obtain the necessary warrants to find those
shears. Come on! You can't conduct search-and-
seizures based on hunches. I shouldn't have to be
telling you this. We shouldn't be having this conversation. I'm saving you from eating a lot of crow. You
know that?"

He swung again. Cracked one way the hell out
there. The automated crowd let out a deafening
cheer.

"But you see how close we are?" Boldt encouraged. "What more do we need?"

"You're *close*, yes, but you're not there. You
need a witness—an employee, maybe." Boldt heaved
a sigh of relief. He was so close now. A little more
. . . "What about those numbers in the database?"
Shoswitz asked. "*Were* they flight numbers as you
suggested? Maybeck and that database—now *there*
is some good evidence. Fuckin' judges and juries just
love anything to do with computers. Can you link
that to any of these vets? You do that, you're one
step closer."

This was the reason for Boldt's being here. Without knowing it, Shoswitz had stepped into the trap.
"Each of the four-digit numbers that are unique to
the laptop database corresponds to a NorthWest Airlines international flight that originates in Vancouver, B.C. Over a dozen flights, but to only two
countries: Argentina and Brazil. Both are known

markets for donor kidneys. The fact that all the flights are with the same two carriers indicates . . ."

"A courier," the lieutenant answered. "A flight attendant, a pilot. Someone hand-carrying the organs for them." Shoswitz lost interest in the baseball.

Boldt felt his skin prickle. So close now. "Exactly. They arranged and kept track of the flights well ahead of schedule because time is an issue with these organs."

"If we identify this courier, you've got your witness. We just might bust this thing."

Boldt could hear the door of his trap slamming shut. Shoswitz was starting to see front-page headlines. "Close, but no cigar," Boldt said.

Shoswitz considered this challenge. He said, "There may be *two* couriers. One transporting the organs between here and Vancouver and then passing the thing off to a second who carries it onto an international flight. The international courier would never know the harvester's identity."

"The harvester remains insulated," Boldt agreed. "But more importantly, they get the organ to someone who is acceptable for bringing in an organ. Flight crew personnel courier UNOS organs all the time. Passengers *never* do."

"Which means we need this *other* courier—the one making the trips between Seattle and Vancouver. "It *would* be a courier, wouldn't it? If they shipped the organs, they'd leave a paper trail."

"Agreed."

Abandoning the bat, Shoswitz tripped some buttons. The screen died, and the lights came on. Compared to Yankee Stadium, this room was tiny. Shoswitz looked foolish in his batting helmet and scuffed wing tips.

Boldt explained quickly, "We need to identify

any passenger who is making roundtrips to Vancouver on the dates of the harvests. We're lucky there because the dates are in the database.''

Shoswitz was catching on. He said, "You've already done this, haven't you?''

"We ran Maybeck's name first—I was all but *positive* that he was the courier. He was the one with the laptop, with the database, but I was wrong. We came up blank. It's *not* Maybeck. We ran the names of the three vets—also blank. I want to run the names of the employees at all three clinics next—past *and* present—through the air carrier manifest lists, but it's an enormous job. Dozens of carriers—dozens of dates. It's a logistical nightmare.''

"Is it even *possible*? The courier would travel under a different name each time, wouldn't he? Pay cash. Travel light.''

"Not different names—we're lucky there. SEA-TAC to Vancouver is *international*—you have to show legal identification. That helps.''

Massaging his elbow, Shoswitz asked, "What about driving?''

"It takes too long. Every hour counts with these organs.'' You're warm, Boldt wanted to say.

"Checking flight manifests for a name common between them? How many carriers between here and Vancouver? A dozen? More? How many flights a day? Fifty? Sixty? How long to cross-check them all? Jesus! A week? A month? I'd say Anna Ferragot died for nothing. We're no fucking closer.'' Shoswitz displayed the same frustrations that Boldt had felt. Daphne had anticipated this. According to her, this was the turning point.

"Impossible,'' Shoswitz mumbled.

"But if we were to narrow the field,'' Boldt suggested. He actually crossed his fingers. He couldn't remember the last time he had done that. Miles started kicking.

"Why are you looking at me like that?" Shoswitz asked, sensing he was missing something. "Give me a second. Just give me a fucking second."

"Seattle to Vancouver," Boldt hinted.

Shoswitz didn't want any hints; he glared at Boldt then snapped his fingers in realization. "Immigration! We *can* search the fed's Immigration computers—it's a *single* database. We can search by date, by the names of the clinic employees. We don't have to deal with a dozen different carriers. How hard can that be? How long could that take?"

"A matter of minutes, if we go in the back door." This was Boldt's moment of glory: Shoswitz had arrived. Boldt said, "It's the federal government. It's red tape a mile long. If we go after it *legally*, it could take weeks. Months, even."

"Why not an end run?" Shoswitz asked. Boldt thought: Why not! Such tactics were fairly common practice: You asked a contact at a credit agency or the phone company—or Immigration—to do a search for you; if something useful was discovered, you were told to make it a formal request, knowing in advance that the formal request would net what you were after. It saved you from jumping through all the legal hoops only to come up dry. Shoswitz finally understood, finally saw his role in all of this. "You want *me* to make the call, is that it?"

For Boldt, it was like fireworks going off. A home run. "You're the only one with the necessary contacts at Immigration. I don't have them. LaMoia doesn't. But you do. I *know* you don't like this kind of thing, Phil, but we need some help here." Boldt had Daphne to thank for this; this technique had been all her doing.

Shoswitz said, "You could have just *asked*, you know."

Boldt offered an inquisitive expression.

The lieutenant considered this a moment. "No," he conceded, "I suppose not." Miles squirmed. He clapped his hands against Boldt's chest.

Boldt said, "LaMoia's working on getting the employee lists. Three clinics in all: Tender Care, North Main, and Lakeview. With any luck, we should have those names by morning."

THURSDAY

February 9
7 A.M.

39

With one day in which to find Sharon alive, Daphne, having slept for only three hours, marched into Boldt's office at seven o'clock Thursday morning and announced, "We overlooked something."

Wearing the same clothes as the day before, Boldt looked up from his desk with glassy eyes and replied, "I wouldn't doubt it."

"I know how to identify the harvester."

He sat up, suddenly more alert, and watched as she passed by him, heading directly to one of several large stacks of paperwork. "Didn't you pull the drivers licenses on the three Tender Care vets?"

"Other stack," he directed. "But it's no good. Shoswitz agrees that we'd be tipping our hand, that we'd give the harvester a chance to close up shop, to destroy evidence, if we interview them. Although the way Maybeck behaved with the laptop, I'm starting to think we're already too late."

"It's not an interview I'm after." She dug through the next pile over and extricated three sheets of paper. "He can tell us who he is without our ever asking a question." She added, "The thing is, Dixie told us the harvester is left-handed. Remember? We weren't thinking."

"But how—?"

"His *signature*, dummy."

She placed the first sheet in front of him. It showed a poor-quality photocopy of a driver's license, complete with name, address, height, weight, eye color, and identification number. Her fingernail ran across the signature. "Right-handed," she stated. "See the slant to the characters and the way the dot on the 'i' trails to the right?" She placed the next sheet in front of Boldt. She was leaning in close to him, and he could smell the shampoo in her hair. "Another rightie," she declared. "He's the one who retained the Tender Care name, isn't he?"

"Yeah, but I don't see how—"

She interrupted again, "This is *my* training, Lou. Not yours." She delivered the last sheet to the table.

Her finger traced along the signature. "A leftie! See the posture of the 'l' and the 'd'? It's *him*!"

Reading the name from the license, Boldt asked, "Elden Tegg? How sure are you about this rightie/leftie business?"

"Put him under surveillance," she instructed, taking charge. "*I* am going to find out who the hell this bastard is."

———

At eight forty-five she re-entered Boldt's office and took a seat across from him. "Dr. Elden Tegg is Canadian by birth—a U.S. citizen now. You want to guess what city in Canada he's from?" When he failed to answer her she said, "Vancouver," and left it hanging in the air like a bomb.

"How do you know any of this?" he asked skeptically.

She slid the faxes over to him, her heart beating quickly. "Just got these." She could feel Boldt's anticipation. "He's a board-certified veterinarian. I ob-

tained his *curriculum vitae* from the Seattle
Veterinary Medical Association. It gets real interest-
ing on page two. Prior to veterinarian school here in
Washington, Elden Tegg attended *medical school* in
Vancouver.''

"As in humans?" Boldt's eyes were as wide as
saucers.

"As in. He didn't make it through his residency,
which is not unusual in itself, the dropout rate being
what it is. He came down here to Seattle and studied
to be a veterinarian—also not that unusual. But it
sure as hell fits the profile. Page three: There's a doctor listed as an attending physician: Dr. Stanley
Millingsford. Lives outside Vancouver. I called him.
What *is* unusual about Elden Tegg is that he was at
the very top of his class. He didn't leave his residency; he was *asked* to leave. Dr. Millingsford was
reluctant to give me *that*. In fact, Dr. Millingsford is
an ardent supporter of Elden Tegg, or *was* until I told
him about the nature of our investigation.'' She
added, ''Would you like to guess Elden Tegg's special
interest in residency?''

Boldt answered, "Transplants?"

She nodded. ''Transplantation surgery. Millingsford is willing to talk but not over the phone. He has
a dislike of phones.''

Understanding her situation, Boldt stated, "You
need a travel voucher signed by Shoswitz."

"You're such a good cop," she said.

"We've established surveillance of the clinic and
Tegg's residence. You're on your way. Now!''

She jumped up. They stood only inches apart. It
seemed he might try to kiss her. Something inside
her hoped that he might at least hug her, but the
moment passed. He hurried out the door, *running*
toward the lieutenant's office. "Lieutenant!" she
heard him shout, "We've got him!''

====

Nestled in a shoreline forest of giant cedar, madronas and pine, Dr. Stanley Millingsford's gray clapboard home was surrounded by a wrought-iron fence with a stone pillar gate. It had a horseshoe driveway made of crushed stone and gave Daphne the impression of an English manor house. As the taxi dropped her off, she faced a nine-foot-high black lacquer door with a polished brass knocker in the shape of a half moon. The sun shone brightly but was not hot. She tapped the moon gently against a polished brass star.

Mrs. Stanley Millingsford, who introduced herself as Marion, was in her late sixties, with pale blue eyes. She wore a riding outfit, complete with high black boots. She led Daphne into the cozy living room where a fire burned in the large fireplace. She seemed upset with Daphne coming here, bothering her husband, and she communicated this in a single, intense expression. She offered tea and went off to prepare it before Daphne had a chance to answer.

Dr. Millingsford walked with a cane. He wore a blue blazer, khakis, white socks, and corduroy slippers. A pair of bifocals protruded from the pocket of his Stewart plaid shirt. He had silver-gray hair and eyes the same color as his wife's. He motioned Daphne to the couch and took the leather wingback chair by the fire for himself. He placed his bad leg on a footstool and leaned the cane within reach. "Sorry to make you come all this way." She didn't say anything. He had that air about him: You didn't interrupt his thoughts. "Your generation is more comfortable with the telephone than mine." He sounded American, not Canadian, but she wasn't going to ask.

"Elden Tegg," he said.

"Yes."

"Organ harvesting?" He glanced at the fire. "*Which* organs?" he asked.

"Kidneys. Lungs. We think it is mostly kidneys. Two of the victims are missing a kidney."

"Victims?"

"At least three of the donors hemorrhaged and died."

He lost some of his color and looked at her gravely.

"He was asked to leave his residency," she reminded him.

"Yes." He collected his thoughts. "You don't forget a man like Elden Tegg. There aren't many that good, which makes them stand out all the more. I don't mean just talent. Talent and intelligence abound in the residency programs. But rare is the individual who rolls the two together and achieves something of a higher level from this combination—call it creativity, call it confidence—when you see it, you know.

"Elden Tegg has as sure a pair of hands as I have ever seen. Brilliant control. He had the *eye*—that's the thing so many lack. Oh, they've read all the texts, they are founts of technical information, but they can't *see*. A surgeon must be able to see that which is *there*. Not just that problem for which he operates, but *everything*. Elden Tegg has such an eye, and the hands to go along with it. But while he was with us he had something else: ambition. The wheels of education moved too slowly for him. He sensed his greatness. He wanted everything, wanted it all. More than anything, he wanted acceptance from his peers. He wanted to belong. It wasn't difficult to see that. He was the *freak*, the whiz kid, and he suffered for it."

Millingsford's wife entered with a rolling tray containing a cozied teapot, cups and saucers, a lemon poppyseed cake and small plates. "You'll have to fend for yourselves, I'm afraid. I'm awfully sorry. We have a sick foal I must attend," she explained. She left.

Daphne poured them both tea and cut some cake for him.

He chewed some cake, looking into the fire. "Have you met him? Tegg?"

"No."

"His problem—and this is a problem with nearly every surgeon, including this one—is his ego. He keeps his nose high. He was quick to put people down. He intimidated most everyone around him. That had its plusses—he effectively controlled everyone, and that sense of leadership is important for any surgeon. The surgeon must be in control. Everyone must know it, must feel it." He glanced at her. Here, he was in control. "The incident that led to his expulsion is what I wanted to talk to you about. We had an open heart to do. Tegg was to assist. I was delayed by another surgery, across town. The patient was submarining—we were losing him quickly. I was nowhere to be found.

"Tegg informed the nursing staff that I had okayed his beginning the procedure without me. He lied: No such conversation had ever taken place. As I have said, he controlled the nurses. They went along with it. Tegg accepted full responsibility. Taking charge was one of his long suits.

"When you perform open heart or any invasive thoracic surgery," he continued, "you open the chest cavity with something called a sternal saw. It's a very useful tool—the sawing used to be done by hand. It's tricky, however. You must maintain an upward pressure at all times—that's the way the blade works." His hands flexed as he spoke. "In my absence, Tegg mishandled the sternal saw. He severed the left ventricle, killing the patient.

"Naturally, Tegg was asked to leave and was told in no uncertain terms that he would never be accepted in *any* residency program. If he applied, all would be revealed. He went on to veterinarian school—I wrote a recommendation for him."

"Was he ever charged for that killing?"

"This is medicine, Miss Matthews. It wasn't murder. It was a mistake. Mistakes happen."

"There were no lawsuits?"

"Yes, there was a lawsuit. That's one of the reasons he was dismissed. The school had to dismiss him immediately in an attempt to defend its position on this. To clarify it. That is precisely why no other program would have ever taken him."

She took some notes while her thoughts were still fresh. She looked up and asked. "Do you remember the patient's name? The one who was killed?"

"You don't forget an incident like that," he explained. "His name was Thomas Kent."

She wrote this down as well. She underlined it.

<u>Thomas Kent</u>

3 P.M.

40

When Daphne cleared the jetway at SEATAC airport she saw Lou Boldt and an airport security patrolman anxiously awaiting her, standing away from the steady stream of departing passengers. Boldt reached out, took her briefcase in one hand and her upper arm in another. They walked fast. He steered her over to a shuttle cart that was waiting for them. The air was electric with urgency. Sharon's time was running out.

Boldt said, "Maybeck's cooling his heels in Interrogation. Shoswitz wants you part of it." Before she had a chance to ask, he answered, "He was busted at a dog fight by the County Police who weren't aware of our investigation or our surveillance. It's a mess. There's a lot of screaming going on."

They climbed onto the cart, and it hurried off almost before she sat down, throwing her into the seat. She said, "We're running out of time. You know that, don't you?"

"We're taking an amphibian to Lake Union to *save* time. Tractor trailer carrying chemicals overturned on I-5. Traffic's been diverted to 99. Nothing is moving. There's an hour delay at least. Don't look at me, it was Phil's idea."

"The lieutenant spending money?" she said over the repetitious beeping of the cart's pedestrian warning system.

"There's a rumor going around that one of the church groups pressured the mayor about Sharon's whereabouts. Whatever happened, the lid is coming off this thing. KING radio ran a story about our finding remains along the Tolt. They're trying to draw Green River comparisons. We're sitting on the rest of it, but Phil suddenly wants results."

"It's about time."

Boldt said, "Yes. That *is* what it's about."

The cart pulled up at gate A-7, where a charter pilot awaited them. Daphne handed her keys over to the airport security man who was going to return her car to the department. Boldt and the pilot shook hands. The three of them hurried down a flight of stairs and out to the waiting plane with its overhead engine, wheels and short pontoons. The plane looked so tiny compared with the huge jetliners.

Daphne shut her eyes in terror as they landed on Lake Union seven minutes later. From the plane, they were chauffeured in a patrolcar, sitting in the back, contained by a cage, the doors without handles.

"You know, in seven years I've never ridden back here," she said.

It had been too loud to talk on the plane. In a strained voice Boldt informed her, "Immigration's computers kicked *dozens* of names. We failed to realize how many commuters travel between the two cities on a daily basis. It's a long list and it's going to be a bitch sorting it out. To make matters worse, we've been unable to get a list of the various employees, and that's the first list we wanted to check Immigration against."

"One step forwad, two steps back."

"Doin' the policeman's polka," he said, making her smile.

The car braked severely. She looked up to see they were already at the Public Safety Building. The driver let them out. Boldt was still carrying her briefcase. The frantic pace lent an urgency that she now felt physically as well. She was taking short, quick breaths. Her heart was racing.

Shoswitz met them on the ground floor; the driver must have called in their position. This kind of treatment was heady. Shoswitz wouldn't allow anyone else on the elevator with them. As the three of them ascended, the lieutenant asked Boldt, "Well?"

"She's pretty much up to date."

"What can you tell us about Tegg?" the lieutenant asked her. "And I want it *all*. Guesses, hunches, *anything*. I've got a meeting with the captain in—" he checked his watch, "ten minutes. Go!"

She had tried to bring her thoughts together on the flight down from Vancouver. These last few minutes had rattled her. The elevator car reached the fourth floor. Shoswitz hit the stop button, preventing the doors from opening. He was waiting for her to brief him.

She said quickly, "Tegg is a paranoid. He's running from his past, trying to prove himself. In his mind, he's better than everyone, yet everyone's against him. Outwardly he could very well be Joe Normal, a good doctor, a good husband, a good father. But inside he's paranoid. He thinks of everyone as inferior to him; he tolerates them, but that's all. He's quick to blame, and he has an explanation for everything. He's Mr. Right. Mr. Perfect. By now he's found some way to put a twist on his killing a man named Thomas Kent—killed him in surgery—but half of him knows that this twist is a lie, that he's lying to himself, and that's been eating away at him a long, long time."

"How dangerous?" Shoswitz asked. "To our people?"

"Violent? I doubt it. But he's worth being afraid of. He was at the top of his class, so he's plenty brainy. He has a scientific mind, which means he'll think in patterns and subsets, very linear and logical. He's always two or three steps ahead—in his thoughts, in his surgery, in his life. He's likely to be obsessive—very few hobbies or distractions to take him away from his work. He's a control freak. Millingsford said he used to intimidate the nurses, that they were afraid of him, and that fits with what I'm thinking. He still intimidates his coworkers. He's lkely to be exceptionally strong-minded, strong-willed. But psychologically speaking, his strengths are his weaknesses. They can be exploited."

The lieutenant nodded and looked up at Boldt. "Okay?" he asked. "Any questions?"

"Okay with me."

She grabbed Shoswitz by the arm. It was the wrong thing to do. "We have to bypass the red tape, Lieutenant. We have to go straight at this guy. And fast."

Shoswitz pulled his arm free, reached down, and punched the Emergency Stop button. The doors slid open. Unexpectedly, they were showered in a blinding array of camera flashes and a dozen questions being shouted at them simultaneously. Shoswitz and Boldt contained Daphne between them, and the three of them, arms raised fending off the lights, surged through the throng of reporters. "No comment," Shoswitz kept shouting back.

As they pushed into Homicide, the press was kept at bay. Shoswitz issued orders to the first patrolman he encountered, "I want them kept in the press room, understand? Not up here." To Boldt he said, "I gotta leave you two now." To Daphne he said, "This is where you earn your meal ticket, Matthews. We need to break this guy. We need for him to give us Tegg in a handbasket. You're the one who said it: Your friend Sharon is running out of time."

She wanted to hit him for saying that. Where had he been this last week?

"Don't worry about him," Boldt said as Shoswitz hurried out of earshot.

"I'm not worried about him," she said. They reached the one-way glass that looked in on Interrogation Room A. "It's *him* I'm wondering about."

On the other side of the glass sat Donald Monroe Maybeck.

Boldt had never seen teeth like that. He and Daphne studied Maybeck through the one-way glass. Boldt said, "As far as he knows, all we have him on is the gaming charge, the pit bulls. But the other arrests were allowed to post bail immediately, so he's got to be wondering why he's still here." Teeth like a junkyard dog, a grotesque gray brown. Despite the no-smoking sign he smoked a nonfilter cigarette, holding the smoke in so long that when he finally exhaled, it left as a thin gray ghost.

"We can book him on a list of charges, but none of them except this pit bull fight is going to stick, and it's a misdemeanor. The laptop was out of his possession—we, a bunch of cops—witnessed it being stolen. He or an attorney can use that to his advantage. Even with the password, he can claim someone put that database onto the laptop while it was out of his possession. Things like that are tricky to prove. Proctor won't go for it, I promise you. I'm betting he killed Connie Chi, but we have yet to connect him to it. ID has that condom—has the sperm. We can make like we're going to run a DNA typing. We can humiliate him: Make him jack-off for the lab boys. But proof? A match? Maybe, maybe not. What I'd like to do is wear him down, crack him open, and get a full confession on his involvement with Tegg and his murdering Connie Chi. Slam-dunk him."

"And we both do the questioning?" she asked. He nodded. A vague smile flickered across her lips. "What do you say I get to play tough?" She unbuttoned the top button of her blouse.

Boldt thought: So she's breaking out the serious hardware. "Sounds good to me."

She waited for him to open the door for her. He did so and said, "After you."

———

"Put out the cigarette," she ordered as she and Boldt came through the door.

"You?" Maybeck let slip, recognizing Boldt from the pawn shop encounter.

This was the fun part for her. This was where it became interesting. It wasn't quite a game, but it was close. Maybeck looked up at her, drank in every curve of her body, and left his eyes boring a hole in her crotch, so she would feel it. So he knew how to play the game too. So what? He smiled; his teeth looked like a rusted garden rake. You hit guys like this. You hit them head on. "Nice teeth," she said. She turned to set her case down, turned to prevent him from trying to vent his anger by communicating with his eyes, turned, as she did, unbuttoned two more buttons so that by the time she swung back around, her blouse sagged open revealing enough cleavage to get lost in. She knew the Maybecks of this world; she worked with them. If men wanted to use her sex against her, then she would use it right back. When Lou's eyes fell for the trick as well, producing a momentary flash of embarrassment in him when their eyes met, she knew she had scored a direct hit. Maybeck wouldn't be able to resist the distraction.

It was a cheap stunt. Nothing more. Who cared? Maybeck was punk trash. She'd seen a photo of Connie Chi taken on her last day on earth. It was enough motivation. "One thing good about correctional institutions," she said, looking him directly in the eye, "they have free dental service." He didn't flinch— stronger than she had expected. Test and probe. He kept his lips pinched tightly shut. Good—embarrassed. Ashamed, even. Nothing as strong as shame to turn the vise. His eyes strayed to her chest again, so she leaned forward to allow her blouse to hang open, giving him a nice long look.

"Nice tits for a cop," he said, striking back. "You fuck your way to the top or what?"

It knocked her back a step. When her eyes met his again she introduced Boldt with, "You guys never officially met, I don't think. This is Sergeant Lou Boldt. *Homicide*," leaning on the word as well as the table. Then she saw in him what she had wanted to see, more than a flicker of panic. She buttoned herself back up.

"You want to tell us about BloodLines?" Boldt asked, clearly knocking the wind out of Maybeck, "Or do you want to do the dance?"

"You look a little *old* for dancing," Maybeck said. "Her . . . she's okay. Have *you* fucked her yet?"

Boldt raised his hand to strike the man, but caught himself. That was what Maybeck wanted: a way to beat the legal system.

She said quickly, "Yeah, the dental work is free in the big house, but so are the condoms. It's kind of a tradeoff. Depends how keen you are on HIV. Some people say AIDS was invented just to keep the prison populations down."

"Come on, man. Hit me," he baited.

Boldt warned him, "We're the front line, pal. We're the ones who will *listen*. The next line of defense is the attorneys. Then come the judges and the jurors, the witnesses—"

"Maybe Connie Chi's sister would make a good witness," she threw in just to catch his reaction.

"Real shame about Connie."

Boldt edged closer.

"*In-mate*. Nice ring to it," Daphne said, worried Boldt might hit him anyway. Boldt was supposed to play "nice guy"; she would play tough—the exact opposite of what Maybeck might expect. Toy with his sensibilities. Turn him upside down and shake.

Boldt looked over at her and rolled his eyes. He was back in control now, she hoped. He was good at this, better than most because he didn't believe he was any good at it, and that made him work harder. Something Daphne appreciated. He listened. He learned. He knew to meet the suspect in the middle, to establish a rapport, to mimic body language, and avoid any outward display of judgment.

"You face a very important decision," Boldt cautioned him, "because the way you play this can mean a difference of *years* for you. Years, Maybeck. Got it? You may want to think about that."

"Maybe I want to call me an attorney."

"You were given your phone call. Don't hose me, friend. I'm telling you: We're the best chance you're going to get."

Maybeck said to her, "You sure don't look like no cop."

Daphne answered, "And *you* don't look very smart, Mr. Maybeck, but I hope I'm wrong about that. We can connect you to BloodLines. We can connect you to Connie Chi. We can connect you to that database. Twenty-seven harvests. Three of them are dead—did you know that? Chew on that with those pretty teeth of yours."

"I think I'm through talking," he said, suddenly restless. A good sign. His veneer was cracking.

"You stop talking, and you're through all right," she said quickly.

Boldt repeated, "Once the attorneys get into this, it's out of our hands. You understand? When have attorneys ever made things simple?"

"If you play dumb," Daphne said, "you *are* dumb."

"Talk to us," Boldt encouraged. "Tell us about Tegg. You give us Tegg, you may just walk away from this."

Maybeck glanced back and forth between the two of them. This was the best sign yet. Indecision filled his eyes, which to Daphne indicated a vulnerability and dictated different tactics.

"Are you prepared to take the heat for Tegg's crimes?" she asked. To Boldt she said, "I don't know . . . maybe he *should* wait for his attorney, because if that's the way he plays this, he's certainly going to need one."

Boldt said, "We're not running a tape recorder. Have you noticed that?"

Daphne cautioned Boldt, "He's not smart enough to understand any of this. I told you he was a dumb shit. I can spot 'em, Lou. You're gonna have to cough up that twenty."

"You're *betting* on me?" Maybeck asked incredulously.

"Betting is for *Vice*," she advised him. "Sergeant Boldt is Homicide. Maybe you missed that the first time around. You think he's here to discuss a pit bull fight? Christ All Friday, get a clue!"

"Tell us about BloodLines. You got the donors for Tegg. You offered them cash for their kidneys and they bit. You delivered them to Tegg. Is that about right? Because if it is, then you've got to think this through, Donnie. Can I call you Donnie? You don't mind? Because you can trade that down to bullshit. Even a first-year PD can get you out of that. See? But kidnapping? Interstate transportation of stolen goods—those are *federal* charges. That's FBI shit. That's three-piece suits and wingtip shoes. You know what you're getting yourself into? For what? Talk to me. Use your head, Donnie, and talk to me. Please."

"Not this one," Daphne said. "He's too stupid. Look at those teeth, would you? That ought to tell you *something*. Shit for brains. The next thing he's going to hear is metal on metal. Boom! That door's going to shut for a long, long time."

"Up yours," he said.

"Oh, no. Not in the big house. Not up *mine*, though they'll tell you it's just as nice. It's up *yours*, Gatemouth. And it's not very pleasant."

That shut him up. Boldt was blushing. Maybeck had allowed his mouth to hang open and his teeth to show. "I bet *you* like it," he said.

She struck him. She open-handed him right across the cheek. He smiled. "Don't forget, asshole," she said angrily. "This is *all* off the record." His smile faded.

Boldt said, "In the eyes of the law, Tegg's crimes are *your* crimes. It is important that you understand that. Do you see any tape recorder, Donnie? It *is* off the record. We're giving you the benefit of the doubt. We're giving you a chance. All we want right now is a little cooperation."

"We want Tegg," she explained, "not you."

Maybeck said through his gray teeth, "I can smell you from here."

Daphne reached down and found some control. "Tegg's using you. He uses everybody, doesn't he?" She tried a different tack. "How much does he pay you? What's he told you a kidney is worth? You know what they pay for them in Argentina, Egypt, India? Between five and *fifteen* thousand." She saw the devastating effect this had on him. When all else fails, play to a person's greed. "How much of that did you see? What do you *owe* him? The remaining years of your natural life? Because that's what you're looking at."

Boldt advised, "How do you think the law reads when it comes to performing surgery without a license? Tegg knows exactly how it reads. We're not even sure we can *hold* him for that. Get it? Why do you think he has you and the others doing his dirty work? Who do you think is going down now that we've busted this thing? Him? No way! Why do you think we were interested in talking to you first, *before* the serious charges?"

"Let me tell you somthing," she said. "The smart ones talk. You may not think so, but that's the way it works. The dumb shits end up investing in a couple cases of condoms and praying like hell they can convince the gorillas inside to use one once in a while." She added, "You haven't done time in this state, Donald. We know that. We pulled your prints off the laptop. We know that four years ago you worked for NorWest Power and Light. We know you haven't filed a tax return—" But she caught herself and stopped. Maybeck had lost a full shade of color. Was it the mention of doing time or the mention of the power company that had that effect on him?

"You got me mixed up with someone else," he said.

She fired right back: "What is it, Donnie? What is it you're hiding?"

"I got a right to an attorney, don't I? So give me one. I got nothing to say to you."

Boldt said, "Who's running the organs up to Vancouver for Tegg?"

A sharp knock on the door caught all three of them by surprise. The door opened. The man standing there was all Brooks Brothers—all business. All attorney. He stretched his arm to Boldt first and then to Daphne. She resented that. "Howard Chamberland," he introduced himself.

Daphne was thinking: *The* Howard Chamberland? Where did scum like Maybeck get money for *those* kinds of fees?

She couldn't believe it. A moment earlier Maybeck had been asking to be *assigned* an attorney. What was going on here?

Chamberland chided Boldt, "I had heard such good things about you. I hadn't expected something as cheap as this. A little gaming? Some dog fighting? You—a *Homicide* lieutenant—"

"Sergeant," Boldt corrected.

"You've been speaking with him, I presume." He shook his head in disgust. "You can forget all that now, of course. You would be wise to forget the *charges*. Pit bulls? What are we talking here, a hundred dollars and animal confiscation? What are you, the ASPCA? Come on! Whatever your intentions, you had better speak to Bob Proctor. *I* certainly am going to as soon as I am done here. Are you bringing additional charges against my client?"

"Your client?" Boldt asked. "At your fee? Or are you doing charity work now?"

"My relationship with Donald is confidential."

Daphne said, "It *must* be. He doesn't like that name. Has anyone even introduced you two?" To Maybeck she said, "You called Tegg, didn't you?" but she watched Chamberland for a reaction. He was

expressionless—worth every penny. Daphne felt the
frustration as a knot in her throat. *So close!* What
were Sharon's chances *now*?

Boldt said, "A few minutes ago *your client* was
requesting to see a *public defender*, Mr. Chamberland. Are you sure you have the right man?"

"Are *you*?" asked the attorney, holding the door
open for them, waiting for them to leave.

41

As Boldt and Daphne headed down
the narrow hallway leading from Interrogation, LaMoia rushed toward
them waving a pink telephone memo, his face a
youthful combination of fatigue and exhilaration.
Before the detective reached them, Shoswitz appeared behind him at the main door and shouted
loudly, "Everybody—and I mean *everybody* but uniforms—in the Situation Room now! *No tears!*" he
emphasized, meaning he would take no excuses.

"I don't like the sound of that," Boldt warned.

"I don't like a sharpshooter with Chamberland's
reputation representing Maybeck." She added, "He's
a heavy hitter."

"Agreed. We've lost Maybeck."

"I'm about to scream."

"Better not." Boldt happened to catch the lieutenant's eye, just a fleeting glimpse that caused him
to make an aside to Daphne. "We're baked." He had
worked with Shoswitz for over eleven of his seventeen years with the department and had learned to
measure even the slightest nuance in his expression.

Such a sixth sense was a prerequisite to a successful career in Homicide; it told you when to shut up and when to push hard. This was one of the times to shut up.

"I think you're right. The last time he called for all of us," she reminded, "was that neo-Nazi thing three years ago."

"LaMoia!" Shoswitz chastised, stopping the man. "The Situation Room is the other way! I said *now*!"

LaMoia switched directions abruptly. He shoved the memo into his pocket. The two sergeants increased their strides, attempting to catch up with LaMoia. They entered the large, open room with its folding chairs and tables.

Daphne rushed to a spot along the wall closest to the room's only other door, hoping to sneak out if necessary. Shoswitz could be long-winded. Sharon couldn't afford long-winded.

The room was in a temporary state of chaos, as investigators of all ranks flooded the seats and established leaning zones. There were two other women in the room besides Daphne, both detectives: Bobbie Gaynes and Anita DeSilva. The two women on loan from Sexual Assault for the pawn shop sting were back on their regular assignments.

"Sit down and put a lid on it!" Shoswitz ordered.

LaMoia reached them and stood behind Daphne, leaning against the door. Facing Shoswitz along with the two men, she said, "What have you got, John?"

"The name of the courier," he whispered. He pulled out the memo again, and Daphne snatched it from him without looking, stunning him. "The employee lists arrived on my E-Mail while you two were in Interrogation. I called over to Port of Seattle Police and they started running the names through the airliner computers. We got luck on two counts:

One, she used an airline early in the alphabet, which was how we started our search—Alaska Air; two, she was greedy—she credited every single flight to her mileage program. It was my buddy's idea, the first place he tried, because the data is essentially already sorted for you, and *bam*: Twenty-some-odd flights stacked right in a row, all to Vancouver International, all on the dates of the previous harvests."

"What's the name?" Boldt asked anxiously, cocking his head just slightly over his shoulder.

"Listen up, people, and listen up good. Come on. Quiet!" Shoswitz roared. "Meyers, put a sock in it! Boldt, you done having *your* meeting? I'd like to get on with *mine*."

Daphne, who was just about to read the name to Boldt, slipped the memo back into her pocket. She felt her face burn.

Shoswitz became intensely serious. "Listen up. Five minutes ago, a little after 4 P.M., a male Caucasian entered the Stoneway Safeway and opened fire with a semiautomatic weapon as yet unidentified."

"The guy or the gun?" an anonymous, disguised voice shouted out. It won some limited laughter.

Shoswitz wasn't having any of it. His face remained rigid and impassive as he continued, "Eleven known dead." A hush swept the room. Maybe no one was breathing. "Including two children, an infant and seven women. One of those women was the daughter of state Senator Baker. SPD and County Police vehicles are presently in pursuit of the suspect—five-foot-eight inches, brown hair, camo clothing, jump boots—believed to be headed north on Aurora around the Eighty-fifth Street crossing. You're all assigned to this one, people." There was a major grumbling of protest throughout the room. "All other investigations, except—" he pulled out a cheat sheet, "the docklands bombing, the ToyLand rape/assault, and the harvester kidnapping take backseat to this. On those cases just mentioned, only, I repeat—ONLY!—the lead detective remains active." More grumbling from his audience. "All support activities, including surveillance, are terminated until notified." That really stirred up the crowd. "Listen! Listen! This is from the top down okay? Don't kill the fucking messenger—excuse the French. I want you all to roll to the crime scene immediately, but watch your driving, especially you, LaMoia—no stunts. We want witness reports, a full ID workup; you know the drill.

"We're going to be under a microscope on this one, people. National news affiliates are already working with Public Information. This has got to be first-class police work. Let's see that it is. Let's zip it up. I will be coordinating along with the Bureau's boys—those experts in homicide." This finally won him some sympathy. A ripple of laughter swept the room. The FBI, who taught homicide investigative techniques, annually conducted fewer homicide investigations on a national basis that a even a small city's police department. The authorities with little experience, they occasionally caused bad blood by exerting that authority.

"Matthews, we'll want you to interface with the FBI on a psych—" He paused. "Where the hell is Matthews? Matthews, pipe up. Raise your hand or something! Boldt!" he hollered, "wasn't she standing right behind you?"

"I'm not sure, Lieutenant," Boldt lied cautiously, his hand curled around the note she had slipped there. He had felt her writing against him, using his back as a desk, just before she slipped out.

"Maybe the little girls' room," LaMoia offered. He knew better.

"Gaynes, find her!" Shoswitz ordered. The detective hurried from the room.

"Don't look too hard," Boldt advised from the corner of his mouth as Gaynes passed. She turned and winked at him. Wherever Daphne was headed, she would make it.

He opened his hand and read the crumpled note, written in mascara on the back of LaMoia's pink memo. It read: "You take Maybeck. I've got *her*." An arrow lead around the note to the other side where the name was boldly circled:

Pamela Chase.

Boldt aimed his back squarely at LaMoia and asked, "Hey, did she get any of that stuff on my coat?"

42

Situated in the northern reaches of the university district, Pamela Chase's apartment building was around the corner from a Greek restaurant, a stationery store and a sewing shop. It looked more like a double-decker motel. Daphne was driving her own Honda Prelude because her assigned vehicle had yet to be returned by the airport security personnel; she would probably never see the car again. As she was checking to make sure her Beretta semiautomatic was secured in its holster up under her jacket, her pager began beeping. She unclipped it from her waist, studied it a moment, and dropped it casually between the seats, muting its tones and distancing herself from it. Shoswitz wasn't reassigning her—that was all there was to it. For several years of her life she had never gone more than thirty days without a trip to the firing range. Ever since that scar, more often than that. Only now, as she faced the possibility of actually using the weapon on a human, did she worry whether or not she could go through with it.

She climbed a flight of cement stairs, a dozen thoughts crowding her brain, paused at the top to catch her breath and clear her head, and approached number six. The mail slot to number six had Pamela Chase's name on it. Daphne felt like a detective now, not just a desk jock: Her stomach was nauseated, her eyes burning, her fingers cold. She had two bold lines of tension running up the back of her neck, as if an eagle had sunk its talons there. Her mouth tasted salty and dry, and she couldn't hear because of the humming in her ears.

Everything seemed to be riding on this moment. If Pamela Chase would go against Tegg, then Sharon might still have a chance.

She knocked on the door.

The woman who answered it was overweight, in her mid-twenties. She carried a surprised innocence in her eyes, a piece of jellied toast in her right hand.

"Pamela Chase?" Daphne asked. Although she looked like a pushover—someone easily broken—Daphne put herself on guard. Maybeck's strength had surprised her. With only hours to go until Friday, February 10, Pamela Chase seemed the last link to Elden Tegg.

There was no time to play sweet, no time to nibble at the edges. Daphne had to take a big bite, right away, and make this woman hurt, make her panic. "I'm with the police, Miss Chase." She offered her a look at her identification. "I'm investigating a kidnapping, four homicides, and a series of organ harvests that date back at least three years."

The toast slapped onto the forest-green shag carpet in a wet landing. She had pinched it too hard. There was still a piece lodged between index finger and thumb. She was far from tan to begin with, but she was paler now. She had locked into a squint as if the sun were shining brightly over Daphne's shoulder. The sun was down, the sky a kind of glowing charcoal gray, like a colorless stained-glass window backlit by a low-watt bulb. Twice, Chase started to say something, tried to get a word out, but something was lodged in her throat. Something like guilt, thought Daphne. The kind of thing, try as you might, you can never swallow away. "What do you say we give your furnace a rest?" The girl didn't get it. "May I come inside?"

"What do you want?"

She felt like saying, *"I want Sharon back alive!"* *"I want more time in which to operate."* *"I want our surveillance people back. A fighting chance."*

She said, "I want Elden Tegg behind bars."

The door swung open. The girl staggered into the center of the dormitory-decorated room, dizzy and disoriented. It wasn't exactly an invitation, but Daphne followed, closing the door behind her. As it thumped shut, the girl glanced over at her, still in that painful squint.

"I don't . . . I don't know anything," she said.

Daphne replied, "It would be nice if we had time to talk about it, wouldn't it? You could lie to me, I could lie to you. We call that 'the dance' in my business. I make promises I can't keep; you repeatedly tell me that you have no idea what I'm talking about. But you're small potatoes to me, Pamela Chase. You hardly count. I haven't got *time* for you.

Neither does my friend—the one you kidnapped. Time is the one I'm chasing now, and you're in the way, and I don't much care what happens to you, as long as you pay for what you've done and I get my friend back. This really isn't like me, but it's the way I feel, and I'll be damned if I can be any different right at the moment."

The girl's mouth sagged open. Dumbfounded, she again tried say something. Again, she failed.

Daphne smelled success brewing. "What it boils down to is whether or not you're willing to go to jail for the crimes *he* committed." Maybeck hadn't responded well to this line of reasoning, but Daphne sensed more chance in a girl like this. "Have you ever seen the inside of a women's prison? You know what they do to each other in there? All we ever hear about are the abuses in the men's prison system, but that's because we're in a male-dominated society. You know what the guards do to the women prisoners? They sell them goods—drugs and cigarettes mostly. And do you know what the women pay with? Why don't you sit down, Pamela? You're going to faint if you don't watch it. That's better. You feel okay? No? You shouldn't. You're not okay. You're in the deep stuff. You're in the stuff that hardens and turns to cement and never lets you go, and you know that all I need from you is a little talk. That's all. How you got into it? What he's done? Just tell me that Elden Tegg is the harvester and tell me you'll sign a warrant to that effect. You do this for me and you may walk away from it. I don't much like that. If it were left to me, I'd make you suffer for what you've done, but the law acts in strange ways. I'll play along, if you will. You buy yourself a big chunk of freedom by cooperating. You buy yourself nothing but trouble if you play it any other way." She took off a shoe and rubbed the sole of her foot.

"Tell me about it, Pam. Tell me how it works. Tell me where Maybeck fits in. And Connie Chi. Did you read in the paper about Connie? She's dead, you know? We think it was Maybeck, but it might have been Tegg. Someone killed her. That could have been you, girl. It *may* yet be you. That's something else I would think about if I were you. Life expectancy in this business of yours is on the backside of the curve." That kind of talk was going to lose her. She looked confused. Daphne didn't want her confused, she wanted her terrified. As terrified as she was. What if she failed with Pamela as well? What then? She spread her fingers into a church steeple, as if she were praying—maybe she was—and stared over nails that needed attention. All of her needed attention. "Sit down!" she shouted.

Pamela stumbled backward and fell to a sitting position on the couch. She was crying.

"Better," Daphne said. She felt about as bad as she had ever felt.

"I don't know what you're talking about," Pamela mumbled again.

"Tell me about your flights to Vancouver. Who asked you to make those deliveries?"

"Am I under arrest?"

Daphne sensed this wasn't Pamela Chase speaking, but Elden Tegg. The girl had been coached. She couldn't arrest her for taking plane flights to Vancouver, and she couldn't very well bring her downtown for further questioning. Not given Shoswitz's edict. The policewoman Daphne Matthews couldn't lie, but she didn't have to answer.

Pamela stood quickly. Daphne instinctively reached for her weapon, as Pamela trundled off toward the kitchen. "Where are you going?" Daphne asked.

"Just a minute," Pamela muttered. The carpet

was worn in a straight line between that couch and the kitchen alcove.

Daphne pulled the weapon now, for Pamela had moved so quickly, she was already out of sight and around the corner. Her heart suddenly in her throat, Daphne edged toward the kitchen. Noises! A cabinet door? A weapon? With the Beretta gripped tightly in both hands, its barrel trained at the floor, Daphne began to level it as she rolled gently around the edge of the corner.

Pamela attempted to hide the large jar of peanut butter, but her cheeks were bulging with it. She swallowed it away, gaping eyes glued to Daphne's gun.

"Did Tegg ask you to make those trips for him?" She returned the gun to her holster.

"I go there for study and research."

"Did he tell you to say that? We know why you go there. We know the flights you connect with there. It's only a matter of time before we uncover the other courier, the one making the international flights. Tegg is going to be mad at you when he finds out how we caught you: It was your frequent flyer miles, Pam. Every trip you took to deliver those organs is listed on your frequent flyer records."

"And why shouldn't they be? I go there for research."

"Kidnapping is a federal offense. A capital offense. You understand that? Prosecuting attorneys will often trade with *one* of the suspects, but only one. The others get the full charges. We already have Maybeck in custody." This shocked Pamela. She reached for the peanut butter and scooped out some with a spoon. Daphne said, "Tell me about Elden Tegg."

When Pamela spoke, her lips smacked with peanut butter.

"He's the best vet in the city. Ninety percent of our new business is based on referrals—cases other vets couldn't solve." This seemed more recited than spoken. Daphne could picture Tegg proudly, arrogantly, announcing these statistics to his assistant and staff.

Pamela Chase had been carefully indoctrinated. Such people couldn't easily be broken; they had to be worn down over repeated sessions, and Daphne didn't have the time for that. Panic seeped through the cracks. Pamela Chase *had* to talk. People on the fringes of criminal activity could often be compromised, but those at the heart proved far more stubborn. Those who stood directly in the shadow of the power were the most difficult of all to break: a dangerous combination of too loyal and too naive. Pamela Chase seemed to fit this latter category.

Daphne quickly adjusted to her new role. Her only hope now was to use Pamela as a conduit, to manipulate her into doing Daphne's work for her. Pamela was anything but cool, calm, and collected; she was panicked inside. They *both* were! Daphne could see it in the woman's frantic consumption of peanut butter, the perspiration on her upper lip, and her nervous eyes. If Daphne pushed her hard enough, if she pushed her over, Pamela would go running to Tegg, whether physically or by telephone, and that would lay the groundwork for an appearance by Daphne at Tegg's home.

She reminded herself that people who served as other people's assistants were accustomed to taking orders. She needed to be more authoritative with this girl. "Leave that on the counter and come into the other room. You're disgusting me."

Pamela's face flushed red. She hesitated.

"Now!" Daphne pronounced.

Down went the jar of chunky.

Daphne didn't carry a purse during working hours; she kept as little on her as possible, divided among several pockets: her wallet, her I.D. and shield, lip gloss, a small comb. The picture of Sharon Shaffer was in the left pocket of her coat, along with some notes, phone messages and her car keys. She handed the photograph to Pamela Chase and watched as those eyes squinted tightly and the girl's neck flashed crimson.

It was Daphne who felt light-headed now. Strangely, until this moment, she had clung to the hope that Sharon's disappearance might be explained some other way—*any* other way—that they had it wrong. But there was no mistaking the recognition in Pamela's reaction, although she also seemed surprised, and this confused Daphne who stated, "Her harvest is scheduled for tomorrow, isn't it."

"Tomorrow?" Pamela questioned, still puzzled. Then she thought better of it. "I d-don't . . ." she stumbled on her words, "I don't know this person."

"That's a lie, Pamela. Lying to the police is a serious crime. You can go to jail just for lying to me. Tell me about Sharon. Where is Tegg keeping her? Why has he kept her for so long, when Cindy Chapman was kept less than thirty-six hours?" There was recognition of that name as well. Daphne's palms were damp, the muscles in her upper back and neck had frozen into an unforgiving knot. So close now . . . She rotated her head trying to free them. Pamela Chase continued to stare at the photograph.

Daphne said, "You think he's wonderful, don't you? You probably even think that what you've been doing is right, at least on some level. You don't strike me as a criminal. Now you're protecting him. Why? He uses you. Don't you see that?"

Pamela's head snapped up from the photo.

"He's using you and Maybeck to do the criminal work while he takes all the money. Do you know the kind of money we're talking about?"

"Shut up!"

"Hundreds of thousands of dollars."

"Quiet!" She dropped the photo and pressed her hands to her ears. The photo glided to the carpet and landed face up. Sharon looked up to Daphne for help.

Daphne asked, "Is she at the clinic? Is that where he's keeping her? If you take me to her, if you helped me to find her, you'll get off scot-free. I promise you." Pamela shook her head no, but Daphne pressed on. "Think! You're a smart woman. You can see Tegg has used you. What laws has *he* broken? But you can take me to Sharon, can't you? You can save her. Take me to her now. What do you owe *him*?"

A look of defiance came over the suspect. Her eyes flashed hatred and she said strongly, "I owe him *everything*! What do you know about it? Nothing! It's all lies. You're the police. You tell nothing but lies. Little people is what you are. Public servants, nothing more. You get out of my house. You get out of my house *now*!"

"I can bring you downtown for questioning."

"Then do it. You're not going to do it, are you? If you were, you would have done it right away, wouldn't you have?" Pamela stepped toward her.

Daphne challenged. She too stepped forward, preventing Pamela from stepping on Sharon's photograph. "She's AB-negative," she said, displaying the photograph once again, "not O. Our experts tell us that her rare blood type indicates the harvester is after a major organ—something that will kill her. A liver maybe. A liver, like Anna Ferragot. Were you part of that?"

Pamela stopped cold. Her eyes filled with tears. Her hurt and horror were palpable.

Sensing a nerve, Daphne pushed harder. "Tell me about Anna. We found her bones, you know? We found them buried by the Tolt River. You can't run away from any of this. There's no running away from this kind of thing. This is murder. At least three others besides Anna Ferragot. You think Elden Tegg is the best? Well, not on humans, he's not. These three died of incompetence—of hermorrhages. They bled internally. Bled to death on the streets. Runaways. No one cares, right? Is that what he told you? Well, he was wrong. We care. I care. Little people? Is that what you called me? Where does that leave you, Pamela? Where in the hell does that leave you and Dr. Elden Tegg?"

"Out! Get out of my house!" She stepped forward and the two of them were face to face, though Daphne stood taller. The girl smelled like a combination of department store perfume and peanut butter.

Given Daphne's present situation, there was nothing more to be done. She ached with this realization. Was Pamela strong enough to act on her own? Daphne decided she wasn't. With Boldt keeping an eye on Maybeck, that left only Elden Tegg. Pamela would have to turn to one or the other.

"You can still save yourself, Pamela."

"Get out."

Daphne slid the photograph into her pocket. As she stood in the open door, the sun now fully set, she said, "If you let her die, if you *help* him, what kind of person does that make you?" She added, "You're the only one who can save her. Tell me where she is. Tell me about Tegg. Tell me *something*. Think, Pamela, think!"

"Go away." Pamela pushed the door closed. Daphne kept her foot wedged in it briefly and the two met eyes. Then the door pushed shut completely. She heard crying on the other side of that door. She lifted her hand to knock—to try one last time, but thought better of it. The phone was quicker than the car.

She had to get to Tegg's as quickly as possible.

43

When Donnie Maybeck returned from his ordeal with the police, he found an unusual delivery awaiting him. Outside his apartment door in the drearily lighted hallway sat a dog cage containing a pit bull. His name and address were written on an envelope taped to the outside of the cage. This cage helped explain a smaller parcel that had arrived earlier, a parcel he had received just prior to heading off to the pit bull fight that had ended in such complete and total disaster. In that earlier package he had found a padlock key and a remote device for a shock collar. The accompanying note, printed by a computer printer, read:

More To Come.

Had to be from the Doc. It was just like him to do something this anonymous. The Doc didn't trust anyone. Didn't trust the phones. Didn't trust nothing. Did he intend for him to use the dog on Pamela? Something like that? No one needed to warn Donnie Maybeck about the danger that these dogs represented.

Donnie lugged the cage inside and shut the door,

taking a second to lock it as well. He tore the envelope off the outside of the cage and ripped it open. The note inside read:

Travel money.

His heart beat a little quicker. Cash? The payoff? The Doc was telling him to get the hell out of Dodge and do it now.

Maybeck practically dove at the cage. He peered into the dark hole, the dog growling at him, and spotted a manila envelope taped to the back wall. *Then* he understood: If you tried to open the cage without the key, without the remote wand to this shock collar, you were toast—you were never going to see that money. Genius! Leave it to the Doc!

Maybeck was beside himself with excitement. He had never been long on patience, and now he found himself moving so quickly he was bumping into things. Fifty? Would the Doc pay him the full fifty? Half would suit him fine. Even ten grand would make him happy for a long time. Why be greedy? But it was greed that drove him to act with such haste.

He found the key and the remote device by the telephone, where he'd left them. He rushed to the cage, the electronic wand at his ready, and frantically went about unlocking the wire door. He was so excited that he forced the key, and damned near broke it off. He tried again and the lock came unsprung. He kept one hand firmly against the cage, to hold the dog inside, and readied the shock collar's wand.

How was he going to do this? He needed to get the dog out, the money out, and then the dog back inside. He hit the button, just to make sure it worked. The collar buzzed. The dog looked terrified in there. It looked mad as all hell.

"Stay," Maybeck commanded. He showed the dog the remote device, believing this would serve as a warning. The dog growled. Maybeck swung open the cage door.

The dog sprang out of the cage like a thirty-pound bullet.

Maybeck triggered the wand. He heard the collar buzz, but the dog was on him now and had him by the forearm. Maybeck let out a roar and hit the button again. Again the collar buzzed, but there was clearly no shock delivered. As a training device, the remote could be set either way—to deliver just the sound of the warning buzz or the sound *and* the shock. The Doc *never* set the remote to buzz the collar *without* delivering a shock, because the dogs weren't that well trained.

But he had this time.

Maybeck knew how a pit bull worked its opponent: fast and dirty. It went for your arm if you were holding an object. Once that object was dropped, it went for your heels and calves. Once you were down, it went for your throat.

It was for this reason he seized the dog by the collar and pulled, struggling with his wounded hand to maintain hold of the wand. The dog's jaws were gripped onto him like a bear trap. How many times had he witnessed this death grip in their backwoods contests? How many times had he wondered what it must feel like to have one of these things locked onto you? And now he knew! If he let go of the wand, if he dropped it, would he have time to get out that door? If not, then what were his choices?

The teeth were through the muscle now and into the bone and nerve, like two saw blades heading for each other. On his knees, Maybeck continued pulling against that collar, trying to choke his adversary to pull him off, but it was useless. The thing was like a pain machine. Instinctively, Maybeck sounded the collar repeatedly, until his fingers stopped working. The remote tumbled out of his hand.

Before the wand reached the floor, the pit bull was already going at the rest of him. It got a good piece of his front thigh. Maybeck deflected its next attempt and made it to his feet. He completed two full steps before the dog severed his right Achilles tendon. Maybeck cried out again, but fear stole his voice. No sound came out. His right foot flopped uselessly, like it didn't belong there. The leg dragged behind him. He stumbled, but bounced back up; if he went down, it was all over.

He danced his way toward the window, trying to give his adversary a moving target, but the dog's re-actions were ten times as quick as his. When he swung his leg left, he felt a bite. The calf muscle. Kicked it right. Calf muscle again. He fell to his knees. The fucking dog bit him right square in the ass and held on tight.

He rolled hard to his left, right on top of the thing. It yipped and briefly let go. Free! Maybeck used every last bit of his strength to come to his feet. He aimed his head low and dove, throwing himself out of the second-story window. Nothing out there but sidewalk, parked cars, and pavement.

The last thing he heard was breaking glass.

44

Lou Boldt was watching Maybeck's apartment when the guy came out of the window doing a swan dive. He was followed by some kind of dog. It seemed to him to happen in a kind of eerie slow motion. The guy was waving his arms as if it might slow him down. Good luck. He looked bloody, he looked bad, even before he hit the fire hydrant.

Boldt didn't have the kind of reactions necessary for field work; he didn't have any business being out here on surveillance. He sprung open his car door, pivoted, and was going for his gun when it occurred to him that maybe it was a bomb that had made the guy jump. Maybe the place was about to blow.

Boldt ducked behind the shield of his car door, waited a beat, and trained the gun on the window from which Maybeck had just exited. Maybe someone had thrown him out. That was more how it looked, now that he thought about it. In situations like this there was no explaining the way he thought. Fragments of ideas attached themselves and then let go, replaced by another consideration. This by another and another. He considered his own self-defense, he considered the welfare of the innocent people on the street around him. The dog flew out the window like a smart bomb. Straight down. It literally bounced off the sidewalk, came to its feet—a front leg bent sideways and broken—and attacked Maybeck. It was like nothing Boldt had ever seen.

There were shrieks of hysteria. There was the sickening sound of the dog at work, of car motors nearby, and a motorcycle in the distance—Boldt was aware of all the sounds. There was this nauseating moment when an active imagination couldn't help but fill in what was happening to the fallen man, and a terrifying moment as Boldt raced across the street, weapon drawn, debating whether or not to shoot the dog.

The decision was made for him: As he cleared a parked car, the dog looked over—actually seemed to focus on the gun, not him—and charged.

He came on low to the ground, and he came fast, as if that broken leg attached to him was nothing but a prosthesis.

Boldt fired once and missed. Fired again and missed. The dog closed the distance faster than Boldt could calculate his next shot. He fired again wildly, missed again. There was blood on its whiskers—he could see that clearly—and a spirited determination in its eyes that pushed Boldt to turn and run.

But Boldt held his ground, his training kicking in. A man with a gun could beat an attacking dog, but not two dogs. The rule was: Two, screw; one, use the gun.

Boldt steadied his weapon—waiting, this time; waiting—preparing to fire.

The blast hit the dog sideways. One minute the dog was there, the next gone—just like that. Dead under the car, if the trail of blood was any indication.

Boldt had not fired.

The boy was no more than seventeen, Asian, wearing a winter overcoat. The brief look Boldt got of the gun convinced him it was a large-bore .45 semiautomatic—the gangs called them Cop Killers after a hit record. The gun was there, then it wasn't—just like the dog. The boy stuffed it out of sight and went off at a run.

Boldt knew the kids in gangs carried guns—sometimes serious guns—but it had never occurred to him that they knew how to shoot at anything but each other. Hitting that dog, even from the side, was no easy shot. But maybe—just maybe—the kid had saved Boldt's life. "Hey!" Boldt called after him; he wasn't sure whether he intended to arrest him or thank him. The kid's pace increased. Boldt ran half a block on instinct but stopped himself when his thoughts caught up to him. What was he going to do, shoot the kid?

A siren wailed in the distance. Someone had called the cops. I am a cop, Boldt thought. Then he took a look at Maybeck. He didn't feel anything. No nausea, no remorse, no sympathy. Nothing like he had felt at the sight of Connie Chi's body. His brain registered that this too was probably a homicide, though it would be one hell of a kill to prove. This mess before him was also a victim. But justice had been served here, at least in the eyes of Lou Boldt, and nobody was going to make him feel wrong about feeling good.

Nobody.

It was later now. Maybe forty-five minutes had passed, he wasn't sure; he had lost track. It was dark. The neighborhood wasn't interested in the killing any longer. He'd been upstairs, had taken some notes. He had bought a disposable camera at a local Quik-Mart and had tried to photograph the scene himself because SPD was so focused on the Safeway killing that only a single patrolcar and a body bag team from Dixie's office arrived to help out. In this light, he wasn't likely to get any decent shots.

He took a picture of the fire hydrant. It was a gravestone now as well. How appropriate that Maybeck had hit a fire hydrant, Boldt thought, taking one last shot. Where this guy was going—maybe he was there already—he'd be putting out fires day and night for the rest of eternity.

His pager rang. He hoped it was Daphne with news of Pamela Chase or Tegg. He had a hell of a time shutting the thing off, but he finally hit the right button.

He called in on his cellular. The message was from LaMoia, who had obviously abandoned the Safeway investigation at some point; LaMoia had a way of getting away with things like that. He was slippery without being sleazy. Nothing from Daphne. That worried him.

The message was read to him by the dispatcher: "Administration building, 8 P.M."

Boldt checked his watch: 7:45.

He jumped in his car and took off. The body bag boys were screaming something at him, but Lou Boldt wasn't listening. Donnie Maybeck was yesterday's news.

45

Dressed in a navy blue cashmere blazer, a white pinpoint Oxford and a multi-colored Italian silk tie, Elden Tegg warmed with the sight of his guests enjoying themselves. He loved the role of host, of provider, although secretly, in his innermost thoughts, he despised the pretensions of these people. Tonight was Peggy's opera dinner. Five of their twelve guests were voting members of the opera board, including its chairman, Byron Endicott. Despite Maybeck's earlier problem with the police and his own discovery that the county police had dug up Anna Ferragot's grave, Tegg attended his wife's dinner, clinging to a plan set in motion earlier in the day with a call to Vancouver. The harvest would take place tomorrow morning as planned. Tegg would deliver the organ himself. He had a noon flight booked out of Vancouver for Rio via Mexico City. His life as a veterinarian was finished; when he hit Rio he would be carrying Wong Kei's money and would have access to several accounts here in the city. If he worked quickly enough, that money could be electronically transferred before the little people had figured out how to even spell his name. That money was his ticket to buying his way in as a transplant surgeon. A new life.

A part of him recognized this as delusion. Fantasy. It all seemed too simple. It all worked out too easily, too perfectly. And yet he convinced himself that people did this kind of thing all the time. He read about them in the paper: Executives vanishing with the entire corporate pension; secretaries disappearing with their bosses; housewives cleaning out the joint accounts, never to be heard of again. All it took was a little courage, a little planning, and a lot of quick decisions.

He was focused on the upcoming harvest and his own escape. All he had to do was maintain a certain pretense of normality for the next few hours—fool everyone—and by tomorrow noon he would be gone, off to his new life. This was the way it was done, wasn't it?

"The way what is done?" the woman in front of him asked.

Had he said something to her? Was he thinking aloud, speaking his thoughts for everyone to hear? "Sorry?" he asked, trying to remember her name, distracted by a piece of mushroom at the corner of her lips.

"What's that?" she asked, her napkin finding the mushroom. Tegg's eyes found her breasts. Right out there for everyone to enjoy. There was more silicon in this room than hors d'oeuvres. More tucks than in a Scottish kilt.

His wife signaled him so that this guest could see. What a lifesaver! He excused himself and dashed off to her side.

Peggy looked radiant, though somewhat awkward, in a Japanese tea dress cut so tightly around her hips and knees that she moved from guest to guest like a hobbled horse. Most of the other women in the room fell noticeably short of Peggy's high standards for presentation, though not for lack of trying.

His wife mouse-stepped past him and whispered, "T.J.'s having trouble with the company, but he won a Pro-Am in Scottsdale last month." She scooted over to the champagne and had a word with one of their white-gloved servers.

Tegg wasn't up to this pandering and politicking. For years he and Peggy had worked so hard to acquire this kind of social acceptance, but now that it was here, especially at a time of such nerve-racking decisions and potentially catastrophic problems, it all seemed so fake to him. They had bought this acceptance, by throwing his harvesting money at the arts—ballet, summer dance, the opera—by being *seen*. By *blending in*. Ridiculous nonsense. What would Peggy say if she found out her substantial contributions to the arts came not from his work at the clinic but from the harvested kidneys of degenerate runaways?

"Wonderful to see you again, Elden. How's the practice?"

Thomas—T.J.—Harper owned the second-largest retail department store in the Northwest. He had white hair, white teeth, and wore a tailored suit from London.

"Keeps me in stitches," Tegg answered, waiting for the rag merchant to see the humor. The man responded with a slight grin, though it seemed forced. Everything was forced at occasions like these. Tegg wasn't sure what to say next. He drank some champagne.

"You did a fine job on Ginger's leg," Harper said.

Ginger was the Harper's terrier mutt. Tegg felt his face flush. These kinds of comments made him feel like cheap labor, a gardener, or a house cleaner. A little person. Tegg felt he was groveling, and he hated himself for it. He forced kind words from his mouth, for Peggy's sake. "I understand your golf game is in top form. Congratulations on Scottsdale."

The man glowed. "We ought to go out sometime."

"I'd love to," Tegg replied. He wasn't much for golf, although they belonged to the club—more for appearances and for Peggy's sake than his own. Tegg excused himself and headed straight for Tina Endicott, whose eyes betrayed a restlessness that Tegg interpreted as sexual urgency. Byron Endicott had incited a great deal of envy in the hearts of the males in his social set by marrying this twenty-eight-year-old stunner, forty-odd years his junior. It was anybody's guess as to how long it would hold together, how much loose play Byron was willing to tolerate. Endicott had asked for a telephone twenty minutes earlier and had yet to reemerge from the study. Tina had legs that didn't stop and lush auburn hair.

As he was revving himself up for his conversation with Tina, his wife again caught his eye and offered a glance at the diminishing caviar that told him his guests had gone through twenty-five hundred dollars worth of fish eggs in half the allotted time. Message received: The soup course would be advanced and served any minute. He and Peggy could work a party the same way he and Pamela could handle a harvest.

It just wasn't as much fun.

Tegg nodded toward the study indicating he would fetch Byron Endicott. Peggy acknowledged and tottered off toward the kitchen.

As Tegg crossed the foyer, a waitress answered the front door. Facing him, her features twisted in anxiety and her swollen limbs trembling with trepidation, stood the piggish Pamela Chase. What was *she* doing here? More problems? Tegg felt a tic coming on and reacted quickly as his shoulder and head attempted to meet, by hurrying to greet Pamela. The young waitress flinched with his tic and glanced quickly away, as if she hadn't seen it. He saw a fear in Pamela's squinty little eyes that he didn't care for one bit.

"Pamela? Problems?" he questioned.

"It's important," she said, maintaining her cool surprisingly well, glancing sideways at the uniformed caterer. "An emergency at the office." The electricity in her eyes told him this required immediate action.

He motioned her toward the study, well aware he would have to evict Byron Endicott. If he didn't handle this carefully, rumors of a scandal would be started before the fish course.

As he ushered Pamela into his study, his mind sorting through possible explanations for her arrival—had Maybeck opened his little package?—he tried to see this young woman through the eyes of Byron Endicott. He knew damn well the kinds of things that would be said about them if he failed to handle this correctly. But he didn't care. Let them talk. By tomorrow, a new life.

Control, he reminded himself, feeling another tic coming on but refusing it, as if slamming a door in its face. Unknowingly, he slammed the door to his study. It made a tremendous crash. Pamela jumped. Old man Endicott mumbled into the receiver and hung up. He rose to his feet and came around the desk with a suspicious, irreverent expression. "And who is this lovely creature?" he asked Pamela.

Tegg experienced a flash of embarrassment. He said, "This is my surgical assistant, Pamela Chase. Byron Endicott," he said, indicating the old man. "I'm afraid something has come up at the clinic, Byron. We'll need the study for a moment if you don't mind."

"Enchanté," Endicott said, taking her hand. "Not Douglas Chase's little girl?"

"Yes," Pamela said, looking to Tegg nervously.

"And such a lovely young woman!" he lied. "Last time I saw you . . . But just look at you!" he said, leering artificially.

She blushed.

Endicott grinned at Tegg. "I'll leave you two," he said, his implication obvious. "But you *must* introduce her around, Elden, or I'll raise a stink. I *promise*." To Pamela he said, "We are all very close friends of your parents. You really *must* say hello before you leave."

Endicott smirked, gave Tegg a teasing, nasty look, and let himself out of the room.

"I'm sorry for coming," she said.

"Not to worry," Tegg replied. "You look awful. What is it?" He closed the door tightly, a dozen thoughts crowding his brain.

"The police came to my apartment asking about my trips to Vancouver."

At first he couldn't be sure he had heard her right, but from her grave expression, from the constriction in his own chest, he knew that indeed he had. He felt the betraying savagery of two tics overcome him—like two sharp bolts of electricity. He fell into a chair. His blood banged so loudly in his ears he couldn't hear what she said next. First Maybeck, now Pamela. Too close. Much too close. There was no time to waste. He began plotting immediately.

"They know about everything," she said. "They offered me a deal if I gave them you."

Had Maybeck *talked*? His attorney, Howard Chamberland, had assured him everything was fine—Maybeck had been released on a misdemeanor charge. His palms went clammy. *Control*! he reminded himself again, answering her perplexed and ghostly gaze with a squaring of his shoulders and a lifting of his chin. The police moved about as fast as languishing sea lions, certainly no match for his latest plans. No reason to panic. Evaluate the situation. Analyze. Indecision was anyone's biggest enemy. He had contingencies.

He looked into her dark, squinting eyes and thought about telling her of his plan to escape. But that would include the harvesting of the heart, and she didn't approve of that—she might even betray him if she knew about the heart. No, better to calm her and be rid of her. Tomorrow morning would come soon enough.

"Sit down," he told her. "Good. Can I get you something to drink? A pop? I want you to relax, calm down. You're with me now, you're all right."

"She's *pretty*. More than pretty. Dark hair. Taller than me. Beautiful eyes."

"A woman?" he asked stupidly. The idea that a woman had questioned her seemed so much less threatening to him than had it been a man. Why, he wasn't sure.

He knew how she hated pretty women. She felt betrayed by her weight problem, failing to see it as a disease, but instead as a weakness of character, an attitude that had been drummed into her by her inept parents.

"I have to interrupt here," he said, doing so. "Forgive me, please, but the details are quite unimportant to me. They didn't arrest you, did they? And there's a reason for that: They haven't got anything of any value on us. Suspicions is all. We've talked about this before, but what's important to remember with the police is that if you don't talk to them, there's nothing they can learn from you. It's hard, I know," he said, reaching over and touching her knee. "Terribly difficult. But true."

"She mentioned the harvests. She said three of the donors had died from hemorrhaging."

He couldn't catch his breath. Failure? Footsteps in the foyer, drawing closer. They wanted him at the table, no doubt. It suddenly felt as if the room were smaller, the walls closing in. Yes. He could feel the walls moving closer. *Control!*

A knock like a knife in his chest. Not now! He glanced toward the door, tried to lift himself from his chair, but couldn't move. Such helplessness was foreign to him: It was always the patient that was paralyzed, never him. Pamela rose effortlessly to answer the door, and this inspired Tegg's limbs to obey. He reached out and stopped her as he came to his feet, reminding himself that the sure sign of superiority is the ability to overcome. Performance—*appearance*—was everything.

When he opened the door he felt relief to find one of the waitresses staring back at him. He had somehow expected his wife and had no desire to face her at this particular moment. He could picture her at the end of the dining table, facing his empty place,

crazed with rage and yet politely fielding conversation and graciously offering the bread basket to her
guests.

"The soup is served, Dr. Tegg. Mrs. Tegg asked
me to tell you."

"Please have them start without me, would you?
Just a little business matter to clear up. I won't be
but a minute." It was an easy absence to explain. As
the only vet in the clinic, he was constantly on-call.
He responded at all hours to emergencies of every
sort. It was perfectly normal for him to be summoned in the evening hours to handle an emergency. Tonight, rather than drag him downtown,
when he was in the midst of an important dinner
party, his assistant had had the good sense to seek
his advice in person so as to occupy as little of his
time as possible.

He shut the door and asked Pamela, "Hemorrhaging? That's impossible! Must be some sort of
trick, saying such a thing. Trying to rattle you."

"I don't think so. She sounded serious. She said
the investigation is being run by Homicide."

The word reminded him of Maybeck, of sending
that package to the man. He regretted that now. He
had regretted that only a moment after he had
turned it over to the delivery boy. But it was done.

"Maybeck's fault," he said, the idea taking hold,
and coming as a great relief. "If he mistreated the
donors in any way . . . Once the patient is out of
our control, out of our care, we can't be expected to
monitor his or her every move, can we? Of course
not! The wrong activity too soon and something is
bound to come loose. They were told how to take
care of themselves. We can't babysit every last patient, now can we?"

Pamela said flatly, "She showed me a picture of
a woman. Sharon, the same woman we did the kid-

ney on last *Saturday*. I remember her name. I remember that night very well, very clearly, as you can imagine I would. And I remember seeing a sponge, and her chest being damp, and now I have to wonder, with Betadyne? Was *that* why her kidney wasn't prepped? Was that why you did what you did to me, what we did, to *distract* me? She said that Sharon had disappeared, and that's not right for a kidney. It's a heart, isn't it, Elden? AB-negative, she said, and all I could think of was a heart."

His own heart responded like a chorus of timpani.

"You don't need to answer because *I know*. How many times have you tried to convince me to do a heart? And just yesterday, you took that dog's heart. What's happening? Have you done it already? Have you?"

"This doesn't involve you," he warned.

"Doesn't *involve me*?" she questioned. "Where is that coming from? Get a clue!"

His anger surfaced but he contained it. She was just a child. "We have talked about this. I don't accept your arguments. You know that. I have heard them a dozen times. What you can't face is that I *might be right*! Admit it!"

"I won't tell them anything. You know I won't. I owe you that. But I'm scared. For you. For me. I'm not sure what to do. They know about the trips to Vancouver. They know about all of it. We have to do *something*! They're not just going to go away."

"You're missing the central point."

"Which is?"

"Which is that if they had anything, you wouldn't be sitting here talking to me."

Panic struck him. What if she had *already* cut a deal with them? What if she were wearing a microphone, the police standing ready outside his door?

He stood and edged around his desk, taking a quick but useless look outside. It was rainy and dark. He couldn't see anything but a driveway full of cars. He approached her from behind then and stroked her hair. She liked it. She leaned her head back and looked up at him. He bent over feigning a kiss and ran his hand over her chest and abdomen, secretly searching for an unwarranted bump that might alert him to a wire or a microphone. He leaned her forward and massaged her neck and back, searching here as well. Nothing. Perhaps she was loyal to him after all.

He continued, "If they had anything at all, they would be doing more than asking questions. They're nosing around, is all. They earn their living nosing around. Our tax dollars, mind you!" He was losing focus. "Granted, they're obviously on the right track. I'll give you that. I'll concede that much. But where are the charges? Why haven't they questioned me? You see? They're tiptoeing around, is all. We mustn't give in to that. And besides, we've talked about this before, haven't we? Of course we have. We have even *anticipated* such a moment. Hmm? The lab at the farm can be dismantled in a matter of a few hours. We're prepared for that. No problem. Where's the evidence to come from?" It was true: If he dismantled the farm's surgical facility, if Pam remained loyal, what was left for the police? He said, "I don't think this is nearly as bad as it looks, my dear. Hmm? Not nearly as bad as it looks. The important thing is to stay calm. With that in mind, stay where you are. I'll be right back."

No matter what his plans, he needed Pamela sedated for the rest of the night. Out of the way. Incapable of fouling the waters.

He hurried out into the garage and rummaged through the veterinarian supplies he kept in the re-

frigerated insert in back of the Isuzu. The only seda-
tives he had on hand were for intravenous use, but
he located an oral supply of Valium in dosages
strong enough for a mastiff. He grabbed two capsules
and hurried back to the study, carefully avoiding the
dining room and his guests.

"There's nothing to worry about, I promise," he
said upon returning. He extended the pills to her.
"Take these, they'll help you relax."

"No thanks."

"Take them. Go on." He handed her his champagne glass. "They'll put your mind at rest. There is
a course through every storm. Go home. Put your
feet up."

She studied the pills. "That's a lot of Valium."

"Trust me."

"I'd rather . . ."

"Pamela, take the medicine!"

She tossed the pills into her mouth and chased
them down with the champagne.

"Drive directly home. Have you eaten anything?"

She nodded.

"Good. Drive straight home for safety's sake,
though you're unlikely to feel them for forty-five
minutes or so. Take a hot bath. Relax. We'll talk in
the morning. Okay?" He lifted her chin with his
finger and looked her in the eye. "It was smart of
you to come here. I'm not mad at you at all. But it's
important to keep perspective. Hmm? You must not
speak with the police again. Not for any reason.
They will only attempt to unsettle you. You mustn't
allow that. Do you hear me, Pamela?"

She nodded again.

"Good. Any problems?"

She shook her head. She looked a little angry. A
little sad. She hadn't wanted to take the pills—that

was it. Or was it? He couldn't tell. "Off you go," he said, offering her his hand.

She said nothing. He had wounded her. Oh well, the Valium would improve things shortly.

He saw her to the front door. She hurried through the rain toward her car.

Tegg heard the idle chatter of his guests from behind him. Could he endure a meal with these people given his present state of anxiety? Did he have any choice?

46

Sitting behind the wheel of her Honda Prelude, taking notes by the limited light of a Shore Drive streetlamp in the Broadmoor Estates, Daphne heard a man's voice call out. She looked up in time to see Pamela Chase hurry through the rain and climb into her car.

Daphne felt impatient, isolated, angry, and even a little afraid. Shoswitz's cut in manpower was going to cost Sharon her life. That was the way it now seemed. The political pressures and responsibilities resulting from the Safeway killings had proved too much for him to bear. The one loser in all of this was Sharon. The frustration of being confined to a front seat, taking notes, drove Daphne into a rage. It was time to *do* something.

Pamela's car started. The lights went on, illuminating the thick landscape vegetation that separated the large, water-view homes from their neighbors. Tegg's house was rich with arched leaded-glass windows, a full turret and a section of battlement along the roof to complete the look of a castle. It had a red slate roof, two chimneys and a weather vane. This wasn't the Volvo and Cherokee set, but the Beamers and Jags. Second homes on Decatur Northwest, twenty-year anniversaries, Ralph Lauren to wear for the Saturday chores, private clubs and political contributions. These were the people that as a cop you were careful with, the kind who knew how to make trouble.

Daphne faced a difficult decision: Pursue Pamela Chase or stay with Tegg? When Pamela had arrived here only minutes after she had, Daphne had felt an initial sense of accomplishment and success in her interrogation of the woman. This was the exact pressure she had hoped to effect: to send Pamela running to Tegg. Her notes carefully marked the time of the girl's arrival, duration of stay, and time of departure. The courts weren't going to catch Daphne on any technicalities. She intended to cover herself well. But now what?

Her impatience urged her to follow, to do *something*. She ignored it, staying with her earlier belief that not Pamela Chase but either Tegg or Maybeck would be responsible for holding Sharon hostage. Her hunch was that Tegg would insulate himself by using Maybeck; Boldt had that assignment, and she, every confidence in him. Pamela had alerted Tegg; now perhaps Tegg would alert Maybeck, who in turn would lead Boldt to Sharon. Maybe they would get lucky. Maybe it was just too much of a long shot to hope for.

She checked her watch: in four hours, at midnight, it would be February 10, the day listed in the database for Sharon's harvest. Sometime in the morning seemed a more likely time for Tegg to do the harvest, given that a party was now under way in his house. She would fight to keep herself awake.

She wished like hell she had either her police radio or cellular phone—being out of communication was the hardest thing of all.

The taillights of Pamela Chase's car receded and then disappeared from view.

Daphne longingly watched them go, wondering whether along with them went Sharon Shaffer's only chance of survival.

47

"Please pass the butter."

Tegg handed the butter dish to the woman with the showy breasts, still unable to recall her name. He had no idea what the table's present topic was and didn't care. Planning his escape occupied him fully. Peggy was happily yukking it up with Byron Endicott. She would do anything for this opera board seat. Strange how petty it all seemed to Tegg now. Why on earth had he ever given that kind of money away? What had possessed him to try to be the philanthropic veterinarian of King County? What an absurdity! All so that his wife would play in the right bridge circles? What did any of it matter? There was life and death at stake here. There was that package he had sent to Maybeck. The police!

Homicide? Had they traced the pit bull back to Tegg that quickly? He refused to believe it! He had taken such care to wipe down the cage, wear gloves, print everything on the HP printer, write nothing by hand; neither the collar, its batteries, or the wand had any kind of serial number. There was no paperwork with the delivery company; he had used one of those fly-by-night outfits in the International District, dropping it off with them to avoid a pickup. He has thought it through so carefully.

"Salt please."

The salt was about six inches from this fool's hand! What did he want, someone to shake it for him? Losing his temper, Tegg did just that. He seized the shaker and sent salt flying all over this man's food. He caught himself, but too late. He apologized, poured the man some Pine Ridge Merlot and, empty bottle in hand, excused himself from the table. He didn't dare look at Peggy.

On his way into the kitchen, he sorted back through his brief but intense encounter with Pamela, searching for any possible mistakes he might have made.

He sat down at a stool in the kitchen. One of the kitchen help said something to him, but he waved him away. Then he thought better of it and asked for some more wine. "And the table's out too," he told no one in particular.

The Valiums were a hell of a good idea, he congratulated himself. That dosage would knock her sideways. He decided that it might be a good idea to check up on her—to make sure she got home okay, to calm her down if the pills hadn't already done so. She wouldn't be feeling them for another few minutes; maybe she needed someone to talk to.

He took his wine with him into the garage, electing to use the cellular in the Isuzu because of his belief in the difficulty the police had listening in on such lines. He eased the seat back, dialed the number, and pushed SND. God, it felt good to be away from those hypocrites in there. He took a big swig of wine and felt his first sense of real relief in hours.

Her answering machine answered.

This troubled him. His heart quickened. He thought himself stupid for forcing the Valium on her while she still had to drive home. He should have just given them to her for her to take once there. But, he recalled, he had wanted to ensure she had taken them. He didn't want her mucking about tonight, messing things up.

Had the cops gotten hold of her?

He sat up and spilled some wine into his lap. In that condition she might tell them *everything*! What had he been thinking by giving her Valium? Another thirty minutes, she'd be a tongue-wagging wreck. He should have stuck with his plan to sedate her! He had wanted her out, not brain-impaired!

A voice from within told him to calm down. Control! She was probably just on the can and couldn't make it to the phone.

He dialed her number again. It rang four times and the machine answered.

"Shit," he said into the receiver.

Maybe, his voice of reason argued, she was high *already* and had simply turned the phone off. Yes, that made some sense. Lying back with headphones on, or watching a movie on the tube. Valium behavior.

He sipped what was left of the wine, not feeling good about any of this. Slowly, his mind reconstructed a vivid memory of their final few minutes together. He could see her, could hear the conversation like a videotape playing inside his head. Had she ever spoken, ever opened her mouth *after* he had fed her those pills? Had she in fact swallowed them?

What if she had *not* taken the Valium but tricked him into believing she had? Where would she go? What would she do?

The police?

The farm!

A tic hit him so hard he heard his neck crack. The wineglass jumped from his hand, struck the gear shift and shattered.

The farm!

He tripped the garage door automatic opener. It groaned open slowly. He couldn't believe how slowly. This thing had never run this slowly! What would he need? Had he forgotten anything?

The party!

The garage door opened far enough to reveal four cars parked in the drive, more out on the road. Trapped?

The door to the kitchen opened. Peggy, in her red Japanese tea dress and her scarlet red face.

What could he say? At this point, what could he do?

Take control.

There was a pretty good gap between the first parked car and the garage. Maybe just enough.

Tegg backed slowly across the wet lawn, the tires cutting deep ruts in the grass, his guests observing him through the window. The four-wheel-drive banged out onto the street, and he was off.

To Pamela's? No, he decided. *Priorities.* He would keep calling. The farm was far more important.

Indeed, the farm was everything.

48

The Isuzu backed across the lawn, its tires spraying mud in all directions. Daphne could barely make out a bearded man's face behind the wheel. Elden Tegg.

She slumped in her seat, dropping low, placed her fingers on the key and waited. His headlights washed the interior of her car, hurting her eyes. She remained absolutely still. She thought her heart might explode.

He passed.

She counted to three and started the car, lifting just high enough to watch his departure in her door mirror. The second he passed out of sight, she dropped the Honda into gear and pulled one of the quickest three-point turns she had ever made.

Only a few seconds later, she was following.

Instinctively, she reached for her police radio and came up empty. Once again, the impact of her isolation from the department bore down on her. She needed to get to a pay phone. She needed a way to alert Boldt or the department that it was going down.

It *was* going down! She could *feel* it: Sharon was at the end of this ride.

It wasn't going to be Maybeck; it was going to be Tegg. It wasn't going to be Boldt; it was going to be her.

49

"I appreciate this, Loraine," LaMoia said to the attractive black woman opening the James Street entrance to the administration building. Boldt guessed her to be in her mid-thirties and just shy of six feet tall. She had beautiful almond eyes and a dancer's figure. She wore jeans and a khaki windbreaker. Boldt knew her face from somewhere—maybe she had worked at one of the civilian jobs for the department a few years back.

"I could get screwed for doing this. You know that, John."

"Yeah, I know."

"Don't ask me why I'm doing this, 'cause I'll be damned if I know."

"And I thought it was because you loved me," LaMoia teased.

"Don't get me thinking about it, lover, or I'll march your ass right out of here."

"We are the police, after all," LaMoia reminded. "It's not as if we're a couple of crooks or something."

"Yeah, yeah. Hey, Ernie," she greeted the security guard coming down the hall to intercept them.

Boldt and LaMoia took out their shields before the man even asked.

"Hey, Lori," the former weightlifter answered. His arms were too big for the uniform he was required to wear. He'd gone a little soft around the middle.

"These here are a couple of Seattle's finest homicide dicks." She introduced everyone all around. He checked their identification carefully. "They need a look-see at some of the records in the assessor's office and can't wait for nothing."

"Homicide? Sure thing," Ernie said. He kept looking at Boldt as if he recognized him. "They got the elevators off, for inspection. You'll have to take the stairs."

On the way up the steep stairs she said, "This place gives me wheebies with no one in it. Know what I mean?" A few steps later she added, "Nah. You guys probably don't know what I mean."

"The deal is," LaMoia said down to Boldt, who was slower going up the stairs than the other two, "it occured to me that the first time I asked Loraine to run a few names into the computer—what was that, yesterday?—I was a little sexist in my approach."

"You?" she said sarcastically. "I can't imagine such a thing."

"I'm talking to him, if you don't mind," LaMoia complained.

"You?" Boldt asked, mimicking the woman's sarcastic tone.

LaMoia continued, undaunted, "I didn't have the time to do the job right. I did check to see if either of the three vets owned land out near where Dixie dug up Farragot, but this was *before* we were tuned in to Tegg. When I got the employee lists I had Loraine try those names as well."

"And that was a *bunch* of names," she complained, as if he owed her something for it.

Boldt was out of shape, that's all there was to it. His legs seemed to weigh a few hundred pounds. "How much farther?"

"Seventh floor, sugar. Two more to go."

"One way to do this," LaMoia explained, "is to use the county maps, because they identify each parcel of private land by name of the taxpayer."

"But that's a *huge* job," Loraine said. "And it's random. There's so much land out there by the Tolt: private, public, private usage, timber lease, water district, you name it." She seemed to be floating up the stairs, barely noticing them. Boldt was beginning to wonder whether he would make it.

She reached the door first. She held it open for LaMoia and waited for Boldt. "You all right?" she asked.

Boldt nodded, too winded to speak. Embarrassed.

"When Matthews nailed it down that it was Tegg for sure, it occurred to me we should try—"

"His wife," Boldt answered, interrupting.

It annoyed LaMoia.

Boldt explained his reasoning as they turned right, then left, and Loraine unlocked the door to room 700A for them. "We know Tegg is originally from Vancouver. He later studied here, married here, and stayed here. If he didn't buy the land, then maybe his wife bought it or inherited it."

"Exactly," LaMoia agreed.

"One name?" Loraine asked. She switched on the lights. The room had a long counter and several oversized signs explaining who was properly served by the assessor's office. In the center of the space allotted to the public was a long table. Against the near wall was a slanted shelf holding three-foot-by-two-foot leather-bound tax maps of the city and King County. According to the gold lettering, they were made by the Kroll Map Co.

Along the far wall were a half-dozen computer terminals and more signs explaining how to use them. The computer screen warmed. Loraine stood ready at the keyboard. "I did this for one name?" She hit several function keys, changing the menu. "Okay, okay. Lay it on me, and let's get out of here before I get a permanent case of the creeps."

You did this to save a woman's life, Boldt wanted to say. You did this to stop a man who has gone mad with a scalpel.

LaMoia handed her a piece of napkin with some writing on it.

"Peggy Schmidt Tegg," Loraine read off, typing it in.

"Just Schmidt," LaMoia corrected. "Peggy Schmidt. This is the info off of her DMV slug—her driver's license. We're hoping like hell she uses her maiden name as her middle name, otherwise we've got to dig up a marriage license."

Loraine protested, "I don't have access to any marriage licenses, John LaMoia. Don't go asking me to get that as well, 'cause that's the second floor, and I've got nothing to do with those people. You want that, you're just gonna have to come back to-morrow."

"Tomorrow's too late," LaMoia said, meeting eyes with Boldt.

"No kidding?" Loraine asked, looking up at La-Moia, the seriousness of the situation sinking in.

"Schmidt," he directed her, pointing to the key-board. "What else could that be but a maiden name?"

"Some other kind of family name," Boldt suggested, hoping he was wrong. LaMoia's face tightened. They both looked on as the woman typed in the name and issued several menu-driven commands.

"Here goes," she said.

The screen went blank.

Boldt felt a sickening depression overtake him. He was exhausted, hungry, and now he was stuck in a dead end.

"Don't get all stinky, lover," she said to Boldt. "This thing can be slow."

The screen filled with a long list of Schmidts, starting with Alfred.

"Next page," LaMoia instructed.

"I know."

Screen after screen of Schmidts. Dozens of names.

"There!" LaMoia said. He pointed to: Schmidt, Priscilla. "That could be her."

Loraine's painted nail ran across a line to a box that was a jumble of dozens of capital letters and numbers. "Legal description of the property," she said. "John, read it off for me, will you?"

She jumped out of her chair. Boldt followed her over to the row of bound maps. She selected the one for King County—North. "Read slow now, lover," she said.

LaMoia read the first coordinates. Loraine found the corresponding latitude number on the edge of the map. She turned to page forty-two. She located the same number here.

"Next," she said.

LaMoia read off the next number.

Spreading her fingers like the points of a drafting compass, Loraine found this number as well. Her fingers closed in on each other, each representing a grid coordinate. There were dozens, *hundreds*, of boxes representing land parcels, each with a name inside. Most read Hollybrook—one of the largest timber/paper companies in the Northwest.

Boldt heard himself say, "Come on. Come on," as he watched her fingers come together. She moved her finger out of the way, and there was the name: Schmidt.

"Skykomish River quadrangle," she announced. "Snoqualmie National Forest, Tolt Reservior. Bingo!"

"We're there?" LaMoia asked incredulously. "We're there?" he repeated excitedly.

She answered, "I'll make you a photocopy, lover. I'll put you in her backyard."

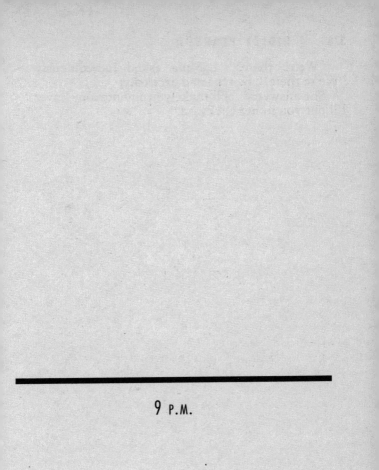

9 P.M.

50

Pamela Chase drove as if she were on her way to a fire. She reached the unpaved county road that accessed Tegg's farm, lost the back end of the car in a skid, and nearly put the car in the trees. He had tried to drug her! She couldn't get over that! She had swallowed one of the Valiums, but had managed to snag the other in her teeth. It was in his front yard now. She was driving fast, not only to reach the farm quickly, but to beat the Valium. It was already taking effect: Her anxiety level had lessened noticeably in the last few minutes—her fingers were no longer welded to the steering wheel; she was no longer grinding her teeth. The more relaxed she felt, the more terrified she became. He had said that he would call her in the morning, but what for? He acted like he owned her, as if she were one of his trained dogs. She felt dirty. She felt foolish. How had she allowed herself to be carried along by him for so long? What kind of person was she?

Not the kind of person to condone a heart harvest, she answered herself. She intended to put an end to that, but quick!

She pulled in to the farm and shut off her car. From the Quonset hut came the ferocious barking of the dogs. Sight of the small turn-of-the-century cabin and its accompanying sheet-metal Quonset hut gave her a renewed sense of the extreme seclusion of this place. She was glad for his dinner party: She wouldn't want him to catch her out here.

She left the car and approached the cabin slowly, despite the urgency she felt. Her feet floated along. The Valium, subtle in its approach, was difficult to resist. Confusion reigned, for she still wanted to believe in him. That belief had given her several years of happiness. By coming here, she hoped as much to disprove her suspicions as prove them. She couldn't get him out of her mind—it was as if he were right here with her, disapproving of each step she took toward betrayal. She could hear his arguments. He could be so convincing. She glanced over her shoulder nervously. The clouds were breaking up; there was a moon out tonight. A black-and-white patch-quilt played over the meadow. She caught herself staring; she was feeling impossibly good.

The spare key was missing. Why would he remove it? Unless . . . She found a rock and smashed it through the window. She had to hurry. The Valium was taking hold. "Things work out for the best," a voice inside her called. "Relax." She tried her best to ignore it. The glass shattered into the kitchen. She reached through the hole, knowing where to find the release, but nicked her forearm in the process. It hurt, but it didn't bother her. The door swung open. To a stranger, the cabin might appear abandoned, the spare amount of leftover furniture from another era. A former hunting cabin, perhaps. Tegg had kept it looking this way intentionally, to discourage trespassers from breaking in. He was paranoid about trespassers discovering the basement lab—the *ad hoc* surgical suite—though she didn't know why. She had never seen another soul anywhere around here.

Although the recovery room they used was in the cellar next to the surgical suite, he could be keeping this woman in any of the bedrooms. She decided to search the cabin top to bottom.

Unless he had fixed them, the upstairs lights didn't work. She tried them. He hadn't fixed them. He kept a flashlight at the top of the cellar stairs. She banged her way through the kitchen and found it, switched it on. She moved quickly through the rooms on the first floor. Nothing. No one.

She climbed the stairs, feeling strangely light and disconnected from her body. Happy. On the top landing, she faced two small bedrooms and a tiny bathroom, the floor of which was an old, chipped linoleum, burgundy red with black fleur-de-lis prints. The sink and toilet were discolored and mineral-stained. The flashlight's yellow beam wandered the walls. The cold faucet dripped into a patinated teardrop. She twisted the handle and it stopped dripping. Something stirred within her—she could *feel* the danger here. Like an animal lifting its head in the forest, she sniffed the air. It smelled metallic, tangy. Worse, she knew that smell: blood. She felt lightheaded as she stepped toward the wicker hamper— the source of that smell. She had never known him to use the hamper, and this added to her confusion and anxiety. Typically, *she* brought the surgical laundry back to the clinic from here. It then went out with the regular service. Standing alongside the hamper now, towering over it, she stopped herself; she didn't want to know what was inside. It frightened her to imagine what she might find. She reached out tentatively, took hold of the hamper's lid, hesitated, and then yanked it open suddenly. She aimed the flashlight inside. At the sight of its contents, she shrieked at the top of her lungs and jumped back. There, in a heap, covered in an unbelievable amount of dried blood, lay his surgical smock. She felt instinctively that this was human blood—Sharon's blood. He had already done the heart. Something had gone horribly wrong with the procedure.

The hamper lid thumped shut. Pamela felt half-crazy, the panic and terror rising from inside her attempting to supersede the ever-increasing medicated bliss of the Valium. As she raced downstairs to confirm her suspicions, she wondered: Was he the only one to blame? Couldn't he blame her, as well, for refusing to assist? Her head swam.

She hurried down the narrow steps that led to the cellar. When she reached the bottom, she aimed the flashlight at the wall switch as she reached to turn on the lights. Dried blood.

The operating room was unlocked! Impossible! Suddenly the various evidence she was collecting added up to something else entirely: the bloody clothes left in the hamper, the unlocked door. Not like Elden. Someone else must have broken in here and vandalized the place.

She was afraid to look any farther. What was on the other side of the operating room door? Tentatively, using the toe of her shoe, she encouraged it to open slowly, prepared for a quick retreat.

Light poured into the room from the bare bulb over her head. A mess! A nightmare. A bloody terror! It looked like a city hospital emergency room after a gang war. She switched on the lights.

The instruments had not been cleaned up. The sternal retractor, the scalpels, the hemostats, the table, the floor, all covered in an unbelievable amount of dried blood. The policewoman had used the term *victim*. Pamela had resented it, had misunderstood it at the time, but now it rang true.

Panic stormed her system, contained in part by

the drug coursing through her veins. She felt pulled in two directions by everything around her. On one level she loved Elden Tegg, but now she feared him; she felt a loyalty to him, but knew she would betray him; she wanted to blame him, but in part she blamed herself; she felt frightened and terrified, she felt impossibly at peace.

A massacre. A *murder*?

A shock collar.

It was resting alongside the hemostats.

She felt a bubble of nervous laughter escape her. A shock collar. It could mean only one thing: a dog. Not a human, not murder. No human victim. A dog! Part of his research?

She had mistrusted him. She had doubted his intentions. She had allowed the police to sway her, just as he had warned. How could she have made such assumptions? How could she have lost her faith in him so quickly? She hated herself for it.

Excited by her discovery, thrilled to prove her earlier suspicions incorrect, she hurried into the recovery room. Its walls and ceilings were also encased in plastic. The flashlight caught the narrow cot pushed up against the wall and then the window to the outside. Even at this distance the barking of the dogs from the kennel sounded unnaturally loud. She had never noticed this before. Perhaps it was the Valium hearing that barking. Perhaps she had never listened.

Why wasn't Sharon here, as she half expected? The flashlight illuminated the painted window again, and she had her answer.

Then the barking of the dogs registered fully: There were no windows in the kennel, no chance at escape.

Out the cellar door. Up the steps. Across the field toward the Quonset hut. She clung to the hope that

the presence of the shock collar *meant* something—
a dog, not a human. Not Sharon. One less dog in the
kennel would prove it. And she, for one, would not
feel too sad about that. These pit bulls of his were
terrors—many of them trained that way well before
he had "saved" them from death. His surgical exper-
iments on them did nothing to improve their dispo-
sition.

Having forgotten the key to the kennel, she had
to run back to the operating room to get it. In the
process she grew more elated at her discovery of the
shock collar. She no longer attributed her bliss to the
drug she had taken; she had forgotten all about it.
Losing her awareness of the fact, she crossed a
threshold. The Valium owned her for now.

Elden had done no wrong. Everything was going
to be fine.

In fact, the way she felt, things were really looking up.

51

The Isuzu rode high in the traffic,
making it an easy target for Daphne
to follow. Wherever possible, Daphne
kept at least one car between herself and Tegg,
though by his hurried, nearly reckless driving, she
doubted he was paying much attention to what was
behind him. He seemed hell-bent on getting to
where he was going.

He took I-5 north but stayed on it only briefly,
heading east on 90. He stayed on the Interstate
through Bellevue, continuing on toward the 901. She

had followed him out of the city limits, had driven right out of her legal authority as a policewoman. She was a Seattle cop; out here police authority was divided between King County Police and the police departments of the incorporated townships. She was technically a civilian now.

He drove seventy wherever possible. The farther away from the city, the more isolated she felt. If he would only stop for gas—if he would only give her a minute or so to make a phone call, to call in some backup. But he barreled along into the night, and she followed a hundred yards back.

At Preston he left the Interstate and took the 203 north toward Fall City.

The farther they went, the more nervous she became. She was in over her head and she knew it. What if he did lead her to Sharon? What then? The gun? A confrontation? In the last six years she had negotiated eleven hostage situations for the department and had a perfect record. But those had been team efforts, team pressures, team resources. The only hostage situation she had failed at—one that wasn't counted on the department records—had been her own. Boldt had solved that one with his weapon, but only after the abductor had drawn his knife across her throat.

Was she capable of using the gun as it was made to be used? Cardboard silhouettes were one thing, a human life another thing entirely.

Only minutes later she followed Tegg into the small town of Fall City, and shortly thereafter he turned south on 202. She was alone with him now, and she worried he would spot her. She fell well behind, but with the increased distance she risked losing him.

They passed Spring Glen, crossed over the dark and sullen Tokul River and turned left toward Snoqualmie Falls. They drove through town, crossed the railroad tracks, and headed south, following the tracks.

Less than a mile later, his blinker signaled a left turn and the Trooper disappeared from sight. Had he taken this turn with the sole intention of losing her? Of trapping her? Was he waiting to see whether she followed? Or was he oblivious to her presence?

There were glimpses of moonlight tonight, the sky a grid of broken clouds. She couldn't continue to follow him as she had been; they were too far off the beaten track for that. What to do? They had passed a tavern on the outskirts of town. Should she go back and telephone for help? Risk losing him?

She slowed, a headache beating unmercifully at her temples.

She switched off her headlights and turned down the darkened lane, following his taillights just barely visible a half-mile in front of her. It was a macadam road, tar mixed with crushed stone. When the moon passed behind the clouds it forced her to slow to a crawl. When it reappeared, she drove quickly, closing the distance between them. Cat and mouse, she caught him and lost him, caught him and lost him. Her headache drove spikes down into her neck. Her calf muscle cramped from carrying the tension there as well.

The road turned to mud. Twice she drove past side roads where his taillights and his tracks said he'd gone. She backed up, worried he might spot the backup lights, made the turn, and followed. It was a spiderweb of dirt roads out here; mud sprayed loudly onto the undercarriage. The front-wheel drive held the car close to the road. A left. A right. She would never find her way out of here. If this was a spiderweb, she thought, then he was the spider and she was the prey. Perhaps he had her exactly where he wanted her. Perhaps he had known she was back here all along.

52 Pamela Chase fumbled awkwardly—nervously—with the oversized brass padlock, finally inserting and turning the key. The dogs were going crazy in there. The lock came open with a loud pop. She leapt away as a dog's nose and teeth jammed through the crack in the door, surprising her. Biting at her. She placed her hand out for the dog to smell. It whined. It tried for her again, and she recognized that nose.

"Felix?" she said. "Did you get out of your cage, boy?" She eased the door open, her hand—her scent—leading her. Felix approached and nuzzled her. A few of the other dogs stopped barking. She closed the door behind her.

It smelled horrible in here. He hadn't been keeping it clean. It smelled *wrong*. Not exactly like dogs. It was dark, and she could not see clearly.

She switched on the lights. The very first pen she looked at was unoccupied, and her mind jumped to the immediate conclusion that this dog had been the one to receive the surgery. Finding an empty pen was exactly what she had hoped for—it exonerated Elden; another warm wave of tranquility passed through her at the sight of it.

Behind her and farther into the structure, she heard a collar sound its warning beep, and one of the dogs smash into the cage wall. She turned to see who was being so rambunctious.

A woman!

Her hair tangled and matted, one eye bandaged, her mouth gagged, lips worn raw, a shock collar locked around her neck.

Pamela screamed. The woman screamed soundlessly. The dogs began barking ferociously again.

A bandage covering a kidney scar. Badly infected, by the color.

"Sharon?" Pamela asked tentatively.

The woman's one good eye cocked toward her suspiciously. Untrusting.

Pamela felt weak, unable to move, without strength. This roller coaster between euphoria and horror was nearly intolerable. Only a moment before . . .

The kidney bandage cried out to her. How could she have done such a thing? Was she to be party to a *murder*? And what did that mean about Elden? Had he *ever* told her the truth about anything? She felt sick to her stomach—the smell, the pleading expression on this poor woman's face. And then another wave of calm swept through her, and she felt much less upset. She could handle this; everything was okay.

And then it struck her again that she was at least partly responsible. Where did her own involvement stop and Tegg's begin?

The woman in the cage—Sharon—laced her fingers through the wire cage and shook, deliberately ignoring the punishment of the shock collar that beeped its warning.

No apparent pain.

The dogs were wild with excitement, but Pamela was used to the dogs, she hardly heard them; it was this woman's exceptional behavior that impressed her and held her interest. Pamela took several steps closer. How could she inflict that kind of punishment on herself and endure it?

"I'm coming," she announced, wondering why she was walking, not running. Wondering how she could feel this comfortable.

Pamela seized hold of the lock attempting to communicate to Sharon that she intended to get her out of here.

Sharon pointed and nodded violently.

"The key?" Pamela asked. "Is there a key in this building?"

The woman shook her head.

"I'm going to get you out," Pamela said confidently, unsure where such confidence came from.

The captive nodded enthusiastically.

She looked around. Without a key, then what? The shovel? Could she beat the lock apart? She walked over to the shovel, knowing she should hurry, but strangely in no hurry. It was okay. Everything was okay.

Sharon became frantic. Shouting. Waving her arms. Slapping the cement floor. Hopping up and down. God, she *looked* like one of the animals.

What was this? Several of the dogs quieted; they all began pacing their cages at once.

Sharon kept slapping the cement, in an ungainly primitive dance.

Pamela struck the lock with the end of the shovel. Nothing.

She tried again.

"I'm trying," she told the frantic woman inside. This woman's behavior was making her nervous. "Stop it!" she said. Only when she identified this fleeting nervousness did she realize what a huge dose of Valium it must have been—there was a gulf between how she should have been, and what she actually was, feeling.

She struck the lock with the shovel again. Nothing.

Now Sharon was shaking her wrist toward the main door. Pounding the cement again and pointing hysterically toward the door.

Finally, Pamela understood as she felt a rumble under her feet.

The dogs barking had covered the approaching sounds, but now Pamela heard them distinctly.

A car!

But if a car, it could only be one of two people: Maybeck or Elden. And if either of them caught her in here doing this . . .

Sharon grabbed hold of the cage again. Her collar sounded and Pamela watched as the collar punished her. She held on an impossibly long time. She pointed emphatically toward the door.

Close the door! Of course!

Pamela moved quite quickly now, surprising herself. First toward the door; then, stopping, she returned to the cage and started in with the shovel again.

She should have never come here, she thought. All a mistake.

She glanced toward the door.

Sharon pointed furiously.

"I know," Pamela said. "I know." What Sharon didn't understand was that there was no way to lock that door from the inside. The only hope now was to get her free of the cage.

She never should have gone against him, she realized. He was too powerful for her.

She dropped the shovel, abandoning her efforts. It clanked to the floor. She felt terrified of him before she ever saw him. The Valium did little to help with this fear.

Sharon let out a muffled, anguished cry.

The dogs went completely hysterical.

Pamela wanted to disappear, to vanish. Anything

but face his wrath. She had glimpsed his anger before. She shook with fear, unable to imagine how he might react to this.

The door creaked.

Sharon retreated, curling back into a ball in the center of her cage.

Pamela felt like hiding, too. She watched as a hand pushed open the door.

She knew that hand.

53

Daphne had the Prelude up to forty, which in the dim light of an inconsistent moon seemed more like twice that. She careened through puddles, sending water up in a torrential spray, blurring her windshield and demanding the wipers.

She had lost him.

A few seconds earlier his taillights had been distant but visible. She had slowed to avoid pressing herself on him. When she caught herself giving him too much leeway, she had sped back up. Now, he was nowhere to be seen.

She pushed the car a little harder, a little faster. Dangerous at best, given the slippery conditions and the lack of visibility. They had been on these backroads for the better part of fifteen minutes—it seemed more like an hour.

There! She just caught a glimpse of some lights out of the corner of her eye. She craned her neck to look out the mud-splattered side window. Was that a road?

A painful cramp stabbed into her neck and locked. She cried out. Her hand just barely tugged the wheel. She forced her head back around as the car began a weightless crabbing to the right, drifting slowly on all four tires, the front end surrendering to momentum and releasing its careful grip. Like a rock tossed out onto a frozen pond. She corrected the wheel to the right. Waited. Nothing. Cut it back. Nothing. Drifting, like a chain was pulling her off the road. She tapped the brakes tentatively, and that did it: The car seemed to snap; the back end swung completely around on her—she was looking back from where she had just come, flying backwards now. Pitch black. Vertigo. Perilously close to the ditch. Mud flying everywhere. The horrible sound of machinery doing what it wasn't designed to do.

She jerked the wheel to the right with authority and bounced her foot off the brake again. A rear tire caught on something. The front end of the car jumped so fast, so hard, that it stole the wheel from her hands. The front end bounced into the shallow drainage ditch. Her head slammed hard against the side glass. The car came to a grinding halt, its engine still running.

She just sat there for a moment collecting herself, checking herself with small movements, the flexing of a muscle, the movement of a joint. She got control of her breathing, though her heart was lost to adrenaline. It took the better part of a minute to get her vision down to one image.

No time! it suddenly occurred to her. In the heat of the moment she had forgotten what she was even doing out here. She forced the car into first gear—it didn't want to go—and let out the clutch. There was a bad noise, but then the front tires suddenly spun. She felt the tire dig a hole in what seemed like a fraction of a second. The front end sank perceptibly.

She tried to back up, tried to go forward: mired. The car rocked once, and then dug in deeply one final time. She climbed out. The car was beached, high-centered on the lip of the ditch, both front tires rutted in up to their hubs.

She grabbed the keys. She kept jumper cables, snow chains, and a heavy-duty black rubber flashlight in the trunk. She grabbed the flashlight, pocketed the keys, and took off at a run through the sloppy mud.

The flashlight showed her the path of her car: an improbable tangle of deep ruts, crisscrossed and pretzled, that led back to two perfectly straight tire tracks and the arching curve of Tegg's tires where the four-wheel drive had turned. She followed Tegg's tracks up a road that quickly narrowed.

She found the edge of the road easier for running, though her Top-Siders became heavy with mud. After about fifty yards it narrowed again, and the texture became more gravel than mud, although it remained spongy. The flashlight caught an occasional boot print, washed by the recent rains, but clearly distinguishable. Now that she caught onto it, it was one long line of boot tracks coming right at her—someone either exceptionally tall or running fast.

It was then that for some reason it occurred to her that this was in fact not a road at all.

It was a driveway.

54

The Keeper stood in the doorway, backlit by moonlight and a finger of fog that reached to the ground. Sharon had witnessed his entry several times, but only once before had he paused there like that, emanating a menace that even the dogs seemed to feel.

Sharon's eye stung badly. A hot, shooting pain bit into her side where the bandage covered her scar. Her neck was hot from the collar. Her ears were ringing.

Only a few short minutes ago she had been on the verge of being rescued, but she shrank from that hope now. The Keeper was too powerful. This young woman was no match for him, even though by the way they looked at each other there seemed to be a strong connection between them.

The dogs remained silent, though they continued to pace anxiously.

The Keeper stepped inside and closed the door firmly behind him. He called, "Heel!" The guard dog obeyed, circling behind the man and sitting quickly by his side.

Sharon, who had lived through hundreds of dangerous incidents while out on the street, felt the impending threat that dog represented.

"I'm sorry," the young woman mumbled, head down. Subservient. "But this isn't right," she dared voice.

"I expected so much more of you," he said, his voice reverberating eerily in the steel building. Sharon felt invisible. He had yet to even glance in her direction. Instead, his full concentration remained focused on this other woman.

The Keeper continued, "You didn't do as I said. You have failed me."

"This is wrong, Elden," she countered.

For the first time, Sharon could attach a name to this man, this monster. It was a strange name and somehow fitting. Strange to be fully prepared to kill a man whose name you don't even know. The needle warmed in her palm.

"You could help me, you know. You could prove yourself. There's work to be done."

"You've gone way too far," she said to the cement. "It's over." She wouldn't look at him; she knew better than to look at him.

Sharon couldn't keep her eyes off him. He drew her into himself like a hypnotist.

"Pamela," he said—and now this young woman had a name as well—"since when do you refuse me?"

The woman looked up at him.

———

Pamela's face felt hot. Her brain was like jelly. She wanted to resist him, but it was so difficult. She had *worshipped* him for so long, and now her anger, mingled with shame and fear, felt like spikes in the middle of her chest. Her emotions wouldn't stay focused for long; another wave of warmth would drive them away.

"Who do you think you are?" she asked, clinging to a shard of righteousness. "A woman's *life* is at stake!"

His face and neck reddened. Felix panted impatiently. "How can you say such things? Hmm? I suggest you consider your situation more carefully," he said, gripping the dog's collar. "Are you frightened? The police frightened you, didn't they?"

The police? Sharon thought. Was it possible?

Pamela stepped up to Sharon's cage and took hold of the lock. "Open it," she said to him.

"Get away from there!" Tegg warned in that sharp voice. He gave the dog's heavy collar a tug, and it came to its feet.

"Give me the key. I'll do it," Pamela said, her voice shaking. "We can give her the electroshock, can't we? Some Ketamine and electroshock. We can leave her at a hospital, no one the wiser. We dismantle everything here and what's there to find?" It took every bit of her strength to address him like this. "You said it yourself: The police don't have anything. They're fishing is all. We can still do this, Elden. We can still get out of this."

"We most certainly cannot. I told you: There's a contract. There are things of which you have no idea. I *have* a plan! It's all settled."

"Settled? It can't be settled. Give me the key."

"Of course I won't. Use your head."

Pamela picked up the shovel. "We can still save her, Elden. Contracts can be broken." She felt as if she were dealing with a child. This wasn't the same man of even a week ago. "You're not well," she told him.

"Away from there!" he roared.

She had chosen the wrong words. Her knees trembled. His strength was overwhelming, almost like a bright light you can't look at. She wanted to please him, to help him.

He stepped toward her. Felix followed. "Stand back," he ordered. Her heart sank, but she felt her feet refuse to obey. What was happening to her?

She raised the shovel and delivered another blow. To her joy, although the lock remained closed, the latch broke a rivet and the door came partially open.

Sharon felt the hair on her arms stand at attention. Freedom? Was it possible?

The Keeper mechanically jerked his head toward her and shouted, "Stay right where you are!"

Sharon thought of the needle in her hand. She'd never managed to come up with a plan for the dog, but one step at a time, she reminded herself.

Pamela said, "How can you justify taking one life in order to save another? What sense is there in *that*?"

The Keeper's expression hardened. "What sense?" His shoulders went military and he shook his head. "Lift your shirt, Pamela."

"What?"

He repeated, "Remove your shirt. Now! Don't question me, Pamela. Show it to me!" His tone was that of a doctor—clinical and authoritative. Pamela stunned Sharon by removing her jacket and unbuttoning her shirt, allowing it to hang open.

From that moment on, Sharon knew it was over. Pamela had given in. She was his.

Below her ribs was a five-inch scar.

"Touch it for me," he instructed.

Pamela shook her head in one last try at defiance. "No, I won't."

"Do it!" he thundered.

Tears came to her eyes. She reached down and traced the long scar with a quivering fingertip.

He nodded. "I saved you. Hmm? I delivered, when no one else was able. Let me tell you this, when one faces losing a young friend as precious, as individual as you, one becomes capable of things he never dreamed possible." He experienced one of those tics then—his head jerking, his shoulder lifting, his eyes squinting shut. Sharon had witnessed this once before. He straightened himself, like a man adjusting his tie, and continued as if nothing had

happened. "I told you a little white lie, a little fib
back then, because to do otherwise would have
caused you undue anxiety and might have interfered
with your recovery. Hmm? Do you remember asking me about where I had located your liver? Hmm?
I may not have done the actual transplant, but I
saved your life—you know that's true. The truth is
inescapable, is it not? It is the biggest burden of all.
Hmm? Did you sense the truth? I suspect you did.
You must have thought at some point that it hadn't
really come from a trauma patient . . . No, of course
it didn't. But I protected you from the truth because
I knew how it would hurt you."

Pamela sobbed and sank to her knees. She was
mumbling to herself, but Sharon couldn't understand a word.

"That's what I'm offering you now, you know.
Protection. But you don't seem to see that. Protection from *them*: the police; your parents; your fears.
But you must join me. Hmm? Not go against me. I
can protect you. Believe me."

"You lied to me?" she asked incredulously.

"What did you think happened to Anna?" he
asked.

Pamela covered her ears.

The man raised his voice to be heard. "Didn't it
ever strike you as odd that Anna just up and disappeared at the same time you were seriously ill? You
must have thought of that!"

He said, "There was an accident—a fatal accident—and there she was." He pointed to the floor.
"What was I to do? I tested her blood type, that's
what! A godsend is what it was. She was *your* blood
type . . . *You* live because another died, and yet you
would deny it for someone else?"

"Nooooo!" she screamed. She came at him with
the shovel raised high.

Sharon broke for the door to her cage.

"Stop!" he commanded Sharon, his finger pointed at her ominously.

The Keeper flickered his wrist next to the dog's eyes. He uttered but a single word: "Hit!"

The pit bull sprang forward. The Keeper dodged the swing of the shovel. The dog leaped several feet into the air and knocked Pamela to the cement.

"Back!" The Keeper ordered, but the starving dog would not obey. *"Back!"* he demanded, sensing his loss of control. "Off of her!!" The dog was wild with hunger and the scent of the blood. The Keeper lifted the shovel and went after the dog.

Sharon looked away.

The sounds of the slaughter echoed throughout the building. The Keeper shouted, he struck the dog again and again, but the dog's will overcame it all.

Sharon fainted.

When she awakened, it was dark in the kennel.

She heard a car racing away.

55

Moving arrows of white light shot through the trees, followed by the growing whine of a car engine advancing steadily toward her. Daphne switched off the flashlight and darted into the trees as that sound grew increasingly louder. Tegg or some stranger? Maybe this wasn't a driveway after all, the way it seemed to go on forever.

She hid behind a tree, standing completely still as the vehicle passed, her breathing competing with

the sound of tires in the mud. It *was* the Trooper—
Tegg. Wherever he had been for the last half hour,
he was now leaving.

She headed back onto the road and took up running again, though this time with the light off,
guided only by the glow of a broken moon. She
checked over her shoulder repeatedly: If he returned
the way he had come, perhaps he was gone for good;
if, however, he turned left at the end of this long
road, he would come across her car and most certainly return.

She ran faster, rounding two long turns.

All at once the road spilled out into a clearing.
The moon played its game of hide-and-seek, disappearing and denying her any sight of what lay ahead.
It was far too dark to see anything clearly, but she
edged her way tentatively out into the muddy, rut-
wormed driveway and followed it slowly up a rise.
A large, heavy shape loomed to her right, another
smaller, more angular shape directly ahead.

The moon cleared the clouds and it was like
someone turning on the stage lights: ahead of her an
old two-story homesteader log cabin; to her right,
the large arcing curve of a Quonset hut.

No lights in the cabin. A single vehicle parked
that she recognized immediately as belonging to
Pamela Chase. A sense of dread filled her—had there
been *two* people in the Trooper? She had seen the
outline of only one. Had it been Tegg or Pamela
Chase? Could she be certain?

She switched on the flashlight and sprinted to
the cabin, drawing her weapon as she went. She
could feel her heart clear up in her throat. She tried
to swallow the lump away. Was Sharon here? She
attempted to blink away the annoying white sparks
that interfered with her vision. It had been two long
years since she had tasted terror.

She climbed the wooden stairs, slipped off the gun's safety, and made herself alert for the slightest noise. A board creaked slightly underfoot.

The Quonset hut exploded in barking. It so startled her that she dropped to one knee and trained her gun in that direction, the flashlight tucked immediately beneath the weapon. For a moment she couldn't catch her breath, she was so surprised and startled. Frightened.

The dogs howled constantly for the better part of a minute and then gave it up to silence. Daphne, winded from the exhausting run, collected herself. She stood and circled the perimeter of the cabin, sliding her back against the logs, rushing quickly across the windows, weapon pointed through the glass. The kitchen door was open, its window broken. She edged it open with the toe of her shoe, and stepped inside, glass crunching beneath her shoes. She moved stealthily room to room, her weapon and flashlight held as a team, jerking around door frames and leveling the gun.

She climbed the stairs to the tightly confined second floor and continued her search. She entered a very small bedroom, the floor dotted with mouse pellets and dust balls. A mass grave of dead flies was collected at the bottom of the window frame from which one of the panes of glass was missing, the wood around it moldy.

She stepped up to this window and looked out on the Quonset hut below, hearing a loud hum coming from the building. At first she couldn't place it. His car returning? she wondered, panicked by the thought. As the moonlight intensified, a shadow raced from one end of the Quonset hut to the other, as if someone had yanked away a huge cover, and she identified the source of the sound as a vent stack plugged into the corrugated roof. A furnace.

Why heat a Quonset hut—even a kennel, if that's what it was? They hadn't had frost in six weeks.

She hurried down the stairs, wondering whether to check the cellar before the Quonset hut. She had to! She descended slowly, her pulse thumping in her ears. It smelled like Dixon's autopsy room down here, and it terrified her. Light from the flashlight played off the stone walls. The storm doors to the outside were open, letting in the night. She reached the bottom of the stairs, gun poised, and turned right. Nudged open a door. Stepped inside.

The light revealed a plastic room, a shiny gray. It found the overhead surgical light and lowered onto the bloodstained operating table.

She was sure then what the furnace was for. She went off at a sprint. Up the cellar stairs, out into the cool night air. She fell to her knees and vomited. She stood and ran harder. The Quonset hut seemed to fade away from her. Her vision dimmed. Hyperventilating. Her feet sloshed through the wet grass.

She reached the door to the shed, the dogs barking frantically, and found an enormous padlock containing it. She stepped back, aimed her weapon, and fired off four consecutive rounds. Two hit the lock but did nothing to open it, boring holes through the metal to no effect. Two others penetrated the galvanized metal, lost to the inside of the shed.

When she heard a rhythmic banging, obscured by the barking, she caught herself immediately and stopped firing. What had she been thinking?

"Sharon?" she shouted, paying no consideration to the possiblity of someone—a guard, Tegg—being nearby.

Daphne reared back and kicked the door repeatedly. It didn't budge. She grabbed hold of the lock. It was hot. One shot had struck it cleanly, damaging the casing, but the lock itself remained intact.

She circled the building, beating on the walls with the butt of her gun. Three quarters of the way down one wall, a return signal echoed back. Tears streaming from her eyes, Daphne shouted to the wall, "I'm coming in!" She came completely around the building: no other doors.

Deciding the structure's only door was far enough away from Sharon's location inside, Daphne elected to use the gun one more time. She placed the barrel's opening directly in contact with the brass lock, stretched her arm straight out, averted her eyes, leaned fully away, and squeezed the trigger. The dogs were barking so loudly that the discharge sounded more like a hand clap.

A piece of shrapnel sliced into her lower leg, barely noticed as she inspected her target. An over-sized bullet hole was bored through the center of the lock, which otherwise remained intact. She slammed it against the door repeatedly, frustrated and angry.

She checked her leg. It was a pea-sized wound, the metal lodged inside. It was bleeding, through not badly. With each passing second, the pain intensified.

She knew then that she had to find another way inside. That lock wasn't coming off. She hurried to Pamela's vehicle and climbed inside. No key! She pounded her fist on the dashboard in frustration. She spotted an old tractor, grass growing up around it, but even from thirty yards away it was apparent that it hadn't run in years.

She came out of the car. Limping, she circled the building again. There *had* to be another way inside.

When the furnace kicked off, she looked up and realized there was.

56

Tegg knew the exact location where his cellular came back into range, a small rise in the road just prior to Maud Lake. He pulled over, leaving the Trooper running, and dialed Wong Kei's cellular number, which was now routed through the Vancouver telephone system. Wong Kei answered coldly, "Speak."

Tegg said, "This is me." He looked down at the hand trembling in his lap and wondered if it really belonged to him, if anything was really as it seemed.

Felix had massacred Pamela, one of the few persons he had seen as a part of his future—his budding young protegé. Had turned her into a bloody pulp. She was now inside the first pen, contained in two black garbage bags. Pamela. Witnessing the slaughter, attempting to stop it, had drained him.

"Our plans are moved forward," Tegg advised.

"What? Impossible!" the man protested. "Tomorrow morning. Tomorrow morning!"

"Tonight. Now," Tegg declared. "I'll call from the airport. Expect me around," he checked his watch, "midnight, maybe a little after. You'll have to move quickly: It will be two hours and counting by the time I reach you. We will have used up half our time."

"Impossible!" the tight voice complained.

"Make it happen. I'm on my way." He pushed: END. He stared at the button's simple message.

He could find ice in Snoqualmie Falls.

He would chain and lock the main gate, use the old fire trail at the back of the property as his escape route. If he got into a panic about time, he could put the harvest off until later; sedate Sharon, hide her in the back seat under a blanket. In the far back of the Trooper he carried everything necessary for field surgery. Why not? Head north—enter Canada through the logging trails, do the harvest somewhere out there. Get the money from Wong Kei—he needed that money now more than ever. Stick with the plan.

The old saying was right: There was more than one way to skin a cat.

A human, too, if it came to that.

57

With the gun returned to its holster and the flashlight protruding awkwardly from her pocket, Daphne used a planter box stood on end as a ladder and scaled the Quonset hut's wall to the roof. The constant howling of the dogs served to remind her what awaited her inside. Optimism fueled her: Sharon was alive!

When she reached the lower lip of the curved roof, she hooked one leg up and over the edge and slid herself carefully onto it. It was cold and wet, and her clothes were immediately soaked through.

Her cheek pressed to the galvanized roof, her fingers groping for purchase, she inched her way up to the ridge, where she pulled herself up to a straddle. With her hands now free, she trained the flashlight onto the vent stack and inspected it, finding her first bit of encouragement: It was surrounded by a poor patchwork of rubber, sheet metal and caulk, all applied haphazardly.

Through the hole, the barking grew louder.

She stuffed the light under her knee, leaned down and pulled on the stack. It popped loose almost effortlessly. She tore at the materials, bending the stack to one side, prying open a hole large enough to stuff herself into. She poked her head into the hole and gasped with the smell, coming up immediately for air. She aimed the flashlight inside, locating the steel frame of the propane furnace suspended from the ceiling. The furnace itself was about the size of a dishwasher. Beneath it she saw the cyclone-wire cage of a dog kennel, the dog's red eyes trained up at her. The furnace's superstructure offered her a platform for her descent.

She lowered herself inside.

Her gun snagged on one of the furnace's angle-iron struts and threw her off balance. The gun ejected from the holster and disappeared into the dark, banging somewhere below her. Instinctively, she reached out to try to catch it, but hit the hot face of the furnace instead and burned herself. She let go and fell, crashing onto the top of the dog cage.

Directly below her the dog leapt up, snapping viciously at her through the wire. She moved and heard the flashlight rolling away from her. She pounced for it, but only managed to knock it off the cage. When it hit the cement floor, it flickered off and then back on as it bounced and rolled.

There, across the room, the light found a woman, stark naked. A bandaged eye. Another bandage on her side. Leather straps around her head holding a gag in her mouth, a heavy collar around her neck. Sharon was up on her knees, her one good eye staring hopefully at Daphne, an I.V. running from a bag overhead. A large bloodstain was smeared in front of the cage. "Sharon?" Daphne called out in horror. Could it be?

Sharon Shaffer cried with joy.

Daphne saw the other dog then; he was not in a cage but loose in the aisle. And he was coming right at her, teeth bared.

58

Unable to stomach these speeds, Boldt chose to look over at LaMoia instead. The blue police light, stuck haphazardly to the dash, pulsed a sterile wash across the car's hood, reflected back onto their faces. The siren wailed loudly but did little to part the traffic ahead of them; people ignored sirens for the most part.

Boldt jerked to one side as LaMoia cut the wheel sharply and passed another slow-moving vehicle. "Asshole," he cursed under his breath. This car honked angrily at them, as if they were in the wrong. LaMoia honked back and flipped the guy the bird.

They had made two stops prior to this: Pamela Chase's apartment and Elden Tegg's home. The former was deserted, the latter in the midst of a dinner party, though the front lawn looked as if some teenager had driven across it.

Tegg's wife had been evasive but under pressure from Boldt had admitted that her husband was not at home, having left about an hour earlier. When LaMoia asked about use of their property in Snoqualmie, the woman said she wanted to phone her lawyer.

"Let me guess," Boldt said. "Howard Chamberland."

"Why, yes," she admitted, her face reddening.

Boldt, worried about Daphne, called a patrol car to check the clinic as he and LaMoia headed for I-90 and Snoqualmie Falls. When it came back to them that no cars were parked in the back lot and that the clinic was locked up tight and dark, he telephoned the King County Police to alert them that SPD Homicide had a possible hostage situation north of Snoqualmie Falls and would appreciate cooperation. Five minutes later a call came back saying that two four-wheel-drive cruisers would rendezvous with them at the intersection of the Burlington Northern tracks and state highway 202. An Air Rescue helicopter, an ambulance, and the local hospital were all on-call. Boldt requested that the ambulance join the cruisers at the rendezvous. "Done," said the dispatcher.

"Not quite," mumbled LaMoia as he cut the car across three lanes and just barely caught the exit for 203 north.

Boldt shut his eyes and said, "Tell me when it's over."

59

Daphne jumped back, avoiding the jaws of the dog. His ear was cut, his face covered in dried blood. Her gun was lost, having fallen *inside* the dog pen through a gap between the two cross supports onto which she had dropped.

From across the room, Sharon attempted to shout at her through the gag. It filled Daphne with a sickening pity. Sharon inched forward on stiff legs and seized hold of the chain-link cyclone fence with both hands. A loud buzzer sounded. Her entire body shook with the jolt of electricity.

She let go and smiled.

Numb to the current? Daphne wondered. Conditioned to the pain?

Sharon nodded proudly. Daphne wondered: Insane? Could she get her out of here? Could this woman be expected to climb through the hole in the roof?

One thing at a time! she resolved.

Her problem at the moment was making it over to Sharon's cage while staying out of the jaws of this guard dog.

She studied her situation thoughtfully, recalling from her training so ingrained in her: *Assess the situation.*

Difficult but not impossible. The roof of the cage stood four to five feet off the cement—low enough that the dog could snap at her but too high for it to actually jump up onto. She had to stay at this level, up above the dog. And she had to get over onto Sharon's side of the building—it seemed her only hope to help her, though by the lock on the cage it wouldn't be easy.

She squatted, prepared to jump across the wide aisle, when Sharon took hold of the cage again, sounding her collar. She did this apparently only to get Daphne's attention, for she immediately let go and gestured toward the overhead funnel light suspended in the middle of the aisle.

Seeing it, Daphne understood immediately that Sharon had considered every possibility of escape—even crossing the aisle. They were a team.

Indeed, the light looked like a good idea. She would try it.

It was deafening in here. Frightful. The dogs

wouldn't stop barking. Had Cindy Chapman once been inside this building? Daphne tried to tune them out, to concentrate, but it wasn't easy. She risked the leaping dog just long enough to reach out and touch the funnel light and get it swinging. With each pass, she increased its arc until she could grab hold of it, which she did. She tested it, giving it a little of her weight, and then tugged down on it. It held firm.

She threw her weight into it and swung across to the other side like Tarzan, letting go in time to land painfully on the top of the opposing cages. The guard dog followed her across—dancing, nipping at her shoes.

The light bulb broke and fell. The pit bull leaped high for it, caught it mid-air, and shattered it in its teeth, unfazed.

Seeing this, Daphne thought: Hungry?

The flashlight barely threw off enough light to see anything but the few feet immediately in front of it: Sharon's cage. Daphne opened her eyes wide and moved from one cage to the next, reaching Sharon's. Unsure how the collars worked, Daphne carefully lowered her finger through the wire mesh, not making contact with it. Sharon, crying now, raised her finger and the two touched. Their fingers hooked and Sharon squeezed.

Daphne fought back her own tears. She had no idea how much time she might have—all night? an hour? a few more minutes?—and knew that she had to make the most of it.

Her top priority was getting the guard dog out of the aisle, so she could get herself down to ground level and Sharon's cage.

Food seemed her most promising weapon.

She discovered that the farthest pen on this side was stacked high with unopened bags of dried dog food. The latches were a mechanism that lifted via a small finger trigger, freeing a steel bar bolted to the hinged door. Sharon's was the only cage padlocked.

Daphne slipped off her belt and fished with its buckle for the gate latch but was interrupted by the dog, who got his teeth on it.

Seeing this, Sharon distracted him by banging on her cage and hopping up and down. This agitated the other dogs as well. The guard dog, head lifted and barking, patrolled the center aisle, irritated and confused.

Daphne hooked the latch, and the door came open. The guard dog approached her, stretching his neck and barking. "Get in there," she said, lowering her hand to tempt him. He snapped at her and she pulled back, but he did not enter the cage, despite the bags of food. He barked erratically, one distrustful eye on the stacked contents, the other on Daphne. She tore loose a bloodied piece of her pant leg and stuffed it between the chain link, landing it directly on top of one of the bags. The suspicious dog stopped barking and edged his way forward, nose twitching. The other dogs went silent as well.

Inside!

Daphne leaped down into the center aisle—reeling from her wounded leg—and slammed the cage door shut, trapping him.

Sharon applauded, hopping around her cage like an ape.

The dog lapped up the piece of pant leg and then tore open a bag of food and gorged himself.

The latch on Sharon's cage was broken, the small padlock now secured to the chain-link wire. Daphne wondered whether, unlike the padlock outside, this smaller one might succumb to being shot open. She turned and studied the placement of her gun inside the occupied cage below the furnace. There was a gap between a vertical post and the chain link that appeared wide enough to shove her arm through. But in the time that would take, it seemed the dog would win the contest.

She retrieved a shovel that was leaning next to Sharon's cage and poked the handle through this gap. The pit bull locked onto the handle, pulling and pushing, preventing Daphne from properly directing it. She wrestled it free and then tried again but with the same frustrating results—the pit bull interfered, and the gun remained at bay.

She hooked the shovel's handle on the gun and pulled, managing to skip the gun a foot closer to her. It was within an arm's length now, within reach, if she dared endure the punishment that dog would give her.

The flashlight went dead. Daphne grabbed for it, shook it, and it came back on.

Sharon hopped up and down again. Frightened. She pointed alarmingly toward the door. She placed her hands against the cement. Daphne felt the cement.

It was vibrating.

The dogs, still quiet, starting pacing in their cages.

A car!

Her thoughts raced ahead: He would see the damaged lock, but it would appear no one had made it inside. She looked up at the furnace's exhaust stack—the ceiling was black tar paper, the hole there impossible to distinguish.

How much time did she have? Seconds?

She took a deep breath, steeled herself for the pain, and went for the gun, shoving her hand into the dog pen.

The dog came after her arm!

Her fingers brushed the weapon's handstock.

The jaws opened. White teeth. A dark throat.

She grabbed hold of the gun—she had it!

The dog took a piece of her arm.

The gun snagged on the wire and bounced back inside. Lost.

The vibration stopped. He was *here!*

The dogs circled their cages.

She had to hide!

She crossed over to the food pen. The guard dog would have to be released in order to return things as they were before.

The flashlight!

She retrieved the flashlight, placed the shovel back, and ran to the far cage where Felix was still feeding. From outside came the high-pitched whine of a car engine revving.

She swung open the cage door and ducked in behind it as the dog spun and charged out.

Sharon shook her cage savagely and briefly diverted the dog's attention away from Daphne, who came around the door and pulled it shut, closing herself inside.

She switched off the flashlight and hid herself between the columns of stacked dog food bags.

There was a tremendous crash.

Edlen Tegg's Trooper broke through the far end of the kennel, blowing a six-foot hole in the wall. He left the headlights on as he climbed out, carrying an oversized pistol that it took Daphne a moment to recognize as a dart gun.

The dogs went absolutely silent.

Daphne's ears were ringing as Tegg said calmly to Sharon Shaffer, "I'm back!"

He glanced quickly and nervously around the structure, waving the dart gun before him. "I see we had a visitor while I was gone. Hmm?" He spun around and faced the Trooper and the headlights, worried that his adversary might attack him from the gaping hole the car had caused. "Off for reinforcements or waiting for me? Hmm?" He remained extremely distracted, jerking his head back and forth between Sharon and the Trooper. "Cat got your tongue?" he asked Sharon, inching toward her cage. "Come on, come on, come on," he encouraged, waving her forward in the cage, clearly intending her for his hostage—for cover. "Hurry!"

He was forced to switch the dart gun to his right hand while he fished for the key, and this made him extremely nervous. He waved the oversized pistol around, attempting to cover both sides of the car. Paranoid.

He managed to get the key in the lock. "Stay!" he directed Felix as the dog edged toward freedom. "Heel!" he commanded. The dog obeyed, though cautiously. Tegg removed the lock, grabbed the collar's remote wand, and shocked Sharon immediately.

Daphne lost sight of Sharon briefly as she fell back to the cement.

"Disconnect the I.V.," Tegg directed, "needle and all."

She obeyed. He shocked her again, apparently to weaken her; and she looked weakened, although Daphne had seen her take much more than this by grabbing hold of the fence. A ruse?

He shocked her yet again. "You'll do exactly as I say," he commanded. She nodded eagerly. "Good. We're going to get in the car, you in front of me. You'll be weak on your feet, but you must not fall. Hmm? I'll punish you," he said, tripping the warning button. She nodded.

He opened the cage.

Sharon moved tentatively forward.

"We're going away," he said. "It's better this way, anyway," he added.

Daphne glanced across at her gun: a second or two to get out of this cage, another one or two to cross the aisle. Yet another to go for the gun. Five seconds at the least, possibly longer—an eternity for that guard dog.

A *lifetime*, she thought.

Without that dog in the equation, she could take on Tegg by herself. Hand-to-hand if necessary. But the dog swung the equation heavily in his favor. Even so, if they made it to the car, Sharon was gone. Everything lost.

Sharon came out of the cage. Daphne could feel her pain as she forced herself to stand. She took one tentative step forward. Tegg, carrying the remote in one hand, the dart pistol in the other, followed her slowly. "Doing fine," he said.

Daphne went for it.

She leapt forward, wormed her fingers through the chain link and opened the latch. She swung the door open and dove across the center aisle, shoving her arm beneath the chain link and straight into the opposing pen. Out of the corner of her eye, she saw Tegg's reaction. Her hand groped for the gun. The pit bull attacked, but this time she got the safety off and fired. The dog squealed and retreated.

Daphne freed the gun and turned in time to aim at the guard dog, who skidded to a stop as Tegg hollered, "Sit!" He had Sharon by the neck, using her as a screen, the dart gun aimed around her. He was at a disadvantage here: He had but one shot, and it wouldn't kill her immediately. His only trump was Sharon.

That dog was aching to charge.

Tegg dragged Sharon toward an adjacent cage.

Two dogs? Daphne thought. "Don't do it!" she advised, her attention split between the guard dog, only a few feet from her, and its master.

His hand groped for the latch—he too, knew that two dogs were nearly impossible to stop.

"Don't!" she warned, switching her aim from Tegg to the dog in front of her.

"Would you actually shoot a dog?" he asked.

She shot Felix dead. Once to drop him. Once more to finish him off.

Tegg cried loudly in protest, "You killed him!" He stared down at the dog in disbelief and repeated it.

"Take your hand off that cage," she instructed.

He obeyed.

Good, they were getting somewhere. She added up her previous shots—five outside, one in the pen, two for the guard dog: eight—only to realize she had but one bullet left. But Tegg didn't know that.

She raised the gun and aimed it directly at Tegg.

Sharon wrestled to get free.

"No!" Tegg ordered.

Two years ago, Daphne had been in the clutches of a madman, Boldt with the gun. Now the roles were reversed. She faced up to the reality of killing Tegg. She glanced down at the poor dog. God! It was still alive! Its paw twitched.

"What's the use?" she asked Tegg. She had to get him talking now. She resorted to negotiation, the only solution she knew to such a standoff. "What if my partner's outside?"

The headlights almost blinded her. Could she get off a clean shot?

"Then he's a little bit slow," Tegg said.

"Slow?" she asked. "How long for whatever's in that toy to take effect?" she asked, indicating the dart pistol. "This is no toy," she said, placing her other hand onto the Beretta, prepared to risk a kill shot to the head. It was a tricky shot, easy to miss even in the best light, the most controlled environment. But no matter what, he wasn't going to put Sharon into that car with him.

"The dog is still alive," she said, "you can help him."

"You've struck a lung. He will suffocate on his own blood. Finish him."

"You can still save him, Doctor. Let Sharon go," she advised. It was a good distance for a head shot—the light was bad, but the distance good.

She couldn't hold the gun up like this much longer. It grew heavy quickly. But with it lowered to her side, she'd have no chance of hitting him cleanly. She kept it elevated. "Tell me about Thomas Kent," she said, using the name of the man he had killed on the operating table in medical school.

Stunned, he loosened his hold on Sharon.

Daphne took another step forward. Another few feet and she could risk the head shot.

"You're a wicked little woman, aren't you?" he said, raising his own weapon. "It was you with Pamela, wasn't it? Of course it was. You killed her, you know? Without you, she would still be alive."

The news of Pamela's death shocked Daphne, and his attempt to stick her with guilt worked, for she understood she had pushed Pamela hard—too hard?—knowingly.

She was going to lose the gun—she couldn't hold it up any longer. If she lowered it, he would shoot her.

Sharon winked her one good eye and looked down.

Only then did Daphne notice the needle in her hand.

Sharon leaned her head back against Tegg and looked up at him. Briefly, he glanced down at her.

She grinned through the leather muzzle and drove the needle into Tegg's eye. Sharon broke loose.

Daphne fired, but missed wildly, as Tegg dropped the dart gun and reached for the needle. He extricated it with an ear-piercing shriek and reached for the shovel. He leveled it once onto Sharon, who had fallen and was crawling toward the car. She buckled with the blow.

Daphne dove at him. He swung the shovel at her and caught her sideways, splaying her against the cage, but lost his balance. He raised it again—this time aiming to come down on Daphne's head.

Daphne seized hold of the dart gun.

The shovel reached its apex. Next stop . . . He was sure to crush her skull.

Summoning the last of her resolve, Sharon sprang the few feet across the cement, going for his legs—one hand slid under his pant leg as the other groped for, and found, the electric fence.

The charge surged through her—through them both—and she would not let go. The buzzer on her collar cried out. Tegg went rigid and with the pain, the shovel suspended above him. Eyes white. Jaws locked open in what began as a silent scream and then turned deafening.

Daphne squeezed the trigger and fired.

The dart gun went off with a dull pop. The white cottony rabbit's tail protruded from Tegg's chest where the dart lodged.

"No!" he screamed, scooting backwards on the cement, as if he could get away from it. Escape it. Only he knew what drug that dart contained. He pulled it out and dropped it onto the cement prior to the first convulsion. "Too much!" he said frantically, knowing the dosage, terrified, staring into Daphne's eyes as if she could help him. "Too much! Too much!" His whole body jumped. Waves of the convulsions passed through him. "Too much!" he repeated, jolted again. But then his mouth wouldn't move. His eyes remained fixed open. Dead? or a result of the drug? His body went limp, then rigid, in an increasing series of convulsions. It stopped completely.

Daphne dragged herself over to Sharon and rolled her over.

She was hemorrhaging.

60

Daphne rode with her in the helicopter, though the paramedic protested against it, claiming there were rules to follow. Once airborne though, he kept trying to treat Daphne as well, but she wouldn't have any of it.

Daphne held Sharon's hand. It was cold, and she worried she knew what that meant.

Several times, a strange weightless feeling passed over Daphne and she wondered each time whether it was the helicopter or Sharon's spirit leaving her body. She would glance at the medic, and he in turn at the various monitors, and he would offer a thumbs-up, and again she would wonder: Does that mean she's gone up, or she's okay?

She wasn't sure exactly what Sharon hoped for in life, and she thought that tragic, because she would have wished it for her if only she knew. What do any of us wish for that really matters? she mused. And she answered herself: another day.

"One more day."

"What?" the paramedic shouted over the roar of the blades.

FRIDAY

February 10

61

Dr. Ronald Dixon, cloaked in a surgical smock, recited his actions as he worked on Tegg's dead body.

Boldt tuned out the autopsy details. As lead detective, his presence was required by law—but no one said he had to pay attention.

It was three in the morning, an unusual time for such a procedure, but Dixie had rallied without complaint. There were six people in the Medical Examiner's waiting room, more expected. Boldt felt thrilled at such a turnout. The world wasn't such a bad place when you knew the right people.

The heat from the overhead light felt like that of a hot sun. It shone down on the naked body. There was nothing pretty about this sight. Bleached skin, pieces of it folded open. Technical words spoken in an unbroken litany. Death reduced to detail.

He had found the three of them in the Quonset hut only minutes after the shooting.

There were more ambulances, a coroner's wagon, crime scene crews—even a fire engine, though no one knew why. The road became impassable. Two tow trucks had been called into service.

Sharon Shaffer had suffered not only a hemorrhage but a ruptured kidney from the blow of the shovel, leaving her without a backup. She had lost a great deal of blood.

A sticker on the back of Elden Tegg's driver's license indicated he was an organ donor. Blood type: AB-negative.

Of the people in the waiting room, one was a woman from the Lion's Eye Bank. Two were part of a lung team that had flown up from Portland. But to Boldt's thinking, the most important was the kidney specialist from the U—Tegg's kidney was destined for Sharon Shaffer.

A cardiac crew was *en route* from Spokane.

Over the next three hours, Elden Tegg would make his final contributions.

"I hate autopsies," said Boldt.

Dixie said, "Just wait until we open those plastic bags."

"Me? No way." Boldt found his first smile in a long while. "I've saved that for LaMoia."

TUESDAY

February 14
Valentine's Day

62

Daphne suggested lunch on Bainbridge Island and Boldt agreed, with Liz's blessings, in part to try to talk her out of quitting. He brought Miles along in a stroller. She accused him of bringing his child as a chaperon, and he allowed that this was partly true. She limped from her bad leg. She wore a blue rain jacket, the kind a backpacker would wear, blue jeans, and two-tone leather deck shoes with rawhide laces. She wore no scarf around her neck, allowing the scar to show, and Boldt knew this was a different woman.

"What's this about a job offer? I thought we were a team."

She didn't answer that. The ferry horn sounded. Miles started crying. Daphne walked over to the rail and looked out across the textured expanse of gray-green water. The city grew progressively smaller behind them. A beautiful skyline and rolling hills covered in toy houses. Boldt and Miles joined her at the rail.

She watched the horizon; he watched her. Miles played with some plastic balls attached to the stroller. This thing was the BMW of strollers. Liz had picked it out after exhaustive research.

"We bought a piano," Boldt said, though he didn't tell her why, not exactly. That reminded him that there were things they hid from each other now, and that was okay. He said, "You get me on the force, and then you quit. That's hardly fair. Shoswitz would cry foul."

She spoke just loudly enough to be heard above the wind and the constant vibration of the engines. "She rejected the kidney."

"Considering the source," he joked, "can you blame her?"

"She's on a list now. Number five on a list."

"I know that," he said soberly.

"What if she's too far down the list? Did she live through all that, just to die?"

"Her? She's a fighter, Daffy."

She nodded faintly and whispered, "This was why he was in business in the first place."

"If anyone can beat this—"

"Yeah, yeah," she interrupted. "You sound just like Dr. Light Horse."

"Well, maybe she's right."

Five seagulls flew just off the rail. Miles pointed. One of the passengers threw a piece of a Hostess Cupcake at them.

"Even seagulls are subjected to junk food," Boldt said to her. But she didn't smile. She didn't even seem to notice. "I brought a kite along," he tried. She stared off.

He said, "Did Einstein tell you about the fish for the kite?"

"He didn't have to. I can smell it."

"It's an old trick of mine. I'm full of tricks. Mostly old ones." She didn't smile at this either. So he had lost his touch. Another sign of change. Or age. Or both. "Even if we should lose her, Daffy, she's made a difference. She has touched hundreds

of lives at The Shelter, more since this story broke.
Organ banks have been flooded with donors. With
more organs, people like Tegg are out of business.
That was *her* doing. You can't knock *that*. We
should all have that kind of effect." He added, "Not
that we're going to lose her."

"I love you," she said, still looking at the horizon. "As a *friend*," she added, smiling for the first
time.

"Likewise. Always will."

"Think so?"

"Know so."

"Once she's better," she said strongly, "I'm off to
London for this new job. Hostage negotiator."

"So I've heard."

"I may stay over there. I don't know. Have you
ever been to London?"

"The way it works," he said, bending toward his
bag and hoping that she hadn't heard his voice catch,
"is that you get the kite up good and high. You get
it way the hell up there. Then you tie the fish to
the line and take up some slack and toss the fish
overboard. The drag on the fish in the water supports
the line and flies the kite. The kite sails out to sea
all by itself. Sometimes for hours. Maybe for days."

"I know you're mad about me quitting," she said.

"We can try it off the stern. The wind is best
there."

She said, "I suppose if you're lucky, it'll sail completely around the world and come right back to
you." This time, he didn't answer. She added, "You
know, it hurt more to kill that dog than to kill him.
Is that possible? What does that make me?"

"Honest, which is more than most of us."

"You think she has a chance?"

"It's all *any* of us have."

"Can I get a hug? Is that allowed?"

Boldt said, "Better ask him" and pointed to Miles, who clapped.

She came into his arms then and held him tightly. She sobbed. People stared. He didn't care. Let them. Boldt cried, too, but for his own reasons. His life was right now. Okay. On track again, and he had her to thank for some of it. "I'll miss you," he whispered.

Miles clapped again, and Daphne laughed. It was good to hear that.

In the end, the kite trick worked. Miles fell asleep in the stroller. The kite sailed off toward the horizon, growing smaller and smaller. People pointed. Some people clapped. Miles slept through it all.

A few weeks later, Daphne followed it into the sky.

Watch for
Ridley Pearson's
next hardcover,

NO WITNESSES

Coming in
October 1994

And now for the good part.

This was where Sergeant Lou Boldt threw out all convention, where the textbooks took a backseat to experience, and where he found out who in the lecture hall was listening and who was asleep.

He raised his voice. A big man, Boldt's words bellowed clear back to the make-out seats without the need of the mike clipped to his tie. "Everything I've told you in the past few weeks concerning evidence, investigative procedure, chain of custody, and chain of command is worthless." A few heads snapped up—more than he had expected. "Worthless unless you learn to read the crime scene, to know the victim, to listen to and trust your own instincts. To feel with your heart as much as think with your head. To find a balance between the two. If it was all in the head, then we would not need detectives; the lab technicians could do it all. Conversely, if it was all in the heart—if we could simply empathize with the suspect and say, 'Yup, you did it,' then who would need the lab nerds?" A few of the studious types busily flipped pages. Boldt informed them, "You won't find any of this in your textbooks. That's just the point. All the textbooks in the world are not going to clear a case—only the *investigator* can. Evidence and information is *nothing* without a human being to analyze, organize, and interpret it. That's you. That's me. There comes a time when all the information must be set aside; there comes a time when passion and instinct take over. It's the stuff that can't be taught; but it *can* be learned. Heart and mind—one's worthless without the other." He paused here, wondering if these peach-fuzz students could see beyond the forty-four-year-old, slightly paunchy homicide cop in the wrinkled khakis and the tattered sport coat that hid a pacifier in its side pocket.

At the same time, he listened to his own words reverberating through the lecture hall, wondering how much he dare tell them. Did he tell them about the nightmares, the divorces, the ulcers, and the politics? The hours? The salary? The penetrating numbness with which the veterans approached a crime scene?

Light flooded an aisle as a door at the rear of the hall swung open and a lanky kid wearing oversize jeans and a rugby shirt hurried toward the podium, casting a stretched shadow. Reaching Boldt, he passed him a pink telephone memo. A sea of students looking on, Boldt unfolded and read it.

Volunteer Park, after class. I'll wait fifteen minutes.—D.M.

Volunteer Park? he wondered, his curiosity raised. Why not the offices? Daphne Matthews was anything but dramatic. As the department's forensic psychologist, she was cool, controlled, studied, patient. Articulate, strong, intelligent. But not dramatic—not like this. The curious faces remained fixed on him. "A love letter," he said, winning a few laughs. But not many: cops weren't expected to be funny—something else they would have to learn.

===

Volunteer Park is perched well above Seattle's downtown cluster of towering high-rises and the gray-green curve of Elliott Bay sweeps out into the island-riddled estuary of Puget Sound. A large reservoir, acting as a reflecting pond, is terraced below the parking lot and lookout that fronts the museum, which had been under reconstruction for months on its way to housing the city's Asian collection. Boldt parked his aging department-issued four-door Chevy three spaces away from her red Prelude, which she maintained showroom clean. She wasn't to be found in her car, which left only one possibility.

The water tower's stone facade rose several stories to his left. Well-kept beds of flowering shrubs and perennials surrounded its footing, like gems in a setting. The grass was a phenomenal emerald green, unique, he thought, to Seattle and Portland. Maybe Ireland too; he had never been. Summer was just taking hold. Every living thing seemed poised for change. The sky was a patchwork quilt of azure blue and cotton white, the clouds moving in swiftly from the west, low and fast. A visitor might think rain, but a local knew better. Not tonight. Cold maybe, if it cleared.

He saw an unfamiliar male face behind the iron

grate in one of the tower's upper windows and waited a minute for this person and his companion to descend and leave the structure. Once they had, he chose the stairway to his right, ascending a narrow chimney of steep steps wedged between the brick rotunda to his right and the riveted steel hull of the water tank to his left. The painted tank and the tower that surrounded it were enormous, perhaps forty or fifty feet high and half again as wide. With each step, Boldt's heart pounded heavier. He was not in the best shape; or maybe it was because she had elected to step outside the system, and that couldn't help but intrigue him; or maybe it was personal and had nothing to do with the shop. He and Daphne had been close once—too close for what was allowed of a married man. They still were close, but mention of that one night never passed their lips. A month earlier she had surprised him by telling him about a new relationship. After Bill Gates got married, Owen Adler became the reigning bachelor-prize of the Northwest, having gone from espresso cart to the fastest-growing beverage and food business in the western region. He leased his own plane, owned a multimillion-dollar estate overlooking Shilshole Marina, and now, quite possibly, the heart and affections of Daphne Matthews. Had her note been worded any other way, had she not chosen such an isolated location, Boldt would have been convinced that her request was nothing more than some lover butterflies.

In another two hours, Volunteer Park would be a drug and sex bazaar. Despite its view, the tower was not a place frequented by the pin-striped set. She had clearly chosen it carefully. Daphne was not given to acts of spontaneity. She desired a clandestine meeting—and he had to wonder why.

He reached the open-air lookout at the top of the tower. It had a cement floor and evenly spaced viewing windows crosshatched with heavy gauge steel to prevent flyers from testing their wings, or projectiles from landing on passersby.

She held her arms crossed tightly, accentuating an anxiety uncommon in her. Her brown hair spilled over her face, hiding her eyes, and when she cleared it, he saw fear where there was usually the spark of excitement. Her square-shouldered, assertive posture collapsed in sagging defeat.

She wore the same blue slacks and cotton sweater as he had seen her wearing at work. She had not been to her houseboat yet.

"What is it?" he asked, worried by this look of hers.

Her chin cast a shadow, hiding the scar on her neck. She did not answer immediately. "It's a potential black hole," she explained—a difficult, if not impossible case to solve, and with political overtones. And then he understood: She had bypassed the proper procedures to give him a chance to sidestep this investigation before he formally inherited it at the cop shop. Why she would have a black hole in the first place, confused him. The department's psychologist did not lead investigations; she kept cops from swallowing barrels, and profiled the loonies that kept Boldt and the others chasing body bags.

She assisted in interrogations. She could take any side of any discussion and make a convincing argument out of it. She was the best listener he knew.

She handed him a fax—the first of what appeared to be several that she removed from a briefcase.

Soup is good food. For some.

She told him, "That was the first threat he received."

"Adler," Boldt said, filling in the blank.

She nodded, her hair trailing her movements. Daphne Matthews had grace, even when frightened.

"Innocuous enough," he said.

She handed him the next, saying "Yes, but not for long."

Suicide or murder. Take your pick. No cops. No press. No tricks, or you will carry with you the blood of the innocent.

"It could be nothing," Boldt said, though his voice belied this.

"That's exactly what Adler said," she replied angrily, lumping them together.

Boldt did not want to be lumped in with Owen Adler. "I'll give you one thing: When you say black hole, you mean black hole." Faxed threats? he thought. In the top left of the page of thermal paper he read a date and time in a tiny typeface. To the right: Page 1 of 1. Good luck tracing this, he thought.

She handed him a third. He did not want it.

"Quite a collection," he said. Boldt's nerves unraveled from time to time, and when it happened, he defaulted to stupid one-liners that seldom won a laugh.

Soup is *bad* food. If Adler Foods is out of business within 30 days, and *all* of the money is gone, and you are dead and buried, there will be no senseless killing. The choice is yours.

"How many days has it been?" It was the first question that popped into his head, though it was answered by the date in the corner. He counted the weeks in his head. The thirty days had expired.

"You see the way he worded it?" Looking down at her feet, she spoke softly, dreamy and terrified. Her lover was the target of these threats, and despite her training, she clearly was not prepared for how to handle it. "The more common threat would be: 'If Adler Foods is *not* out of business within thirty days . . .' You see the difference?"

Her bailiwick, not his, he felt tempted to remind. "Is that significant?" He played along because she had *fragile!* written all over her.

"To me, it's significant. So is the attempt in each fax to place the blame firmly with Owen. It's his decision; his choice." When she looked up at him, he saw that she held back tears.

"Daffy—" he offered, stepping closer.

"Owen and I are not going to see each other—socially—for a while. Me being police and all." She wanted it to sound casual, but failed. "We have to take him seriously now."

Boldt felt a chill. "Do we?"

She handed him another.

> I am waiting. I suggest you do not. You will have to live with your choice. Others will not be so lucky.

"It's the first time he's mentioned himself," Boldt noted.

She handed him the last of the group. "That one was sent four days ago. This one arrived this morning."

> Your indecision is costly. It can, and will, get *much worse* than this.

Below this on the fax was a copy of a newspaper article.

"*Today's* paper," she explained.

The headline read:

INFECTIONS BAFFLE DOCTORS
Two Children Hospitalized

He had read the short article quickly.

"They're *very* sick," she told him. " 'It can, and will, get *much worse* than this,' " she quoted.

He looked up. "This is his offer of proof? Is that what you're thinking?"

"He means to be taken seriously."

"I don't get it," he complained, frustrated. "Why didn't you bring this in sooner?"

"Owen didn't want to believe it." She took back the faxes possessively. Her hand trembled. "The second one warns against involving us."

She meant cops. She meant that the reason for them meeting here, not in the fifth-floor offices, was that she still was not sure how to handle this.

"An Adler employee," Boldt said. "Past or present, an employee is the most likely."

"Owen has Fowler working on it."

She meant Kenny Fowler, formerly of Major Crimes, now Adler's chief of security. Boldt liked Kenny Fowler, and said so. Better yet; he was good police, or had been at one time. She nodded and toyed with a silver ring fashioned as a porpoise that she wore on her right hand.

"I misjudged him," she said so quietly that Boldt leaned in to hear as she repeated herself. Daphne was not one to mumble.

"Are you okay?"

"Sure," she lied.

A black hole. Absorbing energy. Admitting no light—pure darkness. He realized that he had already accepted it, and he wanted to blame her for knowing him so well.

"Talk to me," he said, nervous, irritated.

"You're right about it being an employee. That's the highest percentage bet. But typically, it involves extortion, not suicide demands. Henry Happle, Owen's counsel, wants it handled internally, where there's no chance of press leakage, no police involvement, nothing to violate the demands." This sounded a little too much like the party line, and it bothered him. It was not like her to voice the opinions of others as her own, and he had to wonder what kind of man was Henry Happle that he seemed to carry so much influence with her. "That's why I have to be so careful in dealing with you. Happle wants Fowler to handle this internally. Owen overruled him this morning. He suggested this meeting—opening a dialogue. But it was *not* an easy decision."

"We can't be sure this newspaper story is his doing," Boldt told her. "He may have just seized upon a convenient headline."

"Maybe." She clearly believed otherwise, and Boldt trusted Daphne's instincts. Heart and mind; he was reminded of his lecture.

"What's Fowler doing about it?" Boldt asked.

"He doesn't know about this meeting. Not yet. He, like Happle, advised against involving us. He's looking to identify a disgruntled employee—but he's been on it a month now. He's had a few suspects, but none of them has panned out. His loyalty is to the company. Henry Happle writes his paychecks, not Owen—if you follow me."

Boldt's irritation surfaced. "If this news story *is* his doing, I'd say we're a little late."

"I'm to blame. Owen asked me for my professional opinion. I classified the threats as low risk. I thought whoever it was was blowing smoke. Proper use of the language. The faxes are sent by portable computer from pay phones. Fowler traced the last two to pay phones on Pill Hill. That's a decent enough neighborhood. What that tells us is that in all probability we're dealing with an *educated, affluent, white male* between the ages of *twenty-five* and *forty*. The demands seemed so unrealistic that I assumed our boy was venting some anger—nothing more. Owen went along with that. He put Kenny on it and tried to forget it. I screwed this up, Lou." She crossed her arms tightly again, and her breasts rode high in the cradle. Again she quoted, " 'It can, and will, get *much worse* than this.' "

Her voice echoed slightly in the cavernous enclosure, circling inside his thoughts like horses on a carousel.

A black hole. His now.

"You want me to look into it, I'll look into it," he offered reluctantly.

"Unofficially."

"You know I can't do that, Daffy."

"Please."

"I'm not a rent-a-cop. Neither are you. We're fifth floor. You know the way it works."

"Please!"

"I can't do that *for very long*," he qualified.

"Thank you."

"If either of these kids die, Daffy—" He left it dangling there, like one of the many broken cobwebs suspended from the cement ceiling.

"I know." She avoided his gaze.

"You'll share *everything* with me. No stonewalling."

"Agreed."

"Well . . . maybe not *everything*," he corrected.

It won a genuine smile from her—and he was glad for that—though it deserted her as quickly as it had come.

His frantic footfalls on the formed stairs sounded like the beating of bats' wings as he descended at a run.

The newspaper article had listed one of the hospitals. For Lou Boldt, the victim was where every investigation began.

Island

Let yourself go!

☐	**THE FIRM** by John Grisham	21145-X	$6.99/$7.99 Canada
☐	**PREDATOR** by Jack Olsen	21192-1	$5.99/$6.99 Canada
☐	**MY FAVORITE SUMMER, 1956** by Mickey Mantle & Phil Pepe	21203-0	$5.99/$6.99 Canada
☐	**LIONS AND LACE** by Meagan McKinney	21230-8	$4.99/$5.99 Canada
☐	**BOSS OF BOSSES** by Joseph O'Brien & Andris Kurins	21229-4	$5.99/$6.99 Canada
☐	**A TIME TO KILL** by John Grisham	21172-7	$6.99/$7.99 Canada
☐	**CITY GIRL** by Patricia Scanlon	21275-8	$5.99/$6.99 Canada
☐	**MADONNA: UNAUTHORIZED** by Christopher Andersen	21318-5	$5.99/$6.99 Canada
☐	**HARD FALL** by Ridley Pearson	21262-6	$5.99/$6.99 Canada
☐	**BRIGHT SHARK** by Robert Ballard & Tony Chiu	21405-X	$5.99/$6.99 Canada
☐	**PHANTOM** by Susan Kay	21169-7	$5.99/NCR
☐	**TEMPTED** by Virginia Henley	20625-1	$4.99/$5.99 Canada
☐	**THE PELICAN BRIEF** by John Grisham	21404-1	$6.99/$7.99 Canada
☐	**THE IMPERSONATOR** by Diana Hammond	21416-5	$5.99/$6.99 Canada
☐	**SCIMITAR** by John Abbott	21550-1	$5.99/$6.99 Canada

At your local bookstore or use this handy page for ordering:

DELL READERS SERVICE, DEPT. DIS
2451 South Wolf Road, Des Plaines, IL . 60018

Please send me the above title(s). I am enclosing $_____
(Please add $2.50 per order to cover shipping and handling.) Send
check or money order—no cash or C.O.D.s please.

Ms./Mrs./Mr._____

Address _____

City/State _____ Zip _____

DIS-6/93

Prices and availability subject to change without notice. Please allow four to six
weeks for delivery.